ECSTASY'S TRIUMPH

"Why do you deny your own feelings?" Brock whispered, reaching for Audra's her hand. "Admit you've felt something between us."

His thumb began tracing the delicate veins in her wrist. She felt the pulse beat wildly. If only he would not touch her!

As if he had read her thoughts, he gave a short little laugh of triumph. "You know you felt it, just as I did," he declared.

"No—" she began, but before she knew it he was tenderly lifting her face, and kissing the tears from her eyes. His mouth traced down the soft curve of her cheek and he nibbled at her ear lobe before seeking her lips.

With no seeming volition of their own, Audra's arms crept around Brock's neck and she entwined her fingers in his thick, dark hair, pulling his mouth harder to hers. She felt completely intoxicated by his closeness, by the featherlike kisses he had begun to press on her eyelids, her cheeks, her throat. She did nothing to resist. She wanted him to go on and on. . . .

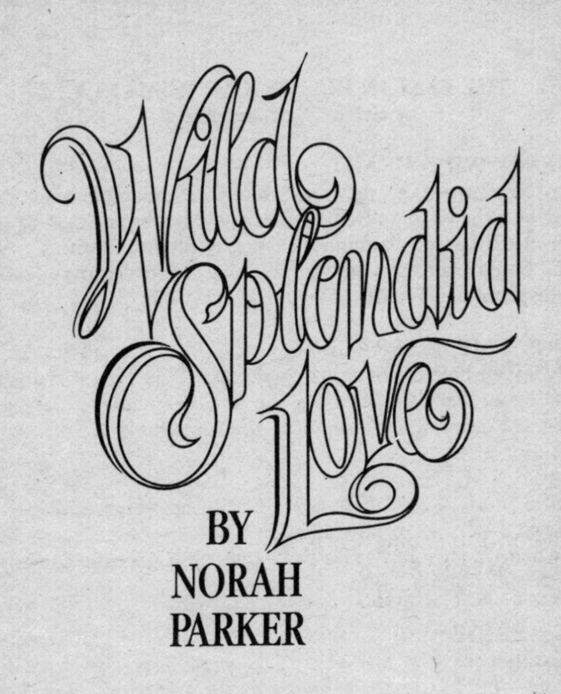

BY
NORAH
PARKER

ZEBRA BOOKS
KENSINGTON PUBLISHING CORP.

ZEBRA BOOKS

are published by

Kensington Publishing Corp.
475 Park Avenue South
New York, N.Y. 10016

First printing: April, 1984

Printed in the United States of America

Chapter One

The spring afternoon was warm, with just a whisper of a breeze. Audra had slipped unnoticed from the house and run to the stables, where she had had her chestnut mare saddled for her. She had declined the escort of the groom who was supposed to attend her, preferring to ride out alone. She had also insisted upon riding astride and had the grooms sworn to secrecy regarding this unbefitting practice. They whispered to one another that one of these days the young miss would be brought home with a broken neck, considering the way she always rode full tilt.

Audra urged the mare into a canter as they left the huge, gray mansion behind and took the riding path she favored, the one that led past the tall yew hedges and out into the open country beyond.

The grass was thick with wild flowers, white daisies, golden buttercups and blue periwinkles. In the distance, the thick woods appeared a verdant green against the clear blue of the sky.

Letting the mare have her head, Audra was soon galloping joyously across the wide open meadow. She had almost reached the trees beyond when a solitary rider came into view, approaching rapidly from the south. She shaded her eyes from the bright sunlight, hoping to determine his identity. Then, with a small cry of recognition, she angled her own horse off sharply in the other's direction. They met at the lower edge of the woodlands, both quickly reining in their mounts.

"It's really you!" Audra exclaimed breathlessly. "When did you arrive home?"

"This morning," the young man said, appraising the lovely young horsewoman before him. The elegant blue riding habit showed to advantage the perfection of her figure. Her long, silvery blond hair in its neatly braided chignon glinted from beneath her little hat and her cheeks were flushed a becoming pink from the fresh air.

Was this beauty really the lanky, young tomboy with whom he had grown up; had raced with across hill and dale, jumping everything and anything that got in their way; had fished and hunted and climbed with before he had entered the army?

Audra was also surveying the young man who now sat so military stiff and straight in his saddle. Paul Chatfield was a boy no longer. He had had two long years of fighting on the peninsula in the war against Napoleon. His warm, brown eyes no longer looked as lighthearted, his fair skin had a weathered appearance and when he had first swept off his hat, she had noticed that his red-gold hair had darkened to almost auburn. He was only twenty, she knew, three years older than herself, but now he seemed much older.

"You were a child when I left," he was saying, "and now you have turned into a young lady. A beautiful young lady, if I may say so."

"You may say so." She flashed him a coquettish smile, her blue eyes dancing.

"Mmm . . ." He raised an eyebrow. "It appears you have now developed feminine wiles as well."

"Naturally," she said, tossing her head, "I have earned a diploma in eyelash fluttering and can flirt quite outrageously from beneath lowered lids."

He threw back his head and laughed. She was glad she had made him laugh. He looked more like the old Paul and not so deadly serious.

"Let us stop here awhile," he said, swinging in one easy motion from his horse's back. "We must bring one another up to date on the last two years."

He helped Audra to dismount and found himself holding her for a moment longer than was necessary before he let her go.

"Do I get a hello kiss? I remember my goodbye one. It was slightly off center."

She smiled. "Of course." And let him kiss her chastely on the cheek.

"*That* could also be improved," he smiled, walking with slim, athletic grace to fasten the reins of the horses around a slender tree trunk. Watching him, Audra thought that it was clear that Paul

Chatfield was an aristocrat. His movements reminded her of a thoroughbred horse.

She sat down on a fallen log and removed her hat and gloves, placing them by her side. "I read in the gazettes that the fighting was very fierce," she said. "I'm glad you were not wounded. Your mother was very worried about you."

"Was she?" He sat down close beside her. "With three other sons, I didn't suppose she had the time to think of me."

"Paul! You were always her favorite and she missed you terribly. She is practically alone now. John is rarely home from Oxford—"

"And Thomas is working hard in the War Office in London, but Milord is here. He has stepped right into Father's footsteps as everyone knew he would." Paul's voice was dry.

She looked at him sharply. "Why do you still call Robert that? I hear he has done a remarkable job with the estate since your father's death."

"He was groomed for it."

"You are still bitter about being the youngest son, aren't you?"

He shook his head. "I've never been bitter. No, that's not true. I *was* bitter, but it was only at the way Father left things. Even if we had not been at war, I would have had no alternative but to buy a commission in the army."

"Your mother thinks he left you no inheritance in order to make a man of you. Do you hate the army so?"

She looked at him, suddenly aware of how lean and hard his slim body looked, how handsome he was in his scarlet uniform with its gold braid.

"I'd rather not talk about it," he said, his finely chiseled jaw tightening. "Tell me about yourself, Audra. I understand your father has married again."

The smile left her face. "Yes. Just after you went away. He met her in London—a pretty, young widow. Her name is Emily."

"And you do not like her," he said perceptively.

"No. How could I? She is practically half Papa's age and he has gone absolutely dotty over her. He spent a fortune courting her and since their marriage, he has fallen deeply into debt due to her extravagances. Now, she has told me, it is up to *me* to make things right."

"Up to *you*? I don't understand."

"I will explain. My stepmama informed me shortly after she came to live here as Papa's wife that I had been allowed to run wild in the country for far too long and she planned to correct that error immediately."

Paul laughed. "Well, you must admit that you drove two governesses away in a state of nervous prostration with your headstrong ways. There are not many young ladies today who can ride and shoot as well as any man, not to mention think and argue like one."

Audra's lovely eyes flashed. "It was not all *my* doing. Papa taught me those things because he had always wanted a son. He seemed happy with the way I was until *she* came along. It was *she* who decided that I should be packed off to London in the care of Great-Aunt Alice to learn proper manners and deportment and all the social graces. It was *she* who said it was high time I became a lady."

"It appears on the surface that Great-Aunt Alice succeeded rather well," he said, his gaze faintly amused as he surveyed her, "although I notice you still ride astride."

"Only here at Greenleigh," she replied, "and only when I can get away with it. But it won't be for long. I have just had my first season in London and my dear stepmama is even now deciding which of several proposals of marriage I received will be the most advantageous financially to the family."

"Surely you are joking."

"No. It is quite true." Audra bit her lip and turned her lovely head away from him.

"Your stepmother cannot force you to marry."

"Of course not." She looked back at him, her eyes full of derision. "*She* is far too subtle. *She* has already started to hint that it will be necessary soon for Papa to sell his beloved Greenleigh which, as you know, has been in the family for generations, and how miserable he is going to be. *She* started to work on me months ago and I will eventually weaken because I love Papa so much, and Mama told me before she died that I must always look after him." Tears clouded the deep-blue eyes.

"Audra. Oh, my dear. Don't cry. I wish there was something I could do."

Strong arms went about her and she turned her face into his shoulder.

"Do you remember what you said to me when you were seventeen?" she asked in a muffled voice. Color rose in her cheeks at the thought, but she went on. "It was after we had gone swimming in the stream."

"I remember. I told you I was going to marry you. But that was before everything changed for me."

On that particular summer afternoon, three years before, the two of them had gone riding and had had several races with their horses across the meadow. There was a stream that made a natural separation between the Wentworth and Chatfield estates. Hot and sticky, they had found themselves in the leafy shade there, cupping their hands and drinking deeply of the cool, clear water.

It had been Audra who had suggested a swim and had waded into the stream quite unashamedly in only her chemise and petticoat. Embarrassed, Paul had left on his breeches, but had removed his shirt and boots.

They had laughed and splashed one another and tried to swim, but the water was quite shallow where they had entered and they had only managed to flounder about a bit. Afterwards, they had flopped down side by side on the bank of the stream, falling back in the soft, green grass.

Audra had been the first to stir, sitting up and ringing the water from her long, blond hair. She had looked over at Paul, still lying quietly beside her. He was staring at her and she saw a strange look darkening his eyes.

It was then that she had realized that the water had made her chemise nearly transparent over her newly developed breasts. She had blushed with shame and had tried to cover them, but Paul had taken her hand away and cupped one, slowly tracing the nipple with his thumb.

Beginning to tremble, she had quickly drawn

away. An unknown feeling had begun to spread through her and although she did not understand it, it was not unpleasant, so she did not protest when he pulled her gently down over him and kissed her.

That first kiss had affected Audra like nothing else she had ever known before. She had felt a thrill as he pressed her close against him and a strange longing to experience more. But he had suddenly shoved her away from him, breaking off the kiss abruptly.

"We'd best be getting back," he had said, jumping up, his voice sounding oddly hoarse. He quickly turned his back on her, and began to search for his shirt and boots.

She had sat where he had left her, her body still shaking with what she had thought to be the dampness of her wet clothing.

When he was dressed, Paul had returned to her. "Come on," he had said, in control of himself now.

"What did I do wrong?" she had asked him, her guileless, young eyes raised to his. "Please tell me, Paul. I have never been kissed before."

"You did nothing wrong," he had growled. "I did." He had held out her clothes to her. "Get dressed, Audra."

Quietly she had slipped into her blouse and skirt and pulled on her stockings and boots. When she had looked up again he was still studying her.

"I'm going to marry you, Audra," he had said very seriously, very determinedly. "When I get my inheritance, I'm going to ask your father for your hand."

"Are you, Paul? Are you?" she had asked, smiling up at him, her deep-blue eyes very wide. "Oh, I think

I would like that. Will you kiss me again?"

"No!" he had said, and he never had until he had received his orders to go to the peninsula. In fact, he had changed completely toward her after that day by the stream. It wasn't just that his father had died, unexpectedly, leaving him no inheritance, it was something else—a self-conscious awkwardness that affected the easy camaraderie they had shared in all those growing-up years together. He had acted toward her as a correct young English gentleman would to a young lady of his acquaintance and she had hated it.

It wasn't until later, when Audra had gone to London and had overheard some whispering female talk, that she had come to understand Paul's behavior that day by the stream and been ashamed at her naïvete.

Now she pushed herself gently away from Paul, looking deep into his dear, familiar face. "Here I am telling you all my troubles and I can see you have been through a good deal yourself."

He smiled. "You have been constantly in my thoughts, Audra. When things were bad, it helped to remember home and the good times, and you were part of that. Now, seeing you today . . . grown so very lovely . . . so very beautiful . . ."

It seemed quite natural that he should lift her face to his. His lips came down on hers, warm and firm.

When they broke apart, she said, a little breathlessly, "I think you have had some practice since you last kissed me."

"A little," he admitted with a grin. "Two years is a long time. But—" his face sobered—"you must promise me something, Audra. Promise me you will not let your stepmother talk you into a loveless marriage."

"But what am I to do?"

"Play for time. I will do my best to think of something to help you."

"You could ask for my hand in marriage yourself," she suggested boldly.

"And have your father laugh me off the estate? I have nothing to offer you. I have no prospects. Only a token allowance and my lieutenant's pay."

"That would not matter to me."

"But it would to me. It would also not help your father to keep Greenleigh." He slapped one clenched fist into the palm of the other. "If only I had more time."

"How long is your leave?"

"Only a fortnight. Audra, there must be *some* way."

"No. Money is the only answer. I will just have to marry the least objectionable rich man who has offered for me."

"No! I cannot bear the thought of you marrying some weak-chinned fop just for his money. So help me, I won't let you do it, Audra. I'll find a way."

As she rode back to Greenleigh, Audra prayed that Paul would indeed be able to solve her problem, but she did not see how. He would surely be too proud to go to his brother, for, although Robert Chatfield was now a very wealthy man, he and Paul had never got along. Robert had seemed grown up and serious when only a boy, always concerned with the estate and the tenants and the farms, while Paul had thought then that the purpose of life was to enjoy every single moment of it.

The army and the war had matured him, Audra realized. He seemed old for his years, yet she still found him easier to talk with than any of the young dandies she had met while in London. She was sure that their only interests were in themselves and in gaming and drinking. With them she could never be her real self.

"They are not interested in what is inside your head, Audra," Great-Aunt Alice had lectured her, "only in your pretty face."

"May I not offer an opinion?"

"No. You must not bore the young men with your ideas. You must charm them with your smile and listen with admiration to what *they* have to say."

She hated playing such a role. She would never be the helpless, fluttering little female, although she was feminine enough to enjoy the lovely gowns and the gay parties and balls and all the attention that was paid to her. Still, she never flirted for she had not liked any of her admirers well enough to encourage his advances.

Nevertheless, the "alluring Audra," as one lovesick swain had dubbed her, despite her lack of a dowry, had gained many admirers.

Sir George and his new wife were to have come to London at this time, but a bad case of pleurisy confined Wentworth to his bed and so it had fallen on Great-Aunt Alice alone to present young Audra to society.

Rising magnificently to the occasion, the widowed Lady Alice Fremont came to enjoy her role enormously. She had been living very quietly since she had lost her dear Horace and adored being back in society's whirl—especially as her grandniece had become such an instant success. She had done her best for Audra, introducing her to the ton, taking her to Almack's and even presenting her at one of the Queen's Drawing Rooms, but it had been to no avail. Audra had not lost her heart to anyone.

When the girl finally returned to Greenleigh, it was to learn, however, that several letters had preceded her, making respectable offers for her hand.

The new Lady Wentworth had taken charge of these, taking upon herself the business of looking into each and every one regarding the merits of the suit. Never once had she consulted Audra as to her own preference.

Audra returned from her afternoon ride later than she had intended, due to her unexpected meeting with Paul Chatfield. She ran up the back stairs to her room only to discover that she had been summoned to join her father and stepmother immediately in the salon for tea.

After a hurried sponge bath, the little maid, Fanny, assisted in dressing her mistress in an afternoon gown of sprigged muslin trimmed with blue and violet ribbons.

"I have no time to arrange my hair," Audra said, tucking a few stray wisps back into the pale blond chignon.

Moments later, she was opening the mahogany

door of the salon. Her stepmother was the first person she saw. Emily Wentworth was graciously pouring tea from the lovely antique silver service that had belonged to Audra's mama. She was a dark and diminutive woman, with the quick, nervous movements of a little bird. Her features were quite pretty, despite a rather sharp nose, and she made full use of her sparkling dark eyes. Unfortunately, she was inclined to overdress. This afternoon, she was gowned in a pale green creation that was trimmed and beruched with quantities of frills and flounces.

Sir George Wentworth, Audra's father, sat opposite his wife in his favorite armchair and rose to his feet as his daughter entered the room. Already standing before the fireplace was a portly gentleman with the round, pink face of a cherub. A thatch of white hair and long, white side whiskers framed his face. Audra remembered him from London. When she had first met him, he had reminded her of Father Christmas without his beard, for he had been dressed in a dark red coat with a velvet collar and white breeches, and one's reflection could be seen in his highly polished black Hessian boots. Now she recalled his name. The earl of Latham.

She dropped him a deep curtsy, noticing that this time the earl's coat was of blue velvet. The bright yellow waistcoat beneath seemed to draw attention to his considerable girth.

"I believe you have met my daughter, my lord," Sir George said.

"Yes, we have met," Latham replied, as Audra smiled at him. His innocent-looking blue eyes twinkled back at her. She remembered he was always laughing at something in his deep, booming way. His whole demeanor seemed to radiate his jolly nature.

He bowed over her hand and Audra was afraid for a moment that he might pop the straining buttons of his waistcoat.

"What a fortunate fellow you are, George, to have two such lovely examples of femininity to look at every day," he said gallantly. He had a low-pitched voice that was wonderfully warm and expressive. "The last time I spied your daughter was at Lady Malmsley's dinner party. I had Margaret change her seating arrangements so I could sit next to her." He patted Audra's hand. "Found out all about you from her, George. Heard you had been ill. That is the reason I decided to drop in and see you on my way north."

"I'm glad you did, Clarence. It has been quite some time since you have honored Greenleigh with your presence."

"I was a friend of your late Uncle William," the earl explained to Audra, sitting down beside her on a settee that protested rather violently as he did so. This caused him to break into his booming laugh. "Have to have all your chairs strengthened after *I* leave, George."

Tea time became very jolly after that with the earl amusing them with stories about his weight and the ludicrous situations it had gotten him into. Sir George insisted that he must stay with them a few days and the earl willingly accepted his invitation.

The supper that evening was more sumptuous than had been served at Greenleigh for some time and it was obvious that the earl enjoyed every morsel of it, refusing nothing, and helping himself to two large portions of the cook's special trifle.

"The Wentworths have always set a good table," he said to Emily, "but you, my dear, have even surpassed the hospitality I have received here in the past."

Lady Wentworth used her wide, dark eyes to convey her pleasure at his words. "Thank you, my lord," she said prettily, then nodded to Audra. "We shall leave you gentlemen to your port."

"Your charming wife does not think I am portly enough, George," the earl said to his host, who laughed with him, his eyes fondly following Emily's diminutive figure to the door.

Audra always felt so tall walking beside her stepmother. She favored her father's side of the family and was over the normal height for a woman. Her great-aunt Alice had told her that it only enhanced her blond beauty, making her appear more regal. Her aunt had done much to bolster a self-image that had begun to suffer at Emily's hands.

"Isn't his lordship amusing?" that lady now said, as she and Audra seated themselves in the salon.

"Indeed," Audra agreed, "he has a very agreeable nature. Has he a family?"

"No," Emily said, "he is a widower. I believe his wife died several years ago. She had been an invalid for some time. They had no children."

"He said he was a friend of Uncle William's."

"Yes. They were apparently at Oxford together. I understand he was present at the fox hunt at the time your uncle was thrown from his horse and fatally injured."

"Papa has never talked to me of it. It always pained him to remember. He had just reached the age of majority when it happened and Uncle William was under thirty. Papa worshipped his only brother."

"So very sad." Emily picked up her needlework. "I am hoping his lordship will stay over with us for at least a week. He seems to be cheering up your father. He has been down in spirits since his illness."

It is the many debts that are hanging over his head that are getting Papa down, Audra thought, looking around the salon. She had always loved this room which was so bright with its French windows opening out onto the garden, but it had been redecorated by Emily, as had most of the rooms in the old country mansion. Thousands of pounds had been spent on new carpeting and wall coverings and furnishings. Some of the most valuable antiques had been relegated to the attics because they were too plain and old-fashioned for Emily's taste.

Now this lovely old room was filled with vivid crimson and saffron yellow brocades and ornate gilt furniture and looked to Audra like one of the overpainted and garishly dressed women she had once caught sight of while driving through one of the less desirable parts of London.

Her stepmother was going on again, as she had so many times since Audra's return, about how disappointed she had been at not being able to go up to town during the season.

"If your father had not let Sir Archibald take him out in that stupid, new high-perch phaeton of his and got drenched to the skin in the rain . . ."

Audra knew that it must have been Emily who had originally encouraged the acceptance of Sir Archibald and Lady Sutley's invitation to spend a few days at their estate. Sir George had always abhorred Sir Archibald, calling him an intolerable braggart.

"I hope you realize, Audra," Emily continued, "that your father spent a great deal of money on the beautiful wardrobe that was purchased for your first season. He was frankly astonished by the bills your great-aunt Alice sent to him. He thought her to be more frugal. Fancy sending you to Madame Bertin for your gowns! I hear she dresses the very leaders of the fashionable world, although I must say those Grecian styles of hers are too severely plain for my taste. No doubt she saves money by not using as much material and trimming. Trust a French woman to think of that!"

There followed a short silence until Audra mentioned casually, "Did you know that Paul Chatfield is home on leave from the continent?"

"How did you learn that?" Emily demanded sharply.

Audra shrugged. "The servants visit back and forth between the estates," she said, quite truthfully.

"Your father told me that you and young Paul grew up together." Audra's stepmother's eyes narrowed. "I hope you won't entertain any thoughts of *him* for a husband. He hasn't a penny to his name, I'm told."

"And that would never do, would it?" Audra said bitterly. "Not when I am to be sold off to the highest bidder."

"You mistake my intentions, my dear," Emily said, her voice noticeably sweetening. "I only want your happiness."

Audra looked up to see her father and the earl entering the room. Emily, she thought, must have eyes in the back of her head.

How much older her father looked since his illness. Sir George was in his early fifties, but she noticed there seemed to be more gray in his thinning, brown hair, more of a slump to his narrow shoulders. He was a tall, lean man who had been very athletic in his youth, but now the vigor had left him and there was a softness to the once-hard muscles, a pallor to the once-tanned skin. He looked like what he was: a tired, middle-aged man.

Beside him, the earl seemed to exude health and well-being. No doubt Emily was right in one regard, Audra thought, as she watched her father laugh at something his lordship said. This jolly man's visit would do him a world of good.

"Clarence is trying to talk me into raising cattle on that eastern pasture land of mine," Sir George said to his wife. "Might be just what we need right now to build up the estate."

Audra looked at the spark of hope in her father's sad eyes and wondered if this might indeed prove to be a way to save Greenleigh. Yet, in her heart, she knew that the earl's suggestion had come too late. There was no money left to purchase cattle and hadn't she heard that while her father lay ill, Emily had got him to sign a document to sell some land?

She met her stepmother's sharp, black eyes and

saw by her expression that it was indeed the eastern pasture land that had been sold. All that beautiful, green countryside lost forever in order to pay for costly ball gowns and fripperies that would be out of style in no time!

Audra lowered her eyes to the hands that lay clasped so tightly in her lap. She could have wept at the dreadful waste!

Chapter Two

It was the next afternoon. Audra had escaped to the garden after tea and was sitting on a marble bench in the shade, contemplating her bleak future, when she heard the crunch of gravel and the earl appeared from around a corner.

"May I join you?" he asked in his warm, mellow voice, and when she nodded he sighed deeply and sat down beside her on the bench, producing a large, white handkerchief with which to mop his perspiring brow.

"Devilishly warm today."

"Yes, my lord, I suppose it is."

"You seem very pensive, my dear."

She said nothing.

"I cannot help but wonder where the smiling young miss I met in London has disappeared to."

"Life is not all smiles and laughter, your lordship."

"Really?" He put a pudgy finger beneath her chin and raised her head to look at him. "At your age it should be," he said, his pale eyes twinkling.

"Not when one has such a heavy responsibility thrust upon one's shoulders."

"Responsibility?" He looked incredulous. "How can that be?" He seemed so kind, his manner so reassuring, that Audra found herself saying to him:

"May I confide in your lordship?"

"I would be honored if you would, my dear."

"It is really a family matter," she said, a little doubtful now of the wisdom of opening up to a man who was almost a stranger.

"If you would rather not . . ." He smiled understandingly.

"It's about Papa, my lord," she finally admitted. "I love him very much and I would not be disloyal to him for the world, but . . . well, Papa has always been a dreamer. He has always preferred riding and shooting, or reading about fascinating, far-off places to tending to the affairs of his estate. Greenleigh has slowly gone downhill and now it has come to the point where Papa has had to sell off part of the land. I believe it was the pasture land you spoke of yesterday."

The earl did not seem in the least surprised. "I'm afraid I guessed as much from certain remarks that were made. I may act the buffoon, Audra, but as far as people are concerned, I believe I am rather perceptive."

"Then perhaps you already know what it is that

distresses me."

"I have an idea," he said sympathetically.

"Papa is deeply in debt, so I am literally to be sold off to the highest bidder. Like a horse at an auction."

"A prize filly, if I may say so," he laughed, "but high-spirited, if I don't miss my guess, and rather difficult to tame."

"It is no laughing matter," she said indignantly.

"I know." His cherubic face sobered. "And I'm sorry, Audra. But I do think you are exaggerating things. You are very dear to your father. He would never force you into marriage. He would not wish to see you unhappy."

"He may have no choice. Where will he go and what will he do if he loses Greenleigh?"

"I see." The earl stroked his several chins. "Well, we will have to endeavor to see that he holds onto it, won't we? Perhaps I can come up with a solution."

Audra sighed. "Paul is already doing his best to find one."

"Paul?" The earl frowned. "Who is he?"

"Paul Chatfield. His family has the estate bordering to the west of Greenleigh. His brother Robert is the new Lord Chatfield. Paul and I have always been the best of friends. We grew up together. He has been away in the army, but at the moment is home on leave."

"I see." The earl nodded. "Are you fond of this Paul?"

"Of course. If it were not that he is the youngest son and penniless, we might have married." She had no idea how her eyes had come alive as she spoke of Paul. "We have always thought alike on so many subjects and he is bright and amusing and very handsome."

"Would you have liked to marry him?"

"Yes, I think I would." Her face fell. "But now that is quite impossible."

The earl took her small hand in his and patted it. "Perhaps things will work out better than you imagine, Audra. You must not lose hope."

She smiled a little shamefacedly at him. "You have been so very kind. I really should not have burdened you with my—"

He brushed her words aside. "It will remain our secret," he assured her.

"Thank you, my lord," she said, rising to her feet. "Now I must be getting back. It is quite late and Emily will be looking for me."

The earl watched her hurry off down the path. She moved so gracefully, he thought. How exquisite she was with her delicate patrician features, her lovely young face framed by those soft, silver-pale curls and her deep and intensely blue eyes. He felt a stab of envy for the Chatfield boy. No doubt he was a perfect specimen of young manhood—lean and broad-shouldered and well muscled. Latham patted his rounded belly as he rose and it began to shake as he started to laugh at himself.

The earl and Sir George were enjoying their after-dinner brandy. Latham had removed a small jewelled box from his pocket and flicked open the lid. He took a delicate pinch of snuff between two pudgy fingers and raised it to one nostril and then the other.

"Your daughter, George, is a delightful conversationalist," he said. "Amazingly well-informed for one so young and beautiful."

"I hope you were not upset by her opinions. I'm afraid she became a bit carried away at dinner. It is my fault that she speaks her mind so freely. I rather encouraged it when there were just the two of us alone here at Greenleigh."

"Upset? I found it delightful. Most of the young chits today haven't a brain in their heads."

There was a small silence as the two men sipped at their brandy.

"George, I have something to say to you and I would appreciate it if you would hear me out before replying."

"Of course." The other nodded.

"I have a confession to make." The earl gave a sneeze from the snuff and fumbled for his handkerchief. "I did not come to Greenleigh solely to see you," he finished, wiping his nose.

Sir George raised his eyebrows in question.

"I am, you see, contemplating a second marriage. I have been a widower for five years now and, as you of all people must know, it is a damned lonely existence."

Sir George smiled. "So, due to my own remarriage, you have come to ask my advice."

"Not exactly, George." Latham regarded him closely. "I have come to ask for your daughter's hand."

"What!" Sir George rose from his chair.

"Hear me out now. I am well aware of the age difference. I am over sixty and the girl is not yet eighteen, but I want to explain the advantages of the union to you. I am a very wealthy man. Few know the full extent of my wealth. I will be able to give Audra everything in the world she could possibly want. Look at me, George. I have always indulged myself with the best of food and drink. How many years do I have left before the old ticker capitulates?" He grinned. "Five? Ten at the most? Still time enough when I am gone for Audra to remarry a man closer to her own age."

Sir George looked across the table at the corpulent, white-haired man. He was old enough to be Audra's grandfather!

"Clarence, you do my daughter a great honor in asking for her hand, but she is so very young. Have you spoken with her? Has she any idea—"

"None whatsoever."

"As you know, Audra has a mind of her own. I am sure she regards you highly, but I am afraid she will consider the age difference far too great."

"How diplomatic you are, George." The earl laughed jovially. "Why don't you come right out and say she would never consider marrying a fat, old man like me."

"Why," Sir George blustered, "I didn't say . . . She wouldn't think . . ."

"Of course she would. What young chit wouldn't? But I have more to offer." The smile left the earl's face, though his eyes still bore an amused twinkle. "What do you say to one hundred thousand pounds to pay your debts and put Greenleigh back on its feet? I'll even supply an experienced estate manager which you seem to lack. With good management, I see no reason why Greenleigh shouldn't become tolerably profitable. I still believe that pasture land would be excellent for grazing cattle."

"I no longer own that land, Clarence."

"Then buy it back. You'll have sufficient funds to pay twice the price if you have to."

For a few seconds Sir George's tired eyes lit up at the thought of seeing his beloved Greenleigh returned to what it once had been, then again he shook his head.

"I will not sell my daughter, Clarence, even to you, despite your tempting offer."

"Sell your—" The earl looked quite shocked. "Forgive me, George. I have apparently expressed myself very badly. Not used to this sort of thing. Been nearly forty years since I declared myself before. But young Audra enchanted me from the first moment I saw her in London. Never went to so many balls and assemblies in my life, just to catch a glimpse of her. I promise you, George, I'll take good care of your little girl if she'll have me."

"I will tell her you have asked for her hand, Clarence. But I can promise you nothing."

The earl rode off the next morning, planning to return in a few days time for Audra's answer. As the large front doors of Greenleigh swung shut behind him, Lady Wentworth turned to Sir George, who stood beside her, and said rather irritably:

"Audra should have been here to bid goodbye to our guest."

"Where is she?"

"Out riding again, I suppose. She likes to go out before breakfast and she does not always take her groom with her. It is quite shocking, George."

"Now, Emily, Audra knows Greenleigh like the back of her hand. She is not likely to get lost."

"That is not the point. What would people say if they saw her out riding alone like that? Even those months in London didn't get the wildness out of that girl. It's really all your fault, George. You let her get away with far too much as a child. Mark my words, her willfulness will be her downfall."

Sir George sighed. "Come with me into the library, Emily," he said, conscious that the servants were in earshot of his wife's quite penetrating voice. "I have something I wish to discuss with you."

He told her then of the earl's proposal of the night before, but he thought it prudent, for the moment, not to mention the enormous sum Latham had offered.

"I told him I would speak to Audra, but of course she will refuse him. She will probably think it quite ludicrous. She told me the day he arrived that he reminded her of Father Christmas without a beard."

"I do not think it ludicrous, George. Why, it would be an excellent match!" Emily said, rising swiftly to her feet and beginning to pace up and down before him, rubbing her hands together. "Audra would be a countess! And Latham is very rich. Why, she would live like a princess! Have everything in the world she might desire!"

"Everything but love," Sir George said wistfully. "Audra is young and beautiful. It is only natural she will want to marry for love."

"Love! Pooh! What has love to do with it?"

He looked at her a trifle sadly. "Why, isn't that why you married *me*, my dear?"

Sir George was still sitting at his desk in the library an hour later when there was a knock at the door.

"Come in," he said, running a weary hand over his brow as he looked up from his papers.

Audra entered the room, still dressed in her riding habit.

"You wished to see me, Papa?"

"Yes, my dear. Sit down a moment will you? This won't take long."

Audra sank down into the chair that was placed before the desk. Her lovely features had settled into a look he recognized. A look of unbending stubbornness.

"I know what you are about to say, Papa. I should not go out riding without a groom. But I have done so for years and you have never minded. It is Emily who is so persnickety. She does not realize that I know every tree and blade of grass around Greenleigh and I—"

"That is *not* what I wished to say, Audra," her father interrupted.

"No?" Her eyes lowered. "Then you found out. One of the grooms has told you."

"Told me what?" He had to smile at her. Her looks were such a contradiction. On the surface there was such a cool, blond demureness about her and yet she was such a little hothead underneath. How those blue eyes could darken and blaze when she was angry about something.

"That I was riding astride. You know I have always hated that stupid sidesaddle. One has no control over the horse while perched like that."

"Audra, will you stop a minute and listen to me. We will discuss your riding habits another time. Right now, I have something much more important to speak to you about."

She came quickly erect in her chair. "What is it, Papa?" she asked anxiously.

"I had a long talk with His Lordship last night after dinner," Sir George said. "It was mostly about you."

Audra frowned. Had the earl told her father about their conversation in the garden? He had *promised* her it would be their secret!

"What did he say?" she asked him warily.

"He said he was enchanted with you." Sir George cleared his throat. "He asked my permission for your hand in marriage."

Audra's blue eyes widened in shock. "He wants to *marry* me! That old man!"

Then it all came to her. Of course. This was the earl's solution to her problem. He was wealthy. He would marry her himself. He was offering to take care of her, that was it. Like a kindly grandfather. She could visualize his round, cherubic face wreathed in smiles when the idea had come to him. What a sweet, generous gesture, she thought. What a dear soul he was!

"The earl of Latham is a very wealthy man," Sir George was going on. "Probably one of the wealthiest in England. As his wife, you would have a high place in society and, as he told me himself, it won't be many years before you will be left a rich, young widow and able to remarry someone closer to your own age."

Tears filled Audra's eyes at this. What a totally unselfish offer for him to make! Yet she could not possibly accept it.

"I don't love him, Papa," she explained. "He is jolly and pleasant and very kind, but marriage to me has always been a sacred trust between two people who love one another, not something arranged for a family's financial or political betterment. I know," her voice caught, "I know this would mean a great deal to you financially, for surely Lord Latham would help Greenleigh, but I just . . . I can't marry him. I'm sorry, Papa." She got to her feet and blindly crossed the room to the door.

"That was what I told him," her father said quietly.

She stopped and slowly turned around. "Oh, Papa!" she cried, running back to him and flinging her arms about his neck. "I knew you would understand."

Audra told no one that she was meeting Paul every afternoon and had been doing so since his return. They always met at the same place, by the fallen tree trunk.

"The earl of Latham has offered for me," Audra told him later that day.

"That old man!" Paul rose from his place beside her on the log. His jaw tightened. "I wondered why he had come to Greenleigh," he said, slapping his boot with his riding crop.

"That was not the reason, Paul. We had a talk yesterday afternoon in the garden, he and I. It was after I had seen you again and things seemed so hopeless. He was aware of my unhappiness and he seemed so kind and fatherly that I confided in him."

"You are very free with your confidences."

"That's not fair, Paul."

He sighed. "I know. I'm sorry."

"The earl spoke to Papa afterwards and asked for my hand. Don't you see? He only did it out of kindness."

"Really?' Paul's voice had a caustic bite to it. "What a terrible hardship it would be for him to have such a beautiful, young wife."

"You misjudge him. He is an old man. He has no family and is quite alone. I expect he thought I would be the daughter he never had."

Paul's smile was faintly cynical, but he said nothing.

"Nevertheless, I refused and Papa was very supportive. He understood when I told him I could never marry a man I did not love."

Paul lifted an eyebrow. "But *I* don't understand," he said quietly. "If I were wealthy, I think you would marry *me*." He looked down at her. "Is it presumptuous of me to think you might care for me?"

He stood there, so proud and aristocratic, so very handsome—a young girl's dream of a husband.

Audra colored, not meeting his eyes. "I am fond of you, Paul," she said, her voice dropping to a whisper. "I don't think it would be difficult to—to care more deeply for you."

He was suddenly kneeling before her, his arms going about her. "Ever since that day by the stream," he said, "when you were but a child and did not realize . . . I've thought about you. Then, the other day, seeing you galloping across the meadow toward me . . . I felt . . . did you not feel something then too?"

"Why, I—I . . ." she stammered.

"I want you, Audra," he groaned, burying his face in the nape of her neck. "I love you and it's all so hopeless. I want you so much and it is no use. Oh, damn!" He pushed himself away from her, resuming his seat beside her on the log, putting his head in his hands. "I talked with Robert last night. All he did, when I explained things to him, was offer to buy Greenleigh. He wouldn't lend me a sou. He is only interested in the estate. Told me I should be looking about for a wealthy bride to marry. One who could sustain a proper mode of living for an officer. Can you believe that? I went to Mother then, but she could do nothing. She has little money and her jewelry is all entailed. It will go to Robert's future wife. You may have heard he is being married in the summer."

Audra nodded. "Thank you for trying, Paul," she said quietly. "It could not have been easy for you."

"I won't give you up. I will find a way for us, Audra. I promise you."

She wanted him to kiss her. Every nerve in her body quivered to feel his strong arms about her again. She waited, but instead he rose to his feet.

Paul was afraid if he remained beside her another moment he might lose his head. She was so incredibly beautiful sitting there, with her soft, silvery hair left free today and flowing in rippling waves over her shoulders, her deep, velvety eyes downcast beneath her thick, dark lashes. She glanced up at last, to see a look of pain on his face.

"Go back home now," he said roughly.

"But it is still early—"

"For God's sake, *go*, Audra!" he ordered.

The earl of Latham returned to Greenleigh a few days later, only to be informed by Sir George of Audra's refusal.

It was obvious to him that Sir George had not told the girl of the large sum of money involved and even more obvious that he had not told the avaricious Lady Wentworth. Perhaps in her he might find an ally.

"One hundred thousand pounds!" Emily Wentworth exclaimed loudly at the magnanimity of the amount. "You offered George one hundred thousand pounds!" Her little mouth drew itself into an angry line. "But he didn't speak of any sum to *me*."

"I didn't suppose he had."

"It would be the answer to all our prayers," she said. "It would not only save Greenleigh, but restore the whole estate."

"Yes, Emily, I believe it would."

"I simply don't understand George. I would have thought he would jump at the opportunity. He loves Greenleigh so."

"Perhaps he is afraid his daughter does not want—"

"I will speak to that selfish little chit. Believe me, my lord, *I* will convince her."

"One hundred thousand pounds, Audra! Do you realize what that would mean?" Emily cried.

Audra nodded mutely.

"And think what *you* will have, my dear," she hastily added. "The earl's seat is in Surrey, but he has several other large estates as well and a splendid London townhouse. You will entertain and be entertained by the *crème de la crème*, and can you imagine the glorious gowns and the jewels you will own? The earl told your father he is prepared to give you anything in the world you might desire. It is like a dream, Audra!"

The girl looked up into her stepmother's glittering eyes. "A dream? And do you think His Lordship a young girl's dream prince?"

"Pshaw! Looks are not everything, Audra. You will find that out as you grow older. And the earl has such a kind and amusing disposition. He is so—so—"

"Fatherly," Audra filled in.

"Yes, that is it."

"He is older than Papa," Audra reminded her.

"What difference does that make?" Emily's voice was sharp.

"You really cannot see, can you?" Audra shook her head. "I do not *love* His Lordship. How can I marry a man I do not love?"

"You are a romantic little fool!" Emily turned away from the girl and strode angrily over to a window of the salon, yanking aside the curtains to look out over the lawn. When she spoke again her voice had lowered. "I really thought you loved your father, Audra. But it appears you think only of yourself. Even after all he has done for you, all he has given you."

"I *do* love Papa. This has nothing to do with—"

"I think it has *everything* to do with it. Haven't you noticed how tired and frail he looks? How worried he has become? You could make him well again. You could make him happy. It is all in your hands, Audra. All in your hands."

"One hundred thousand pounds!" Paul whistled. "He must want you very badly."

"Emily keeps telling me how lucky I am. He will be kind to me, she says, and I will have such splendid jewels and gowns. As if that mattered to me."

"It matters to some women," he said dryly.

"But not to me. Emily tells me I am being selfish, that I am not thinking of Papa, that if I loved him—"

"You would marry this lecherous old man who can hardly wait to get his hands on you!" he broke in. "Damnit to hell!" He thrust a hand through his thick hair. "I can't bear the thought of him touching you, Audra."

"Touching me?" The color went out of Audra's face and she looked up at him in horror. "But he would not . . . surely he is far too old to think of . . ."

Paul snorted. "How naive you are. So long as he is in good health there is no reason—"

"I won't marry him!" she cried. "I had thought he wanted me to be like a daughter to him. But I could *never* be a wife to him in that way. Never!" She was filled with revulsion at the thought of that obese little gnome taking her in his arms, pressing her against his flabby body.

"How your father could even—"

"It's not Father, it's Emily. Oh, Paul, couldn't we just run away together? Leave all this behind us?"

His eyes were very tender as they looked into hers. "I would give the world to do just that, but you know it's impossible. My leave will be up in another week and what would you do when I rejoined my regiment? Where would you go?"

"With you. With you to the continent. I've heard there are women who travel with the army."

"Camp followers," he growled. "Believe me, it is no place for a lady."

"You really don't want to marry me, do you?" Audra cried unreasonably, jumping up and running over to where the chestnut mare was tied. "If you did you would find some way for us." She flung the words over her shoulder. "I don't think you want me at all!" Quickly mounting her horse, she galloped madly off in the direction of Greenleigh.

Paul watched her go, her fair hair streaming out behind her. She had looked so young, so vulnerable, so unhappy. He cursed himself and everyone and everything concerned. He had never felt so completely frustrated. There was absolutely nothing he could do! Nothing, except to find himself a bottle and get thoroughly and insensibly drunk.

Audra rushed into the house, her long hair

dishevelled, the tears still wet on her cheeks, and nearly collided with the earl in the hallway.

He clasped her arm to steady her and she looked down at the pudgy fingers and quickly pulled herself away from him.

He had, however, seen the aversion in her eyes before she had dashed off. She had met that young man again this afternoon, he was sure. What the devil had he said to her?

Latham sighed. He supposed it was necessary now to explain things to Wentworth. It was not something he looked forward to. Damn degrading in fact!

Sir George waited a long moment as the earl sat before him, unspeaking, fiddling with the snuff box in his hands.

"What is it you wish to say, Clarence?"

Latham looked at him. The color rose in his already-florid face. "I am afraid I may have mislead you, George. I should have told you something at the time I asked for Audra's hand." He stopped, clearly embarrassed.

"Go on," Sir George said in a perplexed tone.

The earl got heavily to his feet and walked a few steps away from Sir George, turning his back on him before he spoke.

"I thought you should know, Wentworth, that if the fear of bedding with me is the cause of Audra's refusal, it is all for naught. I am impotent."

Sir George stifled a sigh of relief. Emily had been after him to arrange the marriage ever since she had learned of the sum Latham had offered. Audra was under age. He had every right to arrange her marriage. Now, it was as if a heavy weight had been lifted from his shoulders. He had promised Audra that she should only marry whom she pleased. Now, when the time came, when Latham was dead, she could still go to the man of her choice as untouched and as pure as a maid!

"It was good of you to tell me this, Clarence. I am sure it was not easy to say. Since Audra is but a child and will have many years . . ."

"Then there is still a chance she may accept my suit, George?"

"I would think there is a better chance, Clarence. That is all I can say."

Chapter Three

"You make a beautiful bride, Audra," Emily said as she entered the room.

There were, by this time, several women in Audra's bedchamber, all fussing about her as she stood alone in the center of the floor, clothed in an exquisite white lace gown.

The hairdresser stood back, observing the perfect arrangement of the silvery-blond curls beneath the crown of orange blossoms. The dressmaker knelt at Audra's side, carefully adjusting the long veil, and two little maids giggled together by the dressing table.

Emily, attired in a lavender taffeta gown that almost obscured her in its many ruffles, moved over to hand her stepdaughter a black leather jewel case.

"This came from His Lordship," she said smiling.

She had been smiling with that look of triumph in her dark eyes ever since the wedding date had been announced.

The velvet-lined box contained a magnificent diamond necklace. "I hope you will honor me by wearing the Latham diamonds," the earl had written in the accompanying note.

Audra's hand shook as she read the words. Could this really be happening to her? she wondered. Had her wedding day finally arrived? She had had no word from Paul since their last meeting several weeks before. Yet, even now, even at this last minute, she wanted to believe that somehow, some way, he would appear, bursting in like a knight of old to spirit her off on his white charger.

Even in the carriage on the way to the church, she paid little mind to what her father was saying to her, her eyes at the window searching the faces they passed, hoping . . . hoping . . .

Audra moved up the wide aisle of the London cathedral on Sir George's arm. She felt numb. When her father had explained things fully to her, she felt she could not refuse His Lordship's offer. There was no alternative, and it had made her papa so happy. Up ahead, she saw her husband-to-be, the cherubic faced, little, plump man who awaited her. He was dressed in the very height of fashion from his pomaded locks and his exaggerated shirt points to the intricacies of his neckcloth, the starched frill that protruded between the lapels of his tightly fitting satin coat, the fobs and seals which hung over his obvious paunch, to the rosettes on his pumps.

Latham smiled at her tenderly, understandingly,

and yet Audra felt nothing. She had not heard the gasps of admiration as she had entered the church, for she had never looked more beautiful; nor had she noticed the many guests, and the banks of flowers. She had walked on down the red carpet, one step after the other, a fixed little smile on her lips.

The service began.

Audra's heart gave a lurch as the archbishop's words penetrated her fogged brain: "If any man can show just cause why this man and this woman should not be joined in holy matrimony . . ."

Now! She cried to herself. Now Paul would step forward and demand the ceremony be stopped. Oh, Paul, Paul, where are you?

The service continued.

The question was being asked of her: "Repeat after me. I, Audra Elizabeth . . ."

It was too late! In a shaking voice she did not recognize as her own, Audra said the words. She heard the possessiveness in the earl's voice when he uttered, "For better, for worse, for richer, for poorer, till death us do part."

It was over. She had not been rescued. No miracle had occurred. She was the new countess of Latham.

The ceremony and the reception were over. In the splendidly furnished bedchamber that had been assigned to her in Latham House, Audra looked about her.

Her new lady's maid, Bess, a plump, young redhead with rosy apple cheeks, had removed her lace wedding gown and veil, and had helped her into her modest nightdress. She had brushed Audra's hair until it spread out in a shimmering silver cloud about her shoulders.

"You are very beautiful, milady," the girl said softly, in her country accent, her shy eyes admiring.

"Thank you, Bess." Audra smiled and touched the girl's hand. It was very cold and trembled beneath hers.

"Are you new here?" she asked kindly.

Bess nodded.

"I hope you will not be nervous with me," Audra said in an attempt to put the girl at ease. "I will try not to be too demanding a mistress. This is all very new to me, too," she confessed.

The small smile that had at first lifted the girl's mouth, somehow faded at Audra's last words and she said nothing more until she was dismissed.

"Goodnight, Bess."

"God be with you," the girl murmured, before she closed the door of the bedchamber behind her.

Audra smiled. She had received so many good wishes for her health and future happiness at the reception that was held after the wedding. There had been so many well-wishers. The tables had groaned from the quantities of rich food and there had been toast upon toast raised to her in the finest champagne. She wondered how the earl had managed to obtain so many bottles of the sparkling French wine, considering the trade blockade between England and the continent.

Her head felt a little light from all the champagne, but she did not feel in the least tired. She looked around the room that the earl had told her had been decorated especially for her. Clarence. She must remember to call him by his first name. Soft, blue damask draped the windows and canopy bed. He had picked them, he said, to match the blue of her lovely eyes.

Poor, dear man. He had tried to make himself as handsome as he could for the wedding, but nothing had been able to hide that awful, bulging paunch, brought on by age and overindulgence.

She had caught a few looks of pity that had been directed her way by several of the female wedding guests. A few ill-timed remarks had also reached her ears: "The weight of his pocket is obviously what attracted her"; "A creampot marriage if ever I saw one."

Audra had ignored the looks and the whispered asides. She had made her papa happy and that was all that counted. That, and saving Greenleigh.

The spring evening was cool and a fire had been lit in the marble fireplace of the bedchamber. The flames, Audra noticed, were making dancing patterns over the pale walls. The room was lit by only two candelabra, one at either end of the dressing table.

She moved over to the fireplace and sat down before it on the hearth rug. Her bare feet were cold. She stretched them out to the fire and wiggled her toes. When they were warm, she moved back, clasping her arms about her knees. For several minutes she sat gazing into the flames.

The countess of Latham. Odd, she did not feel any different from when she had been plain Audra Wentworth. She looked down at the gold band on her third finger, and it and the magnificent diamond and sapphire ring the earl had given her winked back at her.

Where was Paul tonight? she wondered. Why had he never communicated with her again after that day when she had grown angry with him and galloped away? The Chatfields had been asked to attend the wedding, but they had sent a polite refusal. Lady Chatfield was not well. Was Paul still in England? She wondered if she would ever see him again and the thought saddened her. Was what she felt for him really love? She had liked to be held in his strong arms. But love? How did it really feel to fall madly in love?

There was a knock at her door. Thinking it to be Bess, she got to her feet. "Come in," she said.

But it was the earl who entered the room. He was dressed in a long, burgundy brocade robe and he carried a silver tray on which rested a bottle of champagne and two crystal goblets. In the candle-light, his heavily jowled face seemed even more florid than usual.

"Good evening, Audra." He smiled his dimpled, cherubic smile. "I thought we might have a glass of champagne together."

Of course, she thought, realizing it would probably look strange to the servants if he did not come to her at all on their wedding night. She sat down in an upholstered chair beside the fire and folded her hands primly in her lap.

He set down the tray on a nearby table and proceeded to uncork the wine, pouring the sparkling liquid into the two goblets.

How like a child she looked, he thought, sitting there so straight and proper in her white, high-necked gown. He wished then that he were a younger man, someone like her Paul, coming to greet his bride.

"Champagne?" he asked, holding out a glass to her.

She shook her head. "I have already had far too much."

"But you must take a sip at least in answer to my toast." He handed her the crystal glass and there was a ringing sound as he touched his own goblet to hers.

"To the two of us," he said, "and our happiness on this, the first day of our life together."

Audra smiled and took a small taste of the wine. Latham had tossed his off and now was gazing down at her. The joviality had left his face, replaced by admiration and something else she could not describe. It was this expression of—could it be longing?—in the pale blue eyes that sent a strange shiver through her.

"Finish your champagne," he said quietly.

"I do not wish any more." Audra set down her glass, and as she did so he moved over to her. Before she knew what he was about, he had reached down and taken her hands, roughly pulling her up from the chair and into his arms. She gave a small cry of surprise. She had never thought him to be so strong. She stood taller than he by several inches, but he had brought her head down and now he was kissing her.

It wasn't the type of kiss she had expected from him. It wasn't a gentle fatherly kiss at all! His wet mouth was moving all over her face and his breath was hot and reeking of stale wine.

He must be drunk, she thought. That was it. There was no other explanation. He would be full of apologies in the morning. And yet, as he lifted his mouth for a second, she noticed for the first time the sensual fullness of his lips and the look of almost cruelty about them. Again they ground against hers and this time his thick tongue probed against her teeth.

She began to struggle, feeling the hard brutality of his arms, the impatient searching of his hands over her body. A wave of revulsion swept over her. This could not be! This just could not be! He had told her father he was not interested in her in *that* way and yet she felt something against her thigh. She tore her mouth away.

"What are you doing?" she gasped.

"What any husband would do on his wedding night."

"No! You go too far—"

"Too far, my dear? Did you not hear the words of the archbishop? We are as one now." And then he laughed. It was a lascivious, bone-chilling laugh. Gone was the jolly, pudgy little man with the Father Christmas smile. Gone was the cherubic expression, the innocent, twinkling blue eyes. All were replaced by the ugliness of raw lust as Latham gazed at the frightened rising and falling of Audra's full, young breasts beneath her modest nightdress.

She stared at him as if transfixed, not believing what she had heard and seen and felt. The fat fingers grabbed at the neckline of her gown, ripping it from her shoulders to her waist in one savage motion.

"Oh, my . . ." he breathed. His pink tongue darted over his full lips as his glittering eyes viewed the high, perfectly shaped, white peaks that were revealed to him. Eager fingers shook as they reached out to grasp and fondle.

"No!" she cried, jerking backwards, trying to cover her nakedness with fluttering hands, her cheeks flaming.

He paid her no mind. She had backed up against the footboard of the bed and he quickly grabbed her again, grunting now in anticipation as he tore away her fingers, hurtfully cupping and squeezing the soft, bare breasts.

"Let me go or I'll scream," she choked.

"And what will you scream, my dear?" he laughed. "That your husband is about to claim his conjugal rights? No one will pay you the slightest heed."

She knew he was right. No one in this house would interfere. But still she fought him.

"Why are you doing this?" she gasped. "I don't understand. You cannot bed me."

"Really?" he asked. His hands moved down to clasp her elbows. "Who told you that?"

"My father. He said you had informed him that you were incapable. He said—"

"So I lied to him." He shrugged.

"What!"

"I lied to him." His lips broke into a lewd grin, revealing his yellowed teeth. "Beautiful women have serviced me all my life. Another weakness of mine, like good food and fine wine. Couldn't have my manhood atrophying on me, could I? I assure you I'm as good as any buck half my age. Probably a damn sight better."

"How could you be so vile and contemptible!" She spat the words at him and freeing her right hand, slapped him hard across his cheek.

He reeled back a little, but the grin never left his florid face. "Good." His mellifluous voice purred. "I like a woman with spunk. Never did like easy conquests."

In that second of freedom, Audra tried to flee, but his hands reached out and grabbed the skirt of her nightdress, ripping it from her hips.

The sight of her naked body instantly inflamed him and he lunged and seized her greedily, lifting her from behind and throwing her face-down across the wide bed.

Audra struggled even when he pinned her down with one large knee pressed sharply into her back. Wildly he groped to unfasten and fling off his restricting robe.

"You're mad!" she cried, sobbing with frustration as she tried to tear herself free of him.

"And you are my wife," he growled, breathing heavily. "I will have you, Audra."

Straddling her thighs with his knees, he rolled her over between them.

Her eyes widened in horror as she viewed the revolting body that loomed above her.

The pink flesh hung from his bloated, flabby stomach in loose rolls of fat, the red, heavy jowled face leered at her, those pale, little eyes that she had thought so kind and gentle now cold and flat like the eyes of a snake. But worst of all was the sight of that monstrous puffy, veined thing rising between his legs.

She bit her lips, wanting to cry out, "No! Oh please, God, no!" but her pride stopped her. He would enjoy that. Instead, she writhed frantically beneath him, pummelling at his shoulders with her fists, twisting and turning to escape him. But for a man of his age and girth, he was surprisingly strong. He pinned her arms to her sides, but she saw that his face was dripping wet from the effort. He lowered it, burying it between her bare breasts and she heard him groan as his hot mouth covered one rose-colored tip and he began to suck at it noisily.

She wanted to scream, but now it was not only from horror. Hot anger was escalating into fury within her. How dare he do this to her! How dare he lie and deceive her into marrying him! She renewed her struggles, her nails raking at him, her teeth biting into his shoulder.

"That's it!" His soft voice was hoarse. "Fight me, Audra! Fight me, you little hellcat!"

But the more she fought to free herself, heaving and twisting, the deeper that hardness pressed against her! It seemed the only hard part of him, except for his arms and legs. The rolls of hot, damp flesh felt soft and spongy as they enveloped her. She shuddered. He was drenched with sweat now, the odor from his ugly, flaccid body nauseating her.

She vowed she would not give in to him without a struggle. In the country she had seen animals mating and knew that very soon now he would try and thrust himself into her. She couldn't bear the thought! She renewed her efforts. She felt she was being dragged down to the very depths of degradation as this fat pig snorted and pawed at her.

Latham's pulpy tongue jabbed into her mouth as Audra gasped for breath. Dazed, gagging from this new violation, she was, at first, unaware that he had forced open her thighs.

She felt little at first, except his hard swollen member poking feverishly at her as he spread her legs still wider. But when he lunged, when that searing rod of fire forced itself deep inside her, Audra was unable to prevent herself from crying out with pain, sobbing with each grinding thrust that threatened to tear right through her.

Latham pounded into her fresh body savagely, using her brutally, while the old bed rattled beneath them.

Writhing and sobbing, Audra tried to free herself from the stabbing length that impaled her.

"That's it!" he rasped. "Move on me, bitch! Move!" He was grunting like an animal in his frenzy, his pumping, panting body mercilessly thrusting deeper.

Oh God, she thought, how long? How long does this go on? She couldn't take much more. She was exhausted from her struggles, but she kept on fighting.

How she hated him! She had never hated anything or anyone before in her life, but she hated this filthy beast with a sense of loathing she did not know she possessed.

She had been betrayed. He had lied to her father. She would never have consented to be his wife if she had known the truth. He had realized that, of course. Oh, he was clever. He had known it was the only way she would marry him.

Latham was jerking faster now, faster and faster and then it came. The final degradation as his hateful juices unleashed within her.

He gave a shuddering sigh as he moved from her and quickly she rolled as far away from him as she could. She was aware now of the tears that had been flowing silently down her cheeks.

If only her first experience had been with Paul, how different it might have been. She knew that he would have been gentle with her. She remembered his kiss, his tenderness, and her heart ached. He would not have pounded into her like a rutting animal!

She wept then, for all that might have been, and did not know she had uttered Paul's name aloud until Latham roughly turned her on her back and raised himself on one elbow to look down at her.

"So it is still Paul, is it?" He laughed. "At least I know now he didn't enjoy you before me."

"Paul is a gentleman," she sniffed. "*He* would never have—"

Latham snorted. "A limp-dicked milksop if you ask me. Perhaps you'll be interested to know that I was able to use my influence in the right quarter to have your young lieutenant's leave cancelled. Shipped immediately back to the peninsula to rejoin his regiment." He chuckled. "Understand he had been drunk for days and put up little fuss about it. I do believe he left some sort of note for you. It came into my hands, but I'm afraid I somehow misplaced it."

"Why, you . . . you . . ."

"Haven't a fitting word yet for me, my dear? You will learn many after a few years. My first wife developed a splendid vocabulary by the time she died." He shook his head. "Too bad she never got pleasure from the act. You, now, are quite different. I think in time you will really enjoy it. Under that snow maiden exterior, I sense a certain wildness. Saw it in you as you galloped across the meadows at Greenleigh. By God, I said to myself, some day she will gallop astride me like that!"

Audra shuddered and scrambled further away from him, sliding to the edge of the bed. In a second she was on her feet, reaching for a dressing gown Bess had left over the back of a chair.

Latham was not surprised by her reaction to him. To be upset after the first time was not unusual for virgins. He had observed this many times before. "I assure you the next time will be better," he said in that musical voice of his that was so cruelly deceptive.

"There will *be* no next time, my lord," Audra said, her chin rising. "I will seek an annullment."

"I think that might be rather difficult since the marriage has already been consummated," he drawled.

"Not by mutual consent," she snapped. "I was raped!" Her hate-filled eyes glared down at him.

"According to our laws, my dear," he sighed, "a man cannot rape his wife. It is a wife's duty to submit to her husband." He sat up on the bed and crossed his legs before him like a fat, little Buddha. "I am going to enjoy breaking you in, Audra, but I have no intention of breaking your spirit. There are so many delightful things I can teach you." He gave a lewd laugh. "So very many things."

Even after the earl had risen and left her, Audra stood in the same position beside the bed, looking numbly down at it. The blue silk coverlet was rumpled and stained where he had taken her so hurtfully against her will. Her groin ached and her thighs felt sticky. Her whole body felt dirty and defiled!

She caught at one of the bedposts and sank to her knees on the carpet, the tears coming again, thick and fast. Feeling a light hand on her shoulder, she started and looked up into Bess's worried brown eyes.

"Are you all right, milady?" the young maid asked.

Audra strove to pull herself together. She had been taught not to show her feelings before the servants. She tried to gulp back the tears.

The little hand patted her shoulder comfortingly. "It may not be my place to say anything, milady, but he's a brute and a beast!" She handed Audra a clean cotton handkerchief from the pocket of her apron and watched as she blew her nose. "I wanted to come when I hears you cry out, but it would have been no use."

"No," Audra said desolately. "I am his wife, after all."

The girl nodded. "I just waited until he left. Can I do anything for you, milady?"

"No, Bess, but thank you." Audra smiled weakly at her.

The young maid put a plump arm about her new

mistress's waist. "You're shivering. You'd best be getting into bed."

Her mistress indicated the torn nightdress on the floor. "I need another gown, Bess," she said.

"Of course."

But before she moved to obtain it, the girl went over to a washstand and came back to Audra with a damp, soaped cloth, handing it to her mistress with a towel before she discreetly turned her back and began to rummage through the chest of drawers, returning, at last, with a clean nightdress.

"Now, into bed with you," Bess said, when this was donned, and pulling off the stained coverlet, she helped Audra climb between the sheets and tucked a warm eider-down comforter about her.

"Will you tell me something, milady?" Bess asked as she folded the coverlet over her arm to take away and sponge. "Something none of us here at Latham House can make head nor tail of? Why in the world did you marry him? You so young and lovely like who could have had anyone?"

Audra knew it wasn't Bess's place to ask such a question, and yet she felt it should be answered.

"My father was deeply in debt and His Lordship promised him one hundred thousand pounds for my hand."

"Your father *sold* you to him!"

"No. It wasn't quite like that. You see, the earl lied to my father. He told him he was too old to bed me."

Bess's eyes widened. "And your father believed that?"

Audra nodded mutely.

"But did he not notice the age of the housemaids

here at Latham House?"

Audra stared at her, uncomprehending.

"Not a one of us is over twenty."

A slow look of horror spread over Audra's face. "My father was never at Latham House until today. Are you trying to tell me? Is His Lordship so foul?"

Bess's stubby fingers twisted a corner of the coverlet. "He chooses for his housemaids young country girls like me who come to the city seeking work. I came from Somerset only a week ago."

Audra swallowed hard. "And has he . . . has he?"

"Yes, milady." The girl nodded, looking down at her hands. "That is why I knows the way it was with you."

"But—but this is monstrous!" Audra sat up, her blue eyes blazing. "This is beyond belief!"

"It often happens in big houses such as this," Bess said quietly. "Lucy told me that the gentlemen often feel it is their right. So kind she was to me afterwards. She's one of the downstairs maids and has been here the longest. His Lordship is right partial to pretty faces, she says, especially if they be virgins."

"Oh, God in heaven," Audra cried, "what depraved creature have I married!"

Chapter Four

The night was dark and cloudy with a steady breeze, all of which had made the crossing favorable. The trim, sleek vessel, *The Peregrine*, named for the falcon of courage and speed, had made the journey to the French coast in record time. Now, the dark shadow of land was fast approaching and the captain was giving low-voiced orders to his men.

A faint light appeared on the shore as a signal to the ship. *The Peregrine*, bearing no illumination, signalled back from its deck. The sails were silently dropped, the anchor lowered and a boat launched almost at once from the port side.

The oarsmen were strong and sturdy men who knew their job well. The captain sat at the tiller himself as they rapidly covered the distance to shore.

The boat was beached in a small cove between a

steep headland and the two men in the bow jumped overboard and dragged it up onto the sand. The rest of the men disembarked then, splashing ashore in the shallow waves. All but one stayed back and waited by the boat.

It was the captain who went on ahead, walking alone into the darkness. If something was to go wrong and he didn't return, the men had their orders to put out to sea without him.

He was thinking of this as he crossed the wide sand beach. A broad-shouldered man of some inches over six feet, he was dressed entirely in black and moved with long, sure strides.

Everything seemed the same as usual this evening, he thought, and yet he sensed something different. He could not put his finger on it, but he had a disturbing feeling that his approach was being watched by unfriendly eyes. The captain shrugged off his suspicions. After all, he reasoned, he was on enemy soil. It was only natural to feel uneasy.

It was not long before he was beneath the cliffs. He followed them to his left a little way and then, rounding some rocks, arrived at the spot from where he had been signalled. It was the mouth of a cave, hidden conveniently from the shore.

The captain gave a low whistle and a figure appeared in the door of the cave, shading a lantern with his hand.

"Peregrine," the captain said in a deep voice and the other man nodded and disappeared back into the cavern.

Following him through the opening, the captain had to duck his tall frame. What he saw made him break into a broad grin. There were dozens of kegs of brandy and gin, bales of tobacco and tea, crates that he knew contained fine silks and laces and satins, all piled neatly near the beach entrance of the cave. There would be quite a cargo tonight, he thought exultantly.

"*Bon soir*, Captain," said a voice from the shadows beside him. He could only see the bright eyes of the man who had spoken, for he was almost completely covered in a long, dark cloak, his hat pulled low over his brow.

"*Bon soir*," the captain returned in perfect French, eyeing the merchandise around him. "I see you have managed to get us the very best this time."

"Don't I always?" The other laughed. "I have the best thieves in all of France working for me."

"All goes well with them I hope?" There was an anxious note to the captain's voice.

"*Tres bien*!"

"Good. You are all doing a commendable job." He nodded to the other men who stood silently by. "Now, we must get this lot down to the boat. These spring nights are short for this business."

"You take a great risk, Captain."

The captain smiled. "There is often an early morning sea mist at this time of year."

The man with the lantern was now instructed to signal the men who waited down by the shore. They came on the run to help the men in the cave load the goods into the boat. The captain checked every item that was carried out of the cave on their husky shoulders. When it was all loaded into the boat, he paid the man he had spoken to in gold, concealed in a heavy belt he wore around his waist.

"Your next cargo will be lighter," the Frenchman said significantly.

The captain raised an eyebrow. "It is all set, then?"

"*Oui*, Captain. Two nights hence if the weather be favorable."

"We will be here."

The captain, anxious to be on his way, raised a hand in a farewell salute and ducked out through the cave's entrance.

He quickly retraced his steps below the cliffs and was just heading down to the sea where the boat and men were waiting, when there was a shout from above of "*Les Anglais*!" and a volley of shots broke out, directed at the beach.

The captain yelled to his men to put out to sea and broke into a run. Halfway across the beach he was hit. He fell hard, pitching forward on his face in the sand.

His men did not hesitate in obeying his orders and quickly launched the boat, leaving their captain where he lay. Despite continued shooting from the beach, they were able to transfer their cargo to the larger vessel on the wayward side, and weigh anchor. True to the captain's prediction, once out to sea they were enveloped by early morning mist and despite their heavy cargo were able to reach their destination quickly and unobserved.

The man in the long cape had followed the captain to the base of the cliffs and before the hostile group above could descend to the beach and reach him, he had dragged him among the shadowy rocks and half-carried him back toward the cave.

The other men in the cave, hearing the shots, were more than anxious to be on their way, but as soon as their leader had entered with his burden, they quickly obliterated any marks in the sand at the entrance to the opening and rolled back a heavy rock to obscure it.

It took three of the well-built men to carry the big English captain as they hurried to the back of the cave. The man with the lantern led the way through another opening and along a dark passageway that seemed to run straight back into the cliffs. The air was damp and cold in this tunnellike corridor. It was hewn from solid rock and curved and twisted, sometimes opening into other caverns, sometimes becoming quite narrow, but always, it seemed, rising slowly, but steadily upwards.

The men who carried the captain were breathing heavily as they ascended. After leaving the lower cave, the French leader had allowed more lanterns to be lit so they could better see their way, but after another one hundred yards, when the passage suddenly curved, he ordered them extinguished. A faint light could now be seen up ahead. The men had exchanged the odd word as they moved along, but now all became silent. The leader went on ahead, signalling the men to wait as he approached the exit.

He slipped through the opening, pulling back the strategically placed branches that shielded it from view and made his way through a small stand of trees to where he could almost see the road that lay before him. He listened for perhaps three or four minutes, but other than the usual night sounds, there was nothing to be heard. Quietly he returned to the cave and after paying the men generously for their night's work, he urged them to disperse as usual.

Then to those who had carried the captain he instructed: "Take one of the carts that was left in the woods. Cover him with straw and bring him to the rear gate of the château. I will meet you there."

The English captain had been brought into the large kitchen of the château and deposited on a settle before the fire. He was too long for it and his legs hung over one of the wooden arms.

The man in the long cloak removed it and his dark hat and placed them on a wooden chair inside the door. He was a sturdy man in his early thirties with a bright, intelligent face and an air of command about him. His name was Jean Paul Beaudette.

Beaudette trusted the two men he had brought with him implicitly. They were old friends and with him still held a grudge against Bonaparte.

General Brune had created a holocaust along the coast, a few years before, because of an anti-Bonaparte uprising. The village in the Pas de Calais near the château had been fired, as a lesson to all concerned, and many had lost their lives. Fortunately, a heavy rain had helped save the village from total destruction, but the three men present had all lost members of their families.

"Get a basin of clean water," Jean Paul told one of the men who had carried in the wounded captain. "Do not light more candles, Louis. The lantern is enough. Above all, be quiet!"

He took the one tallow candle which he had lit and

disappeared through a door to a hallway beyond. Only a few minutes passed before he returned, a young woman, who was still adjusting her hastily donned clothing, beside him.

"Marie will help us," was all the man said, drawing her over to the wounded Englishman.

Marie, who was ladies' maid to the lady of the house and sister to Jean Paul, gave a nod of her head. She and her brother had grown up at the château, but now he lived in the rebuilt village, which lay a little way down the coast, having become a trusted local official.

Marie gave a start when she looked down at the captain, known to her by the name of his ship. Peregrine. He lay very still and there was a great deal of blood down the side of his strong-featured face that now appeared to her to be unnaturally pallid.

"*Mon Dieu*!" she murmured. "Is he dead?"

"*Non*, but I still don't know the extent of his wound," answered her brother.

Marie pushed him rudely aside and kneeling down beside the settle proceeded to wring out a clean cloth in the tin basin that had been filled with clear water. She gently wiped the congealed blood from the captain's forehead and cheek, noticing that some was still flowing down from his temple.

"Will you hold up the candle, Jean Paul, so I may see him better?" she asked her brother.

Gingerly she pushed back the dark, curly hair and felt the area along the side of the captain's head. "He does not have a bullet in him," she said.

"The bullet hit him from behind," Jean Paul explained. "I think it seared its way across the side of his head, as he was running at an angle."

"*Oui*, it singed his hair above his ear," Marie noted. "Still, it has dug a nasty little trench. Does one of you have some brandy?"

Her brother nodded, producing a flask from the pocket of his coat. "I doubt you will get much down him until he comes around," he said, handing it to her.

"I am using it to cleanse the wound," she returned scornfully. She poured a little over the area and with the pain of it the wounded man groaned and moved his head restlessly from side to side.

"Hold his head still," Marie ordered her brother as she deposited the flask in the pocket of her apron, first removing some thread, a needle and a roll of linen she had managed to gather up after she had been awakened. Where the blood flowed the most deeply, above the temple, a white section of bone could be seen through the torn flesh. It would require several stitches. With Jean Paul's assistance Marie accomplished this very neatly.

She tore off a strip of linen and made a thick, narrow pad, placing it over the wound to staunch the bleeding. Again with Jean Paul's help, she managed to wind the rest of the linen bandage twice around the captain's head, while keeping the pad in position over the deepest part of the wound. Tucking in the ends, she sat back on her heels.

"I knew you could do that better than I," Jean Paul complimented her.

"Don't ask me why I help you," she grumbled. "I think you are mad getting mixed up with these smugglers."

"But the gold does much good, *ma petite soeur.*"

The captain let out another groan. This time it was louder.

"We must get him out of here," Jean Paul said, his voice low and urgent.

"But where?" one of the men asked.

"I had thought of *le nid d'amour* of which you told me," Jean Paul smiled at his sister. "Do you think your mistress would object?"

Marie shook her head. "*Non.* The love nest is the very place!"

"We must hurry." His glance went to the kitchen window. "The dawn is fast approaching."

Marie took the candle from her brother to lead the way and Jean Paul nodded to the two men to pick up their burden once more.

The little maid led them from the kitchen down a long hallway that lay beyond. When they had reached the end of it, she turned off at a right angle along another corridor. In the silence of the sleeping château, it seemed their footsteps must be heard, although they moved with infinite caution, for the men trod heavily under the weight of the big man they carried.

Marie motioned with her head to Jean Paul who walked beside her. She indicated a closed door at the end of the corridor. Upon reaching it, she quietly turned the handle and opened the door, revealing a deep, almost empty cupboard that lay behind.

Marie held the candle up to a panel at the back of the cupboard and with measuring fingers searched for a hidden spring.

All at once, with a soft murmur it gave way and

fell open before their eyes. In the light of the candle a narrow staircase could be seen leading almost straight upward.

"*Mon Dieu*! We can't get him up there!" muttered Jean Paul. "It is too steep and too narrow."

"It will take the three of you," Marie considered. "You and Louis must go up backwards, lifting him from beneath his arms and Henri can take his feet, *n'est-ce pas*?"

Up they started, slowly, very slowly, only a few steps at a time. The three men breathing hard from their exertion.

"I will go back and see that all is well in the kitchen," Marie said. "Rest at the top of the stairs and I will join you there." She closed the panel and hurried away.

The men were sitting on the upper landing, still breathless, when she returned. She thrust her brother's cape and hat at him.

"There is now no trace of us having been there," she assured Jean Paul.

The captain was starting to regain consciousness and mumbling incoherently from where they had propped him up in a sitting position.

Marie approached the low doorway that was positioned to the right of the landing and thrust the door inward.

A small room lay beyond, furnished with an enormous canopy bed, beside which was a table bearing a branch of candles. The only other furniture in the room was a small washstand in the corner and a straight-backed chair. The walls were stark except for a portrait on the wall opposite the bed. The early morning light penetrating through a skylight in the sloped ceiling revealed the portrait to be of a naked man and woman in a close, intimate embrace.

Jean Paul who was the first through the doorway after his sister, grinned as he surveyed the portrait.

"Madame la Comtesse, *certainment*, but which of her lovers was that one?" he asked Marie.

The young woman shrugged her slim shoulders.

The men by this time had carried in the wounded captain and now were depositing him on the big bed.

"Wait!" Marie cried, stripping back the richly embroidered red silk covering from beneath him and revealing the gleaming satin sheets and eider down beneath.

"Such luxury," laughed Jean Paul, as he stooped to pull off the captain's boots. "Perhaps I should endeavor to become one of the comtesse's lovers myself. What say you, Louis?"

The other man gave a loud guffaw and Marie was forced to hush them both. Jean Paul grinned at her and went about removing the outer clothing from the wounded man, leaving him clad only in his shirt and drawers. He thrust the covers over him and looked questioningly at his sister.

"I will stay with him until it is time to wake Madame." Marie nodded. "*Allez-vous en*! And be sure to close the cupboard panel when you leave. I can open it from this side."

The men were not long in making their departure and Jean Paul, after quietly thanking his sister, followed them from the room.

Marie fixed the covers more neatly under the

English captain's chin and stared down at him a moment. He seemed to have lost consciousness again. It worried her, but there was little she could do about it. He had lost so much blood, she thought, and was bound to be very weak. She sat down on the straight-backed chair to wait.

One hour passed. Then another. It was quite bright in the little room now. Marie got up from the uncomfortable chair and stretched her arms and shoulders. It was then that the captain's eyes opened.

"Where the devil am I?" he muttered.

She turned back to the bed. "You are at the château, monsieur."

A frown creased his brow and he winced at the pain even that small action created. "Can't remember . . . Was starting down the beach . . ."

"You were shot. The bullet grazed your temple. Jean Paul does not know who the men were. He brought you here to the château. I am Marie, Madame's maid and Jean Paul's sister. Do you remember me?"

He looked up at her and smiled a rather weak smile. Despite his pallor, he was a disturbingly handsome man, she thought. No wonder Madame was attracted.

"I recognize you, Marie," he was saying and then a look of puzzlement filled his eyes as he regarded the canopy above his head. A dozen faces stared down at him with bandaged heads. My God, he thought, I must be delirious.

"It is the mirrors, monsieur." Marie smiled at him. "We have you hidden in the love nest."

"The love nest?" He looked bewildered.

"I thought Madame would have brought you—" she started to say, and then stopped, coloring.

"I was not so privileged." The captain grinned. "Mirrors," he started to laugh, "sewn into the canopy. Celeste is quite *sans pareil*." The laughing, however, seemed to have increased the pain and Marie saw his mouth tighten.

"I have some brandy, monsieur," she said, bringing out the flask from the pocket of her apron.

His hazel eyes lit up and he reached for it eagerly.

"*Non*!" She drew back. "I will lift your head first."

She puffed up the soft, down pillows and raised his head gently upon them before holding the flask to his lips.

He drank deeply and gave a sigh as she removed the flask, grasping her small wrist with his big hand.

"May I keep it?"

She nodded, relinquishing the flask to him. "I really must go now. Madame will wake soon and I will tell her you are here."

"Thank you for all you have done for me, Marie."

The young maid blushed under his intent stare. "What you need now is rest, monsieur. I will bring you some breakfast later."

Marie expertly dodged the candle holder that was snatched from the nightstand beside the bed and thrown at her.

"Why are you waking me up so early, you *imbécile*?"

"If you will permit me to come nearer, madame, I will explain," Marie said from where she crouched beside a chaise longue. She had just pulled back the heavy draperies that covered the windows of her mistress's bedchamber.

"*Voyons*!" Celeste said irritably. "But I hope, for your sake, that your explanation warrants this early intrusion."

Marie hesitantly approached the large gilt bed that sat on a dais between two enormous swaths of rose silk that descended from a small gilt canopy in the high ceiling. The whole bedchamber was richly decorated in rose and white and gold, colors that became the dark-haired, white-skinned comtesse becomingly.

"Well?" that lady now demanded.

"It's the English smuggler, madame. He was wounded on the beach last night and brought here."

"Peregrine? Wounded!"

"*Oui*, madame. He was shot in the side of the head, but the bullet only creased him. He lost a good deal of blood, but I have bandaged him and my brother and I have hidden—"

"Where is he?" Celeste interrupted. "Where did you put him?"

"In *le dit d'amour*."

"And no one saw you?"

"*Non*, madame."

Celeste let out a sigh of relief. "You used your head, Marie. That is the very place for him to hide."

"Do you wish to go to him, madame?"

"As soon as I have breakfasted."

Celeste, la comtesse de Lascalles, with Marie's help, spent a full hour on her appearance before she felt she looked well enough to leave her room and visit her English lover.

Her gown was of a soft sea-green shade that set off her jet-black hair to perfection. Marie had drawn most of it back in a Circe knot, leaving a few soft curls about the face that would have been classical in its beauty except for the full, rather sensual mouth. Her eyes were dark, reminding one of the sea on a wintery day and depending upon her mood could become as stormy or as serene, sparkle with a coquettish challenge or smolder with passion. She was a beautiful, volatile and highly desirable woman.

Marie opened the bedchamber door for her mistress, but before Celeste ventured forth, she nodded to a connecting door to her right.

"My husband?" she whispered.

"He should not wake for hours, madame. He was very late to bed."

"And no doubt very drunk," the comtesse's lip curled. "Let us hurry, Marie. Peregrine will be wanting his breakfast." She said it as if it were her maid's fault that they were late.

Celeste waited for a moment at the top of the stairs, carefully regaining her breath before opening the door to the little room. Marie had gone off to fetch some breakfast for the captain without arousing undue suspicion—a difficult task at so late an hour in the morning.

"Peregrine!" the comtesse cried, as she burst into the room. "Oh, *mon cher*, what have they done to you?"

The captain had had several hours of sleep and, wakening, had pushed himself up on his pillows and polished off the remainder of the brandy in the flask. He didn't feel too badly at all, except for the constant throbbing pain along the side of his head.

"Good morning, Celeste." He even managed his engaging grin.

"Oh, Peregrine, you look so drawn and pale." She leaned over him to kiss his cheek, giving him a delightful glimpse of full, white breasts straining at the low décolleté of her gown.

"That is because I am desolate, Celeste," he said, trying to keep his mouth from twitching.

She sat down beside him on the edge of the bed. "Desolate?" she asked anxiously. "Why is that?"

"You have never thought me worthy enough to bring here before." He grinned, indicating the room about him.

She burst into a charming, low-pitched laugh. "What do you think of it, *mon cher*? It was built with the château, of course, but I believe I am the first to use it as a love nest."

"The mirrors I can accept," he said thoughtfully, "but the portrait on the wall will have to go."

"*Vraiment*?" She raised a shapely eyebrow. "Does it disturb you?"

"Yes. The artist hasn't captured my likeness at all."

"Oh, Peregrine." She laughed. "How I have missed you, you rogue. You promised you would return to me weeks ago."

"There is a small matter of a war between our countries."

"A dreadful bore! It seems to go on and on and what good has it done anyone?"

"It brought us together," he reminded her.

She smiled. "If my horse hadn't lost a shoe . . ."

"And if the man I was to meet hadn't been delayed . . ."

Her smile became provocative. "It was fate, *n'est-ce pas*?"

He was about to make a rejoinder when there was a knock at the door.

Marie entered with the captain's breakfast and placed the tray on the table by the bed. As she turned to leave, Peregrine stopped her.

"Will you tell me something that has been bothering me?" he asked her. "Did my men get away?"

"*Oui*," she answered, "with no trouble."

"Good," he sighed.

"I think it shameful they left you lying there on the beach," the comtesse broke in.

"They were only following orders, Celeste."

"Bah! Cowards, all of them!"

"I owe my life to Marie and her brother," the captain said, smiling at the little maid as she made her way to the door. "And to you, of course, Celeste," he quickly added, seeing her frown at the departing girl, "for allowing me to remain here."

"And remain here you will until you are quite well again," she murmured, leaning over to kiss him tenderly on the lips. "Let us hope your head heals quickly," she said, running her fingers inside the open neck of his shirt and caressing the smooth, hard flesh.

"What the devil has my head to do with it?" He gave her a meaningful grin.

"You might jar it," she said. His shirt was open now and she could feel the rock-hard muscles along his shoulder. "You are such a violent lover, *mon amour*."

He reached up and captured her two hands in one of his, pushing them aside. "Will you leave me to my breakfast, you tempting little baggage," he growled.

"On one condition." She got to her feet. "Do not attempt to leave this room. Philippe is in residence here at the château."

"Philippe!"

"*Oui*. My dear husband has been here for over a week, but he should be leaving any day now."

"I gather he does not know of the existence of this room."

"Of course not." She smiled. "This was *my* family home not Philippe's. His estates were stolen during the revolution, but not his fortune, thank God. His claims have finally been acknowledged by Bonaparte and soon his case is to be heard in the courts. That is why he is so much in Paris." She put a hand to his cheek. "That is also why I have never brought you to this room before. There was no need. Philippe was away from the château and my own bed quite, quite empty."

"And today? Has he already risen that you were able to come?"

She shook her head. "He sleeps late in his own bed. He devoted last night to cognac and not to me."

"More fool he."

"I care not." She shrugged. "His lovemaking is so unimaginative—so mechanical."

"Yet he loves you to destraction, from all I

hear. Has he no suspicion that you are unfaithful to him?"

"Philippe?" she scoffed. "He has such an exalted opinion of himself and his abilities as a lover it would never occur to him."

"Nevertheless, under the circumstances, *ma petite cherie*, I would appreciate it if you would bring me a weapon of some sort to protect myself. I feel quite defenseless in this room."

"I mean you to be." She smiled. "Quite, quite defenseless, my darling Peregrine."

Chapter Five

Audra slept little on her wedding night, lying awake and staring into the darkness. Her mind was in a turmoil, emotions crowding in on her—anger, fear and disgust all ran the gamut, but only served to strengthen her resolve. She would not stay with this foul old lecher who had demeaned and abused her, who lived a life of hypocrisy with his pleasant, jovial manner that belied the vileness beneath.

She would escape! But lying awake in the small hours of the night, she wondered where she could go. She could not go back to Greenleigh. Not now. Her father would listen to her, she felt sure, and would not force her to return to Latham, but his honesty would also require him to give back the settlement to the earl. Sir George was not well, and the resulting conflict and humiliation might well bring about a relapse. She could not risk that.

Should she seek refuge with her great-aunt Alice? No. She was of the old school and would never countenance a woman leaving her husband for whatever reason. "You did take marriage vows committing you, no matter the disillusionment and pain," she could imagine her aunt saying. "Many are unhappy in their marriages, but manage a brave front in public." It was obvious to Audra that in this instance Great-Aunt Alice would be of no help.

Paul. She could go to Paul. Despite his negative feelings about joining him on the continent, she felt sure he would look after her.

But would the earl pursue her? Audra had no doubt that he would. Relentlessly. She had visions of spending the rest of her days looking over her shoulder. Tossing and turning in the big bed, it was dawn by the time sleep finally claimed her.

Bess brought her breakfast on a tray and pulled back the heavy, blue curtains to let in the bright spring sunshine.

"It is a beautiful day, milady," she said to Audra.

"Is it?" her mistress asked, turning her pale face with the mauve smudges beneath the lovely eyes to look at her maid. She felt a hundred years older than when she had awakened the previous morning—the morning of her wedding—the wedding that had made a travesty of the sacred vows of love and trust and honor.

"Eat your breakfast," Bess urged, plumping up the soft pillows behind Audra's head. "His Lordship has gone for the day. Some sporting event, Abel said. Abel is His Lordship's manservant." Her voice lowered. "I think he and Lucy are in love." Bess might have been at Latham House only a week, but she had been quick to learn many of its secrets.

Audra had little appetite for her breakfast. While she quietly sipped at her hot chocolate, her mind was alive with the knowledge that the earl was away from the house for the day. She would pack what she needed in a bandbox, tell the servants she was off to the dressmaker with something to be altered, and make her escape from Latham House forever! What did she care where she went so long as it was away from that ugly, despicable man?

She tried to keep the excitement from her voice as she said to Bess, "Will you help me dress? Since I am left alone for the day, I think I will visit Madame Bertin. I have a new gown I am not pleased with. The seams need some adjusting."

The smile left the young maid's face. "I am sorry, milady, that will not be possible."

Audra was indignant. "I beg your pardon?"

"His Lordship has left instructions that you are to remain indoors today."

"He has . . . what! What right has he . . ."

Bess looked at her helplessly. "If you should try to leave the house, milady, Abel has his orders to lock you in your room."

Audra's blue eyes darkened in anger. "How dare he!" She slammed her cup down hard into its saucer, splashing chocolate onto the eider-down comforter. "How dare he treat me like a prisoner! I am his wife. I am . . ." Her voice faltered.

"Yes, milady, I know," the young maid sympathized, quietly removing the tray from Audra's lap. "Perhaps you would care to look about your new home today, meet the rest of the servants."

"New *home*!" Audra exclaimed. "This will *never* be my home! I am not going to remain here any longer than I have to. The first chance, the first opportunity . . ."

"That is what we all say, milady," Bess sighed. "You see he has a hold on every one of us. Those of us who work here have no other place to go. Without references, we would end up on the streets."

Audra stared at her. "Even the male servants? What of them? What keeps Abel here?"

"Abel has a prison record, my lady. He was accused of stealing by his former employer, although he swears his innocence to this day. If he ever tried to leave, His Lordship would quickly have the law down on him and—"

"Accuse him of thievery, I suppose," Audra broke in. "Why this is nothing but a house of slaves, Bess! We are all slaves to that fiend!" she cried, her voice rising.

"Please don't upset yourself, milady," Bess said anxiously. But Audra was on her feet now, angrily pacing up and down beside the bed. Suddenly, she stopped and looked at her young maid, who was quietly laying out some underclothing for her mistress to wear.

"Where do they go?" she shot the question at her.

"Who, milady?"

"The female servants when he tires of them?"

"We do not know. No one speaks of it, milady. The day I came, an upstairs maid called Annie was missing. Disappeared during the night, they said.

They all just looked at one another and it made my flesh crawl it did to see their eyes."

"The earl could not just dismiss them," Audra pondered, "or they would spread the word about him. And no word could *ever* have leaked out for his reputation has never been questioned. My father," she scoffed, "was sure it was quite above reproach."

The young maid was regarding her mistress with wide, fear-filled eyes.

"Oh, my lady, do you think he has taken them to those—those houses?"

Audra had heard of such places when she had been in London before. "Brothels?" she considered. "No. There are certain dandies of the ton who frequent them, I'm told. A remark dropped to them and His Lordship's reputation would be blackened in no time. No. I fear even worse, Bess," she shivered at the thought. "Behind that warm, jolly appearance, His Lordship is an evil, conniving man. I don't suppose you have ever heard of White Slave Traders. . . ."

Audra awoke with a start. A dark shape was standing beside her bed holding a branch of candles.

"Good evening, my dear," said that deceptively beautiful voice, causing a chill to run down her spine.

With an effort, Audra kept her own voice steady. "Get out of here!" she commanded, raising herself up in bed and pointing to the door.

"You would order your husband from your room?" he asked, placing the candelabrum upon the dressing table. "I have every right to be here, my dear."

"There is no way you will force your foulness on me again!" she spat. "I loathe and abhor the very sight of you!"

"I don't doubt it," he said, undisturbed by the vehemence of her outburst. "But you are my wife and I am going to have you whenever and however I like. What is more," he purred, "I am going to make you love it."

She glared at him, her blazing eyes declaring how completely impossible that would be, that she hated him and would prefer death to his embrace.

Her attitude excited him. She could see the excitement growing in his eyes as he unfastened his robe and flung back the bedcovers.

In that moment, Audra reached beneath her pillow and withdrew a knife she had taken from her dinner tray and hidden there.

"Get back!" she cautioned him, the blue eyes spitting fury.

Latham did just that, moving slowly backwards, keeping his eyes warily on the hand that waved the weapon, but as he moved, he reached down for the robe he had dropped.

Thinking he meant to put it back on, her eyes flicked from his face to the robe. It was a mistake. In that small second, he swung the robe at her hand, entangling it and making the weapon useless. Instantly, he was clutching the wrist that still held the knife.

"Drop it, Audra," he cried, his fingers increasing the pressure until she had no course but to do as he asked.

He flung the robe and knife aside and they dropped to the floor. She tried to jerk away from his hold, but he held her fast with his right hand while his left tugged at her nightdress, finally yanking it over her head.

Before she could make another move, he had thrown his pink, fleshy body atop hers. She was pinned, but her hands were now free. She struck at him, clawed at him, and he brought back his head and laughed in her face, a glittering, avid look in his pale eyes.

"That's it, Audra," he urged. "Fight me!"

In that moment it became clear to her. Her efforts to escape him only added to his pleasure. This was what he wanted. Her struggles simply increased his lust. This was how this old man became aroused enough to take her.

Immediately she stopped fighting him and let her arms fall limply to her sides. She willed herself to lie completely still.

The slobbering lips closed over hers. He pulled her roughly against his fat, sweat-drenched body, his mouth striving to part her lips. He was wildly intent on making her respond and at last his lips forced hers to open and he rammed his thick tongue within.

She offered no resistance. She lay as one dead, having steeled herself to feel completely detached from what was being inflicted upon her.

"So that's your plan, is it?" he growled. "We shall see."

Gently he began to kiss and caress her, intent on bringing the response she refused to give, all the while whispering words of love to her in that warm, melodious voice. His only reward was a convulsive shudder that racked her cold, rigid body. The soft love words turned to salacious obscenities as he tried a different approach. Revulsion might cause her to struggle and resist him again, but still she did not move. She lay like a rag doll beneath him and he could not take her! Weak and limp against her belly, he was unable to achieve the erection he craved.

He struck her hard across the cheek. The force of the blow brought tears to her eyes.

"Don't be indifferent to me, you little bitch!" he growled. "You'll regret it if you do!"

The imprint of his hand was flame red on her pale cheek, yet she did not move. Her expression remained remote and uncaring. It was her second mistake.

Latham scrambled from the bed and grabbed for the robe he had discarded. Reaching into one of the capacious front pockets, he withdrew a thin, coiled coachman's whip.

"Now, I will see you move." He smiled, gloating down at her as he unleashed the whip. It was odd that that musical voice seemed its warmest when he was planning something vile and abhorrent.

Audra gasped and squirmed to the other side of the bed as the lash came down, missing her by inches.

"You're insane!" she cried, springing from the bed and darting around the side of it, but he was there before her, anticipating her move. She heard the whistle of the whip as it swept through the air and then a searing pain bit into her thighs as it neatly encircled them. So quickly was she yanked toward him that she lost her balance and fell heavily to the floor. The breath was knocked from her and in that moment he was upon her.

All thought of indifference to him vanished and Audra again fought desperately to restrain him, but more weakly now, more ineffectually. The brief struggle ended with Latham's mocking laugh of triumph.

Shivering, Audra knelt before the fire, trying to stir up the dying embers.

"I hope you have learned a lesson tonight," the earl said, standing over her, his hands thrust deep into the pockets of his robe.

She turned her head and looked up at him. There were still traces of tears on her cheeks. She ached from all he had inflicted upon her, yet her blue eyes pierced daggers into him as she sat up, her back ramrod straight, her head held high.

"You've had your pleasure," she spat at him. "Now, for the love of God, leave me alone!"

She clasped the afghan she had thrust about herself closer, but her movement had briefly revealed one shapely thigh and the ugly, red welt along it.

"I truly disliked bruising that lovely skin," he said regretfully.

"You lie!" she snapped. "You enjoyed every moment of it."

"You needed to learn that my rights as a husband are not to be denied. You will do as I wish from now on, Audra."

"Your rights as a husband! Is it part of those rights to degrade and torture your wife so you may satisfy your own lusts? If you only wanted to use me, why did you marry me? Why? You have your servant girls who are virtual slaves to you. Why did you bother to marry *me*?"

"You mean you have not guessed?"

"No. You have no love in your heart for me. You love only yourself."

"It's very simple, my dear. I want a legitimate heir."

"An heir!" She looked incredulous. "You think at your age you could possibly—"

"Yes!" he cried. "I am not too old." His chest went out proudly. "In this past year two of my housemaids have given birth to my bastards!"

She stared at him for a long moment and then a mocking smile touched the corners of her mouth. Oh, how she wanted to get back at him! "And of course you believed them. How they must have laughed behind your back."

"What do you mean?" A slow flush of anger was slowly creeping up his face. She should have been warned. Twice that evening she had misjudged his reactions, but now she was past caring. Unable to injure him physically, she took aim at his ego.

"Your manservant, your butler and your footmen, my lord, are all much younger men than you, and undoubtedly more virile."

"Are you suggesting—"

She had gone too far! Latham erupted with a roar, cursing her viciously as he grabbed for her, his strong fingers fastening themselves around her throat. His face was purple now with rage, his pale eyes black with fury.

"They were *mine*! They swore they were mine!"

His hands closed tighter about her neck, squeezign steadily. Desperately she clawed at him, trying to break their murderous hold on her windpipe. She strained and squirmed, feeling weak and dizzy. He was a madman! His eyes gleamed with an insane light as he increased the pressure on her throat.

She felt something fall across her leg and realized it was the poker she had used on the fire. Reaching down, her fingers grasped it and with her last ounce of strength she lifted it and swung it hard at the side of Latham's head.

His fingers relaxed on her throat and he fell over sideways with a crash. There was a look of surprise on his face as he went down, striking his head on the corner of the heavy brass fender.

He lay very still.

Gasping for breath, Audra knelt there, head bent, her throat raw with pain, her lungs bursting with pinpoints of fire. The dizziness passed and she looked over at the figure by her side.

A small pool of blood had formed beneath where he had hit his head. Had she killed him? She leaned over him and felt his pulse. He was still breathing.

Now she was deathly afraid. She had to get away! Fast! If she were still here when he regained consciousness, he would surely murder her!

Audra got unsteadily to her feet. Should she call Bess and get the girl to help her? No. She must not involve the little maid. It would only get her into trouble. She must make her own escape.

But she felt so terribly weak. She ached from Latham's brutal assault and she was shaking with fear and fatigue. Hurry! cried her brain. You must hurry!

She dragged herself across the room to the big, carved wardrobe and with trembling fingers fumbled inside it for a warm travelling dress and pelisse. On the floor she discovered a small portmanteau.

Every breath caused an agony of pain, but she forced herself to dress as quickly as she could. She shoved extra clothing into the bag and in a reticule placed all the money she possessed and the small amount of jewelry that the earl had not locked away in his safe. Quickly she tied a poke bonnet over her dishevelled curls.

She was ready.

A groan from the dark form that lay before the fireplace galvanized her into action. She must be away from Latham House before he recovered! Then she stopped. It wasn't fair to leave Bess here and the rest of the servants who might want to make good an escape.

Audra rang for the girl and then flew to the door. It opened to her touch and as she peered out into the dimly lit hallway, she saw Bess crossing the gallery and hurrying toward her.

Slipping out of her bedchamber, she closed the door behind her. The key was in the lock and she turned it.

"Milady!" Bess exclaimed, seeing her dressed for travel, with the portmanteau at her side. "What—"

"The earl is inside," Audra quickly silenced her, although her voice shook. "He—he nearly choked me to death, but I managed to hit him with a poker and break free." She cleared her hoarse, raw throat. "He is lying in there unconscious, Bess." She removed the key from the door and handed it to the girl. "I locked him in."

"You are leaving here?"

"Yes, and I must hurry. I—"

"Oh, milady, let me go with you, I pray you!" Bess pleaded, grasping Audra's arm as she started across the hall toward the stairway.

Audra took less than a moment to consider. "You may come, Bess, but there is no time to lose." They hastened along the hallway and crept noiselessly down the stairs.

Audra had left her bedchamber that day and had made a tour of the entire house. She had wondered at that time how she might escape if the chance ever presented itself, and had discovered that the French doors in the drawing room were locked from the inside. She explained this to Bess when they reached the lower hall and the girl nodded.

"Wait just outside for me," she said breathlessly. "I will only stop to get my cloak." Then she paused. "I owe it to Lucy to tell her. There may be others who will want . . . Shall I give her the key?"

Audra nodded. "But hurry, Bess! Hurry!"

When the girl had gone, Audra grasped a lighted candle from a wall sconce and made her way to the drawing room, silently opening the double mahogany doors. She left them ajar for Bess and crossed the room. The latch on the French doors opened with a faint click and within seconds she was outside the silent house.

Audra breathed a sigh of relief. It was cool and dark in the garden, but all she was aware of was a sense of freedom. She was free of that madman she had married! Never, she vowed, would he ever get his hands on her again! If she had to travel to the ends of the earth to escape him, she would!

She waited impatiently on the terrace for Bess. As the minutes passed, she grew more and more frantic. Where was the girl? What was taking her so long?

All at once the light of a candle flickering across the drawing room inside caught her eye, and soon Bess was beside her, her face as pale as death.

"Run!" she cried. "Run for the garden wall! Milord is bellowing upstairs and pounding on the door!"

Fortunately, it was not a pitch-black night, and holding up their skirts they raced across the grass as fast as they could go. Audra felt a searing pain in her bruised throat, but she did not stop.

The starlight and a faint quarter moon illuminated the stone wall before them. It was about six feet tall, but to Audra, the former tomboy, it would normally offer little difficulty in scaling. Tonight, however, her whole body ached from the beating she had suffered. Could she manage it?

Audra gave Bess her portmanteau and reticule to hold and, hoisting her skirt above her knees, she found a toe hold in the stone and reached for a sturdy vine. Holding tight to it, she struggled to pull herself up to the top of the wall. One foot slipped and she thought she would fall, but the vine held and slowly she pulled herself to the top, grasping the edge with eager fingers. Her knees were both skinned, her fingers raw, but she had made it!

Audra would have liked to stop long enough to catch her breath, but there was no time to waste. Anxiously Bess was handing up her belongings to her and a small parcel of the maid's own. Audra dropped them on the other side of the wall and then, leaning over, reached down to grasp Bess's hands. Fortunately, the young maid proved to be quite nimble and was soon up beside her. In another moment they were both safely over the other side of the wall and standing in a short private lane. It was deserted. Bess pointed in the direction they should take and the two young women set off.

Luck was with them. They had barely reached the dimly lit street beyond the lane when an empty hackney carriage rumbled around the corner. This they promptly hailed and were soon on their way to the White Horse Inn in Fetter Lane where, the sleepy driver assured them, they could catch the early morning mail coach to Dover.

At last Audra felt able to breathe freely again.

Chapter Six

The English captain was feeling better. He had lain for several days in *le nid d'amour*, waited on and nursed by the little maid, Marie, and visited briefly by the beautiful Comtesse de Lascalles.

He put his hands beneath his head and grinned up at the mirrored canopy above him. It amused him to think that he lay in the very home of the man he hated above all others, and would soon resume an affair with that gentleman's adored wife.

Celeste knew him only as the head of a band of English smugglers, as Peregrine, the name of his ship. He knew it excited her to take such a rogue as her lover.

Philippe de Lascalles was not aware of his existence. They had yet to meet face to face. Yet, thinking of the reason for his hatred, the captain's face darkened.

His brother, an escaped prisoner of war, had been recaptured on this estate, just outside the château, so very close to the channel and to freedom! He had been tortured on de Lascalles's express orders. The compte had been convinced he was carrying secrets back to England and felt a confession from such a high-ranking prisoner would be looked upon favorably in Paris. The captain's brother had taken a long time to die and he had died an agonizing death. These facts the captain had learned a year before from his good friend Jean Paul.

He had thirsted for revenge, but a quick killing of the compte would, he knew, bring him no personal satisfaction. He had learned of de Lascalles's beautiful wife, Celeste, learned how her husband loved her to such distraction that he kept her hidden away in the country—far from the eyes of any would-be admirers. It was no accident he had met Celeste the day her horse had lost a shoe. It had all been carefully arranged. It had taken even less time than he had imagined to gain her bed.

The captain was modestly aware that women were attracted to his rugged good looks, but he could not have said why. Normally, he did not purposely set out to charm them, but when he smiled, which he did frequently, something happened between his teasing eyes and his insolent grin that convinced them he had something wonderful to share with them. Many had discovered, to their delight, that he did.

He was a man who enjoyed giving pleasure as much as he enjoyed receiving it. Not desiring marriage, he avoided young, unwedded females like the plague and confined his attentions to married women or those of experience who freely offered their favors.

Now that his head wound was healing well, the captain was becoming restless. He felt like a prisoner in this confining room. He rose and dressed and sat down in the chair by the table. Celeste had sent him several books to read, but they were all romantic French novels, which he found ludicrous and implausible. As the afternoon came to a close, he began to pace the small room. He was bored and longed to do something. Anything. He was not used to inactivity. He had no idea how long he would be forced to hide out in the château.

The night before Jean Paul had come to him with the news that his men had returned on *The Peregrine* as had been arranged to pick up their human cargo, but he had felt it too dangerous, and had signalled them off before they could launch a boat. The earlier attack on the captain and his men, Jean Paul was quite sure, had been instigated by the Compte de Lascalles himself, but the reason was unknown to him.

When Jean Paul had left, the captain pondered this.

The compte did not seem in any great hurry to depart for Paris. Celeste, not wanting to arouse his suspicions, was playing the role of the devoted wife. Therefore, she was only able to slip up to see him for very short periods of time. Now that he had almost regained his health, this was beginning to prove quite frustrating to them both.

The captain poured himself another glass of

brandy. Damnit, in his boredom he was drinking too much of it, which certainly did nothing to help his injured head. He longed to do something positive, hating the inaction.

He began to pace the floor again and as he did so he stumbled over a loose, braided rug at the foot of the bed. Reaching down to straighten it, he noticed something unusual about the oaken floorboards beneath.

He threw back the rug. Underneath was what he had suspected—a triangular section that formed a trap door! The oaken boards were so perfectly joined together that only a close inspection revealed the fact that the floor was not solid. He got down on his hands and knees and examined it. Where he knelt, there seemed to be space enough to insert his fingers and lift the section up. This he did, with little difficulty.

The dusty cavity below was dark and narrow. It appeared only large enough for one person to squeeze in, and he would be required to lie down flat. The captain grinned. This was obviously the perfect spot to hurriedly hide a lover for the brief period of time it would take to search the room.

He decided to get into the space himself and see how it felt. He lifted himself down into the dark, cramped area, realizing that it had not been constructed for a person of his size. He was too tall, for one thing, and had to lie on his side and bend up his knees. His shoulders were also too wide and fitted uncomfortably tight. He was about to pull himself out when he heard voices talking below him.

The captain realized then that there was a

breathing hole in the corner by his head. He twisted himself until he could put his eye to it. He could not see clearly, as the light was dim below him, but he did see that there were two—no, three men in the room that appeared to be a library or a study. One of the men was speaking to the other two.

"Are you sure every building hereabouts has been thoroughly searched?" he asked.

"*Oui*, Monsieur le Compte. The wounded smuggler is not in the village. It is our belief he was picked up later that night by his own men."

"How could that be? There have been men guarding the entire five miles of beach since it happened. Would they not have seen something?"

"In the dark, Monsieur le Compte, it is sometimes difficult—"

"*Sacré bleu*! That is why the men were hand-picked. I wanted men who were used to night work and could shoot well. What do I get? Incompetent paysans who shoot at a smuggler!"

"There was no sign of a human cargo that night, Monsieur le Compte. The report by your informer was not correct."

"So you chose instead to shoot one of the smugglers. Sots! Smugglers are encouraged by Bonaparte. All that is done by him is to relieve them of their gold and send them on their way."

"It was the smugglers' leader who was shot and wounded. It was hoped he might have knowledge of this escape route your informer spoke of."

"But he too has escaped it seems. Bah! I have delayed my return to Paris by several days due to the hope you might unearth him. Now I cannot waste any more time. I must set out tomorrow. While I am gone, Etienne, you are solely in charge of this operation. Pierre, of course, will assist you."

"*Oui*, Monsieur le Compte."

"You still have no suspicions as to who from the village may have helped the English smugglers?"

"*Non*. The villagers here are very closemouthed."

"There are ways, Etienne. There should always be one or two men stationed in the taproom at the inn. Free drink has been known to loosen many a tongue."

The compte and the two men left the room. The captain waited a few minutes and then crawled quietly out of the hiding place. He carefully replaced the door and the rug.

It was the first time he had seen his enemy and he had not had a good view. Richly dressed, a well-built man of what he judged to be average height, the compte had thinning hair, carefully arranged to hide a spot that was balding. His long, thin nose was apparent, but the rest of his face had not been easily seen from the angle in which the captain had been forced to lie. He would also have trouble identifying the other two darkly clad men, but he did know their names and the fact that Etienne was tall and thin and Pierre, short and stocky.

By the time Marie came with his dinner, the captain was lying propped up in bed, contemplating several possible plans.

She lit the branched candles beside him. "I am sorry I am late," she said, "but I could not get away any earlier. The compte has guests tonight and I had to help madame to dress and—"

"That is quite all right, Marie," the captain broke in. "Having no exercise, I am not particularly hungry." He smiled at her.

It was impossible for Marie not to be terribly aware of this man, for she was seeing him constantly. How handsome he was, she thought, a soft blush creeping up her thin cheeks. She had enjoyed caring for him these last few days, pretending to herself that this giant of a man belonged to her alone. She had almost convinced herself that he really did not care for her beautiful, selfish mistress. Surely he could see through her, see that he was only the latest of her many lovers.

Before him had been a lieutenant in the Dragoons, stationed for a time in the village, and then there was a young fisherman, followed by the head groom at the château. Marie shook her head. This captain was different. There was a commanding presence about him that seemed to fill the little room. He was his own man—so distinctly masculine. The comtesse was mistaken if she thought she could manipulate *him*.

How wonderful it would be to feel the thrill of those strong arms closing about her, of demanding lips covering her own, of warm flesh pressing against warm flesh. Her soft blush turned to crimson as she realized he was addressing her.

"Would it be possible for me to see your brother? I have something I wish to tell him."

"I will contact him, monsieur. He may be able to come sometime during the night."

"Thank you, Marie. By the way, I have not seen your mistress today. Is she well?"

"She is well," Marie said so brusquely that the captain gave her a strange look. "She sent her apologies to you, monsieur. The compte has been very demanding of her time today."

He nodded, but the motion triggered a sharp pain in his head and he closed his eyes.

"It still aches, monsieur?"

"A little, but I have much to thank you for, Marie." He smiled that devastating smile of his. No woman on earth, she was sure, could have resisted that smile. It made her feel decidedly weak in the knees.

"There has been no infection, so the wound is healing well," she managed. "I think you will only have a slight scar."

Jean Paul came just before dawn and he and the English captain discussed what the latter had overheard from the hiding place. The captain urged the Frenchman and his men to be even more vigilant, warning them of the informer. The men were taking turns each night at the smuggling cave in order to signal away any approaching vessel. These men must be doubly sure they were not followed either to or from the cave.

Jean Paul told the captain that in two nights a fishing boat would be putting out to sea with the human cargo of three men who had been forced to hide for the last few days in the cave. The fishermen would signal *The Peregrine* and transfer this cargo directly to her. Was the captain interested in joining them at that time?

The captain assured him that he was indeed, but wondered how this was to be arranged. There were many men guarding the beaches.

Jean Paul smiled. It seemed the mayor of the village had a daughter who was to be married in two days. There would be a great celebration. That was why that particular night had been chosen. It had already been decided that the compte's men who guarded the stretch of beach close to the cave would receive liberal quantities of wine quite early in the evening.

"They may also not be as vigilant with the compte away in Paris," the captain said. "Perhaps," he suggested, "it would be an added precaution to invite the head men to be guests at the wedding reception." He had described these men to Jean Paul who had instantly recognized them. "Could that be arranged?"

Jean Paul grinned. "Very easily, monsieur."

"Then I shall look forward to leaving this comfortable prison in two days time," the English captain said, shaking the other's hand.

"Peregrine, my love, he has gone! He has finally gone!" Celeste cried, rushing into the love nest late the next afternoon. "Look, I have brought us some champagne to celebrate." She produced a magnum, which she set down on the table.

Celeste looked ravishing in a crimson-colored gown. Her jet-black hair flowed freely down her back in rippling waves.

Freshly shaven and feeling better than he had in

days, the captain was sitting on the bed, his long legs crossed at the ankle, struggling to read one of her risqué French novels.

"It has taken him long enough," he grunted.

"Have you been impatient, Peregrine?" Celeste asked coyly, sitting down on the edge of the bed and removing the book from his hands. There was a feline sensuality in the dark eyes that slanted up at him from beneath the long, sweeping lashes. "Have you missed me?"

"You know I have," he said thickly, his arms going about her shoulders, drawing her almost roughly back to him as he hungrily sought her mouth. The book fell unheeded to the floor.

Her tongue was hot, darting between his lips as she worked at a button of his shirt. He gave a growl of pleasure, yet he pushed her away from him. "Let us not rush it, *ma petite.* Let us slowly savor this long awaited time together." I intend to have the upper hand was the message he conveyed.

She looked a little disappointed, a pout forming on her lips, but he paid her no mind. He reached for the bottle of champagne and proceeded to uncork it, pouring the sparkling liquid into the two goblets that had been sitting beside the brandy bottle on the table.

Celeste kicked off her shoes and lolled back against the pillows beside her lover.

They touched glasses.

"To Philippe's departure." Celeste gave a meaningful smile. "Long may he remain in Paris."

They drank deeply to that and then the captain toasted Celeste and she him and they went on to toast Jean Paul and his friends, the captain's crew, the comtesse's horse who had lost her shoe and soon there was much laughter as the toasts became more and more ridiculous and the level of the champagne in the bottle became lower.

Gently the captain removed the empty goblet from Celeste's hand and set it with his own glass on the table beside him. When he turned back to her, Celeste had already unfastened the bodice of her revealing gown. He helped pull it over her head. Her body lay before him, naked and voluptuously inviting.

His hands cupped her full breasts and his head lowered to taste each perfect orb in turn, teasing the erect nipples with his tongue. She arched her back with delight, giggling softly.

"I really feel quite tipsy," she admitted. Then she looked at him. "But you are still dressed." The laughter left her dark eyes to be replaced by a smoldering look of desire.

It took her only seconds to remove his shirt and he grinned as he helped her slide his breeches over his slim hips.

The sight of his already turgid manhood increased her growing passion. She wanted to feel it hot and hard between her thighs. She began to rub her lush, warm body against his in sensual delight, purring like a cat.

None of her lovers had ever equalled this one. Not only did he possess the body of a Greek god, but he never rushed like the others to seek his own fulfillment. Instead, he preferred the slow, sensuous enjoyment of building up their mutual desire.

Together they explored every lustful pleasure, until wild and writhing against him she cried out for him to take her. Even then he held himself back, urging her on to the very pinnacle of agonizing pleasure before allowing his own release.

The captain was the first to move from the entanglement of limbs. He stretched his arms to regain their circulation and settled back more comfortably on the pillows. One hand moved to idly stroke the smooth shoulder that lay against his chest.

"*Si bon*!" Celeste sighed.

The captain grunted.

A few moments passed.

Celeste began nibbling at the hairs on his damp chest. "I'm thirsty again," she murmured.

"You're a voracious wench," he choked. "Give me a little time."

"Thirsty for more champagne," she giggled, a teasing look appearing in the sensuous dark eyes as she looked up at him. "Although I have no objection to an encore, *mon amour*."

"Then I will endeavor to make love to you as often as you wish, madame."

"What a stallion you are!" Her laugh was husky.

They did not bother with the goblets this time, but passed the wine back and forth between them, laughing when in tipping up the big bottle the champagne spilt down their chins.

"How deliciously decadent." Celeste laughed, slurring the words a little as she flung back her head.

"Oh look, *mon étalon*!" Above them their naked bodies were mirrored a dozen times. "See, a veritable orgy!"

He laughed, his warm, deep laugh and saluted their reflections with the bottle, taking a long drink. He held it out to her, but she shook her head.

"*Non*! I am already quite dizzy."

"Good." He gave her a wicked grin. "Then I have you where I want you." He bared his teeth. "And I intend to ravish you, my fair maiden!"

She drew back with a feigned look of horror. "Oh no, Monsieur Stallion, I pray you!" she squealed.

Monsieur Stallion indeed! He said an ugly word to himself. Damn the rapacious wench! So all she saw in him was a stud to perform at her will. Well, perhaps it was just as well. She was not the one on whom he wished his revenge. It was better that their affair remain only physical for her as well as him.

Afternoon turned into evening. Sexually sated at last, the two lovers slept. It was Celeste who awoke to hear the knock at the door.

She untangled herself from the captain's arms, her lips brushing him with a kiss, and rose from the bed. Walking over to it a little unsteadily, she opened the door.

Marie stood on the threshold with the captain's dinner tray in her hands. She took in the scene at a glance, quickly lowering her eyes from the sight of her naked and dishevelled mistress.

"Is there enough for two, Marie?"

"*Oui*, madame."

"Then bring it in and put it on the table," Celeste said impatiently.

"But—"

"*Tiens*! He's sound asleep." Her mistress scoffed at Marie's suddenly burning face.

The little maid hurried quickly over to the table and set down the tray, trying to avert her gaze from the bed. She did not want to see him. She wanted to flee as fast as she could from this scene of love she ached to have shared. Why then did her eyes flick to him as she turned from the table? She saw only the bronzed blur of his broad back amongst the rumpled covers.

Celeste, however, had caught her furtive glance and met her eyes with a mocking smile as she headed for the door.

"Wish you could take my place, Marie?" she jeered at the girl. "I'll confess something to you. The handsome captain is even better than he looks."

Lewd laughter followed the little maid as she ran from the room and fled quickly down the steep staircase.

Chapter Seven

On the early morning coach to Dover, besides Audra and her young maid, there were two men, who appeared to be tradesmen, and a fat older woman. They had barely left the outskirts of London before Audra realized that the woman was a loquacious busybody intent on learning everybody's business. As she did not wish to reveal her destination, or any personal details, Audra excused herself from the conversation, stifled a yawn, and then began to feign sleep until that state actually did overtake her. She was completely exhausted from all she had experienced in the last few days and slept on until they had nearly reached their first stop at Maidstone.

Audra awoke to sense someone's eyes upon her and became aware that one of the tradesmen sitting in the seat opposite was gazing at her with open admiration. Ignoring him, she turned her head and proceeded to stare out of the window at the passing countryside.

"Uppity!" she heard the fat woman murmur to the tradesman and had to keep herself from smiling.

At the small wayside inn at Maidstone, Audra purchased some refreshment for herself and Bess.

"You are sure you do not wish to return to Somerset?" she asked the girl.

"No!" Bess said hastily. "I could not go back home."

"But would you not be happier with your family?"

"No! There is no room for me now. I must make my own way."

"But surely you have friends in your village who would help you find employment there?" In a way Audra envied the girl. She only wished that *she* might return to her home—to Greenleigh.

"You do not understand, milady." The young maid swallowed and looked down at her lap. "There was a young man who wished to marry me. Despite the urging of my family, I refused him. I had always dreamed of getting away from the village, of seeing a bit of the world. All I could see of my future if I married was just another cramped, little cottage and a pack of children. My ma was very angry at me she was. 'Then go!' she says and thrusts me out. 'You'll be sorry,' she says, 'but don't come cryin' home to me'"

There was understanding in Audra's eyes as she looked at the young girl. "But what of that young man? Have you changed your mind about him?"

"He wouldn't have me." Bess sniffed back the tears. "I'm soiled now. I cannot wed."

"Why not?" Audra cried. "If this young man loved you I do not think he would reject you for a fault that was not your own."

"No, but I would not come to him dishonored." Bess set her little round chin proudly.

Audra shook her head. "I think you are being very foolish."

"Oh, milady," Bess begged, "pray let me travel with you wherever you are going. You will need someone to care for you."

Audra regarded her. "It may be dangerous where I am going, Bess. I would not want anything to happen to you on my account."

"I don't care—"

Audra held up a hand to interrupt her. "Wait until I tell you what I plan. I wish to obtain passage on a packet going to France. I have a very dear friend who is an officer in the army on the peninsula and I have decided that I am going to join him there."

"To France!" Bess's eyes widened. "But we are at war with the French."

"I speak the language rather well, Bess. Years ago my father became friends with an elderly French aristocrat, a widower and an émigré from the revolution. He had purchased an estate not far from Greenleigh, which was my home. I was quite small when he died and Father employed two of his servants, an old married couple, who spoke not a word of English and had been turned out by the new owners of the estate.

"I learned to speak French from them, but it

wasn't until I went to London last year and spoke to a French gentleman in his own tongue that I discovered that my accent was strictly that of the servant class and not at all aristocratic." She laughed, remembering the haughty lift to the gentleman's eyebrows as he had given her a crushing set-down. "I feel," Audra went on, "that this will help, rather than hinder me in this undertaking, if I am to pose as a Frenchwoman in order to join my friend."

A light had come into Bess's eyes as Audra had explained her plans. "It will be a great adventure! Oh, do take me with you, milady!"

Audra smiled at her. "I would be delighted to have you with me, Bess. I have never had to do for myself before and I am quite ignorant about many things."

It seemed, upon their arrival in Dover, that one of the things of which Audra was ignorant was the knowledge that there were no longer any packets sailing from Dover to France.

Audra, dragging her young maid behind her, made several inquiries around the town. All to no avail. At last, she obtained rooms for herself and Bess in a respectable-looking inn.

She even questioned the innkeeper about passage to the continent, using as a reason for her eagerness the tale she had fabricated of an unwell grandmother, but he also shook his head. If she had been astute enough to recognize it, she would, however, have caught the flicker of indecision in his eyes.

Audra decided to dine in her room and Bess had just returned with a tray for her, when there was a knock at the door.

It was the innkeeper's wife with a message. There was a gentleman downstairs who wished to speak with Mrs. Worth, as Audra was calling herself.

Audra looked puzzled. "But I don't know—"

The woman lowered her voice. "I believe it is about some transportation," she whispered, then proceeded to stare so pointedly at her open hand that Audra realized that the woman expected some remuneration for her trouble. Giving her some coins from her reticule, Audra turned back to Bess and instructed her to remain in the room. She then followed the innkeeper's wife out the door and down the narrow stairway.

A dark gentleman of slim build and medium height approached her as she reached the bottom of the stairs.

"I believe we have something to discuss, madam," he said, bowing slightly. "There is a private parlor where we may speak undisturbed."

Audra hesitated a moment, but the man appeared to be a gentleman and quite businesslike in his manner, so she allowed him to lead her down a short hallway and into a small room.

They sat down opposite one another at a table. The innkeeper himself entered almost immediately with a bottle of claret and two glasses. Nothing was said until he had discreetly withdrawn.

Audra refused the glass he poured out for her and the gentleman did not touch his own until he asked:

"You are looking for a boat to take you to France?" His face was expressionless, but Audra was aware of the fact that he had a slight French accent.

"Yes, I am," she said, observing him more closely.

"May I ask why?" He took a sip from his glass.

"My grandmother is French," she lied, sticking to the story she had invented. "She has not been well and I have had no word from her in over a year. I am naturally most anxious. . . ."

"May I ask why your husband has not made inquiries?"

"It is of no interest to him. He—he—" she stammered. Then she stopped, looking at him desperately. Could she trust this stranger? She decided that she had no choice. "I will be honest with you," she said, swallowing hard. "I have run away from my husband. He—he ill-treated me."

Although it was quickly masked, she caught his look of disbelief.

"Look!" she cried, unfastening the scarf at her neck and moving closer to the lamplight. "Look at my throat!"

"*Mon Dieu*!" he exclaimed, seeing the nasty bruises around her slim neck. "Did he try to throttle you?"

"He is mad!" she shuddered, sitting down again. "That is why I have run away from him. My grandmother is the only one I can go to. She will understand." She looked at him anxiously. "You *do* see, don't you? That is why I *must* go to France!"

He nodded. In his mind there was no question of the young lady's sincerity. Englishmen were such barbarians. He made his decision.

"I have made arrangements for a small boat to take me across the channel tomorrow night," he said, lowering his voice. "Would you be interested in travelling with me?"

"But of course!" she exclaimed. Then a puzzled look came into her eyes. "But why are you so anxious for another passenger?" She bit her lip. "If it is money, I have very little. . . ."

"That is not why I have asked you," he said, studying the tabletop for a moment before he looked up. "Let us just say I would find it expedient at this time to travel with a wife. Would you object to pretending you are my wife for the length of the journey?"

"So long as it was only for appearance's sake," she considered.

"That is the only reason, I assure you, Mrs. Worth." Although, he thought to himself, as he observed the little beauty who sat so demurely opposite him, you are very lovely. It is too bad we did not meet under better circumstances. Perhaps, when we reach France . . .

Audra was about to question him further when something occurred to her. Could it be that this man was travelling to France on a mission for the government? It would explain the whole thing. He might even be an agent! Who would suspect a man travelling with his wife to be a spy?

"May I ask you something before I give you my answer?" she said and at his nod she continued. "Are you journeying to France on an assignment?"

He caught the spark of excitement in her wide, blue eyes. "Yes," he said very seriously, striving to keep his lips from twitching. Her naïvete delighted him. He was positive now that he had made no mistake in approaching her.

"Am I to be told anything about it?"

He shook his head. "I am afraid not," he said even more soberly.

She was thoroughly convinced now that her assessment of him had been correct. The man *was* a spy! She had heard in London that many of the émigrés from the revolution were eager to serve England as their adopted country. Perhaps he was one of them—travelling surreptitiously to France to gather information. She felt honored to play even a small part in helping such a man.

"What do you wish me to do?" she asked him conspiratorially.

In a low-pitched voice he began: "As soon as it becomes dark tomorrow night . . ."

Audra and Bess sat in the bow of the fishing boat as it headed out across the channel. It was a warm evening with little wind and the men at the oars appeared to be making good time.

The owner of the boat, a big, rough-looking individual named Jock was at the tiller and the Frenchman sat beside him.

Audra thought back to earlier in the evening when she and Bess had been hustled into an old carriage at the door of the inn and had started out down a coastal road in the direction of Dymchurch. In that town, they had abandoned the carriage to ride horseback. The Frenchman had led them across the Downs until he reached a small creek. It was there they were met and introduced to Jock, who had hurriedly helped them into the quickly launched boat. They shoved off almost at once.

There was little talking during the trip. The time passed without incident until in the far distance they could see the dark outline of the French coast.

It was then that Audra thought she heard a faint noise off to their port side. She turned her head. Was it another boat?

Jock quietly barked out the order. "Lift your oars!"

The men obeyed him, now aware that another vessel was fast approaching. Its dark shape was slowly becoming discernible in the gray light.

"Heave to!" a voice shouted in English from across the water.

"A revenue cutter!" one of the men near Audra cried.

"Row, damn you!" came the command. "We'll make a run for it!"

Panicking, the crew thrust their oars back into the sea, but began to pull discordantly.

"Heave to, or we fire!"

"Row in time, damn you! Faster! Faster!"

The boat seemed to take off across the water, but there was a sudden explosion and a bullet whizzed over them.

"Keep your 'eads down!"

Audra pulled Bess down to the bottom of the boat. The young maid was shaking in fear and clinging to her mistress's arm.

"My God!" exclaimed the man at the tiller, recognizing the vessel that bore down on them. "It's not revenue officers, it's *The Peregrine*!"

Immediately indecision seemed to break out

amongst the men. Some continued to row, while others slowly raised their hands above their heads.

More shots were fired as the approaching ship drew closer. All rowing stopped as the men at the oars lifted their arms in quiet surrender.

Jock was cursing bitterly now. He should never have taken his boat out. He should have known better. Now he was likely to lose it and even worse! He did not notice for a moment that the Frenchman beside him had stripped off his outer clothing and was divesting himself of his boots. Now he rose and in one smooth motion dove over the side of the boat and into the sea.

The Peregrine was nearly beside them now and someone aboard shouted: "One of them is trying to make it to shore!"

"Stop, or I'll shoot!" a deep voice bellowed out after the swimming Frenchman.

But the man swam on, flailing his arms and legs as fast as they would go, desperately striving to reach the distant beach.

"Fool!" was heard from the ship that was now abreast of the fishing boat. There was a loud report and as Audra watched, peering over the bow of the boat, she saw the Frenchman's arms rise in the air as he was hit.

"No!" she cried out in horror.

Immediately someone threw himself over the side of the larger vessel and stroked rapidly in the direction of the man who had been shot. He was quickly lost to Audra's view as the hull of the ship closed in against the fishing boat. A rope ladder was let down and they were commanded to ascend it as quickly as possible.

"Oh, milady," Bess trembled beside Audra. "Be they pirates?"

"Smugglers, I think," Audra answered her, having overheard some of the murmurs of the men. "It appears we have broken some agreement."

The two women were helped up the ladder and soon found themselves on the deck of a trim little sloop.

A man of great height with a wide breadth of shoulders stood with his back toward them. He still held a long-barreled pistol in his hand and as Audra watched, he shoved it into the pocket of his greatcoat and turned to face the little group that had come aboard.

"Who is in command?" he asked. His voice was rich and deep. The same voice that had cried out to them from across the water.

Two men with lanterns had come up beside him as he spoke.

"I am," Jock mumbled, stepping forward. Gone was the hard and resolute look he had borne earlier; he was plainly nervous of the formidable man he faced.

"It was *your* fishing boat, Scalley?"

"Aye, Captain," the man admitted. "What do ye plan to do wi' her? She be all I have—"

"I'm afraid she has already been cast adrift and it serves you bloody right. You know the rules, Scalley."

The fisherman's face whitened. "But what will I do now?" he wailed. "'Ow will I make me livin'?"

"The gold guineas you got for this crossing will no

doubt console you and your men," the other grunted.

He had moved into the lanternlight and for the first time Audra saw his face clearly. It was that of a man in his late twenties, or early thirties, strong featured, but lacking the refinement of a gentleman. Instead, it was the sort of face one might well imagine for a pirate—rakishly good-looking and a trifle frightening. The scarf tied around his forehead only added to his wicked countenance. All he needed was a gold ring in his ear and a cutlass in his teeth.

She caught his surprised glance as his eyes rested on her for a moment. She knew he could not see her clearly beneath the shadowy brim of her poke bonnet.

"Who is this?" he asked the man he had addressed as Scalley.

"The Frenchman's wife, sir, and her maid with her. They were accompanying the man who jumped overboard. I swear they were our only cargo, sir. Ye may search us all. The only gold I have is what the Frenchman paid me to take them to France. This is not a smuggling run. I have no extra guineas to trade with the Frenchies for brandy and tobacco."

The captain turned from him and gave an order to several of his men. "Take them below and search them, although I doubt you will find anything. From this man's anxiety about his boat, I believe any gold he might have brought with him was hidden under her floorboards and is now resting on the bottom of the sea."

As the men were led off, there appeared a slight movement on the starboard side of the sloop where the rope ladder had been lowered. One of *The Peregrine*'s men went over the side and a moment later came back into view carrying a dark shape over his shoulder. A man in dripping wet clothing followed him. The first man let his burden down gently on the deck. It was the body of the Frenchman!

"Is he dead?" the captain asked the second man.

"Aye, sir. Shot through the back of the neck."

The captain swore. "Tried to aim for his shoulder," he said angrily. "Search his clothing thoroughly, Ned."

All at once he remembered Audra, who had not moved but was looking at the dead man in shocked silence.

"My apologies, madam," he gave her a little bow before turning to the man who had deposited the Frenchman's body on the deck.

"Take the lady and her maid below to my cabin."

The captain's cabin was small, but neat and well-appointed. The walls were panelled in dark mahogany and were covered with several large, framed maps. For furniture there was an enormous desk and several comfortable chairs.

Audra urged Bess to sit down in one after the man had left them. The girl was white with fear and clutched her elbows close to her body.

"What is going to befall us, milady?" she moaned, rocking back and forth.

"You must let me do all the talking, Bess," Audra told her as she paced up and down before the desk. "This murdering captain must never learn my true identity or you may be sure he will be quick to seek a reward from the earl for my return."

This statement only caused Bess to look more terrified.

Audra was immediately contrite. "Don't worry," she said, patting the girl's shoulder. She was doing her best to appear in complete control, but her heart was hammering wildly. "We are headed back to England, and there isn't very much we can do about that, but we will manage to figure out something when we get there."

"*If* we get there," Bess cried, tears spilling down her freckled cheeks.

It must have been a full hour later that the low door of the cabin opened and the tall captain ducked his head and entered. He had removed his coat and was dressed all in black from his shirt to his tall, gleaming boots. To Audra it made him look all the more sinister. By this time her nerves were raw and she was struggling to retain her composure. She had stopped her pacing, but she was still standing as he crossed the carpeted floor to her.

He looked down at her from his great height, his intense gold-flecked hazel eyes seeming to look right into hers. Somehow Audra managed to return his gaze, unsettingly conscious of something passing between them.

"I am sure this has been a most distressing time for you, madam," he said, a touch of sarcasm in his deep voice.

"Distressing?" she shot back. "Why on earth should I become distressed over such a trifling matter as cold-blooded murder!"

The captain ignored her thrust. "May I offer you some sherry?" he asked, turning his back to her and walking over to open a small cupboard beside the desk. He removed a bottle and some glasses. "Do sit down," he said to Audra as he poured out the wine.

She took the chair nearest the desk, sitting down on the edge of it and holding her back very stiff and rigid.

"Madam?" he offered her a glass and Audra accepted it. The young maid looked to her mistress before she took her glass and at Audra's nod, her fingers reached gratefully for it.

"Your name?" the captain said to the maid.

"Bess, sir."

"Well, Bess, I wish to speak with your mistress alone for a moment. If you would kindly withdraw to the adjoining room?" He took her elbow, helping her from the chair and opening a door in the wall opposite to the cupboard, ushered her into his sleeping quarters.

When he had closed the door, he turned back to Audra.

"You look most uncomfortable, madam. May I take your cloak?"

"I think not," Audra said tightly.

"Will you at least remove your bonnet?" He smiled—it was a very attractive smile, but she was instantly wary of it.

Nevertheless, the bonnet was hot and heavy so she set down her glass and wordlessly reached up, unfastened the ribbons and removed it. Her soft, silvery blond curls were crushed and unconsciously her hands went up to tidy them.

When she looked up at him again, he had undone the scarf from about his head and she could not fail to notice the recent scar along his temple. Had he been in a duel, she wondered, or was the wound caused by the path of a bullet?

Their eyes met, hers a little anxious, his faintly amused as he appraised her.

She was very lovely, he thought, the delicate features perfectly formed around large, deep-blue eyes, her pale skin as smooth as fine silk. There was an unmistakable well-bred air about her that was confirmed by her speech. When she had lifted her hands to her hair the soft blue pelisse she wore had opened and he had caught a glimpse of firm, high breasts and a slender waist. The Frenchman's eye for beauty could not be questioned, but the lady's character, he thought, was another matter.

Audra did not blush or flinch from his frankly admiring stare. She simply reached for her glass and took a sip of her sherry.

He raised his own glass to her. "You are a cool one, madam," he said, his eyes narrowing. "Your husband is killed before your very eyes, dragged out of the sea and dumped at your feet and you do not flick an eyelash or shed a tear." His lip curled in disgust. "I have never in my life seen such a heartless wench!"

She gasped at his words. "I was quite horrified by his murder!" she cried, her voice shaking. "But the man was *not* my husband."

He frowned. "Do you really expect me to believe that?"

"It is the truth."

"Not according to Scalley. That man has just told me that a Frenchman by the name of Fornier engaged him to take his wife and himself over to France. He gave the fisherman some story about an elderly relative who had not been well."

"*That* was not the truth," Audra said, thinking to herself that it had been *her* made-up story the Frenchman had used.

"Since you were not his wife," the captain went on, "were you then his mistress?"

"Certainly not!" Audra said hotly. "I did not even know the man's name! Why, I only met him last night."

"So that's your story," he snorted. "Quite inventive. An innocent little doxy whose client offers her more money if she will pose as his wife and travel to France with him?" He gave a harsh laugh. "You'll have to do better than that, my dear. Whores don't usually travel with an abigail in attendance."

She sprang angrily from her chair and without thinking slapped the cynical grin from his face.

He had thought she was beautiful, even while she was pale and her large eyes filled with anxious fear. Now that the fear had gone, replaced by this fierce indignation, he thought her irresistible.

Before she realized what was happening, he had caught her arm, forcibly pulling her to him. She struggled furiously, but she was as helpless as a child in his grasp as his arms tightened about her, holding her close against his rock-hard chest, making it impossible for her to escape.

He kissed her then quite ruthlessly, holding her chin firmly in his big hand as his mouth crushed her lips in a kiss that bruised and demanded and explored, wresting the very breath from her, making her dizzy and weak in the knees.

It all happened so swiftly. Her body responded instinctively to the wild urgency that transmitted itself to her and arched itself brazenly against the tall, muscular frame. Strong hands slid down to pull her hips closer and a disturbing sensation spread through her loins, a delirious heat that threatened to engulf her as he rocked her sensually against himself.

Recent ugly memories made her jerk her body back, but she could not bear to tear her lips away. She felt as if she were slowly dissolving in the passion of his scorching kiss. Horrified, realizing what was happening to her, she pushed roughly against his chest. Abruptly he released her and she fell back against the desk, angry, panting, struggling to still her pounding heart.

"You loathsome brute!" There was a noticeable break in her voice and the fear had returned to her blue eyes, for there was no sign of mercy in the wickedly grinning face that stared down at her. At that moment he looked more fiendish than her wildest imaginings of a bloodthirsty pirate!

He took a step toward her and with a last, desperate effort she swung at him, but he grabbed her wrists and deflected the blow.

Fighting the tears that filled her eyes, she gasped, "Dear God, am I to be ravished again?"

"Again?" He lifted a mocking eyebrow as once more he released her.

"Twice," she cried, rubbing her wrists, "twice in the last few days."

It was the first time since her wedding night that she had broken down. Exhausted, acutely aware of an emotion she could not understand, Audra was no longer able to hold back the tears. Furious at herself for her weakness, she turned to hide her face.

The captain looked at her askance. That she was a lady, he now had no doubt. She was much younger than he had at first taken her for, and he now wondered about the gold band on her third finger. He could have sworn when he had kissed her that he was kissing a maid, so inexperienced were the lips beneath his. Now she was desperately struggling to control herself.

He put a gentle hand on her shoulder, but she recoiled from it sharply. "You have no cause to fear me," he said shortly. "I am only a smuggler. I do not ravish women."

"And I am to take your word for that?" she said scornfully, gulping back a sob. "The word of a murderer?"

His lips tightened. "Murderer or not, my dear," he replied, "I do not force myself on women. Not even ones as lovely as you." Unexpectedly he grinned, an insolent grin that made him appear quite boyish. "I have never found that necessary."

"You are clearly no gentleman, sir!"

"What did you expect of a smuggler, madam? The manners of a London dandy?"

She sat down in the chair she had vacated and began to hunt through her reticule for a handkerchief. He reached into his own pocket and handed her a folded linen square. She blew her nose on it a little defiantly. "I don't usually indulge in such weakness."

"I don't believe you do," the captain said quietly, watching as she put the handkerchief away. "I think you should begin at the beginning," he sighed, sitting down opposite her and spreading out his long legs before him. It had been a long day and he was tired. When she said nothing, he continued, "Who gave you those bruises on your neck?"

"My husband," she admitted. "We were married four days ago. It was an arranged marriage. He was old and I did not think he would want . . ." Her voice broke. "He had to prove his mastery over me in every way."

"There is no need for you to go on if it distresses you," he said, so gently that she glanced at him sharply, his new attitude confusing her. Who was this man with the contradictory behavior? Who calmly committed murder one moment and grabbed her like a brutish lout, and yet appeared, beneath it all, to be unusually sensitive to her feelings.

She did not elaborate any more on the horror of her marriage, but went on, "I took Bess with me and ran away. We arrived in Dover yesterday. I decided I would go to the continent and seek a friend, an officer who is with Wellesley's army in Spain. We grew up together and—but that is of no consequence," she dismissed that line of thought. "My plan turned out to be a foolhardy one as there were no longer packets running between England and the continent. I questioned many about passage, but I believe it was the landlord of the inn who put the Frenchman in touch with me."

"And what arrangements did you make with

him?" the captain asked.

"I would simply act as his wife for the journey and in exchange he promised that once we reached France he would help me to get in touch with my grandmother. You see, that was the story I gave him for wanting to travel to France. I thought I would find some way to get to Spain from there."

"And you took this Frenchman—this stranger—at his word?"

"I had no reason to doubt him. He was a gentleman."

"*And* a Bonapartist agent."

"What!"

"We discovered some valuable papers sewn into his clothing. A memorandum regarding some of our navy's future plans. You can imagine how Bonaparte would like to get his hands on *that* information. It was no wonder the Frenchman made such a desperate attempt to reach his native shore."

"So he really *was* an agent," Audra exclaimed. "But an enemy one! I thought he might be going to France on a secret mission for *our* government, but I never dreamed . . ."

"Fornier was not his real name. I believe he may have been the scion of a distinguished émigré family. It was too bad he decided to throw in his lot with Bonaparte."

"A fine way to pay back the country who had befriended his family after the revolution," Audra sniffed.

"Spoken like a loyal Englishwoman."

"Which I am, despite you taking me for the wife of a French spy, or—or even worse!"

The captain gave a slight smile. "It is fortunate for you, I think, that *The Peregrine* managed to come along before you and your so-called husband reached France."

"Surely you don't think he would have turned me over to the French authorities?"

He shook his head. "No, my dear." His eyes slipped over her. "But I think he fully intended to have his way with you, before bidding you adieu."

She looked stunned. "He may have been a traitor, but I don't believe *that* of him."

"Why? Because he was a gentleman? Apparently a gentleman is the beginning and end-all for you."

"You would not understand."

"Of course not. I am no gentleman."

"Through no fault of your own. It is a question of birth, sir."

"Really?" He laughed. Like his voice, his laugh was rich and deep. "And no doubt that adoring husband you spoke of is a gentleman of the first order."

Color flared in Audra's cheeks and she looked away from him. "You have made your point, sir," she allowed.

"I only wished to illustrate to you that you should be careful not to take people at face value. A gentleman is not always a gentleman. He may be a foreign agent or a ravisher beneath his impeccably cut coat."

"I think I have learned that lesson, sir," she said bitterly. "My husband has the round, innocent face of a cherub and a warm, mellow voice that could charm the most skeptical man alive into believing in him. He is also not what he seemed. I will not trust so easily again."

She raised her large and luminous eyes to him. The hazel eyes that met hers had lost their wicked glint of amusement and now appeared to have softened and become dark and penetrating. She felt unexplainably drawn to them and stared at him as if transfixed for a long moment. Then she shuddered. This man was a common criminal! Not only was he a smuggler, but a murderer besides! What had come over her? She flushed as she remembered how it had felt when he had kissed her and held her fast in his arms.

"What is your name?" he asked, his voice even deeper than before.

"Audra," she whispered, noting that his face bore no wicked signs, was very attractive, in fact, when he smiled, as he was doing now.

"And I am Brock," he said, for some unaccountable reason giving her his real name.

A silence followed, interrupted only by a sudden noise from the deck above.

"I believe we approach the English coast." The captain rose from his chair and crossed the room to the door. "You and your maid will stay here until someone comes for you," he said.

As if to make sure of this, she heard a key turn in the lock when he had vacated the cabin.

Chapter Eight

The Peregrine was slowly approaching the coast of Kent, a dozen or so miles to the east of Dover. There was a heavy sea mist obscuring the landscape and the poor visibility made it necessary for the lookout to use all his powers of observation, as he clung to the bowsprit, peering intently through the wet, swirling mist for a familiar landmark.

There were many creeks dissecting the south coast, but *The Peregrine* was heading in the direction of a particularly narrow channel that was situated between high, rocky cliffs. A channel that was deep enough to allow a sloop of *The Peregrine*'s size and low draft to travel up it for a good half mile, although it narrowed between the clifflike banks until there was barely a six-foot clearance on either side. The crew never got used to it. It felt to them as if they were in a dark tunnel which was slowly closing in upon them.

Out of the mist, almost as if by magic, the familiar rocky landmarks appeared and the lookout gave a shout. The seamen quietly went about their jobs, although their tenseness was evident as the captain slowly nosed the ship in between the high cliffs.

Unexpectedly the gentle wind began to lift the blanketing mist as they headed up the channel. Sails were carefully lowered until only the jib was left to carry them along. *The Peregrine* came to its anchorage at last, having reached the point where it could go no further.

Off the starboard bow stood the gaping mouth of a subterranean cave. In this deep rock opening the cargo was usually unloaded and stored. The next day or night it was transported upwards through winding passages that interlocked with other caves and tunnels in the hillside. It ended in an ancient crypt which lay below the ruins of a chapel almost a mile away.

The cargo could be stored there wholly undetected for as long as necessary before being hauled above, loaded onto carts covered with straw or farm produce and driven to secluded areas where London agents met and transferred the goods.

The operation was smoothly run and had thus far succeeded in evading the law. The principal reason for this success was the captain of *The Peregrine* himself. Two years before he had taken it upon himself to organize the greater part of the smuggling trade in this region of Kent. Due completely to his efforts none of the boats that plied the English

Channel in his name had ever come in contact with the coast guard or revenue officers.

This, of course, meant a great deal to the local members of the smuggling trade, most of whom were decent fishermen and farmers only out to make a few extra guineas for their families.

Being caught by the revenue officers meant hanging or being transported for life, and before the captain had come, the decent fellows had been slowly frightened off and replaced by rough and lawless types who were constantly fighting amongst themselves and terrifying the countryside by their thievery and drunkenness and taking of innocent women. The captain had changed all that. He had been responsible for the chasing off or rounding up of the undesirables and for bringing back the local men into the trade.

Having proved his authority and influence, he had become the ideal controller of the smuggling boats. It was he who decided on the night each boat should make its run, depending on the weather conditions, he who arranged and bought the cargos, determined where to safely store them and planned for their disposal.

Known for his honesty and fair dealing, the captain was well thought of by those who worked for him. However, he would not brook any disobedience to the rules he had set down. If a man were discovered to have misappropriated goods for himself or attempted to make an extra run (as Scalley had done this particular night), that man was likely to mysteriously disappear from the district. It served to put sufficient fear into the men to make it a rare occurrence.

When *The Peregrine* was safely moored, the captain called the crew together on the deck before they disembarked. This had not been a smuggling run, but the arranged pickup under the command of Ned Walker, *The Peregrine*'s second in command, to transport the three men who made up the "human cargo" back to England. The crew had been overjoyed to discover, when the fishing boat had met them offshore, that their wounded captain was accompanying this cargo.

This time, thanks to Jean Paul, there had been no trouble from the French and it was not long afterward that the captain stood on the deck admiring his graceful sloop as the wind filled her sails and she headed out to sea. It was only a few minutes later that they had encountered the fishing boat belonging to Jock Scalley.

The three members of the human cargo had been on deck with the captain when the boat was sighted and he had suggested Ned Walker take them below where they would not be observed. They had remained in Walker's quarters for the rest of the journey. Now, the captain spoke briefly to his men, congratulating them on a well-managed crossing and thanking them for all they had done on his behalf. At this point, he turned a leather bag over to his second in command to pay them twice their usual wage for the crossing.

Most of the men then dispersed, entering the large mouth of the cave and making their way through the passages to an exit that opened out in the woods above the village. There were some, though, who stayed behind on *The Peregrine* to guard Jock Scalley and his men who were to be kept in the hold overnight. The captain knew only too well how anxious they would become as hour after hour passed with no hint of what they might expect in punishment.

Ned Walker led the three men who had accompanied the captain from France out of his quarters and up onto the deck. After a word with the captain they were taken off the ship and followed Walker into the cave. He led them down the passageways in a roundabout method that they would never be able to remember and at last they exited from a gorse-bush-hidden opening. Before them lay a large, darkened mansion that was built just back from the top of the cliff. They could hear the sea far below them as they made their way along a gravelled driveway.

Approaching wrought-iron gates in a brick wall, they could see that the driveway continued beyond, winding back into darkness where the stables were located. Walker opened the gates and tugged at a bell-pull. When they reached the imposing front door of the mansion, it was opened almost immediately by an elderly butler who appeared to have dressed very hurriedly. He held a branch of candles in his hand.

"The captain wished me to bring his guests here straightaway, Barrow. They have had a long journey and would seek their beds as soon as their rooms can be made ready," Ned explained.

The butler's face brightened. "I am happy to learn that the captain has returned, Mr. Walker. If you will come this way, gentlemen."

When the captain opened the door to his cabin, he discovered a sleeping Bess, but her mistress was wide awake and staring at him anxiously.

"We are safely moored and you may come ashore now."

"Where are we?"

"Back in England, madam." He said no more, but when Audra had awakened Bess and the two women had put on their bonnets, he picked up the portmanteau. "If you will follow me, please."

The captain lit a lantern and preceded them off the sloop, leading them into the entrance of the large cave. Holding the lantern high before him, he continued on ahead while the two women stumbled along behind him. Down the winding passages, they went, up stone steps cut from rock, along more damp tunnels and through low archways of rock that made it necessary for even the small Bess to bend her head. On and on they progressed with the captain not slackening his lengthy pace. It seemed to Audra that they had walked for miles underground before they reached the bottom of a wooden staircase. Ascending this in single-file, they came face to face with a solid stone wall.

The captain approached one of the large squares of stone that bore a metal ring embedded in it and, clasping it, pulled hard. A door, cut from the stone swung slowly outward revealing a dark corridor beyond. He stepped through and beckoned to the two women to follow.

It was apparent now to Audra that they were in a cellar of a house. They ascended more stairs and came out at last in what appeared to be a large pantry.

"My housekeeper will have been told to have your bedchamber ready," the captain said to Audra as they made their way down a corridor to the front of the house.

Audra looked around her curiously as they crossed a lofty front hall. Down the broad staircase, a little white-haired woman hurried toward them.

The captain nodded to her. "Mrs. Barrow will show you to your rooms," he said perfunctorily before the housekeeper could speak.

"But—" Audra began.

"We will discuss everything in the morning," he said to her. "I am sure you must be very tired." He gave her a little bow and was soon lost in the shadows of the dark hall.

Audra was conducted to a bedchamber quite as large as her own at Greenleigh, but the furniture was heavy and old-fashioned and the curtains and carpet almost threadbare. A servant girl was passing a warming pan between the sheets of the bed and a fire was burning rather smokily on the hearth.

The housekeeper assured herself that all was in order, insisted Audra ring the bell if she should require anything, bade her a goodnight, although it was closer to dawn, and withdrew.

The servant girl showed Bess the small room adjoining that was to be hers and also took her leave.

"Well, I never," Bess said when they were alone. "It appears a respectable house. What do you make of it, milady?"

"I don't know, Bess, and right now I do not care. I

just want to climb into that warm bed."

It was almost noon before Audra awoke. Bess had entered her bedchamber carrying a breakfast tray and was delighted to see that her mistress was finally stirring.

"I have so much to tell you," she said eagerly.

"Have you been up long?" Audra yawned.

"Several hours. This is a fine, old house, milady, but it is not in the best condition. I don't think it has been much in use of late."

"Really?" Audra stretched, pushing herself up on her pillows. "Did you discover the owner?"

"Yes, I did," Bess said proudly. "It is owned by a Lord Deverell."

"Lord Deverell?" Audra looked puzzled. "Is he in residence?"

"I don't think so, milady. There are dust covers over the furniture in most of the rooms."

"So . . ." Audra mused. "A house beside the sea. A perfect hiding place for smugglers with or without its owner's consent. Considering our captain, I venture to say it is the latter."

"Do you think so, milady?"

Audra nodded, her lips tight. "Are there many servants, Bess?"

"No, milady. A bare minimum I would say. The Barrows—she is the housekeeper and he the butler—a cook, and a young housemaid. It was she who warmed your bed last night. There are probably grooms at the stable, but I have not seen them yet."

Audra had to smile. It had taken no time for Bess

to gather all this information. She had given the young housemaid only a cursory glance the night before, but she remembered a pretty face and a low-cut blouse. No doubt by nightfall Bess would know which of the smugglers was the girl's lover . . . unless—could she have been waiting to warm the captain's bed with more than the warming pan?

For some reason the thought served to make Audra angry. Why had he brought her to this place? What did he intend to do with her? She turned the anger inward. What a fool she had been! After warning Bess, it was she who had stupidly told the captain about running away from her husband! If he had overheard Bess addressing her as "Milady," he would naturally have put two and two together and decided that a titled gentleman would pay well for the return of his wife. At least he did not know the name of her husband and she vowed that that was something he would never learn. Quickly, Audra made Bess promise that on *no* account would she divulge her mistress's true name to anyone. Then she threw back the covers and got out of bed.

"I am going to dress and seek out the captain, Bess. I wish a few words with him."

"I think you should know, milady, that he is very well thought of in this house," the young maid told her.

"No great recommendation considering everyone employed here is probably a felon of some sort."

"If I may say so, milady, I think you are perhaps being a little harsh with the captain. He has shown us nothing but kindness."

"Kindness! How gullible you are, Bess! It is no

wonder you were taken in by the earl." This, of course, was a little unfair since Audra had been taken in by him herself.

But Bess would not be daunted. "You must not compare the captain to the earl, milady. The captain helps people. Mrs. Barrow says the captain will know what is best for us."

"The captain! Best for us!" Audra exploded, following these words with a string of bitter vindictives against the arrogant blackguard of a captain and his outrageous behavior.

"He is a criminal, Bess, and I would advise you not to forget that for a moment. Last night he murdered a man without the slightest compunction and you must remember that at the time he was completely unaware that the Frenchman *was* an enemy agent." She had told Bess all about the spy.

"But he was trying to make for the enemy shore, milady. Would a loyal Englishman do that?"

Audra stopped long enough to consider this fact. "Nevertheless, Bess," she went on, "I don't trust that captain. Mark my words, he is already planning how best he may use us."

A half hour later Audra started down the wide front staircase. Before she reached the bottom, she heard a door opening and closing and the sound of firm footsteps crossing the hall.

The captain came into view below her, dressed for riding in fawn breeches, a dark brown whipcord coat and resplendent black boots. He glanced up at her, looking most disturbingly handsome, despite a tiredness about his eyes.

"Good morning, Audra, or should I say, good afternoon?"

"Good day, sir." This was said very crisply.

He smiled, making him look all the more attractive. "I was hoping to see you before I left."

"Left? Where are you going?"

She looked even more lovely in the daylight, he decided, observing the shimmering glow cast upon her by the sunlight streaming through the tall, diamond-paned windows that flanked the front door.

"To London. I shan't be gone more than a day or two."

Audra looked dismayed. "I was hoping you might be able to arrange passage for us to the continent with one of your smuggling friends."

"Really?" He cocked an eyebrow at her. "And what makes you think you are free to go?"

His words brought angry color to her cheeks. "Through no fault of my own, my journey to France was interrupted and I was brought back to England. Surely, you don't propose to keep me here against my will?"

"No. You are quite free to roam about the house and grounds until I return. Then I will decide what is to become of you."

"What is to become!" Audra's blue eyes struck sparks of fiery indignation.

"I can hardly allow you to rush off to the nearest authorities and report me and my smuggling operation, can I?"

"I would not . . ." she began and then she wisely

stopped, biting back her angry retort. She could see it was useless to argue with him. "You don't waste much time, do you?" she said loftily. "Off to London already to sell your contraband."

"I am not selling *this* cargo," he told her. "Nor do I expect any reward for returning to the proper authorities the memorandum stolen by the French spy."

"You mean you intend to return it yourself?" she looked incredulous.

"Of course." He flashed white teeth in a quick grin.

"I do believe you would walk straight into the War Office and hand the papers over to Viscount Castlereagh himself."

His grin widened. "Why not? Do you know His Lordship personally?"

"No, but I have read of him and I would caution you not to treat the man lightly. He has done much to rid this country of those slimy, foreign agents who work to undermine our troop and ship movements."

"Slimy foreign agents like your so-called husband?"

"I admit I did not judge his character very well," she said, not meeting his eyes.

"Only through lack of experience." He smiled. "May I now hope you have reversed your poor opinion of me? That you no longer consider me a murderer but, instead, someone working for the well-being of our country?"

"Well-being?" she scoffed. "I would hardly say that, considering the loss of revenue to Britain due to smuggling is nearly sixty thousand pounds a year!"

He stood a few steps below her, regarding her

rather lazily, one booted foot resting on the first stair.

"You are remarkably well-read," he murmured.

"For a woman, you mean," she challenged. "Bonaparte has boasted on more than one occasion that the golden guineas which have crossed the channel to buy brandy and tobacco and all the other goods you smuggle into England have helped immeasurably in dressing and feeding his army."

He clicked his tongue and shook his head mockingly from side to side.

"But what of *our* army, sir?" Audra's temper was rising at his apparent indifference. "What have *you* done to help the men who are fighting so hard against the might of Napoleon?" Her blue eyes flashed angrily at him. "Since you are such a good sailor, Captain, why have you not joined Admiral Collingwood in the navy instead of adding to his problems by conducting this illegal trade?"

He shrugged. "I'm afraid I'm not much of a military man, Audra. Never been very good at obeying rules and regulations."

"Unless you make the rules yourself," she snapped. "Tell me, Captain, what did you do to poor Mr. Scalley and his men for disobeying them?"

"Mr. Scalley's men have all been transported back to their villages."

"And Mr. Scalley himself?"

"He will not return for some time," the captain said, the sudden coldness in his voice warning her that she was now on dangerous ground.

She disregarded this. "Surely you did not kill him?"

A brief silence. "No, Scalley is alive." He dropped

his voice but the command in it was not to be ignored. "Do not ask any more questions, Audra. You are an intelligent woman, but I must warn you not to use those brains of yours around Southcliffe. That is the name of this house. Do not question the servants, or probe into matters that do not concern you. Accept things as you see them." He took her hand in his and bowed over it. "Now, if you will excuse me."

Why did he have such a disconcerting effect upon her? Audra wondered. At the moment she was keenly aware of the strong fingers grasping hers.

"I must be on my way," he said, relinquishing her hand and beginning to draw on his gloves.

"You mean I am to—to just wait here for your return?"

"Precisely," the captain said. "As I mentioned earlier you are free to roam the house and grounds. I must warn you, however, that Southcliffe is well-guarded by my men."

"Then I am to remain here as a prisoner?"

"If that is the way you consider it. I prefer, instead, to regard you as my guest. A very beautiful guest." His hazel eyes had warmed again.

Audra did not notice. She had never been more furious. "You have no right to keep me here against my will!"

"I have *every* right!" he said imperiously. "I am a smuggler, remember? You, my dear, are valuable goods."

"I don't belong to you!" she cried in irate indignation, "and I don't intend to remain here. I warn you, Captain, I will do everything in my power to escape from this house while you are gone."

"Thank you for the warning," he said, with unimpaired calm. "I will make sure the guard is doubled."

Her lip curled. "I suppose kidnapping is minor compared to your other list of crimes."

"Infinitely minor."

"Smuggling, murder, trespassing," she started to tick them off on her fingers.

"*Not* trespassing," he interrupted.

"I wonder if Lord Deverell would agree with you?" she said, looking around her. "Does he have the slightest idea that his premises are being used for such nefarious purposes?"

"I gather Lord Deverell's reputation is unknown to you." The captain's eyes glittered. "He is a notorious rake and is part of a decidedly degenerate set of the ton. My lord drinks too much, is an inveterate gambler and has been involved in several disastrous duels over ladies who apparently had little honor to protect. Country life is *not* his style, far too dull and bucolic for such a profligate."

"Your words are hardly reassuring, Captain," Audra retorted. "What if, by chance, due to one of his reckless deeds he is forced to repair to his country estate? What pray should *I* do if he arrived here while I am alone?"

"In that case I would strongly advise you to keep to your room," he said, with a sardonic twist to his lips. "Unless, of course, you desire a romp in his bed."

Chapter Nine

Audra spent the afternoon after the captain had left wandering aimlessly around Southcliffe. She noticed that Bess had been correct in her assessment. The dark, heavy furniture in most of the spacious rooms on the first floor were covered with holland covers. Ivy and creepers overhung a great many of the windows, making the rooms appear dark, even in the bright sunshine. Nevertheless, despite a coating of dust, she felt Southcliffe must at one time have possessed an atmosphere of warmth and close family life. Perhaps this was due to the many ancestral portraits of parents and children which decorated the walls of the mansion.

The library, Audra discovered, was the one room that showed signs of being scrubbed and polished. Since it faced south, the spring sunlight coming through its leaded windowpanes (the vines had obviously been stripped away outside) gave it a more cheerful aspect.

She spent some time looking over the titles of the old leather-bound volumes on the book shelves before she walked over to the large window behind the heavy flat-topped desk and looked out. A neglected garden lay beyond, filled with overgrown shrubs and plants. She was mentally weeding around the rose bushes when she heard the door behind her open, and turned to see the man who the captain had addressed as "Ned" standing there, a little startled to see her.

"I'm very sorry to disturb you, madam," he said politely.

He was a man of medium height and sturdy build with a shock of unruly brown hair and brown eyes that reminded Audra of a shy puppy she had once owned. She smiled at him.

"Your name is Ned, I believe."

"That's right," he answered, giving her a formal little bow. "Ned Walker at your service, madam."

"Come in, Ned. I am just leaving," Audra said, starting across the room. "But if you are hoping to find the captain, he departed for London several hours ago."

"Of that I am aware," he retorted, advancing into the room. "I come here most afternoons to attend to the account book for the captain."

"I see," she said. "Don't let me deter you." Sarcasm crept into her voice. "Smuggling being such a profitable enterprise, no doubt you have many hours of work ahead of you."

He stopped abruptly in the middle of the room and eyed her closely, a look of keen discernment replacing the placid, puppy-dog look in his eyes. "I can see that you are angry with the captain for keeping you here," he said quietly.

"Why on earth would you think that?" marvelled Audra. "I am forced to remain a virtual prisoner in this house for as long as your captain decrees. I can't think why that should make me angry, can you?"

"If the captain has decided you should remain here, I can assure you it is for the best."

"And the captain always does what is best. Is that it?" she scoffed. "You poor, deluded man. I suppose he is using you too."

She saw the color rise up in his face, but he did not lose his composure. "Despite how it may look to you at the moment, madam, the captain always knows the right way to go about doing things."

"Really?" Audra's hands went defiantly to her hips. "And do you consider smuggling to be the right and lawful way to go about doing things?"

"Not lawful perhaps, madam," Ned returned in his soft country voice. "But all of us on the estate and most in the village have benefited from the smuggling activities the captain has organized."

"Including Napoleon himself who is desperate for our gold!"

"Don't you think, madam, that people are more important than gold?" he chided her gently.

"I wonder if you will change your tune if Britain is invaded by Bonaparte?" Audra snapped, stalking from the room.

* * *

The next two days it poured rain and Audra's plans to reconnoiter the grounds of Southcliffe for a possible means of escape were foiled.

Bess had worked her way into Mrs. Barrow's good graces by offering to help her about the house. She told Audra how much the captain was liked and respected by his staff and how this knowledge had put her own mind at rest.

"We have been treated most kindly, milady. Is that the way of an outlaw?" she asked. "I believe we be in very good hands."

"Very good hands!"

But Bess had seen the fury in her mistress's eyes and hastily made her escape from the room before another tirade could descend upon her.

How could all these people be so taken in by that high-handed, overbearing man! Audra thought to herself, seething with rage. It was as if he had mesmerized them all with the force of his personality.

Well, he had not mesmerized *her*! She still smoldered from the arrogant way he had dictated to her. She would continue to fight and deny the indefinable attraction that she had unwillingly sensed from that first moment their eyes had met in his cabin aboard *The Peregrine*. She would *never* admit the extraordinary effect his kiss had had on her and how he had the power to make her heart pound at the very sight of him. Yet his handsome face continued to mock her, even in absence. She saw again his indolent grin, heard his deep, rich laugh, felt again the taste of his hot, demanding mouth, was tormented in the dark hours of the night by the memory of his strong, muscular body pressed close to hers. He had given her a glimpse of a passion that had first budded with Paul and now, with this man, was struggling to surface again. Desperately she fought to keep the compelling thoughts away, all too aware now of the fire that lay banked within her, the desire that she must never give in to.

She had made a vow to herself not to trust any man. Not ever again! Paul had let her down. Both the earl and the Frenchman had lied to her. Men, it seemed, only used women for their own ends. No doubt the captain had already decided on how best he could use her. Likely he would hold her for ransom and collect a generous reward for her return. But he would not use her body! That, she vowed, no man would ever do again.

Brock was closeted with Viscount Castlereagh for the better part of two days. The body of the French spy had been brought to London in a hastily constructed pine box and carried in a separate coach behind that of Brock and the three men who had accompanied him from France.

The spy had been identified by a member of Castlereagh's staff as one Charles de Fehr, the eldest son of the compte d'Abreau. The compte had remained an ardent Royalist, waiting patiently in Britain for the defeat of the upstart Corsican and the return of the rightful monarch to the throne of France. His son, however, had grown impatient, and had, apparently, been easily enticed into following Bonaparte.

Charles de Fehr had proved to be a valuable asset to the French cause, being employed in the War Office as a translator. Although his position was of a minor capacity, he had somehow managed, with his charm and family connections, to gain the confidence of those higher up. It was believed there had been a leakage of information, which Charles had carefully pursued and had thus discovered the important memorandum which he had stolen.

It was all most unfortunate, Castlereagh told Brock, but it had proven a good lesson to the department to tighten its security. Brock was duly commended for the return of the lost memorandum.

"I only wish my aim had been better and I had been able to bring the traitor back alive," he said quietly. "I thought he looked familiar and am almost certain now that I met him at a card party at Lord Fairclough's last winter."

"Fairclough, you say? Might be an idea to keep an eye on him and his friends," Castlereagh said. He steepled his fingertips on the top of the desk and studied the big man sitting across from him.

"Your wound is healing well?" he asked.

"Yes, my lord."

"You would not be adverse then to taking on a mission for us?"

"No, my lord."

"Through the escape route you and that Frenchman, Beaudette, organized, we were able to get De Leon and his friends out of Paris in time. You see, it had become known to use that he was under suspicion and was being watched very closely. He is a valuable agent. It will take a little while to obtain a new identity for him, but we want him to return to France."

"There is one thing I must impart to you before

your plans are made," Brock interjected. "I feel it almost certain that there is an informer amongst Jean Paul's men. Someone had to have informed the compte de Lascalles of the human cargo being picked up. I believe that was why I was shot. Men were brought in to intercept De Leon and the others."

"Have you or Jean Paul any suspicions as to who the informer might be?"

"Not as yet. Perhaps by the time I return to France with De Leon, Jean Paul will—"

"You will *not* return with De Leon, Brock. I wish you to go *before* him to obtain contacts for him from France to Vienna."

"Vienna!"

"We have it on good authority that the Austrians are considering re-entering the struggle. Our government has already begun to send supportive funds through to them but a route and a better communication system must be established."

"I see." Brock nodded. "It was my intention to return to Southcliffe tomorrow, my lord. Would you prefer I remain here?"

"No. That will not be necessary. We can send word to you there. But make no smuggling runs yourself. We need you, Brock. You have proved yourself to be irreplaceable."

"Tell that to Colonel Dawson." Brock laughed. "You have no idea how it irks him to curtail his coast guard on the nights of our crossings."

Due to the constant rain, Ned discovered Audra reading in the library on the next two afternoons. Ignoring the captain's advice, she asked innumerable questions of him about the smuggling operations.

Ned, however, remained tight-lipped over everything except his praise of the captain. "No one is starving at Southcliffe now," Ned said proudly, "or in the village either. You must understand, madam, that a lot of the inhabitants hereabouts make their living by sheep farming. With the blockade on there is no export of wool and things were going from bad to worse in the district. Smuggling became our only recourse."

"But what happens to the men if one of your boats is caught by the coast guard or revenue officers?"

"The gallows or transportation," Ned said quietly.

"Isn't that a terrible risk to take?"

"Not since the captain started running things. Not one of the boats that has gone out under his orders has been taken."

"That is quite a record," Audra admitted.

"It is indeed. We all have faith in the captain, madam. He is a fine man and he knows the local farmers and fishermen are decent and honest. He is working for a cause and not just personal gain. Not like those cutthroats that came in and started to run the smuggling before."

"Cutthroats?"

"Yes. Not much better than animals they were! Crafty brutes. Taking whatever they wanted, however lawless, and quite prepared to slit another's throat or turn him over to the law if bribed with a guinea or two. Thank God the captain arrived and saw what was happening. He changed all that. Got rid of the lot of them almost overnight it seemed.

Made the whole district a safe place to live in again."

"It appears you admire your captain very much."

"Admire him! I'd give my life for him, I would," Ned said with quiet conviction. "The hardest thing I ever did was to leave him on that beach in France. Saw him shot from behind and fall face-down in the sand. Thought he was dead for sure. He'd given orders to return to the ship and I had to obey him. Hardest thing I ever did," he repeated.

"So it was a bullet that creased his forehead," Audra mused. "I wondered about that."

"Yes. Lucky he was hit at an angle or he would be in a French grave."

"Ned," Audra asked, looking puzzled, "what is your *real* profession? Are you a sailor or a bookkeeper?"

"I grew up here on this estate, madam, but I have always loved sailing. My father worked for his old lordship as his steward, buying and selling the wool and the sheep and seeing to the tenants. I received more education than most around here in preparation to take over my father's position, and, when he died, I managed things for a year under the new lord. He was already in the army and off fighting on the continent when he gained the title. He was killed in France. A fine man he was too. Terrible shame. His brother, the present lord, is nothing like him. A society popinjay, who has allowed this estate to go down more and more every year. Bleeds it to death. Cares nothing for it or the tenants. We could all have starved to death and it wouldn't have mattered a whit to him."

"And it was then that the captain appeared?"

"That's right."

"But where did he come from?"

Ned smiled at her shyly and shook his head. "That is for the captain to say, madam. If he—er, wishes you to know."

"All right, Ned," Audra sighed. "I won't question you on that score, but what did he do when he got here and saw what was going on?"

"He took charge right away. Organized the local men in no time at all. It seemed only natural to make Southcliffe our headquarters. The captain made me his second in command. 'Ned,' he said to me once, 'there is no one I trust more than you.' Proud I felt then and proud I feel now to work for the captain."

"I'm sure your loyalty is very admirable, Ned, but I hope it is not ill-placed. The captain, after all, is working outside the law. He is a criminal."

"Don't say that!" Ned cried, rising from his chair and for the first time Audra saw real anger in the soft, brown eyes. "The captain's the finest man who ever lived. Ask anyone!"

"I have no need," Audra said, throwing up her hands. If she heard any more praise exalting the captain she would scream!

For the second night in a row, she lay awake, unable to erase the thoughts of her captor from her mind. She seemed to be the only one at Southcliffe who dared to question his motives or speak out against him.

She had talked with Barrow and his wife and the servant girl, Polly, and had come to the conclusion that Brock was, without question, considered the great man of the neighborhood. It appeared that the captain's word was law and his actions regarded as above criticism.

Audra had to bite her tongue as she was told again and again of the captain's good deeds, feeling she was listening to the praise of a veritable saint and not the arrogant leader of a band of smugglers who was not above murder and kidnapping to gain his ends. Nevertheless, she was not blind to the fact that in order for the captain to endear himself so completely to those who worked for him, the man must have some estimable qualities. When sleep finally claimed her, Audra found that the tall, handsome smuggler was a major part of her dreams.

What was the matter with her? she thought upon awakening. Why did the man spark such conflicting emotions within her? He was a common criminal, a contrabandist! There would always be an immeasurable gulf between Audra, the countess of Latham, and Brock, the captain of a band of smugglers. They belonged to totally different worlds. And yet . . . There was that magnetic attraction. She could not completely forget that night in his cabin, the touch of his warm lips on hers, causing a tingling delight to spread throughout her whole body. Even Paul's kisses had never made her feel that way.

Paul. Since she had met Brock she had not thought of him at all. What had ever made her decide to go to Spain and join him? It was madness, she realized now. He had let her down once. He had promised to do something so she would not be forced into marriage to the earl, but he had done nothing. He had even been helpless to prevent Latham from sending him prematurely back to his regiment.

If a man of Brock's strength and determination had been in Paul's place, she felt sure, under no condition would he have allowed her to marry someone she didn't love. He would have taken any measure—however desperate—to ensure that her father kept Greenleigh and she did not wed the old earl. However desperate? She sat up in bed. Something illegal, perhaps? Something like smuggling? It came to her then. Perhaps that was Brock's real reason for becoming a contrabandist. Perhaps there was something desperate for which *he* needed the money!

For the first time she thought of his manner—his way of speaking. It was no different, she realized, from that of Paul or her father. Why had that fact not occurred to her before?

She remembered the day he had left for London. There had been a casualness about his riding clothes, and yet, by the cut of them one should have noticed immediately the hand of an expert tailor.

The arrogant way the man moved, the crispness of his orders to his crew, all bespoke a man who was no stranger to command. Yet, he had admitted to being no gentleman. Brock was clearly a mystery. What was his full name? Where did he come from? What would his plans be for her on his return from London? Suddenly Audra felt a bit unnerved at the prospect.

The captain drove back to Southcliffe in a light

chaise, changing horses twice on the road and arriving in record time in the late afternoon. It was still raining.

On the way he found himself thinking of Audra. In fact, the blue-eyed beauty with the quick temper had not been absent from his thoughts for very long since she had first come into his life. Who was she? Who was the husband from whom she had run away? A miserable brute, apparently, and clearly undeserving of her lovely charms. He had kept his ears open in London, hoping to hear even a hint of gossip concerning a runaway wife, but he had heard nothing. No doubt the husband would wish to keep it quiet for as long as he could. Especially if he were a nobleman. Brock remembered the frightened voice of Audra's maid in an especially dark tunnel of caves where he had lead them. "Oh, hold my hand, milady," the girl had cried out in fear.

Milady. It had only served to confirm what he had immediately surmised. With those clear, blue eyes which looked directly into his, that graceful carriage, that haughty lift to her chin, he had known she had breeding.

Audra's bedchamber overlooked the front of the house, and hearing the chaise pull up, she glanced surreptitiously through the rain-splattered window and saw the captain alight, hand the reins to a rather elderly groom and make a dash up the steps.

It did not surprise her to receive a message shortly afterward that he requested her company at dinner that evening. She thought to refuse, disliking to be ordered about, but curiosity overcame her initial hostility, curiosity and something she would never admit—a quickening of her heart at the prospect of seeing him again.

She brushed this unwelcome feeling aside, determined to use all her feminine wiles on him tonight. Perhaps she could prevail upon him to let her go; if he was as decent a person as Ned and his servants claimed the captain to be, he would release her without trying to claim a ransom. If only she could manage to keep her temper!

Audra had brought only two gowns with her in her haste to pack her portmanteau. A simple, gray cambric gown edged with lace, which she had worn every day since her arrival at Southcliffe, and a silk afternoon gown in a soft shade of moss rose that complemented her delicate pink and white complexion. Bess had fortunately pressed this gown before hanging it in the old, carved wardrobe and now she laid it out for her mistress.

Audra wore only a single strand of pearls, which had been her mother's. Upon leaving Latham House, she had vowed never to wear any of the jewelry the earl had bestowed upon her. Instead of the prim, braided chignon in which she had previously worn her long hair, Audra had allowed her natural ringlets to fall becomingly from a knot placed high on her head.

Brock was leaning nonchalantly against the mantelpiece when she appeared in the doorway to the library, his physical presence so dominant that she felt a strange ache inside. He had changed from his riding clothes into evening wear. His coat of dark green velvet fitted him superbly and his snowy cravat was tied in the most intricate of folds. She saw the glint of a signet ring on his little finger as he raised the glass he was holding in a silent tribute to her.

"What a lovely vision you make, Audra. Do come in."

It seemed only natural to move toward him and take the seat he offered her on the couch beside the hearth.

"A glass of sherry?" He smiled at her. There was an amused twist to his lips.

"Thank you."

He handed her a goblet of wine and then seated himself beside her on the velvet couch, stretching out his long legs.

"You seem strangely subdued from the indignant little female I left here a few days ago."

"Captivity sometimes has that effect on people."

"But surely not on you. I would have thought it would have brought out all your inherent restlessnes." She said nothing, so he went on, "I am amazed to hear you have been quite content to spend afternoons quietly reading in this room."

"There are some fine, old books on the shelves."

"And some ponderously dull ones too." He grinned. "Speaking of dullness, I have been keeping such serious company the last few days, I was quite hoping you would have sharpened up that stinging wit of yours for me. Am I do be disappointed?"

"I fear so. It did not take me long to discover that in this house it did little good to rail against the estimable captain," she said a little waspishly. "You have a very loyal camp here. Even my maid defends you to my face."

"Really? And does that not tell you something?" His grin deepened.

"Oh, you *are* odious!" she cried, forgetting herself, and he burst out laughing.

"Now, there's the Audra I know," he said, but the laugh died out of his eyes as they met her furious ones. For a long moment hazel held blue, the intensity of his gaze compelling.

It seemed to Brock that from the first moment he had seen this lovely young woman revealed in the light of his cabin, he had desired her. It rather amazed him. He had never been particularly attracted to fair, blue-eyed females before, preferring sultry, dark-eyed brunettes or an occasional flaming redhead. Now, he wanted above all else to take this beauty, who so epitomized the perfect English rose, in his arms, to rain kisses upon her until he could replace that cool, haughty look in her eyes with one of soft and yielding passion.

Audra found she was holding her breath, knowing she should move away from this man, but unable to do so.

Still looking into her eyes, he reached out and drew her gently to him. Remembering how it had been before, Audra could not make herself resist. He folded her into his arms and kissed her. His mouth moved lovingly over her soft lips and she shivered uncontrollably, slowly melting against him.

At that moment, Barrow knocked discreetly at the door in order to announce dinner.

The meal was served in the large, empty dining hall. Seated at the head of the long mahogany table, the captain looked even more impressive and overpowering. Audra was placed to his right. She had not spoken since they had been interrupted in the library. She had felt such a strange feeling then. Surely it had been relief, for it could not have been disappointment. He had released her with a grin and merely shrugged. There was no apology, but then, of course, he was no gentleman.

Audra had taken refuge in anger, but this time it had been directed at herself. What had come over her? How could she have been so weak-willed? She sat straight in her chair now, careful not to catch Brock's eye, her gaze following Barrow as he waited upon them.

When, at last, the butler had left the room, Brock addressed her. "Do you think we could pretend we have just met for the first time and start all over again?" He smiled a smile that reminded her of a naughty little boy trying to make amends.

"Perhaps," she would not commit herself.

"Won't you tell me a little about yourself?"

"You already know my first name." That was all she was going to tell him. He would not learn from *her* lips that she was the countess of Latham. That information would only prompt him to send a ransom demand to her husband.

"Brock is my nickname," he admitted. "My real name is James Brockington. I am twenty-eight years of age, have all my own teeth and am a smuggler by trade."

Audra's lips twitched a little at that. "You are ten years my senior," she said, and then, relenting a little, "I grew up in Surrey and am a good horsewoman."

"Do you ride to the hunt?"

"I have, but I hate fox hunting. All that mob charging down upon one small, defenseless animal. I can shoot as well as any man, though," she said proudly.

"I will consider myself forewarned." He smiled. "I have no wish to have my skull creased by another bullet."

She frowned. "Ned told me how you got—"

He held up a hand. "We have just met, remember? You know nothing about me."

They continued this game all through dinner, talking as politely to one another as two people seated together at a formal London dinner party. It seemed that neither wished to reveal much about his life before their meeting, yet Audra soon found that she was conversing with this man, this smuggler, quite easily and naturally. As for Brock, he was fascinated not merely because Audra was beautiful, sitting beside him with the candlelight playing on her soft, silver-blond hair, but that she was also most intelligent. Unlike most of the females of his acquaintance, Audra's manner was refreshingly natural and honest. (But then she had completely forgotten that she was supposed to be using her feminine wiles on him.) She quite enchanted him with her opinions, often strongly expressed as when they discussed the war with France.

"I feel England could have avoided it," Audra said earnestly.

Brock cocked an eyebrow at her over his wineglass. "How is that?" he asked her.

"She should have stopped Napoleon one way or

another before he had the chance to sweep across all of Europe. Despotism should be dealt with swiftly, before it has a chance to grow."

"I think Englishmen in general are too inclined to a 'wait and see' attitude," he said. He smiled at her, shaking his head. "Audra, you are quite a remarkable young woman. I thought I knew your sex, but I was wrong."

"I'm afraid I have a hard time holding my tongue when I have something to say. I'm told I don't behave as a delicately bred lady should."

"Who told you that?"

"My stepmother. She thinks I had a lamentable upbringing, because my father treated me as he would a son."

"She is wrong. It has made you quite unique."

"Do you think so? Then you are different from other men. As a matter of fact, you are the first man, other than my father, who has ever really listened to my opinions, without an amused or patronizing air."

He smiled. "Perhaps that is due to my grandmother. She is a very perceptive and intelligent woman. I believe she possesses more common sense in her little finger than most of our statesmen."

"I would like to meet her," Audra said.

"Perhaps some day you will."

They talked on through several dinner courses, expressing their various opinions, clearly in agreement on many subjects. The longer they talked, the more often their eyes met, and caught in Brock's gaze, Audra again felt that strange, soft warmth spreading through her.

When they had finished, Brock moved Audra's

chair back for her and suggested they enjoy their brandy in the more comfortable confines of the library. He was surprised by Audra's instant hesitation.

"Does the prospect of being alone with me worry you?"

It did but she wouldn't admit it. "No," she said, the color rising in her cheeks. "It is just that I do not . . . care very much for brandy." That, at least, was the truth.

"A glass of sherry, then?"

She nodded weakly in assent.

More wood had been added to the fire and it burned quite cozily in the library grate. They seated themselves as before on the couch beside the hearth, but Audra made sure there was a comfortable distance between them this time.

"Don't worry." He grinned. "Barrow won't disturb us again."

Audra ignored the implication. She took a long sip of her wine. "What do you plan to do with me?" she blurted out what had long been on her mind. "Are you after a ransom?"

He stared at her, bemused. "Is that what you think of me? That I am so low as to return you to that brute of a husband of yours in exchange for some paltry sum?"

"You did say I was valuable goods," she reminded him.

"And so you are. Too valuable, I think, to send you back to him or off again to the continent when I have heard that Napoleon is again moving on Madrid."

"I realize now that my proposed journey was a foolish idea."

"I'm glad to hear you have changed your mind, but what of your army officer?"

"He is not 'my' army officer. I don't believe he ever cared for me at all."

Whether it was due to the wine, or their new relaxed relationship, Audra could not have said, but she found herself recounting to him the full story of her father's remarriage, of her need to find a rich husband, of Paul's return and the earl offering for her hand. She left out only the correct names of those concerned, finishing with the day of her wedding and her disappointment that Paul had done nothing to stop it.

"I think, perhaps, you are being unfair to the young officer," Brock considered, watching her set down her empty goblet on a tea table before them. "What, under the circumstances, did you expect him to do?"

"Anything! Everything! Oh, I don't really know," she confessed, "but I *do* know that if he had been *you*, *you* would have thought of something!" She stopped, blushing furiously, painfully aware of what she had said and all it implied.

"You flatter me," he said, moving over to set his own glass down beside hers. His voice had lowered and when he turned back to her, those penetrating hazel eyes seemed to have probed and uncovered all her innermost secrets.

The next moment she was in his arms and he was lowering his face to hers. Their lips met in what was at first a tender kiss, but soon became harder and more demanding as he pressed her body more firmly against his own. There was again that powerful responsive current that had passed between them in the cabin on board *The Peregrine.*

With no seeming volition of their own, Audra's arms crept around Brock's neck and she entwined her fingers in his thick, dark hair, pulling his mouth harder to hers. She felt completely intoxicated by his closeness, by the featherlike kisses he had begun to press on her eyelids, her cheeks, her throat. She did nothing to resist. She wanted him to go on and on. She did not even care if . . .

The searing touch of his fingers as they slid below the low neckline of her gown and gently caressed one breast brought her to life. All at once she was trembling, pushing him away from her.

"Are you still afraid of me?" he asked. "You are very lovely, Audra, very desirable, but I assure you I would never . . . not unless you wanted me to."

"Wanted you to!" A look of horror crossed her face. "I would *never* want that! Not ever again! It was so ugly—so degrading! I hated it!"

He studied her a moment. "I am not talking of ravishment, Audra. I am talking of lovemaking. There is a world of difference."

"Is there? Whatever its name, men are the only ones who enjoy it."

"You have that on good authority?" His eyes regarded her, softening as they saw the silky eyelashes blinking back the tears. She looked so very young, so very vulnerable.

"Why do you deny your own feelings?" he whispered, reaching for her hand. "Admit you've felt something between us."

His thumb began tracing the delicate veins in her wrist. She felt the pulse beat wildly. If only he would not touch her!

As if he had read her thoughts, he gave a short little laugh of triumph. "You know you felt it, just as I did," he declared.

"No! Don't say that! Oh, why are all men the same? You only want to use a woman—to debase her!" Tears stung her eyes.

He shook his head. "You're wrong, Audra." His voice was soft, persuasive. She was so beautiful it caught at his heart. It was obvious to him that this child-woman had been badly bruised by her stupid brute of a husband. He must move slowly if she were to share his desire. "Let me show you how wrong you are," he whispered.

"No—" she began, but before she knew it he was tenderly lifting her face, and kissing the tears from her eyes. His mouth traced down the soft curve of her cheek and he nibbled at her ear lobe before seeking her lips. It was as the sweet kiss deepened that Brock felt Audra's first answering tremors. He pulled her close and held her shaking against him until her body quivered no more, his very gentleness reassuring her.

His hands began to softly caress her. Such big, strong hands, she thought, but so extraordinarily gentle. He stroked her hair, drawing the pins from it, letting it fall in a silvery cloud about her shoulders in loose array. He lifted a handful of it and kissed it, moving his lips to the pulse in her throat.

Brock sensed that Audra was like an injured

animal that might spring away in panic if he moved too fast. Yet he wanted her so, wanted to be the one to show her that all men were not brutal beasts, that lovemaking could be as fulfilling for a woman as a man. He must be patient with her, although he realized his own patience might be sorely tried before she was ready for him.

He began to tease her mouth to open to his tender search. She trembled at the delirious sensations beginning to rise within her, making her dizzy and weak.

"Don't be afraid of me, Audra. I would never hurt you," he whispered, murmuring soft love words as his hands moved delicately over her breasts, cradling them, feeling them tauten beneath the thin fabric of her gown.

The sweet tenderness with which he caressed her stirred a pleasure deep within her. She felt her will receding, felt everything begin to fade about her. There was only herself and Brock locked in an embrace she hoped would never end.

Audra strained against him, her heart pounding wildly, half in fear, half in anticipation. She would allow herself a taste of this—just a taste! She wanted so to be loved. Even for a little while. Soon she would make him stop. In just a little while.

He moved her down on the couch, adjusting the cushions beneath her head. His firm and knowing mouth closed over hers, savoring the sweet, fresh taste of her. Breathlessly, her senses swimming, she opened to his probing tongue, feeling the stroking deep in the very core of her being.

Slowly, with infinite care, he began to undress her,

stopping once to growl angrily at the weal marks that were still apparent on the silken skin of her thighs. Then his breath caught in his throat as he gazed down at her full beauty, at the high, pink-tipped breasts that only emphasized the smallness of her waist, at the gently rounded hips, the long, shapely legs, the silver-blond triangle.

Audra lay naked before him on the couch and he came to her the same way. As his big, strong body stretched out alongside her, the trembling she felt inside spread rapidly through her. He bent over her, taking his time, his lips descending in a delicate sensual trail from her mouth to the whiteness of her throat and shoulders. His light, caressing fingers cupped an upthrust breast and his warm tongue slowly encircled the nipple. She let out a small moan as it hardened beneath his touch and he teased and sucked gently at it.

Audra felt as if all her bones were melting and becoming fluid. She was in a dream, floating helplessly as he leisurely explored her. No matter where he touched her with his hands or his mouth his caress was like velvet. She gave a deep, shuddering sigh as he continued to arouse her beyond anything she had ever believed possible, awakening every inch of her body, setting her aflame with his touch. Any thought of stopping this man was long forgotten. She exulted in the tumultuous sensations he was awakening. She wanted him. Wanted him to do anything he liked with her!

Brock continued to prolong the pleasure, holding himself achingly in check. Audra had never been loved before, only used and used brutally. She must be completely ready. It was too beautiful, too perfect to spoil.

He began to stroke her trembling thighs with the tips of his fingers. Audra gasped as he found the warm hollow between her legs and instantly recoiled.

"No, my love," he whispered huskily, "don't be frightened. I will be gentle." He began reassuring her with his soft, caressing touch, stroking her reverently, arousing her with delicious torment. She twisted and thrust against the featherlike touch that was slowly driving her wild. The warm fingers traced and teased, taking infinite time as his lips and tongue tasted her more and more intimately.

"No! Oh please, Brock, don't!" But her body was quivering with her need of him, her thighs moist and open to welcome him.

She felt him move up and over her then, felt the hard length of him brush against her. He kissed her lightly and wanting her to be sure, murmured, "Do you want me, Audra?"

"Yes!" she moaned, not able to deny the aching, agonizing need a moment longer. "Oh, yes!"

He made a low noise in his throat and she felt the pressure of him bear down onto her, felt the hot strength slip gently into her. It was all so easy, so right. Unhurriedly, with the utmost control, his firm stroking manhood began to move within her, thrusting deep, filling the whole of her. She fell at once into the rhythmic pattern in which he paced himself, straining against him, shuddering as he plunged even deeper. Her nails dug into his muscled back, her teeth nipped his shoulder and she began to utter mindless little cries of rapture.

Concentrating on giving her pleasure, Brock found it was being returned in full. Her body twisted uncontrollably under him as she clung to him, rocked with him, lost in the incredible sweet anguish that engulfed them both. By deliberately holding back, Brock intensified the pleasure he gave her until a great wave of ecstasy broke over her and she was swept away in a soft, floating tide of joy. Only then did he allow his own release, and with a husky growl he spilled himself deep within her.

He lay over her, languid with the aftermath of love, gazing down at her with a look of puzzled disbelief. Having considerably more experience than she in such matters, he knew that what they had just shared had been something quite beyond casual lovemaking. What a fool her brute of a husband had been to make her despise what she was so clearly made for. What a delightful, hot-blooded creature had been hidden beneath that cool, ladylike exterior.

Audra's lovely eyes looked up at him. They were no longer bewildered and fearful, but luminous with happiness. What was he thinking? Surely no human being could arouse such feelings in another and not be aware of them.

He moved to withdraw herself, but she snuggled closer, holding him to her, reluctant to part from him. "Don't leave me," she murmured.

"I wasn't going far." He smiled down at her tenderly.

"It was only . . ." She blushed. "I can't bear it to be over."

Her artlessness delighted him. He gave a deep-throated chuckle. "What gave you the idea it was over?" His warm lips closed over hers and soon she was rising with him once more, desire quickly renewing itself. His big body again drove to possess hers and again she felt the exquisite ecstasy of fulfillment.

Afterwards she lay still in his arms as the trembling ebbed away. He bent to kiss her brow and saw the teardrops that lay on her long, sweeping lashes like tiny diamonds.

"Audra?" He was suddenly concerned. "Did I hurt you?"

She shook her head. How could she tell him that it had been so wonderful that she was saddened by the thougth that it could not last. She knew that to Brock, the illusive smuggler, this was only one night of pleasure, but to her it was the end of fear and the awakening of something she had never felt before in all her life. How beautiful it had been. Brock had been right. It was not ugly. It was warm and tender and perfect. But it had been this man who had made it so.

He wound a finger about a soft, silky curl of her hair. "My lovely, lovely Audra. We could not have gone on much longer denying our feelings. I've wanted you since the first moment I saw you."

"I tried to fight it and now . . ." She looked up at him wonderingly. "I suppose I should feel guilt."

"Why?" he asked. "It was meant to be."

She watched as he raised himself from the couch and began to dress. She knew, somehow, that he was right. She had been forever changed from the first moment she had met this man. It must have been meant to be!

Brock accompanied her to her bedroom door and kissed her goodnight. Although the kiss was warm, there was no longer any passion in it. She longed for him to draw her into his arms and reassure her that their lovemaking had meant as much to him as it had to her, but he turned away.

"Good night, Brock," she whispered and slipped into her room.

He stood for a long moment in the hallway. He had had to keep a tight rein on himself, wanting desperately to sweep her up into his arms and bed her once more, but she would probably have thought him as lecherous a brute as her husband if he had. She trusted him now. He must not do anything to betray that trust.

Chapter Ten

By the next morning the weather had cleared. Brock rose very early and rode out with Ned. There were already laborers working in the soft, green fields that bordered the estate. He stopped long enough to talk with them before continuing out across the undulating countryside, where on the slopes the sheep quietly grazed.

Looking back, Brock caught a glimpse of Southcliffe lying below; the sunlight glancing off its diamond-paned windows made it look like a sparkling jewel nestled in the velvety green woodland of chestnut and beech, planted to shield it from the cold winds blowing in from the sea.

He thought of Audra still asleep in her bed. Imagined her fair cloud of hair spread out over the pillow, smelt the sweet scent of her velvet skin, tasted the softness of her lips, felt the warmth of her supple, young body. Aware that his own body was responding accordingly, he swore and urged his horse forward, quickly overtaking Ned. There was work to do, work he had lately neglected, and long ago he had learned to put his own desires second.

Brock spent almost the entire day in the saddle, inspecting what had progressed on the estate in the past weeks when he had been away. By the time he returned to Southcliffe, it had almost reached the dinner hour. He sent word to Audra, asking her forgiveness for his lateness and suggesting she join him in the library for a before-dinner glass of sherry.

Then he bathed and began to dress. He was struggling alone with the intricacies of his cravat when there was a knock at his door and Barrow entered.

"Excuse me, sir, but I am afraid the lady will not be joining you for dinner this evening."

Brock scowled and tore the offending neckcloth from his throat. "Why is that? Is she ill?"

"I do not know, sir. Her maid says she locked herself in the bedchamber after breakfast and will see no one."

"What! Locked herself . . ." He stalked across the room to the door and flung it open. In long strides he covered the upper gallery and started down the opposite corridor, meeting Bess outside Audra's door.

"I wish to see your mistress," he demanded.

The young maid looked distressed. "She won't see anyone, sir. Locked herself in since morning and refuses to open the door, even for food and drink.

Something is terribly wrong, sir!"

Brock stared at her a moment in silence.

"Did this come on suddenly, Bess?" Had his actions of the night before been the cause of it?

"She was fine when she awakened, sir. Glad to see the sunshine again after so much rain and chatting happily to me. It was after breakfast when she went into the library."

"The library! Was anyone there?"

"Not to my knowledge, sir."

"She did not appear ill, Bess?"

"I did not see her go to her room, sir, but she passed Polly on the stairs and Polly says she looked very strange."

"Strange? What do you mean?" he growled.

"Like she had had a shock, sir. Her eyes were blank-like and her face white."

"Are there no other keys to her bedchamber?" Brock turned back to Barrow who had followed quietly behind him.

"No, sir. Bess asked me that, sir, and I looked, but a number of the keys are missing."

"Isn't there a door from her bedchamber into yours?" Brock questioned the maid.

"Yes, sir, but it is also locked."

"But it is not as sturdy a door," he mused. "Barrow, go and fetch some brandy and don't fret, Bess. I'll attend to this."

"I'm ever so glad you are here now, sir," she said, feeling much comfort from his big, authoritative presence.

They continued down the hall and around the corner to the door to Bess's small room. Brock entered and, observing the door in the opposite wall, went straight toward it and turned the handle. It was locked, as Bess had said, from the other side.

"Audra!" he called through it, his manner peremptory. "This is Brock. Are you going to open this door?"

There was no answer.

"Audra! You're acting like a spoiled child. Open this door immediately or I'll break it down!"

Still no answer.

A sudden fear filled him. He moved back and took a short run at the door, hunching one of his massive shoulders. The lock gave under the pressure and the door flew open. He straightened himself and entered the room, the little maid hesitating in the doorway.

The fear left him when he saw Audra sitting primly, hands clasped in her lap, on a settee positioned close to the hearth. There was no fire in the grate, nor had there been for hours and the room had a decided chill to it.

Brock strode angrily across the room toward her. "Audra, what the devil is this all about? You've frightened Bess half to death."

She said nothing. She did not even look at him as he stood glaring down at her, but two large tears rolled unchecked down her pale cheeks.

His expression changed immediately and he dropped down beside her on the settee. "What is it?" he asked, his voice softer, full of concern. "I can't help if you won't tell me."

She turned to him then and he thought he had never before seen such desolation in anyone's eyes.

"You can't help me," she said despairingly. "No

one can help me."

He made a move to draw her to him in consolation, but she put up her hands. "Don't come near me!"

He moved back. "So that's it," he sighed. "Look, Audra, you can't undo what we—"

She shook her head. "It has nothing to do with us . . . with . . . Oh God, Brock, I've committed murder!"

"Murder?" He frowned, and then the corners of his mouth began to twitch. "And when, pray, did you align yourself with *me*?"

"I'm not jesting, Brock. The man you killed was, after all, an enemy of our country. My deed was much worse!"

"Who was *your* victim?"

"My husband! I've killed my husband!" She put her hands to her face. "It—it's there in the copy of the *Times* you brought back from London."

Looking about him, Brock saw the newspaper lying on the floor beside the settee. He reached over and picked it up, hastily scanning the headlines.

"I see nothing about a murder."

"It's a funeral notice," she murmured.

He saw it then, read it aloud: "The Fifth Earl of Latham's funeral was held this morning, at eleven o'clock, in St. George's Church in Hanover Square. His Lordship died early Thursday morning at his residence.

"Latham!" he exclaimed in surprise. "Good lord, you were married to that fat, little toad?"

"Did you know him?" she asked, lowering her hands from her face.

"He was pointed out to me once," he quickly covered himself. "So it was Latham who treated you so abominably."

Audra nodded.

"I think you should be delighted that you are free of him."

"But it was *I* who killed him, don't you see?" she cried, her expression full of pain.

From the corner of his eye Brock saw Barrow enter the room with a brandy decanter and a goblet on a tray. He motioned the servant over.

"I want you to have a drink of this, Audra," he ordered. "And then you are going to tell me the whole story." He poured her out a small draft of brandy. "Swallow some of this. You will feel much better if you do."

She choked over it, but she managed to get some of the pungent liquor down.

"A little more," he urged.

"I'd rather not," she begged. "I hate brandy."

"Nevertheless, it will do you good."

Obediently she sipped a little more. "I have had nothing to eat all day and it's very strong. I may get tipsy."

"A state highly preferable to your present one."

"You *are* odious!" she cried. "Completely odious!"

"A favorite word of yours." He grinned.

Brock motioned for Barrow and Bess to leave the room. "I will ring if I want you," he said quietly. The door swung to behind them, then opened a little, unable to latch. Brock rose and went over to it, placing a straight-backed chair against it.

"We won't be disturbed," he said, coming back to her.

Audra had finished her glass of brandy. He took it from her fingers. "All right, start at the beginning," he said, sitting down beside her again.

"Must I?" she asked piteously. "Must I dredge up all I've been trying to forget?"

"Just tell me about the last time you saw your husband."

He hated making her remember, hated the picture that sprang to his mind of that foul old man hurting and abusing her.

Suddenly she found herself pouring everything out in almost incoherent bursts.

"I had been asleep. I awoke to see him standing at the end of my bed leering at me." Her voice shook. "I vowed after the first time that he would never force himself on me again. I was going to escape . . . but he was clever. He made sure I couldn't leave the house. I managed, though, to steal a knife and I hid it beneath my pillow. When he came toward me I threatened him with it." She gave a little sob. "I don't know how it happened . . . somehow he threw his robe over it and snatched it away from me and then . . . then he was all over me again and . . . oh please, Brock, don't ask me to . . ." She was pleading now, the anguish from the ugly memory clouding her lovely eyes.

He could no longer keep his hands from her. One arm went about her shoulders, drawing her gently against his comforting bulk. "Get it all out," he soothed, his warm eyes full of understanding and compassion. He realized that she had bottled it up inside her—the vileness and abasement—and now she must get it out—all of it—like an ugly infection. Only then would the wound heal.

"He—he tried to make me respond to him and when I would not he—he took out a whip." She stopped talking, her eyes staring blankly into the fireplace. Then she took a deep breath and let it out slowly. "He lashed it out at me and the whip encircled me and I crashed down and . . ." Silent tears began to slide down her cheeks and she struggled to continue.

Brock turned to the table and poured her a little more brandy. Anger had risen in him at her words. He remembered the ugly weal marks on her soft skin and he nearly snapped the stem from the goblet as he held it to her lips.

Audra recruited herself with a deep swallow before going on. "Besides the pain, the worst part of it was the degradation. I—I tried so hard to fight him, but I couldn't prevent . . ."

"The filthy bastard!" Brock swore. He didn't want to hear any more. The sordid, brutal scene was all too vivid to him.

"Afterwards, I crawled over to the fireplace," Audra went on, her gaze far away. "I remember being cold. So cold. And I saw an afghan over the arm of a chair and wrapped it around me. Then I tried to stir up the fire with a poker."

"And Latham?" Brock spat his name.

"He just stood there gloating. I don't believe I will ever hate anyone as much in my life!"

"Oh, my dear," Brock said, his comforting arm tightening about her shoulders.

"I had found out from Bess that the young female servants in the house had all been forced to service him and so I asked him why he had bothered to marry me." She swallowed. "He told me he wanted an heir."

Audra's delicate profile was turned toward Brock as she talked and he watched it closely, each quiver of the soft lips, each flicker of the long lashes. It was a good thing Latham were dead, he thought, or he would gladly have killed the son of a bitch himself!

"He boasted to me," Audra went on, "that he had fathered by-blows by two of the young housemaids in the last year. I wanted so much to get back at him and like a fool I implied that they might not be his, that there were younger, more virile men employed in the house. Of course, it only served to set him off. He became like a madman! Before I knew it he had his hands about my throat and was pressing them deeper and deeper." Audra shuddered again. "I managed to grab the poker from the fireplace. I hit him as hard as I could on the side of the head. He fell back against the fender with a dreadful crash and then he just lay there."

"He was dead?"

"Not then. I checked and he was still breathing. He even groaned several times while I was getting my things together. I knew I had to escape from the house before he regained consciousness. Bess came with me and we ran away." She stopped a moment. "But now he *is* dead, Brock! He must have died from that blow to his head! I killed him!"

"It was self-defense."

"But there were no witnesses to prove that."

"What of Bess?"

"She did not see him. I met her in the hallway after I had locked him in the bedchamber."

"You locked him in?"

"Yes. I gave Bess the key and she . . . I think she gave it to one of the other servants before we left. He—he must have died lying there in that locked room. I killed him, Brock! I killed him and I don't know what to do!" She burst into deep sobs.

"Audra, don't!" he said firmly. "The swine deserved to die and I will see to it that nothing happens to you. I swear it!"

"But—but how can *you*, a smuggler, do anything?"

"I have friends," he said tersely. "You must trust me, Audra." Then, with comforting gentleness, he gathered her to him, pulling her close, and it seemed the most natural thing in the world for her to turn to him, to sob against his throat, to be held in his strong arms. For the first time since she had left Greenleigh she felt safe and secure.

Then slowly, as if in a dream, she sensed everything changing for them. Feelings of comfort and compassion quickly disappeared, dispersed by the same compelling emotion that they had experienced the night before.

For several seconds Brock did nothing more than slowly caress her arms and shoulders while his lips gently brushed her forehead, her eyelids, the hollow in her throat. When at last his mouth closed over hers, she gave a shuddering sigh of relief. Eagerly she returned his kisses, reaching up to cup his face and bring it down closer to hers, holding it to her mouth.

There was no longer any fear felt within her, no inhibitions, only a fiery renewal of the hunger she felt for this man, this passionate smuggler who had shown her such joy.

She felt him lift her up in his arms as easily, as effortlessly as if she had been a child. He moved over to the bed and laid her down on the soft couterpane before he began to divest himself of his clothing.

"Brock," she murmured, "surely you don't—I'm a murderess!"

"You frighten me to death." He grinned, with gentle insistence, beginning to slip her gown from her shoulders.

His eyes, now dark with passion, swept over her, savoring the beauty he was unveiling. Her breasts, full and white and exquisite. He kissed each in turn, tonguing the nipples until she thought they might burst. Lips and hands left a trail of delicate flame as they moved teasingly, enticingly down over the softly rounded curves of hips and belly.

Her blood singing, Audra writhed beneath his touch, waves of such intense pleasure rising within her that she wanted to scream aloud.

This was what she needed to block out the ugly memories. Although there were no guarantees of tomorrow with this man, there was this moment and his touch, a touch which could do such devastating things to her, which could evoke responses from her body so compelling that she felt herself whirling into an oblivion of sensation.

Desperately she clutched him back. His flesh was warm and smooth beneath her finger tips as she began to explore him, running her hands over the strong muscles of his shoulders. Her lips moved down to teasingly pull at the dark, curly hairs on his broad chest, to graze the nipples. Her fingers traced the rib cage and flat belly, then hesitated as they encountered the rigid strength.

"Go on," he urged, his deep voice thick as he guided her unsure hand to him. Trembling at first, she slowly began to stroke the wondrous length, the delicious sensation of her touch making him growl with pleasure.

The desire had now grown unbearable between them and urgently she guided the ready flesh between her silken thighs, opening wide to welcome his first searing thrust.

Straining to absorb all of him, she arched high, digging her fingers into the hard muscles of his flanks as he moved within her, urging him on, rocking wildly beneath him, making soft, little cries of ecstasy that served to drive him to even greater passion, glorying in the power of pleasing him as he pleased her.

With one voice they cried out their delight as the floodgates opened and they were both swept gloriously away.

"Oh, Audra, love," he breathed hoarsely. "You learn quickly."

Basking in the warmth of their lovemaking, they lay contentedly in one another's arms. Languidly Brock stroked her cheek with his lips.

"You may think me insensitive for saying this," he muttered, and with his words, Audra tensed. "But I'm absolutely starved!" he finished.

She laughed with relief. "So am I," she admitted.

"Then I think it is time I was off to raid the pantry."

"Oh Brock, you wouldn't." She giggled.

"I shall bring back a veritable feast, milady," he assured her.

He rose, collecting and dressing in the clothes he had flung aside so hastily. Audra watched him, a great tenderness for him rising within her. It had been so easy to confide in him. He had listened with such understanding and compassion to her recital of the horrors she had suffered at Latham's hands. Her fears had slowly melted as he comforted her, melted into something neither had been able to deny and she had so desperately needed. He had been so gentle with her, so loving, so sensitive. She would never regret a moment spent with this man. If this was living for the moment, it was all the happiness she needed.

"Now, stay where you are," he ordered from the doorway. "I won't be long."

He was true to his word. Almost before she knew it he had returned with a tray on which rested a plate of cold chicken, some thick, crusted bread and butter, cheese and a bottle of wine. He set it down on a table by the fire which he then proceeded to light.

Audra, having drawn on a dressing gown in his absence, joined him on a settee and they eagerly began to partake of the contents of the tray, saying little, perfectly content to gaze and smile at one another.

"We will leave for London in the morning," Brock said, at last, filling their glasses once more before settling back on the settee.

She looked at him sharply. "What are you saying?"

"I am taking you to London."

"But I don't understand."

"I think it essential that we learn more about Latham. How he died. What has been said about your absence. You can't run away from this, Audra. Not anymore."

"But what if I'm accused of murdering him?" she exclaimed, the fear burning again in her eyes.

"Then we will prove it was self-defense," he said quietly. "But, somehow, I do not think it is being thought of as murder. There was no hue and cry. I would have at least heard something when I was in London."

"Not necessarily. I doubt you move in the same circles."

Something flashed in the hazel eyes, but he gave a mocking laugh. "How stupid of me, forgetting I'm no gentleman."

She stared at the cynical twist that had come to his lips. "You are the most gentle man I have ever met," she said softly, reaching over to take his hand. "I would never wish you to be like those inane fops and dandies. You are worth ten of them."

"You flatter me, Countess."

Her face clouded. "Don't call me that! Don't *ever* call me that! I hate my title and everything connected with it."

He raised an eyebrow. "Don't forget you are now a very wealthy widow, Audra."

"I don't want Latham's filthy money! I will never

forget that it was because of it I was encouraged to marry him."

"Nevertheless," he said resolutely, "we will go to London and get this settled before—" He stopped. He had been about to say, "Before I go to France."

"I will not go back to Latham House," she said defiantly.

"Of course not. You will stay with my grandmother."

"Your grandmother?"

"Yes. I told you about her. She will enjoy assisting you. She loves nothing better than a little intrigue."

"Oh no, Brock. I could not impose myself on her. My presence might prove an embarrassment or—or even worse!"

"Nonsense. You don't know the old girl. I think it is quite the best explanation of where you have been this past week."

"Visiting her? But why would I go to visit . . . Oh, I think I see what you mean. I could say she was my old nanny or something."

"Old *nanny*! Grandmother!" Brock broke into a roar of deep laughter.

Audra looked a little perplexed.

"I'm sorry, my dear, but you see—" He couldn't help laughing some more. "Well, you will meet her and judge for yourself."

Piqued by his amusement at her expense, Audra rose from the settee. "If I am to leave in the morning, I must get my things together," she said.

"Bess will do that. Don't be angry with me, my love." He grinned up at her with that beguiling smile that made him look so young and boyish.

"I'm not angry with you," she sighed. "I just hope I am doing the right thing."

"By trusting me? You are," he said positively. He leaned back on the settee. "Come here," he said gently, his warm gaze probing hers.

Before she knew it, she was again in his arms and he was rising to his feet, scooping her up with him.

"What delightful booty you are, my sweet," he whispered, burying his face in her fragrant hair as he strode toward the bed. "A rare prize for a common smuggler."

"You are no common smuggler, Captain," Audra murmured. "Not to me."

Throughout the long night, they made love again and yet again. He couldn't seem to get enough of her and Audra reveled, shamelessly, in the joyous demands of her smuggler lover. As the dim light of early dawn stole around the edges of the curtains, sleep at last claimed Brock, but Audra lay curled up beside him, still awake and purring with drowsy contentment.

She had let this man—this smuggler—have his way with her as if she had been a common little trollop! It might be wrong and wicked, but she had never felt so alive! She ached from his fierce lovemaking, but it was a delightful ache. She hugged herself. What a perfect lover he was! With so little effort he could arouse her to fever pitch, craving to become part of him again. Just to feel him inside her, filling the whole of her, whispering his delight in her, made her happier than she had ever dreamed possible.

The fact that Brock's expertise at lovemaking must have come from much practice did not deter her, for she refused to think about the other women in his life. It was enough that today, at this moment, he belonged only to her. The future ceased to exist. Only the present mattered.

Chapter Eleven

Again clad in her blue pelisse and bonnet, Audra sat beside Brock as he drove his light chaise at a smart pace northward toward London. Looking back, Audra saw that, at a respectable distance, Bess and the small amount of luggage followed them in the light travelling coach. The chaise was soon out in the open countryside heading past soft, green fields.

"Are you warm enough?" Brock asked. "Tuck that rug well around you. The air is cool this morning."

"I am quite comfortable, thank you." Audra smiled at him. "But it was thoughtful of you to ask. Under that overbearing exterior of yours, you are a very kind and sensitive man." Then she couldn't help adding, "The woman in your life is very lucky."

"Do you think so?" He grinned. "Do you consider

yourself lucky?"

She stared at his profile, watching the impudent grin widen. "I am not so naive as to think I am the *only* woman in your life," she said quietly.

He slowed the horses and looked at her, his hazel eyes soft and discerning before they turned back to the road. "And if I said you were?"

"I wouldn't believe you. I know you've known many."

"But none who has affected me as you have, my sweet."

He said no more and she knew she must be content with that. She had the feeling that such admissions did not come easily to Brock.

Earlier in the morning, before they had risen, he had gently touched her cheek with his hand and had murmured, "I think you have bloomed overnight. You seem even more beautiful."

"It's because I am happy," she had sighed. "I never dreamed it could be like that. You were so . . ." She had stopped, blushing. "I won't say any more. It will only make you conceited and you are arrogant enough as it is."

He had laughed and whispered that he adored her and everything about her.

But for how long? she wondered now. She was the current woman in his life. His latest conquest. But he had as much as admitted that he had had other conquests. Had he ever truly cared for any of them? She shook her head. She must not think of that. This was only a romantic interlude after all.

Now she watched his hands as he effortlessly guided the horses around a difficult turn in the road.

"It appears you are a competent whip," she said admiringly as their speed increased.

"Do you drive yourself?" he asked.

"I used to. My father had a two-seated curricle like this that I used to drive."

"There is still so much I don't know about you, Audra. Will you tell me your father's name?"

"Sir George Wentworth."

Brock considered a moment. "I believe I have met him. A tall, distinguished-looking man."

"Yes." She nodded, frankly puzzled by his knowledge of those who moved in a society he was no part of.

"You must care for him very much," he said, thinking of what she had suffered to help her father.

"I do indeed. He has not been well of late. I hope now that his financial worries have lifted, his health will improve."

"When things have been settled in London, and I have no doubt whatsoever that we can settle them easily, you should go home and visit him."

She looked at him keenly. "And you? Where will you go?"

"I am needed at Southcliffe. I will return as soon as I am able."

"To take another smuggling trip to France?" she asked, her voice a little sharp.

"Perhaps."

Audra became angry then. "To risk being shot at again? I can't imagine why you would put your life in jeopardy just for some brandy and bolts of cloth." In agitation one hand grasped his arm.

"Careful!" he cried, his eyes on his lead horses as

the jolt affected the pressure on the reins.

"I'm sorry," she apologized, but she did not drop the subject. "You have the smuggling all organized, Brock. Why must you go yourself?"

"Sometimes it is necessary."

"Ned told me that you take the local wool to sell in France."

"Yes. With the spring shearing completed, we have transported a good deal of wool."

"But don't you think it wrong to sell to Napoleon?"

"We do not sell to government procurers, Audra. I would never wish to assist Bonaparte in any way. It was because of him that my brother was killed."

It was the first time he had mentioned a member of his family other than his grandmother.

"Are your parents still alive, Brock?"

"No," he said, with quiet finality.

"Your grandmother—does she have any idea that you are a smuggler?"

"I don't know. She may have guessed something of the sort. Nevertheless, I would appreciate it if you would not speak of it to anyone in London."

"Of course not. You know you can trust me and I will caution Bess."

A small silence.

"Your grandmother must worry about you."

He turned slightly to grin at her. "And you? Will you worry about me now?"

She lowered her head so he could not see her face beneath the brim of her bonnet. "Why should I do that?" she asked.

"Because I will worry about you," he said

truthfully. "As Latham's widow, every fortune hunter in town will be after you, and you are very young and vulnerable." His voice softened. "My conscience, you see, still tweaks me. You were very close to being a virgin and I have never despoiled a virgin."

"I have no regrets," she told him. "I feel as if I had never truly existed before. Now I intend to savor life's every moment."

"That is the way of a smuggler," he declared. "Living for the moment. Not thinking of the future or the past. We will have a week or two in London together, Audra. Let us make the most of it."

She agreed. If she never had any more, she would have this short time with him.

It was evening before they reached London. Audra soon realized that they were travelling through a part of the city with which she was vaguely familiar. Brock pulled up the horses before a gray stone house in Grosvenor Square.

"Here we are," he said, assisting her to alight.

With a puzzled frown, Audra entered the marble hallway. Brock greeted the major-domo, whom he called Fletcher, and allowed him to show them into a large salon. Audra observed in the evening twilight that it overlooked a garden at the back. The room was furnished with priceless antiques and there were several large vases of beautifully arranged flowers. A fire was burning in the grate; Brock led Audra to an armchair before it and smiled reassuringly at her.

"Grandmother will have retired to her sitting

room upstairs. I had best have a word with her alone first."

He excused himself and left the room.

Audra removed her bonnet and pelisse and fixed her hair before a gilt-framed mirror. A glass of sherry was brought to her and she sat down, warming herself before the fire, sipping the wine, her thoughts in complete confusion.

If Brock's grandmother lived in this lovely home, then she must not be in any dire need. Had this all come from the proceeds of smuggling? She thought not. It was obvious this had been a family home for many years.

She gazed about her. On closer inspection, she saw that the furniture coverings and carpets were faded and showed much wear, but everything was spotless and gleamed with polish.

A half hour later Brock re-entered the room. He was smiling.

"My grandmother is delighted to have you as her guest," he announced to Audra. "There is nothing she enjoys more than a little excitement in her lonely life. She wishes to meet you as soon as we have dined."

"And I to meet her," Audra exclaimed, rising from her chair. "I don't—" she began, but the elderly butler entered just then and she was soon being shown to her bedchamber where Bess awaited her. The little maid helped Audra to freshen up and change into the rose silk for dinner.

It wasn't until Audra was seated opposite Brock at the long mahogany table in the dimly lit dining room, which, she surmised, saw little use, that she had a chance to speak her mind.

She waited until Fletcher had departed and they were alone before she said, "I don't believe you have been entirely honest with me, Brock."

He grinned at her over his wineglass. "I may have omitted to tell you a few things, but I have not lied to you."

"You told me you were no gentleman," she chided him.

"As I have explained to you before, Audra, being born a gentleman does not automatically make one a gentleman. Surely my lawbreaking profession and my treatment of you, a lady, only serve to emphasize that fact."

"You have always treated me as a gentleman should."

"No. You are wrong," he contradicted. "I took advantage of your weakness in an unguarded moment."

"You showed me great pleasure," she whispered, her lovely eyes lifting to his.

They were met by the dark, brooding look that desire always brought to his face.

"So you would tease me, would you, woman! Are you at all aware that you have been placed in a bedchamber as far removed from mine as possible?"

Audra's lips twitched in amusement. "I have a feeling your grandmother is very astute."

"Devil take it," he growled. "It is not as if I had ever brought another woman here."

"I should hope you would show more discretion. Do you always stay here while in London?"

"No, rarely. I have my own small suite of rooms. I—" He nodded slowly as a thought came to him. "Of course. I will have another key made tomorrow. We can meet there."

Audra regarded him closely. "How delightfully clandestine," she remarked, with soft irony.

He frowned. "I'm afraid for the time being that is how it must be."

For the time being? she thought. Until he finds out I am a murderess? Until he tires of me? What was the time being to Brock?

At their entrance into the small, upstairs sitting room, an elderly lady rose from her chair before the fire to greet them.

At eighty, she still stood regally erect with the evidence of her past beauty still clearly apparent in the classical features, the luxuriant white hair.

"Grandmother, I would like you to meet Audra, the countess of Latham. Audra, my grandmother, Lady Deverell."

"Deverell!" Audra could not help exclaiming in surprise as she gave a little curtsy to the older woman.

"Apparently my grandson has neglected to tell you my name," Lady Deverell said in a strong, well-modulated voice. She was carefully observing the fair-haired young beauty before her.

"Your grandson told me his name was James Brockington," Audra said, giving Brock an accusing look.

"James Brockington *Deverell*," the older woman

finished, her eyes twinkling. "I see you are still trying to divorce yourself from your family, Brock."

"Where I live Deverell is not a popular name," he retorted.

"And how *is* our country seat?" his grandmother asked, indicating two chairs near to her. "Do sit down. Fetcher will bring us some tea. Oh, and some good French brandy for you, Brock." She smiled. "Thank you for the anonymous gift." Lady Deverell still had all her own teeth and her charming smile reminded Audra of her grandson's.

"Southcliffe is slowly coming into its own again, Grandmother," Brock said, ignoring her last remark. "The tenants have their crops in and with the mild winter the flocks in the hill country have increased."

"I should like to see it again before I die," she said, a little wistfully. "I have many happy memories of Southcliffe."

"With Napoleon's plans unknown, the seacoast is not the safest place to be. When things are settled, I will take you," Brock promised.

Lady Deverell turned to Audra. "My grandson told me briefly what you had been through, my dear, and why he has brought you back to London. You are a very courageous young lady. One after my own heart, if I may say so. I hope all can be settled happily for you."

"Thank you, Your Ladyship."

Fletcher entered with the tea and brandy and had hardly left the room before Lady Deverell shot Brock a question, her shrewd eyes regarding him closely.

"Why, when you were here to see me two days ago did you not mention that this charming young lady was at Southcliffe?"

Audra answered for him. "At that point I don't think he knew what to do with me."

"Then he's no grandson of mine," Lady Deverell laughed, a delightful, silvery laugh.

Audra found herself blushing, but Brock began to explain to his grandmother that he had not known Audra's full name at the time and whether he should return her to her home or allow her to continue on her journey to France.

Lady Deverell then questioned him about stopping the fishing boat Audra was on. Brock would have passed it off as simply apprehending smugglers, but Audra explained about the Frenchman being a spy and how Brock had retrieved a valuable memorandum the man had stolen.

The older woman's eyes had become bright with excitement. "Why didn't you tell me that, Brock? A spy! And you *shot* him!"

"It was not something to be proud of," Brock mumbled. "I should have brought him back alive for questioning."

Lady Deverell was regarding Audra. "Pray tell me how you came to be travelling with this spy?"

Audra thought it best then to tell her the complete story. She told the older woman as briefly as possible of her father's financial problems and her subsequent marriage, of Latham's brutality, although she avoided the graphic details, and his attempt on her life, of her striking back and her manner of escape. She explained to Lady Deverell just why she had made the trip to Dover with her maid and of meeting the Frenchman and of Brock stopping the fishing boat and taking them back to Southcliffe.

"Now," Brock said, "we must find the true cause of Latham's death and produce an explanation of where Audra has been all this time." He looked at his grandmother, who immediately responded to his lead.

"Why, she has been *here*, of course, with me." She smiled. "For the sake of propriety, Audra, it must not be known that you have been gadding about with my grandson."

Audra nodded, coloring again.

"But what reason are you going to give," Lady Deverell said to Brock, "as to why she did not communicate with anyone or did not attend her husband's funeral?"

"She has been very ill and you, Grandmother, did not think her well enough to hear the news of her husband's unfortunate death until she was feeling better."

The older woman frowned. "But why did I not send a message to Latham House of her whereabouts?"

"Because she had told the earl she was going to visit you. He died before he could let anyone else know."

"Mmmm. It might work." Lady Deverell turned to Audra. "We must find out more details of your husband's death before you see Latham's solicitor. What about your maid? Could she not visit Latham House in the morning and talk to the servants?"

"The very thing!" Brock agreed.

"Bess reminded me today," Audra said, "that when she and I escaped from Latham House the earl was bellowing at the door of my bedchamber where I had locked him. He was obviously very much alive then and I know she will swear to that."

"There was never any doubt in my mind about whether you had killed him," Brock said. "I do not think we will need her testimony. As Grandmother suggested, it would be wise to send Bess around in the morning to learn the actual reason for Latham's death."

Lady Deverell had noticed the anxiety that had appeared in Audra's face with the talk of Latham. "I wouldn't worry, dear." She leaned over to pat Audra's knee. "Once Brock takes charge of something he does not let it go until it is finished to his liking. He is a very stubborn and determined young man."

"Traits that are not altogether foreign to *you*, ma'am." Brock smiled, bowing his head slightly in his grandmother's direction.

"Insolent pup!" Lady Deverell cried, her bright eyes flashing.

Brock laughed. "We will not tire you any longer, Grandmother." He rose, holding out his hand to Audra. "It was a long drive from Southcliffe and I am sure Audra is anxious to retire."

Lady Deverell nodded. "I will see you both tomorrow."

She watched them cross the room to the door. "See that you *only* see her to her bedchamber, Brock." She wagged a finger at her grandson. "I will be listening for your return footsteps."

Hearing what Brock mumbled under his breath,

Audra was forced to stifle a giggle as he closed the door behind them.

Audra lay in her bed drowsily waiting for sleep to claim her. It had been a long day and she had slept little the night before, but she could not rest. She found herself pursuing the tangles in her mind, tangles Brock had created about himself. She remembered his words in the chaise that morning.

"I would never wish to assist Bonaparte in any way. It was because of him that my brother was killed."

When she had questioned him he had told her that his parents were also dead. Apparently there was only his grandmother. A grandmother who had turned out to be the Dowager Lady Deverell! No wonder Brock had laughed at her when she had compared the woman to an old nanny! Lady Deverell was every inch a gentlewoman!

Other words returned to Audra. Ned's words: "I managed things for a year under the new lord. He was already in the army and off fighting on the continent when he gained the title. Killed over in France." Was he the brother of whom Brock had spoken?

He had also said: "I gather Lord Deverell's reputation is unknown to you. He is a notorious rake and is part of a decidedly degenerate set of the ton."

But if his brother, Lord Deverell, had died in France, who was the new Lord Deverell?

Audra sat bolt upright in her bed. There was nothing to unravel here! It was all quite clear and simple! Brock, himself, was Lord Deverell! He *had* to be! His brother was dead and he had gained the title! Perhaps it was his grief over that death that had led him into becoming the man he had warned her about, into seeking forgetfulness in drinking and gaming and womanizing until he had bled Southcliffe dry.

She lay back on her pillows and, gazing at the ceiling, tried to imagine Brock as he might have been in those days. Something must have occurred then to have caused him to travel to the estate, to see for himself the deplorable conditions, to become the captain of *The Peregrine* and proceed to make restitution. It all made sense. Perfect sense. And yet it was difficult for Audra to picture Brock as the society popinjay Ned had described. He was so strong and so sure of himself and his goals. She could not imagine him as a drunken and dissolute gambler, risking his life in a duel over some painted little trollop.

How glad she was that she had not known him then. The Brock *she* knew was gallant and courageous, with a tenderness of heart that had reached out and claimed her.

It was at that moment that she realized she was totally, irrevocably in love with him! She *had* been, she now knew, even when she had thought him to be but a common smuggler. What a fool she was! He had never said he loved her. He had only made it clear that he wanted her. There was no commitment there. Yet what they had shared had changed her forever. There was no going back now, even if it didn't last, even if he broke her heart.

Chapter Twelve

Bess went to Latham House in the morning. She discovered that the only servants left in the house were the housemaid, Lucy, who had befriended her, and Abel, who had been the earl's valet.

"We did not tell the authorities the whole truth," Lucy admitted to her. "We did not want Her Ladyship to get into trouble. Her being so young and so ill-treated by him. We just told them she had left with you to visit friends and we didn't know where to reach her."

"His Lordship, you see, Bess," Abel added, "pounded and pounded on that door for a good quarter hour while some of the more timid of the servants tried to decide whether to run off or to stay. Finally, I got the key from Lucy here and opened the door. By that time His Lordship was crazed with anger! He came rushing out into the upper hall, yelling for Her Ladyship, and when I told him she had gone, he seemed to go even more berserk. He snatched a whip of some sort from the pocket of his robe and thrashed the air about him, shouting, 'I'll get her! I'll get her!' Then, he started to dash down the stairs. His robe was long on him, him being such a short man, and he tripped over the hem of it and down he went! Over and over, head over heels, cracking his head on the newel post at the bottom! It snapped his neck outright and killed him. Can't help but think it served him right."

Bess's eyes were like saucers as they stared at Abel. "What did you do then?"

"We didn't touch him, except to remove the whip from his hand. I put that away, I did. It was a funny thing. When he came flying out of milady's bedchamber, the left side of his head was bleeding as if he'd been struck, and when he fell, he cracked the very same side of his skull. I thought it best not to mention the first wound to the authorities."

"Bless you for that, Abel," Bess exclaimed. "You see, milady was forced to hit him with a poker—"

"I told you I cleaned that poker up and the hearth too," Lucy interrupted. "I didn't know whose blood it was and I wasn't going to ask. Better, I thought, to let sleeping dogs lie. His Lordship's death was never questioned. They smelled liquor on him and it was obvious he tripped, the robe being torn at the hem."

"All has been quiet since the funeral, except that a little clerk from His Lordship's solicitor's office keeps coming around to ask if there is any word of Her Ladyship."

"Milady will want to contact the solicitor. What is his name, Abel?"

"Sir Henry Browne," Abel replied.

"Sir Henry Browne," Lady Deverell murmured, "that old reprobate."

Bess had just left the salon after telling the dowager, Brock and Audra the story.

"Do you know him, Grandmother?"

"Know him. Of course I know him. Old fool. Jumped out of the bushes at me once at a garden party. Tried to kiss me. There I was, married with children and he more than ten years my junior. No doubt someone dared him."

Audra could not help but smile and Brock broke into a roar of laughter. "Grandmother, I hope I have as good a memory when I am your age."

"The trouble is that one remembers such idiotic things." Then her face sobered. "Just see that you *get* to my age," she told him, her eyes full of meaning.

It took Brock some time to convince Audra that she must take whatever Latham had bequeathed to her. She had suffered enough at that bastard's hands, he insisted, and deserved every penny she might be left as his widow. Audra was finally forced to agree. She would not, however, she stated firmly, take anything that had belonged to the earl, anything he might have touched or looked upon.

This did not strike Brock as being unusual. He could quite understand her wanting to alleviate herself of any memory of him.

Lady Deverell sent word to Sir Henry Browne

that the countess of Latham was with her and having suffered a serious illness had only recently been thought strong enough to learn of her husband's death. It was the same explanation that Audra had written to her father and Emily.

Upon reading Lady Deverell's missive, Sir Henry was persuaded to leave his large, comfortable offices off Temple Court for the Grosvenor Square address.

The solicitor arrived late the next morning with a little law clerk so close behind him he was almost treading on his heels. They were shown into the library where Audra and Brock awaited them.

Sir Henry Browne was a balding gentleman in his late sixties with exaggerated sideburns and a decidedly pompous air. He offered his condolences to Audra, who sat as if convalescing in a chair by the fire with an afghan wrapped about her knees. She had appropriately donned a dark gown for the occasion, most of her clothing having been sent over from Latham House the afternoon before. Brock suggested that the solicitor seat himself before the large, mahogany desk.

"Thank you, Deverell," Sir Henry said, motioning to the little clerk to sit by his side. "I don't suppose you remember meeting me with your brother at White's one evening?"

"I do indeed, Sir Henry," Brock said quietly. "It was in the early days of the war."

The solicitor nodded. "Your brother was about to depart for the continent, I believe. Shocking loss." Sir Henry shook his head sympathetically before turning to Audra. Knowing Lady Deverell, he said to her, he could well understand her decision not to inform the countess of her husband's death until she felt she was well enough to hear the news. He hoped she was convalescing well.

Audra assured him that she was, thanks to Lady Deverell and her grandson's kindness.

Sir Henry got right down to business then, producing Latham's last will and testament, from a leather case the obsequious little clerk handed him. It had, he said, been drawn up only a few days before the earl's marriage. In almost a monotone he read it completely through. It appeared the earl had possessed considerable holdings all over the country. Everything, it seemed, had been left to Audra and any heirs that might have resulted from their union.

"Were there no other relatives?" Audra asked, surprised.

"Only a cousin who has been in charge of the Latham family seat in Sussex for many years. He and his sons have run the estate most proficiently."

"Then he must have it," Audra said quietly.

"Have it?" Sir Henry's eyebrows rose. "You mean, of course, that he should continue to run it."

"No. I mean that he and his family should be given the estate. All these years he has probably existed on a pittance from the earl for his hard work."

"But—but—" Sir Henry sputtered, "it is the most profitable of the earl's properties and it is, after all, the family seat."

"More reason than ever for it to remain in the family. After all, Sir Henry, this cousin must have been the earl's heir until his marriage to me."

"Well, this is all very generous of you, Your

Ladyship, but—"

"That is the way I wish it," she said decisively.

Sir Henry looked over at Brock, as if for support, but that man only shrugged his broad shoulders.

"All right," the solicitor sighed, "if that is the way you wish it, but there is now the matter of several other properties and houses." He listed them.

"I wish them all to be sold," Audra said when he had finished.

"All?" Sir Henry looked amazed.

"All. I do not wish to live in or hold onto any of them."

Sir Henry shook his head. "But, Your Ladyship, there are many wise investments among—"

"Sell them," Audra instructed. "I will invest the money as I see fit."

"Your Ladyship." Sir Henry carefully set the papers down before him and pursed his lips. "I do not like to say this, but you are very young and perhaps you should think this over for a little while and take the advice of older and wiser men, who are more knowledgeable about investments."

"I fully intend to seek others' advice about investing, Sir Henry, but I will not change my mind about liquidating all my assets."

"Deverell, do you think you could—"

"Her Ladyship has a mind of her own, Sir Henry. I would not dream of trying to dissuade her."

"As you wish," Sir Henry said tightly. "Then, if I might just have your signature, Your Ladyship. Here . . . and here."

The solicitor and his assistant rose to leave shortly after Audra had affixed her signature to several documents.

"I hope you will not be sorry that you have made such hasty decisions, Your Ladyship," Sir Henry admonished her.

"I am sure I will not," she said, gazing at him levelly. "Thank you for coming so promptly, Sir Henry."

As he reached the door, the solicitor turned back to Brock who had accompanied him and in so doing almost collided with his little clerk who scurried out of the way.

"Are you in town for long, Deverell?" he asked.

The other shook his head. "Only until some business of mine has been completed."

"I see. Have you seen Jason?"

"No." Brock's face darkened. "We do not frequent the same haunts."

"You might like to know that it is rumored he may be getting in over his head again."

"Stupid ass!" Brock growled.

It was afternoon of the same day. Brock had excused himself after luncheon. An appointment, he told his grandmother. Only he knew it was to see Viscount Castlereagh, who had been informed of his return to London. However, when Brock arrived at the War Office, it was to learn that the viscount had been called away to attend an important meeting of the government and would not be available to see him until the following morning.

Leaving the War Office, Brock headed straight to his suite of rooms, which were empty as he had arranged, his man having discreetly left for the afternoon.

It was pouring rain. Lady Deverell had tried to dissuade Audra from going to Latham House to collect a few personal belongings that had not been sent over with her clothes. Audra had insisted. The older woman had shrugged, but she had watched Audra closely from her window, observing that she had left the house unattended.

Dressed in unrelieved black from shoes to veiled bonnet, Audra had taken Her Ladyship's carriage, but dismissed it upon her arrival at Latham House, insisting the driver return home and not wait in the downpour. She did not know how long she would be and she would get someone from Latham House to transport her home.

Audra had been welcomed by Lucy and Abel, had chatted briefly with them and retrieved her silver brush and comb and some other small articles from her bedchamber. Then she had asked Abel to call her a hackney carriage.

He had protested that the earl's horses were still in the stable and he could quickly arrange for them to be harnessed to one of several vehicles, but Audra insisted she could not wait. When he returned from putting her into a carriage, Abel winked at Lucy.

"Do you think Her Ladyship has an assignation?" he asked.

She nodded. "There is always a man involved when a woman looks that radiant."

Audra used the key Brock had given her to enter

the suite of rooms at the quiet address. She had barely closed the door when Brock was beside her, sweeping her into his powerful arms.

"I thought you would never come."

His lips closed over hers hard and demanding and then more tender as she yielded to him. Her arms went about his neck, straining to draw him closer, but his hold loosened and he stepped back.

"You're shivering," he said, proceeding to remove her damp cloak and untie the ribbons of her bonnet. "Come warm yourself." His voice was soft as he placed her things on a chair and led her over to the fire. He bent down and set another log on the grate, watching a moment as the flames curled up around it.

"Did you miss me?" he asked, rising and drawing her to him again.

She nodded. "It's been two long days."

"And two even longer nights."

"Oh, Brock," she murmured huskily, "it's been—"

"Torture," he finished, his voice roughly taut, "living in such close proximity and yet unable to even touch you."

His fingers went to her hair, pulling out the pins, tangling in the pale cloud that tumbled down over the shoulders of the severe black gown. He looked at it in distaste.

"I hate you wearing those reminders of death." His breath was hot against her cheek. "I long to see you without them . . . smooth and soft and white."

Audra felt again that sweet, warm suffusion beginning deep inside her, frightening and thrilling her. Due to its illicitness, this meeting seemed all the more exciting to her.

He pressed her closer to him, his lips claiming hers, his kiss deepening until the pressure of his mouth opened hers, and their tongues met and tasted.

"I want you like the very devil!" he groaned, the hunger mounting as he unfastened the tiny buttons at the back of her gown, slipping it from her creamy shoulders, removing the rest of her clothing with equal ease until she stood proudly naked before him, as motionless as a beautiful, marble statue glowing in the firelight.

He took a step backward, his gaze shifting from her face to her breasts and down the full line of her lovely body. His hazel eyes gleamed with the reflected light of the fire and the hunger that was in him. She trembled as he reached to touch her, her eyes partially closed with pleasure as he ran his hands gently over her shoulders, down over the firm, young breasts that peaked and hardened beneath his caress.

"It's my turn," she murmured, beginning to unbutton his fine linen shirt. She had to stand on tiptoe to pull it off, and the taut breasts brushed tantalizingly against his muscular chest.

His hands went to his breeches, but she whispered, "Let me."

Unsure, trembling with anticipation, her fingers fumbled with the buttons.

"I don't think you have undressed many men, my love," he teased, his voice deep and amused.

Tentatively she touched the mound that bulged against the fabric before setting the swelling flesh free. His breeches fell, were kicked aside.

Bathed by the flickering flames, they stood looking at one another, feeling the pleasurable tension grow between them.

Slowly, like two people in a trance, they came together. Their eager bodies touched, warm flesh meeting warm flesh, pressing closer, soft breasts crushed to tautly muscled plains, swollen manhood against tender loins. Softness inviting hardness, slow, sensual, touching, rubbing, giving in to growing hunger, mouths conveying their fierce need, bodies yearning, straining, moving erotically against one another. Without a word, lost in desire, they sank to the thick, fur hearth rug.

In burning torment Audra knew that the fire that raged within her could only be assuaged by the man who now rained kisses in a hot trail down her twisting body. She moaned at the touch of his lips and his hands, crying out for him to hurry. She wouldn't let him linger in his lovemaking. Not this time. She craved him so deeply. Longed for him to become part of her again.

Feverishly she reached for him, grasping and guiding him to where she was moist and ready. She gripped his wide shoulders hard as that wondrous length entered, stretched and filled her with fiery heat.

Blind to everything but her need of him, Audra urgently directed one who needed no direction. Hazel eyes gazed down at her, and a little half smile played at Brock's lips at her eagerness.

Like a flaming rocket she found herself soaring higher and higher, meeting each searing thrust as his big body drove ever deeper into hers. Her fingers dug into his buttocks, challenging him to plunge harder, faster, as she arched herself closer to him.

The frightened little child-woman had become a demanding savage, writhing beneath him, urging him on and on. In wild abandon they thrashed about on the soft, thick fur, revelling in the exquisite ecstasy their lovemaking produced. Lost in the agonizing pleasure, they strove upward, upward, until with a sunburst of dazzling light the climax came, so shattering in its intensity that Audra cried aloud.

Gasping, Brock held her shuddering body against him. "Dear God," he breathed, "that was worth all the waiting."

They lay on the hearth rug, tangled in each other's arms and she drew in the warm scent of him, mingled with the smell of the burning wood on the grate. She pressed her cheek against his damp chest, nestling closer to him. His arms folded around her protectively.

"My adorable Audra," he murmured, "I had never thought to find one such as you. I can't get enough of you."

The soft throbbing against her thigh betrayed his renewed desire. He kissed her lovingly, brushing aside a stray tendril of fair hair from her cheek, his lips finding the pulse in her throat. Her breathing quickened as his kiss lingered. Desire began to course through her veins once more.

This time they came together slowly and leisurely, without urgency. The blazing fire had been banked and there was a gentle sweetness to their lovemaking, tenderly caressing, cherishing each other.

Afterwards, they lay curled together before the

flickering fire, murmuring their delight in one another until sleep claimed them both.

Audra was the first to wake. Despite Brock's closeness she was cold. Only embers of the fire glowed in the grate. She struggled to raise herself on her elbows and Brock awoke.

"It is late," she said. "I must go."

He pushed her gently back. "Not yet!" He couldn't bear to part from her and end this perfect afternoon.

Again they loved and later, lying sated and exhausted in the shelter of Brock's arms, Audra thought she lacked the strength to rise and leave. Nor had she any wish to. How blissful to stay forever in this private haven, closed off from all the world and be made love to by the man you loved.

It was her feelings for Brock, she knew, that made the act so wonderful. Oh, how I love you, she thought as she gazed adoringly at the handsome profile beside her. It wasn't a whim or a fancy that would go away after he left. He was the man she wanted forever—so strong and virile, yet so gentle and loving. If only she could be with him always!

Reluctantly he pulled her to her feet. They dressed silently, helping one another, stopping to kiss more than once. On their hands and knees they searched laughingly for her hairpins in the deep fur of the rug.

"Tomorrow?" he said to her at the door, before he went to hail a carriage.

"But what excuse can I—"

"Tomorrow," he said determinedly, and she knew she would find a way.

Chapter Thirteen

Brock sent word to his grandmother that he would not be returning to the family residence that evening. Upon learning this, Audra was both relieved and disappointed. Relieved, because she was sure she could not have sat across the table from him without her feelings becoming immediately apparent to Lady Deverell, and disappointed because she would miss him terribly.

Brock, sitting in a comfortable chair before the fire in his rooms, sipped at his brandy and, glancing down at the hearth rug, remembered the lovely young woman who had lain there in his arms. What was he going to do about her?

From that first moment in the cabin of *The Peregrine*, when Audra had stood proudly before him, trying to hide her fear, he had been attracted to her. She had made her dislike of him so clearly apparent, and being unused to women reacting in such a negative manner to him, he had become intrigued. Despite the anger that was quick to leap to her eyes, despite her haughty manner and her cutting tongue, he had soon become completely captivated. Not for him a meek little complacent mouse! He had always enjoyed spirited women, women with intelligence and minds of their own, women who would eagerly respond to his lovemaking. But until Audra, he had not realized that something had been missing. It had taken one bruised and lonely young woman to show him.

Damn it! He was in love with her! His blood quickened at the very thought of her. He remembered her luminous eyes, her soft lips, her lovely breasts, her sweet smile. The moment when her fear had turned to trust in him, when she had bared her soul to him and thrown all pretense aside. She had shown herself to him then, beautiful and frightened and starved for love. In trying to make her happy, he had become happier than he had ever dreamed possible. Damn, but this was not the time for love! Why had he allowed it to happen? He did not have the time. It would only complicate matters. He had to have his mind and heart totally free to concentrate completely on the work that lay ahead.

The first thing in the morning, Brock went back to see Castlereagh.

"Good morning, my lord. You wished to see me?"

"Yes, Deverell. Please sit down. We received some

news yesterday that is quite disturbing." Castlereagh sat forward in his chair. "We learned that word has reached Napoleon that Austria is thinking of re-entering the struggle. As you know, we have begun to supply her with English money. Now we must send much more and help the Austrians in every way to push forward their preparations as quickly as possible. Naturally, Napoleon will warn his three commands in Germany—Davout in Prussia, Oudinot in west central Germany and Lefebvre in Bavaria—that Austria is arming for an attack."

"In what way may I help?"

"You must make a message through to the Archduke Karl Ludwig urging him to take the initiative to strike before Napoleon can augment his troops. We understand that there are only about sixty thousand men at present withdrawn behind the Rhine. It is the perfect time. Even Metternick, the Austrian ambassador to France, agrees. Ludwig must not delay!"

"When do you wish me to leave?" Brock asked him.

"As soon as possible. Can you set sail tomorrow evening?"

"Yes," Brock answered succinctly. "I am already holding all smuggling runs in abeyance until the French informer is uncovered."

Viscount Castlereagh rose and, taking a key from his pocket, opened a safe set into the wall behind his desk. From it he withdrew a securely wrapped packet that he handed to Brock.

"Contained in here are also your new identity papers. You will be Jacques Sabourin, a wine merchant from the Loire Valley."

He swung the steel door shut and tested it to make sure it was securely locked before again pocketing the key.

"If I may have pen and paper," Brock said, "I would like to write two letters to be placed in your safe. I wish them to be delivered only on the event of my death."

"I pray that will never be necessary."

"I rather share your sentiments." Brock grinned.

Castlereagh moved to the door. "Use my desk. Do not hurry. I wish to speak with my undersecretary and I will be some time."

"Thank you, my lord."

"God go with you, Brock."

Arriving back at his suite of rooms an hour later, Brock was given a missive from Audra to the effect that she could not dissuade Lady Deverell from taking her shopping that afternoon. His grandmother had insisted that she must obtain certain accouterments for her mourning. Audra sent her love and hoped she would be seeing him that evening for dinner.

The thought that shopping for hypocritical trappings was keeping them apart made Brock angry. Damnit, they had so little time.

He arrived at the Grosvenor Square address in the early evening. Lady Deverell caught the soft flush that rose in Audra's cheeks when Brock was announced. He strode into the salon, crossing the room to where the two women sat, enjoying a pre-dinner glass of sherry.

The dowager was growing very fond of the lovely young widow who had been brought into her home. They had struck an immediate rapport and had enjoyed one another's company greatly that afternoon. Audra had not hesitated in making it very clear to Lady Deverell that she intended to dress as she pleased when not in the public eye.

"It is too hypocritical to be in mourning for a man I despised," she said as they drove off to the shops.

"I couldn't agree with you more," Lady Deverell congratulated her, saying she was glad to find a young woman with some backbone. She had thought the breed had all died out.

The dowager, however, had seen Audra returning from her outing the previous afternoon and the young woman's radiance had not been lost on her. She had put two and two together and now, seeing the way Audra greeted Brock, her heart sank. The young widow had been through a nasty experience with her bestial husband. Lady Deverell did not wish to see her hurt again. And hurt she would be if she fell in love with Brock, the dowager was afraid. She was not blind to the fact that her grandson had known many women, but to her knowledge his affairs had all been short-lived, his desire cooling quickly at the slightest sign of entanglement. She thrust these thoughts aside as she became aware that Brock was discussing her with Audra.

"Did you know that Grandmother was quite a madcap in her day? What did they call it then? Full of 'gig'?"

"I had a good time," Lady Deverell admitted with a little smile of remembrance.

"Good time indeed. Grandmother was the toast of St. James in her day. Widely acclaimed for her beauty and wit." He turned to his grandmother. "I have heard about the large *cicisbeo* you attracted."

"*Cicisbeo*! Well . . . maybe one or two admirers."

"Don't be so modest. You admitted only a day or two ago that Sir Henry Browne was panting at your heels."

"I never encouraged one of them!" His grandmother wagged a finger at him. "But your grandfather was such a dashingly handsome man that I found if I kept him off balance a little it served to keep him away from the muslin company." She smiled. "He was so like Jason in appearance, but more authoritative in manner like you, Brock. He was a man who went out for what he wanted and would not rest until he got it." Her eyes twinkled. "I suppose that was how he got *me*."

Dinner that evening turned into a gay and happy affair and Audra found herself thoroughly enjoying Lady Deverell's amusing and sometimes outrageous stories of her youth. It was easy to see why she had been noted for her wit. As for her beauty, she was still an arresting-looking woman at eighty, with her bright blue eyes, her luxuriant white hair and her regal bearing.

"I only wish you were not so recently widowed," Lady Deverell said to Audra over dessert. "I would love to entertain for you. Would she not be a sensation, Brock?"

"She would indeed." His eyes regarded Audra with admiration. She wore one of Madame Bertin's gowns and she knew by his expression that he had perceived its elegance and how well it suited her. Now his eyes, regarding her over his wine glass, told her much much more. She blushed becomingly at the open desire she read in their darkened depths.

It was later than her usual hour when Lady Deverell indicated that she wished to retire. Seeing the two ladies to the bottom of the stairway, Brock gallantly kissed first his grandmother's and then Audra's hand, wishing each in turn pleasant dreams.

Lady Deverell regarded him a long moment before she quietly echoed his words and with Audra's assistance ascended the wide staircase.

Audra found she couldn't get to sleep. She lay in bed, staring at the flickering light on the ceiling of her room made by her bedside candle. She had never been so happy, she thought, living each day for the sight of Brock, enjoying every moment she spent with him, even in the company of his grandmother.

They had only had that one precious afternoon alone, but knowing Brock, Audra felt sure he would arrange more time with her before he left. In the back of her mind she feared his inevitable departure, but she would not let herself dwell on it. They had at least another week together.

For the hundredth time she pictured the two of them together on the hearth rug, before the fire in his rooms. She felt again the gentle touch of his lips and his hands, saw his dark, tousled hair, his devastating smile, as he lowered his head to hers, as his broad shoulders blotted out the whole world.

Her breath quickened as she remembered the wildness of their passion. Did anything matter anymore except this smuggler with the rakish smile who had, in such a short while, become her very reason for existence?

Audra felt a stirring deep within her loins. She wanted him so! Now! This very minute! The idea that came to her was flagrant . . . wanton . . . but she didn't care! She would go to him.

She slipped from her bed and grasping the candle in one hand flitted across the room, noiseless in her bare feet. As she opened the door she started and nearly dropped the flickering candle!

Brock stood before her in a long burgundy robe with his hand raised as if to knock. He gave her that familiar wicked grin.

"I decided propriety be damned!" he said.

"You shouldn't have come," she whispered. "Your grandmother . . ."

He eyed the candle in her hand and his grin deepened. "You were on your way to visit *her*, I presume?" He pushed her gently back into the room and closed the door. "Forget my grandmother." The deep timber of his voice sent a shiver through her body. "Forget everyone and everything. Tonight there is only you and me."

She set down the candle and let him lead her to the bed. He sat down on it and drew her between his knees. Her fingers went to untie the ribbons at the neck of her nightdress. He helped slide it down over her shoulders, down to fall in a heap at her feet.

"You're so beautiful, my love," he said, almost in awe, as the soft candlelight revealed the smoothly molded shoulders, the full, high breasts and the slim curves of her waist.

He leaned forward and buried his face between the lush breasts and for a long moment he didn't move, glorying in the warmth and the scent of her body.

Audra's hands went to entwine themselves in his thick, dark hair, pulling his head up to hers, fitting her eager mouth to his. The kiss was tender, melting into a deeper, growing passion.

His hands found her breasts, caressing them gently and she reached toward him and pulled at the cord of his robe. He shrugged it off and, as it left his shoulders, she kissed his neck, his chest, with its dark mat of curling hair, making little circles with her tongue on his skin, licking at the nipples. He groaned and fell back on the bed, taking her with him so that she was stretched full length on top of him.

A sweet, familiar fire raced through them as he grasped her buttocks, pressing her closer to his hard body. Their mouths and tongues eagerly sought each other, their breathing quickened. His hands moved to roll her over.

"No, don't!" Audra whispered, rising to kneel over him, reaching for him with trembling fingers, encircling him, caressing the velvet strength, wanting, aching, to have it buried deep within her.

She lifted herself, guiding the eager shaft between her thighs, up into the welcoming heat. Slowly, deliciously, she lowered herself upon him. The feel of the throbbing length sliding deep within her sent waves of pleasure searing through her body. She moaned aloud and he raised her gently by her hips, almost allowing the entire length to withdraw before lowering her down on him again. She thrilled to the delightful, delirious sensation, and began to move on him, increasing the pleasure, lifting, plunging, rocking from side to side. He pulled her closer, his hands on her slim hips as she rode him faster and faster. Her long hair fell in a soft curtain about his face as she leaned over to kiss him, her eyes closed, her mouth open with the joy of it.

She could have cried aloud as the exquisite pleasure heightened, but he covered her lips with his own, pulling her tighter when the frenzy could no longer be contained. He groaned and she felt his deep shudder as together they erupted in exploding rapture, perfectly attuned as always.

They lay locked as one as the tremulous thrills subsided. Each time they made love it seemed to be better. They were more aware of the other's preferences and desires.

"Sweet little rider," he murmured now.

She blushed at his words. "Oh, Brock, I'm so glad you came to me!"

"I had to come. I couldn't stay away another moment." His mouth brushed her eyes, her lips. "Damn it, our time is so short."

She slid off him then, curling up against him and he pulled her even closer to his side, kissing her lingeringly.

Only a week more, she thought, and then this will end. He will leave me. She felt a chill of fear and tried to ignore it. He was here with her now and she would not spoil it by thinking of the future. When he gathered her into his arms she felt safe and secure. There was no tomorrow, no partings, no loneliness, only Brock.

"My adorable Audra," he was saying, cupping her cheek gently with one hand. "How am I ever going to leave you?"

"Don't talk of leaving," she pleaded. "We still have days—"

"I wish we did." He shook his head sadly. "I leave in the morning."

"The morning!" She struggled from his arms. "But I thought—"

"So did I, but something has come up."

"Another smuggling run?" Her voice caught in her throat.

He nodded.

It came to her then. It was so clear and simple. She could prevent his leaving.

"Oh, Brock, don't you see, there is no longer any need for you to smuggle."

He raised himself on one elbow and looked down at her. "There is still Southcliffe to consider and the tenants and villagers."

"But remember Sir Henry said I would have millions. Millions! It was *you* who insisted I take the money. Let me help you with your plans, help you with Southcliffe."

She felt his body go rigid beside her. "I don't think you understand, Audra," he explained. "Southcliffe is not mine. The tenants are not really my responsibility, although when I discovered their plight I took on their welfare."

"What do you mean? Does Southcliffe no longer

belong to the Deverells?"

"It belongs to Jason Deverell, my brother." He said the words as if they were a source of anguish to him.

Audra looked at him in amazement. "Your *brother*! But I—I thought he died in France, that *you* had inherited . . ."

"Now, I see." Enlightenment filled his eyes. "You were under the impression *I* was Lord Deverell." His lips twisted into his old mocking smile. "I'm sorry to disappoint you, my dear, but you seem to make a habit of aligning yourself with younger sons."

She seemed a little dazed. "Your grandmother mentioned Jason, but I—I just naturally thought that he was your dead brother."

"No. *His* name was David. I suppose I should have told you. There were three of us. Jason is the middle son. It was a sad day when *he* gained the title. He is a gambler and a wastrel who has nearly used up the entire family fortune. Bled poor Grandmother dry. She's been living on the gradual sale of her jewelry and treasured possessions," he growled. "I did not become a smuggler as a lark. The risks I take are necessary for my very existence."

Audra's eyes searched his face. Her voice trembled a little as she said, "You need no longer take those risks. I have all the money we will ever need."

Her soft words lingered for a moment in the quiet room. Then a bitter laugh burst from Brock's throat.

"Devil take it, I do believe I'm being propositioned," he chuckled. "I'd never thought to be kept by a woman."

Audra recoiled as if she had been slapped.

"It might be quite delightful at that," he went on, the muscles flexing in his cheek. "Set up in a house of my own, clothed like a Corinthian, showered with little gifts. And all I'd have to do—"

He caught at her arm before it could inflict the blow to his face.

"Get out!" she cried, fighting tears of anger and humiliation as she tried to wrest herself free of him.

"No!" He forced her to look at him. "Goddamnit, Audra, what do you think of me? Don't you suppose I have any pride?"

"Stupid, senseless pride!" she lashed out. "Instead you would rather go out and risk your life in some nonsensical smuggling run."

"Hardly nonsensical." His voice was harsh. "A lot of people depend on me."

"Really? Oh, I forgot. They would suffer greatly, wouldn't they, without their precious French brandy," she scoffed. "And what on earth would they do without French lace to trim their silken gowns?"

He didn't answer for a minute, but he let her wrist go. She began to rub it, still glaring at him.

"I don't expect you to understand all the reasons behind what I do," he said quietly.

There was something about his face that stemmed her sharp rebuttal. A determined look. The look of a warrior going into battle. It frightened her. What if something happened to him? The anger left her as quickly as it had come.

"Don't go, Brock," she pleaded.

"Do you think I want to leave?" he rasped. "When I hold you in my arms how easy it would be to say,

'To hell with my obligations and promises, to hell with everything and everyone in the whole damn world!'"

He gathered her to him, burying his face in her hair. "I'm sorry for what I said to you. You're the best thing that's ever happened to me. Do you know that?" His grip tightened as if he never wanted to let her go. "It will be awhile before I return," he said finally. "There are new contacts I must establish."

He made no move to release her. How long would it be before he held her again? Would he *ever* hold her again? He had known many women, but he had never known anything like this before. He wanted to be everything to Audra, her protector, her companion, her lover. Damnit, he swore to himself, he could not be any of them. Not now. Tomorrow he would be gone to God knows where and only God knew if he would return.

Gradually Brock's hold relaxed and he looked deep into her eyes. "I have to go. I can't help it, Audra."

Of course you can't, she thought. You're a smuggler and to a smuggler there is no future, only a present. How many others had loved him? she wondered. How many hearts had he broken? How many women, whether simple barmaids or titled ladies lay awake at night remembering this handsome smuggler, so skilled at lovemaking, yet as elusive as the bird for which his ship was named.

You went into his knowing it was only a romantic interlude, she reminded herself. Even if it is only desire and not love on his part, take what you can! You still have tonight. Don't waste it!

She had never been more aware of his closeness, his every caress, the wondrous ways in which he aroused her as they passed the long night in love. Exhausted, they would sleep an hour or two only to wake and seek each other once again, unable to quench the fires of passion and desire.

As the gray of the dawn broke the darkness, Audra lay, pale and weary, encircled by Brock's protective arms. He leaned over to kiss her cheek.

"You must sleep," she whispered to him, "or you will not be able to keep your eyes open on the drive to Southcliffe."

"How can I sleep," he murmured, "when I hold someone so delectably warm and soft in my arms?"

He brushed her neck, her cheek, her temple with velvet kisses and slowly, as if in slow motion, they melted together and became one again. With exquisite gentleness he moved in her, increasing the lazy rhythm until she clung helplessly to him. Their bodies drank deeply of one another and again the ecstasy rose and broke over them.

When Brock next woke it was daylight and he quietly slipped from Audra's side. He did not wish to wake her. She looked so peaceful and so beautiful with her cloud of fair hair spread out over the pillow. She gave a little mew and one hand reached out for him as he left the bed, but she did not appear to waken. He shrugged into his robe, then felt compelled to return to touch his lips to hers one last time.

Blue eyes, shadowed with fatigue, blinked and looked up into his. "You're leaving?" she murmured.

"I must. It's morning."

Suddenly wide awake she pushed herself upright. "Kiss me just once more," she whispered.

"You know where that will lead and the servants are already stirring."

Instead, he threw her the kiss she had asked for and strode toward the door.

"Be careful, Brock."

He gave her a grin. "Miss me," he said, and was gone.

Chapter Fourteen

It was late in the morning when Audra again woke, only to receive an urgent message brought by Lady Deverell's abigail that her mistress wished to see her in her bedchamber.

She found the dowager sitting up in her enormous four-poster bed, wearing a cap of lace on her head and a frilly lace-trimmed bed jacket.

"Ah, there you are," she exclaimed as Audra approached her. "Come and sit down on the end of my bed. I wish to speak with you."

She waited until Audra was seated before she continued. "Brock must be well on his way to Southcliffe by now."

Audra started. "He told you he was leaving?" she asked.

"No . . . not in so many words. I knew it last

evening when he bid us goodnight."

Puzzlement showed in Audra's eyes.

"There is something about the way he looks up at me when he kisses my hand," the dowager explained. "It's as if he wonders if it will be for the last time." It was not lost on her how Audra paled at her words. "Was that, perhaps, how he looked at *you*, my dear, when he left your room this morning?" Lady Deverell's voice was purposely casual as one hand smoothed the satin coverlet before her.

Audra stared at her, the color rising in her cheeks.

"Well, speak up! How long have you two been lovers?"

"Your Ladyship!" Audra jumped to her feet.

"Why do you look so shocked? It's the truth, ain't it? I may be old, but I'm not yet blind and deaf. Nor am I such a prude, missy. My grandson is a devilishly attractive buck. In your shoes, I'd have gladly opened my door to him."

"Your Ladyship, I—"

"Still, I've become inordinately fond of you, Audra, and I think you should be made aware of a few facts." She pointed to the end of the bed. "Sit down. Sit down. You make me nervous."

Audra reluctantly did as she was told.

"Attractive bucks," Lady Deverell went on, "unfortunately are inclined to have reputations. Our Brock is no exception. He is considered a bit of a heartbreaker. Though he usually has shied away from respectable females, there *have* been a few who thought they had snared him, only to find to their sorrow that he had no intention of marrying them."

"Your Ladyship," Audra began again, her eyes

beginning to darken, "I really have to—"

The dowager shrugged. "I only thought you should be aware that you might be wasting your time."

"Thank you very much for telling me," Audra said stiffly, rising again to her feet. "But I was quite aware from the start that there was no commitment on Brock's part—as—as there was none on mine. He offered only a sympathetic shoulder, a temporary—"

"Fustian! You're a poor liar, my dear " Lady Deverell shook her head. "It's obvious to the thickest head that you're in love with him."

Audra turned away from the older woman's intent gaze. "Does it show so much?"

"Only to those who care." The dowager's voice had softened. "I knew it the minute I saw you with him. He admires you. I saw *that* in his eyes, but whether it is anything deeper I cannot tell. Brock hides his feelings well."

There was silence for a moment before Audra turned back to Lady Deverell, her chin proudly raised.

"I presume you would like me to vacate your home."

"Whatever for?"

"Considering my illicit relationship with your grandson."

"What has that to do with anything? You were discreet. I doubt the servants are aware of it, unless your maid is a gossip."

"But—"

"Farradiddle, people are so namby-pamby these

days. Everything so hush-hush. Good lord, you're a widow, not a simpering, little virgin. You can be your own woman now. Take as many lovers as you please."

"But I don't—"

"I know." Lady Deverell waved a ringed hand at her. "You don't want a flock of lovers. You only want Brock." She gave a deep sigh. "More fool you, my dear."

At Lady Deverell's words, a sudden sense of despair came over Audra. "I'm more of a fool than you know," she said. "I practically threw myself at him—offered him money—begged him to say."

"*That* was a mistake," the dowager said. "He's as proud as a peacock, that one."

"But to risk his very life smuggling stupid, non-essential goods—"

"Audra," Lady Deverell said, her voice lower, "look at me. You know my grandson better than most. You were on his ship, saw him with his men. He commands well, doesn't he? Has the respect and affection of those who work for him?"

Audra nodded, wondering what this was leading to.

"Did you know that Brock was briefly a captain in the navy? You must have met Ned at the estate. He was Brock's second in command. It was *me*, Audra, who forced him to come back from the war after his brother was killed, after Jason . . . but that's another story. I needed Brock and he soon became interested in Southcliffe, taking on certain responsibilities there. I have always wondered why he became connected with the smuggling. I put it down to restlessness, frustration at not being able to fight, but I think now that I was wrong."

Audra regarded Lady Deverell more closely.

"I want you to think on this. Did it ever occur to you that, considering Brock's lawbreaking activities, it was pretty bold of him to go to Viscount Castlereagh himself with that stolen memorandum?"

"No. At the time I thought his audacity rather in character."

"True." Lady Deverell smiled. "But remember Castlereagh is no fool. Why did he not detain Brock for more questioning? Why did he not ask him what the devil he was doing on a ship off the French coast so late at night?"

Audra nodded. She was following the dowager's words carefully.

"There was no way Brock could have lied his way out of that," Lady Deverell went on. "Castlereagh must have known *why* his ship was there! He must be aware that Brock is smuggling! That is the only answer. Think it over. You're a needle-witted chit."

"But if he *is* aware of Brock's activities, why hasn't he stopped—"

"He hasn't stopped them because Brock is working for him. It's as simple as that. Brock's smuggling is a mask for something far more dangerous."

Audra felt the quickening of her heart as understanding dawned. That *had* to be it!

"My guess is that Castlereagh had another mission for him and that is why Brock left so quickly."

"It all makes sense when you explain it," Audra said slowly.

It made too good sense. She could hear Brock's voice the night before: "I don't expect you to understand all the reasons behind what I do," he had said. She remembered that determined expression on his face. She had compared it to a warrior going into battle. Brock was risking his life for his country and she had once had the temerity to call him a traitor!

"I think you realize, Audra, that what we have just discussed must not go beyond this room," Lady Deverell said meaningfully. "Brock's very life may depend on our silence."

Somehow Audra managed to get through that day and the next. She visited Sir Henry Browne at his offices and managed to straighten out a few more details concerning Latham's large estate. One such detail was to settle a generous amount on Lucy and Abel for their loyalty to her. But no matter how busy she tried to keep herself in the daytime, there were still the agonizingly long nights to get through. Sometimes, when the memories came, she wondered dully which was the worst, the memory of her happiness with Brock, or the fact that it might be all over? Would he come back to her? He had only asked her to miss him, not to wait for him.

The very thought of that big, rugged man caused her heart to beat faster, caused a quickness in her loins. Would he always affect her that way? She could so clearly picture him. His dark, tousled hair that she had loved to lose her fingers in, his mocking hazel eyes, his lips twisted in an insolent grin. Please keep him safe, she prayed. Please bring him back to me.

It was the second afternoon after Brock had left that Audra, seated reading in the salon after luncheon, heard a repeated pounding of the front door knocker.

She saw Fletcher hurry past the open salon door on his way to answer the summons and then a drawling masculine voice met her ears.

"Hello there, Fletcher. Not dead yet, I see. Grandmama at home?"

"I should have known it was you, milord, by the way you demanded entrance," the old servant said stiffly. "Her Ladyship is resting at the moment, if you haven't disturbed her."

The new arrival strode past him, flinging the words over his shoulder. "I'll wait in the salon, then. Bring me some claret. That's a good man."

Audra stared as a tall sprig of fashion entered the salon. His skintight pantaloons were of a delicate shade of yellow and his boots a mirror-shiny black Hessian, with gold tassels. He wore a long-tailed coat of bright blue superfine with stiffly wadded shoulders and enormous breast flaps. Topping off his dandified costume was a Mathematical Tie over extremely high shirt-points.

Audra watched as he crossed the room and upon seeing her he stopped in his tracks a few feet away. He gave her a graceful bow.

"I beg your pardon. I was not aware the room was occupied." He lifted his quizzing glass and surveyed her. "Are you a guest of my grandmother?" he asked with a smile of pleasure. Why, the chit was a real beauty!

"Yes, I am."

"How unusual. Let me introduce myself. I am—"

"Lord Deverell," she finished.

"How did you know?"

"You resemble your brother a little," she murmured.

But you are not quite as tall and much slimmer in build, she thought. In fact, had she not heard how dissipated his lordship had become, she would have thought him unwell. His face was pale and weary looking and there were dark pouches beneath his eyes that aged him considerably, yet he could not be more than a few years older than Brock.

How different this dandified man was to his brother! There was a quaint distinction about Brock's dress, she realized. His plain, close-fitting coats always fitted him superbly, but perhaps this was due to the splendid physique they covered. Other men were forced to use more padding in the shoulders or larger lapels to disguise their imperfections. Lord Deverell was one of these. He was slim almost to the point of gauntness.

"And who are you, my dear?" he was asking.

She introduced herself.

"Latham's widow? Well, I'll be hanged. How do you come to be here?"

As Audra began the explanation that she had told so many times before, Lord Deverell pulled a comfortable chair up across from her. She was just finishing her story when Fletcher entered with the wine for His Lordship, and was full of apologies at not being aware of Audra's presence in the salon.

"It is quite all right, Fletcher." She smiled at him. "We have introduced ourselves."

She politely refused a glass of claret, and Fletcher poured out one for His Lordship and, with a scowl in his direction, made his departure.

"So you have met my brother," Jason Deverell said, taking a sip from his stemmed glass.

"Yes. He was in London for a few days earlier in the week."

"He told you of me, I'll be bound."

"Yes, he did."

"And none of it good."

She had little use for this man and decided to speak the truth. "None of it," she agreed.

He looked a little taken aback by her frankness, then shrugged and took a deep swallow of his wine. "He's right, of course," he said. "Can't say I blame him for being bitter. Dragged out of the navy because Grandmama couldn't bear to lose another grandson to old Boney. Forced to live in the country and make a go of that dilapidated old estate when I refused to set foot there. Brock isn't averse to taking responsibility, you see. Myself, I'd rather have a good time and let others do the worrying."

Audra's blue eyes flashed. "How admirable of you," she scoffed, rising from her chair, determined not to spend any more time with this detestable man.

"Sit down, my dear. Didn't mean to pique you." His slightly hooded eyes swept over her. "You're a pretty little thing, y'know, despite your obvious temper. What is your Christian name? Mine is Jason."

"Audra."

"Audra," he repeated. "Of course. Heard tell of you. 'The Alluring Audra' you were called, weren't you? Quite the rage of town last season. Not that I often frequent Almack's, mind you."

"Nor would they welcome you," said an imperious voice from the doorway.

"Grandmama!" Jason rose and went forward to meet her. "How good it is to see you!"

Lady Deverell met him halfway across the room. He gave her a charming smile and lifted her hand to his lips.

"As usual you look very dapper-dog," she said, regarding his apparel. "Run into Dun territory again, Jason, that you come to see me?"

"Grandmama! How can you say—"

The sharp, old eyes met his and he had the grace to color. "I'm afraid you're right. I've come to beg you to take me in for a little while . . . until I can straighten out my affairs."

"Faith, Jason," the dowager said, letting him help her to a chair. "I swear you'll be the death of me. I told you the last time—and you gave me your solemn word you would not again indulge in so many excesses."

"Must we go into such sordid matters with such a beautiful young lady present?" Jason said, smiling across at Audra.

Audra did not return his smile.

"I'll wager that fancy piece I saw on your arm last week had something to do with this," Lady Deverell declared, her bright eyes never leaving her grandson.

Lord Deverell gave a little choke. "Grandmama! Surely your guest is not interested in my little peccadillos." He proceeded to offer the older woman a glass of claret.

The dowager waved it away. "You drink far too much, Jason," she said tartly. "Always have."

"I never did like to do things in moderation," he laughed. "Makes life so mediocre and dull."

"God forbid that you and those reprehensible cronies of yours should ever become prosaic. Tell me, Jason, have you ever gone twenty-four hours without gambling, drinking or womanizing?"

Jason looked helplessly at Audra and shook his head. "You see before you a foul degenerate, my lady. A dissolute monster."

Audra rose to her feet. "Would Your Ladyship please excuse me?"

Lady Deverell nodded to her. "I am afraid we have made you feel uncomfortable, my dear, and I apologize. Of course you may be excused."

As soon as Audra had left the room, Jason broke into a laugh. "All right, Grandmama, how much is she worth? I know Latham was full to bursting in the pockets."

Lady Deverell stared at him. "I have no idea."

"Oh, come now, don't play innocent with me. I don't understand why you took her in initially, but it was certainly an astounding piece of good luck on your part. Latham dying like that and you with his sick, little widow on your hands and two impoverished and eligible grandsons."

"Why must you think everyone has a mind like your own, Jason?" his grandmother said sadly. "I am very fond of Audra."

"Hard not to be. She's very lovely." He rubbed his

chin, considering. "I think I could put up with the temper and a great deal more to get my hands on that fortune."

"You will not have the chance, Jason," his grandmother said sharply.

"Really? And why not? Have you picked Brock for her then?"

"I have made *no* arrangements for Audra's future. It is none of my affair. Besides, she has scarce been a widow more than a few weeks. I hardly think she is thinking of remarriage."

"Damn! I suppose propriety dictates a year's mourning and that, I'm afraid, will be a little too late to—"

"How much, may I ask, are you clipped this time?" Lady Deverell questioned.

"Not much, a mere trifle."

"How much?" the dowager insisted.

"How should I know? I'm not a bank clerk. Around fifty thousand or so, I dare say."

"Jason!" The old lady's hand went to her heart.

"Brock will help me, won't he? I'll send a message down to Southcliffe. You said the estate was beginning to show a profit again."

Lady Deverell looked at him hard. "Brock will not help you. He is pouring what profit there is back into the estate. I told you that the last time. I also told you I am barely getting by on what I have."

"So my dear brother doesn't care if I am done up and dragged off to the Fleet, eh? Doesn't care about the family name being besmirched."

"Do *you* care, Jason? I really don't think you care tuppence for anything or anyone anymore."

Chapter Fifteen

Audra climbed the stairs to her room thinking about Jason Deverell. What a narcissistic man he was! How could his grandmother pander to him? Sell her jewelry and possessions to pay his debts and feed his lusts? Could she not see that this was not the way to save him? She was only helping to ruin him by continuing to come to his assistance.

Audra was sure Brock would rather do the most menial work than ever appeal to his grandmother for a sou. He would never live off a woman. He had made that perfectly clear. He had his pride and he was a man, she thought. Oh yes, Brock Deverell was *all* man! She blushed at the memories that now filled her. Memories of his lovemaking—so gentle one moment, so wildly passionate the next. Would she ever feel his strong arms about her again?

Audra met Lord Deverell in the salon before dinner. That he had been drinking steadily through the afternoon was apparent by his flushed face and his slight stagger as he rose to greet her.

"Grandmama has sent her apologies. She is a little indish-indisposed and will not be joining us."

No doubt she is consumed with anxiety over the new debts you have run up and how she will manage to pay them, Audra thought, regarding Jason scornfully.

He was thinking that the young chit standing before him with such a look of disdain on her beautiful face was one of the most exquisite creatures he had ever seen.

"You don't like me, do you, Audra?"

"No," she admitted, "I think you are insensitive and selfish and stupid. How can you go to those gaming-halls night after night and lose all that money? What is the point? Can you really enjoy it? Are you foolish enough to think you can win back all that you have lost?"

He took a pinch of snuff from the delicate Sevres box in his hand before he answered her.

"You do not understand gambling, my dear. It is an addiction. It gets in one's blood."

"Are you so weak you cannot conquer it?"

"Why should I conquer that which I find enjoyable?" he asked, laughing.

"Because people depend on you." She glared at him. "It is your duty. You have your estate tenants and the people you employ to look after, not to mention your family. You should be caring for your grandmother. Not she for you."

Jason's air proclaimed his unutterable boredom with the subject. "Brock is running the estate and he seems to be doing an excellent job of it."

"He is risking his very life to help—" Audra stopped. She had nearly mentioned his smuggling runs.

"That is going a bit far, isn't it?" He gave her a mocking smile. "Farming and sheep-raising are hardly life and death propositions."

"But looking after the estate is *your* job," she hastily declared. "*You* should be the one putting it to rights, not Brock."

Lord Deverell yawned. "I find that sort of thing infinitely boring."

"Then, far be it for me to bore you any further, Your Lordship," Audra exclaimed, the color rising in her cheeks. And before he could say another word she had swept from the room.

It was the next morning that Audra, prepared to descend the stairs for a quiet walk in the garden with Bess, heard the loud chatter of voices rising from the downstairs hall.

She stopped and looked down at a throng of men, noticing that poor Fletcher was beside himself, trying to hold them back. It appeared they were tradesmen, and various other creditors, clasping accounts in their hands. They had heard that Lord Deverell was now residing at this residence, they said, and insisted upon seeing him.

Fletcher was protesting that this was the home of the Dowager Lady Deverell and not her grandson, but they would have none of it and as their voices rose, Audra became alarmed.

She felt someone at her elbow and, thinking it to be Bess, remarked, "I believe we are about to see Lord Deverell obtain his just desserts."

"No!" cried a trembling voice beside her and Audra turned to see Lady Deverell standing there. She looked her age and more this morning. She could not have passed a good night.

How could His Lordship do this to her? Audra thought angrily. She loves him and he is making her suffer for his stupidity.

"Surely he should be told they are here," Audra said. "Let him get himself out of this muddle if he can. Poor Fletcher cannot—"

"No. *I* will handle it," Lady Deverell said quietly.

She was about to start down the stairs when she went suddenly white and her knees began to give way. Fortunately, Audra was close enough to catch the frail form. Bess came running up to them at that point, having darted back to her mistress's room for a forgotten glove. Between the two of them they managed to carry Lady Deverell back to her room and help her to bed. The dowager's abigail was frantically trying to remember where she had placed the hartshorn when Lady Deverell spoke.

"Audra?"

"Yes, Your Ladyship, I am here. I want you to rest and I will deal with those men downstairs. I will return when they are gone."

"Thank you, my dear. Queer. I suddenly felt so dizzy. . . ."

"Good morning, gentlemen," Audra said a few minutes later as she descended the stairs. "Can I be of any assistance? Lady Deverell is not well."

The men gathered below looked up to see a young lady dressed in widow's weeds slowly coming toward them.

"I am the countess of Latham," she introduced herself. "A friend of Her Ladyship."

"'Tis not Her Ladyship we wishes to see," shouted one burly man loudly. "'Tis that no-good grandson o' hers. Owed me for nearly two years he has. Heard he'd lost everything over the turn o' a card. Figured to get something from him, at least, before he ends up in the Fleet."

"I can quite understand your concern," Audra said truthfully.

The voices had now died down and Fletcher was looking gratefully, but inquiringly, at Audra.

"I think this can be settled quite easily," she said with quiet authority. "Please leave your accounts with Mr. Fletcher and I will see that you are paid within the next few days."

"How can we be sure of that?" one distrustful man growled.

"You have my word," Audra said quietly.

The man's eyes fell before the intent stare that dared him to question it.

With no more protests, the men did as Audra suggested and mumbling to themselves began to shuffle off. Fletcher closed the door on the last of them and shoved in the bar. Wiping his forehead with a handkerchief, he turned back to Audra, who still stood at the bottom of the stairs.

"Come into the salon a moment, Fletcher. I would speak with you alone," she said. "And bring those accounts with you."

"I want to thank you, milady," the old butler said as he followed her into the room. "When I opened the door, they pushed their way in. I don't think I could have held them back much longer and I shudder to think what they would have done."

Audra went over to a table by the fireplace that had been turned into a grog table by Lord Deverell. She poured out a glass of brandy and offered it to the servant.

"I think you need this, Fletcher."

"But, milady, I couldn't—"

"Drink it," she said.

The butler, looking a trifle embarrassed, took a long sip of the brandy.

"That was very brave of you to defy that ugly-looking mob," Audra told him.

"But what are we to do with these?" Fletcher said, waving the wad of bills he still clasped in his left hand. "Her Ladyship has sold the most valuable of her possessions and I would hate to see—"

"She will sell nothing more, Fletcher," Audra said firmly. "I will pay His Lordship's debts."

"You? I beg pardon, milady, but why should you—"

"Because Lady Deverell has been very kind to me. I am certainly *not* doing this to help her useless grandson," she added hastily.

"That is very generous of you, but I am sure when Her Ladyship hears of this—"

"I do not wish her to hear of it, Fletcher. It is to be our secret. Yours and mine. We will simply tell her that I have talked those creditors into another extension. In the meantime, I wish you to discover the owners of His Lordship's gambling markers as I would also like to take care of them. In a few days, when everything is settled, it will be learned that an unknown friend has come to Lord Deverell's aid and kept him from ruin."

"Milady—" The old butler smiled at her—"you not only look like an angel, you are one."

Lying in bed that night, Audra said to herself, "You wouldn't let me help *you*, Brock, but you cannot stop me from helping your grandmother."

She had gone to see Sir Henry Browne that afternoon, with little Bess in tow, and had made all the arrangements for paying Lord Deverell's debts, explaining her reasons to the formidable solicitor.

"Her Ladyship has been so kind to me and she has become ill with worry over this matter," she had said. Surprisingly, Sir Henry had understood and agreed to attend to it.

Again Brock entered her thoughts. Where was he this night? she wondered with a shudder. She could not keep from thinking of the dangers he might be encountering, the risks to his life. Was he deep in French territory now? Perhaps hiding out? Bonaparte had ordered the immediate imprisonment of any British citizen found on French soil. Pray God Brock had not been captured or wounded or . . . worse!"

There was a quiet knock at her door and without waiting for an answer someone entered the room.

Audra sat up in bed, the candle was still burning on her nightstand. She expected to see Bess standing in the doorway, but to her astonishment she saw it was Jason Deverell. He was wearing a gold, brocade robe with a high, stiff collar. It caught the light as he crossed the room and approached the bed.

"What do *you* want?" she asked him sharply.

"Don't look so shocked. I came to thank you personally, Audra, for procuring an extension from my creditors. I don't know how or why you did it, but it was very good of you."

"I did not do it for *you*," she snapped. "Your grandmother was so clearly distressed—"

"Nevertheless, Audra, you have done me a great service and that is why I felt I must come. . . ."

Audra could see that he had again been drinking heavily for he reeled a little and caught hold of the bedpost for balance.

"To thank me," she finished.

"No, to offer you . . . *my* services."

"Your services?" she asked, clearly puzzled by his words.

"Yes. Once a woman has been married . . . has known a man . . . she feels the need. And as it has been weeks since Latham died . . ." He looked at her. Her pale blond hair soft and loose about her shoulders, her skin white and glowing in the candlelight.

To his amazement, she suddenly threw back her head and started to laugh. She couldn't stop herself. Peels of silvery laughter filled the room.

"What's so damn amusing?" he growled.

"Your conceit," she choked. "That you should imagine, that you should even think . . ." She laughed even harder.

His face darkened with anger. "You find the idea of me making love to you amusing?"

"No." She shook her head. "Only your way of going about it."

The anger began to drain from him. "I can assure you that you would find it highly enjoyable." He gave her a supercilious smile. "I am not inexperienced in pleasing a lady."

He was beside her now and bent forward as if to take her in his arms, but she moved quickly beyond his reach.

"I am quite sure you have had plenty of experience, Jason, but if you touch me, you will regret it." She said this very firmly, the smile having left her face.

"If you can stand that fat pig Latham in your bed, I don't see why . . . or do you like to play games? Is that it? Like to pretend you don't want me, spout a stream of protestations until I have overwhelmed you." He snorted. "Damn waste of time, if you ask me. I want you and if you'll only admit it, you want me too."

"You really *do* believe that, don't you, Jason?" she said, shaking her head.

"I *know* you do. Why play this cat and mouse game?"

Audra didn't answer.

"Don't tell me you're a little prude?"

Still no answer.

"Is it marriage you are holding out for?" he pressed her, clearly exasperated now. "I'd be glad to marry you."

"I'm sure you would." She tried to keep the corners of her mouth from twitching. "Brock told me I should beware of fortune hunters. I wonder if he realized that the first one to offer for me would be his brother?"

"Brock?" He lifted an eyebrow. "He must be acquiring some subtlety. I would have thought he would have barged right in and declared himself."

"He *did* declare that he would never let a woman support him."

"Really? How noble. Don't believe a word of it, my dear. To my knowledge Brock has had several very wealthy paramours. Doubtless they were not averse to lending him their support."

He saw by the pained look in her blue eyes that he had struck a chord. So that was how it was, he thought to himself. Brock had already laid claim to her heart. Well, no matter. It would all be in the family. All those lovely millions!

He bowed and wished Audra a pleasant good night, heading jauntily, if a little listingly, toward the door, completely unaffected by her refusal of him. It never occurred to Jason that she did not really want him. That thought never entered his head. Brock had got there first was how he rationalized her refusal, and Audra would not play false with him, however much she wished to do so.

Across the channel, in a hidden bedchamber, another countess faced another Deverell.

"My husband is suspicious," Celeste said. "He was informed that *The Peregrine* was sighted last night and that it was thought a man had come ashore."

"Do you know his informer?"

"*Non.* I just overheard Philippe speaking of this to two men in the lower hall. He was demanding the whole countryside be searched."

"Do you think you could discover who the informer might be?" Brock asked, adding, "It is for your best interests as well as mine, Celeste."

"I will try. Have you not questioned Jean Paul?"

"He seemed nervous having to bring me here. He is afraid the informer may be a servant at the château."

"*Mon Dieu!*" Celeste looked suddenly afraid. "If Philippe should find out I've been hiding you . . . that we are lovers . . ."

"Then you would direct him to me. It is time, I think, that we came face to face."

She saw something in the narrowed hazel eyes that she had never seen before. A dark, blazing hatred that sent a convulsive shiver down her spine. "You have something personal against Philippe, *n'est-ce pas?*"

"You are his wife."

"*Non.* It is more than that. More even than the fact that you are enemies in war," she said perceptively.

Brock hesitated only a moment. "You're right," he admitted. "Your husband was responsible for the slow and painful death of my brother." Each word he uttered was said like a curse. "He tortured David right here in this château!"

Celeste turned chalk white. "Then . . . from the very first . . . you came here to . . ."

He said nothing, but she could see the truth in his eyes.

"You deliberately planned the whole thing! You used *me* to get at Philippe!"

"One always searches for one's enemy's Achilles' heel, Celeste," Brock said quietly. "You, *chèrie*, are Philippe's."

"But he is an insanely jealous man!" Celeste cried. "Have you not thought of what he might do to *me*?"

"Nothing will happen to you if you will only lead him to me," Brock assured her. "It is me he will want. I ask only for my revenge, Celeste."

She turned on him then. "*Bâtard*!" she screamed. "Pretending to care for me when I meant nothing to you! Nothing! *Pourquoi*, all I've ever been to you is a willing body!"

His voice was a deep rasp. "Was I any more to you, madame? A stallion, you called me. A bloody stud is more like it!"

Her bitter rejoinder was silenced by his mouth coming down hard over hers. He had to stop her! She was angry enough now to do something foolish. He grasped her shoulders and drew her roughly to him. His hands moved over her and without even a token resistance, she began to respond to his expert touch. She pressed herself against him, her mouth opening to return his kisses.

Moments later he laid her back on the bed and impatiently she helped the strong fingers loosen and remove the sheer gown. Slowly, delightfully, his trailing hands and mouth brought her body to life in flaming arousal. The passion grew, totally consuming her. She cried out for him to take her, but abruptly, cruelly, he broke away and rolled out of reach.

"You don't want *me*," he taunted her. "As you said, I've only used you to get at Philippe. You'll get another lover soon enough to relieve your boredom"

"*Non*!" she gasped, reaching for him, clawing wildly at him. "*Non,* Peregrine, I want *you*! Only *you*!"

He felt nothing but disgust for himself as he exacted her promise to discover the identity of the informer, as he finally allowed her feverish fingers to tear at his clothes, as he blanked all thoughts of Audra from his mind and gave in to the purely physical response.

Chapter Sixteen

There was a letter for Audra from her father in the morning post. In it he expressed his relief that she had recovered so rapidly from her illness. It made Audra feel guilty that she had had to deceive him with this lie. If he had not been married to Emily—but there was no use in thinking of that. He ended his letter by telling her that Paul Chatfield had arrived home, wounded, and was coming to London to see her.

Paul. She put down the letter. A crowd of memories came back to her. Happy memories of their youth together, unhappy memories of the last time she had seen him and how angry she had been at his inability to help her.

Poor Paul. It had not been his fault. She had only made it worse for him. Why, if it had not been for her, Latham would not have had him sent back so quickly to the peninsula. Perhaps he would not have been wounded. Was it a serious wound? Was his army career over?

All these thoughts went through her head as she sat in the sunny little morning room and again read over her father's letter. There was a sudden knock at the door and Fletcher entered.

"A gentleman is here to see you, milady," he said, handing her a card.

She read the name and caught her breath. "Lieutenant Paul Melville Chatfield." Her father's letter must have been delayed in reaching her. Paul was already in London! He was here!

Audra realized she was not dressed in appropriate mourning clothing, but the soft mauve gown she wore was suitably plain and unadorned.

"Show him in, Fletcher."

Paul was wearing his uniform and his limp was quite pronounced as he entered the room. His face came alive when he saw her.

"Audra!"

She rose to greet him, smiling as he came toward her. He took both her hands in his, raising each in turn to his lips.

"You are more beautiful than ever."

"It is good to see you, Paul," she said a little formally, wondering why she did not feel as she had only a few months before when they had met on the meadow at Greenleigh. This time the old, familiar ease was sadly absent. She could hardly believe she had been quite prepared to marry this man, if he could have found a way. She realized now how very little she knew him. She saw before her a pale, good-looking young man whose face still bore the signs of pain and fatigue, a young man of whom she was still fond, but could never truly love, for Brock held all her love now.

They sat down opposite one another in the bright little room.

"I was so sorry to hear you had been wounded," Audra said, her face showing her concern.

"A bullet shattered my knee. The surgeons removed it, but I am to have another operation soon. If it is successful I will not have this stiff leg."

"Then I pray that it will be," she said, smiling warmly at him.

"I don't want to talk about me," Paul said. "Did you get the letter I sent to you before I left?"

"No, I did not. *He* conveniently lost it."

"The earl?"

"Yes. I suppose you realized it was he who instigated your return to your regiment before your leave was up?"

"It did not matter. It was better for me to get back into the thick of things. It gave me less time to think." His eyes met hers. "I poured out my heart to you in that letter. Rather stupid of me. No doubt he read it and thought better of letting you see it." His gaze held hers. "Was he . . . was he good to you, Audra?"

"We were married only two days before he died, Paul."

"You did not answer my question."

She got up and moved to stand before the

fireplace, turning her back to him for a moment. When she faced him again there were tears in her eyes.

"I cannot lie to you. No, he was *not* good to me. In fact, he was brutish and cruel. I am not sorry he is dead."

"Oh God," he groaned. "I was so afraid—"

"We will speak no more of it," she said brusquely. "My father must never know, Paul. It is over and I intend to block those two days forever from my mind."

His gaze fell. "It was all my fault," he murmured. "If only—"

"The world is full of 'if onlys,' Paul. Please let us not mention it again."

There was a moment of awkward silence. Audra looked down at Paul who seemed consumed with guilt. Why had she told him? Was she unconsciously trying to hurt him because he had not measured up to her expectations, had not rescued her in time from Latham's clutches? That was totally unfair. Yet she could not help comparing him to Brock. Brock seemed so much stronger in character, so sure of himself, and yet Paul was no weakling. He was an officer in the army and had probably led men into battle. He was bravely enduring the pain of his wound.

"What are your plans now, Audra?" Paul was asking her.

"Lady Deverell has kindly insisted I stay here with her until my affairs are all in order. Then I may visit my father at Greenleigh."

"Do you plan to take up permanent residence in London at Latham House?"

"No. I am selling the house. I want no property or possession that was *ever* in Latham's hands."

Her hate was very deep, Paul realized. Audra had changed considerably since he had last seen her. She was a woman now, clearly more confident, and there was something else about her. He had seen how her eyes had softened as she thought of something or someone while she stood silently before him.

"You may wonder why I am even taking his money," Audra was now saying, "but someone convinced me that I deserved it."

"And so you do. You can return to Greenleigh now and flaunt it over Emily." He smiled at her, looking more like the old Paul. "Wouldn't you like to do that? Put her in her place once and for all?"

Audra shrugged. "Not really. I simply don't care about that anymore."

A frown creased his brow. "What *do* you care about now?"

She was silent. She could hardly tell him that all she cared about at the moment was Brock's safe return.

"We had something once between us," Paul went on, his voice softening. "Our hearts and our minds were so in tune. Can we not bring it back, Audra?"

He rose and she saw him wince as his weight came down on his bad leg. He walked over to the fireplace where she stood.

"I adore you," he said. "You must know that. As soon as it is proper I wish to marry you."

She looked at him, the surprise showing in her

eyes. "So you *are* taking Robert's advice," she said dryly.

"What do you mean?"

"Was it not he who urged you to find a wealthy bride? One who could sustain a proper mode of living for an officer?"

Audra heard his denials, his vow that he had loved her long before she married Latham. But she also sensed that he would give the world to flaunt it over Robert that he was no longer the impoverished younger son. She heard again Brock's words to her on their drive to London. "Every fortune hunter in town will be after you," he had said. Why, she thought, this was her second proposal in less than twelve hours!

"Thank you, Paul," she replied, "for the honor, but you must realize that I will be in mourning for some months yet. I think you are a trifle premature."

"I have to be," he said, a little desperately. "I will be having my operation soon and if all goes well I will be shipped right back to my regiment."

He reached for her then, pulling her to him, pressing his mouth over hers. She did not respond, as his kiss deepened. She felt completely detached from him and at last he released her.

"I'm sorry. I should not have rushed this."

"Can't you see, Paul," she said sadly, "what we once shared is no longer there."

"No. I won't believe that. It's Latham who has changed you. It will take time, but it will come back if you'll let it."

He gave her a little bow and headed for the door. "I will call again tomorrow."

"No, Paul, I beg—"

But he was gone.

With Bess to accompany her, Audra left for Southcliffe early the next morning in Lady Deverell's light carriage. She had explained to the dowager the previous afternoon that she could no longer stay in London and why.

"But where will you go?" Lady Deverell had asked her anxiously.

"I think . . . to Southcliffe," Audra considered. "If you will agree."

"A wise choice." The older woman smiled. "You will be there when Brock returns."

"Do you think it too presumptuous of me?"

"No. I think you should follow your heart, child."

"You won't tell anyone where I am going?"

"You have my word. I shall miss you very much. And—" she gave Audra a wink—"I will be very disappointed if when I next see my grandson you haven't managed to get him to declare himself."

Audra had been at Southcliffe for a week. On her previous visit she had compared it unfavorably to Greenleigh. Now, as she sat on the back of a little mare and gazed down at the mansion from a grassy slope that overlooked it, she thought it very lovely indeed.

Unkempt gardens bloomed about the old house and the woods that sheltered Southcliffe from the winter storms that blew in from the sea seemed so green. The spring breeze was soft today and there was barely a cloud in the sky. She watched the gulls dipping and soaring high above the cliffs. She wished she could borrow their wings and fly across the channel, follow Brock's route and glide down to land before him wherever he might be.

There had been no word from him and he had been gone for nearly two weeks. How much longer would it take him? "Miss me" had been his last words to her. Oh, how much she did!

She turned the little mare back in the direction of Southcliffe. Brock would be surprised when he entered the old house again. Her eyes suddenly shone when she thought of his expression.

She had told the servants that she had been staying with Lady Deverell in London and that Her Ladyship wished to come back for a visit to Southcliffe very soon. She had, Audra told them, so many happy memories of her old home. The Barrows and Polly had appeared pleased and when Audra had suggested they fix up the house in anticipation of that visit, they had all set to with a vengeance.

With Audra in command, dust covers had been removed, dark curtains had been flung back, heavy and ugly articles of furniture had been consigned to the attics, windows were opened to let in the spring sunshine and the darkening ivy cut back from them. Little by little, Southcliffe's oppressive somberness and its feeling of desertion disappeared. It had become a home again.

Ned came nearly every afternoon to work in the library and he and Audra soon became good friends.

She spoke of Brock easily and naturally to him and if he wondered about the relationship between the captain and Her Ladyship, he said nothing. It was no surprise to him that the captain had won her over. He had yet to meet a female who could resist him.

He, himself, had discovered the gentle charms of young Bess, and that young woman had finally consented to go for a drive with him the next Sunday afternoon.

"Was I wrong to accept?" Bess asked Audra that evening as she was helping her mistress to undress for bed.

"Of course not. Ned is a very admirable young man."

"But he is not . . . He is not a servant, milady. He is far above me."

"Nonsense. I won't hear you talk that way."

"But what if someday . . . what if some man should want to court me? I can never marry."

"Is that foolish notion still in your head? Why can't you marry? If a man really loves you he will understand what you were forced to endure and love you all the more for it."

"The way the captain loves you?" Bess asked.

Audra's eyes fell before her young maid's. "I don't know how the captain feels about me," she said honestly.

"But you love *him.*"

"Yes, God help me, I do. That is why I am waiting here for his return. I have to know how he feels—if there will ever be anything more between us." She sighed. "I am probably a fool, Bess."

* * *

Brock was at last in Vienna. He was frankly exhausted from his breakneck pace across Europe, barely having time to establish the contacts that were so vital to him and those that might follow, riding hard and sleeping little.

He had turned over the packet he had carried from England to the proper authorities, but had unfortunately learned that the Austrians had delayed too long. Metternick, the Austrian ambassador to France had tried and failed to hide from Napoleon the rearming of his country.

Napoleon had not delayed. He had summoned two divisions from Spain, called up conscripts and troops from the Rhine Confederation and now had 310 thousand men under his command. It was rumored that he had already left Paris to join his main army.

Brock would remain in Vienna for a little while at least to gather more information. He did not feel his journey to have been in vain. If the new contacts could be kept secret, a good many people might be able to escape Napoleon's ire by using the route.

However, due to the unknown informer, it had become necessary for even stricter secrecy to be maintained. The complete route was now known to him alone. Not even Jean Paul was aware of it.

Lying in the first comfortable bed he had slept in since leaving the château, Brock thought of Celeste.

Had she been able to discover the identity of the informer? He again felt guilt at using her. How empty their lovemaking had been compared to what he had shared with Audra. He now knew what it was that made the difference. Something that he had once ridiculed and disdained. Love.

He could see Audra so clearly lying before him, her cloud of fair hair fanning out over the pillow, her deep, blue eyes dark with passion, looking up into his. He could feel her skin as smooth and soft as fine silk as he caressed her. Her lips . . . damnit! He wanted her so, needed her so. Would she be waiting for him at his grandmother's when he returned?

And even if she were? He gave a snort. What was the use? He could not ask for her hand. He had neither wealth nor title. He had nothing to offer her.

The message came from France by way of a French smuggler. It was delivered to Ned at Southcliffe early in the morning.

Jean Paul Beaudette, it seemed, had been arrested for treason and was being held at the château. He must be rescued as quickly as possible. A plan had been decided upon, but it would require the help of *The Peregrine*. Would it be possible for the sloop to lie offshore five miles south of the usual rendezvous tonight at midnight? The message was signed, Louis.

Audra discovered Ned reading this note in the front hallway when she came downstairs preparatory to her morning ride.

"Is that a message from Brock?" she cried, rushing toward him.

"I'm afraid not," he said, hastily shoving the paper into an inside pocket of his coat.

"Don't lie to me, Ned. I could see by your expression that it was important."

"It only concerns *The Peregrine*," he said honestly, "and a voyage I must take."

"Brock is not involved?"

"No. The captain has nothing to do with this. That is the truth, Your Ladyship."

Audra let out a sigh. "Did the captain tell you he would be gone this long?"

"Yes, Your Ladyship. I told you before it would likely be several weeks—a month at the very least."

"I can't help but worry about him."

"The captain can take care of himself." But it worried Ned that Jean Paul had been arrested. It appeared the captain had been right and there was an informant working within the group of men Jean Paul had so carefully selected for his work. The escape route might no longer be safe and Brock might walk right into a trap on his return to the French coast.

Audra paced the front hall, waiting for her horse to be brought around. Ned had disappeared into the library. He seemed to have a great deal on his mind.

She heard the knocker sound on the front door and, not waiting for Barrow to answer it, flung it open.

A tall man stood before her, quietly and unobtrusively attired. He asked it he might see Mr. Walker.

Audra invited him in and, as Barrow had by now appeared, sent him to inform Ned of the man's arrival.

A groom, in the meantime, had appeared in the open doorway to announce to Audra that her horse had been brought around.

"Return her to the stable, Croft," she said airily. "I have changed my mind. I shan't ride this morning."

The groom looked a trifle surprised, but nodded and departed.

Barrow was now ushering the tall man into the library. Audra hung back, appearing to be looking for something she had dropped, but as soon as Barrow had let the man in and had departed down the hall to the back of the house, she hurried over to the library door. Very slowly, so as to make no noise, she opened it a crack and put her ear to it.

"Mr. Walker, I am representing Viscount Castlereagh of the War Office. Captain Deverell left word with him that in the case of an emergency you were the man to contact."

"There has been an emergency?" The anxiety in Ned's voice was clear to Audra's ears.

"I am afraid so. As the captain's orders were secret, I presume you have no idea why he is on the continent."

"None whatsoever."

"He was sent to Austria, Mr. Walker. The reason need not be discussed at this time, but I tell you of his destination because of what has occurred. Your captain should have arrived by now. He is travelling with papers describing him as a wine merchant, Jacques Sabourin by name. His identity and papers were taken by one of our agents from a man he found robbed and wounded by the side of a road near Paris. The agent tried to help the poor fellow and was told by him that he was from an obscure town in the Loire Valley and had no family. He died soon after and our agent helped himself to his papers, thinking that under the circumstances they might prove useful to us. He thought no one would be able to trace the man. He was wrong. Apparently Jacques Sabourin was not an obscure wine merchant at all. He was one of Napoleon's most important agents! In looking for identification of the corpse, papers were later discovered in his boot verifying this. Now an extensive search is in progress for the person using Jacques Sabourin's papers as it is thought he is guilty of his murder."

"Oh, my God!" Ned exclaimed.

"Someone must leave immediately for the continent and contact your captain before he tries to recross the border into France again."

"But who?"

"His Lordship thought you would know the captain's French contacts. That they could—"

"Damn!" Ned swore. "Sir, the man who should be sent has just been arrested and imprisoned. I was informed of this only this morning and I must leave tonight on a mission to rescue him."

"Is there no one else—"

"Perhaps, but I don't— Well, you will have to leave this with me. I will get word to the others tonight. I would go myself, but I must command *The Peregrine* and, furthermore, I speak little French. This is a devil of a coil!"

"Time is of the essence. A day or two might be wasted if Viscount Castlereagh has to locate someone else. You *must* get word to someone on French soil *tonight* and even then he must ride with all speed."

There was a brief silence.

"Take this," said Castlereagh's man. "Inside this belt are the new identity papers for Captain Deverell."

"I will do all I can, you may trust me for that," Ned said, but there was a terrible hopelessness in his voice.

"God help your captain if he is caught, for it is certain *we* will not be able to," the other said chillingly.

Chapter Seventeen

Audra had heard every word that had been exchanged between Ned and Castlereagh's man. She was filled with fear and horror for Brock. Could someone be found to get to him in time?

Ned was asking the man if he would care for any refreshment, but the other refused, saying he must return to London by evening. Audra heard the scrape of Ned's chair as he rose and hurriedly she closed the door and darted around a corner so she would not be seen when the men left the room.

She watched as Ned saw the stranger to the front door, watched as they shook hands and Castlereagh's man departed. She let Ned return to the library before she approached the door again. This time she knocked.

Ned's voice, sounding most unlike his usual

cheerful tone, bade her enter.

Sitting at the desk, Audra saw him raise his head from his hands and try to compose his face as she entered the room.

"May I help you, Your Ladyship?"

"I think so, Ned."

She came over to the desk and laid her hands flat on the top of it, looking down at him. When she spoke her voice was steady.

"I am not going to waste any time pretending I don't know what is going on. I listened at the door, Ned. You may think it reprehensible of me, but I do not care. All I care about is Brock. We've got to save him and you've got to let me help you."

He shook his head. "There is nothing you can do, Your Ladyship. Nothing at all."

"Stop it, Ned! Of course there is something I can do. I can take the message to him myself."

"What! Are you mad!" he cried, before he realized what he had said and hastily apologized.

"No. I am quite sane. I can ride as well or better than any man. My father taught me to use a pistol and I speak perfect patois French."

Ned shook his head. "It would take you far too long to get to him. You could not travel unattended and a coach would take days—"

"I would go alone and on horseback."

"Impossible, milady," Ned said firmly. "Utterly impossible. A beautiful woman travelling alone—you would not get a mile before some footpad or worse accosted you. I realize you are trying to help, but the captain would have my head if I allowed you to go. You know that."

"And the captain may *lose* his head to Madame Guillotine if I *don't* go! Pray give me a chance to show you, Ned." She considered a moment. "Meet me at the north crossroads at three this afternoon," she suggested.

"But why—"

"Just meet me, Ned."

Ned Walker sighed. "I will be there, Your Ladyship," he said, deciding to humor her, "but I will *not* change my mind."

True to his word, Ned Walker rode out that afternoon to meet the countess, although he had no idea why. Was she going to prove her skill at shooting or her horsemanship in the open fields nearby? He reached the north crossroads at five minutes to three and waited on horseback until fifteen minutes after the hour, but there was no sign of Her Ladyship.

The local doctor's carriage rushed by on its way to an emergency as did a young country lad on an old nag with a bag of seed across his saddle. He called to this youth as he went by.

"Boy, did you by chance see a lady coming this way?"

The lad shook his head. "No, sir," he said in the clear country tones of the region and rode on.

Ned had just decided to dismount when he again heard the noise of horse's hoofs on the hard road and looked up to see the same young lad returning. He brought the old nag to a standstill before Ned.

"Well?" said a voice that struck Ned as being most

familiar, and then the large-brimmed hat was snatched from the lad's head.

Ned Walker's mouth fell open.

The countess of Latham sat before him dressed as a youth in a frayed coat and breeches. Her long, silvery-blond hair had been cut short and now clustered in feathery curls about her head, her deep, blue eyes looked down at him, twinkling with merriment.

"You didn't recognize me, did you, Ned?"

"No," he admitted, still astonished by her appearance. "I never thought for a moment—"

"There. You see. I can pass for a youth. I am slim and tall for a woman. I should have no difficulty at all."

"But it is too fantastic a scheme. It will never work. I cannot let—"

"It is the only answer, Ned. There is no one else to send. I *must* go!"

"But, my lady—"

"I love him, Ned," she said despairingly. "No one else would have as single-minded a desire to reach him in time."

"But it is a terrible risk, even for a man."

"Then get me a small pistol for my protection. I assure you, I know how to use one."

"Oh, milady, if something should happen to you, I would never forgive myself."

"Nothing will happen to me. I will be taken for a scruffy, country boy. No one will think I have anything to rob or will suspect me of being other than what I appear."

"We will have to obtain identity papers for you.

That may present a problem," Ned considered.

"Can they not be obtained from your friends in France?"

"Possibly, but tonight they must arrange for Jean Paul's escape. There will be no time to think of other things."

"You will anchor *The Peregrine* offshore, will you not? And they will ferry this Jean Paul out to you?"

Ned nodded.

"Then it is simple. I will take his place in the boat on their return trip." She laughed. "There, Ned, don't look so glum. It is all settled. Now ride with me back to old Mr. Patterson's farm so I may return his nag and pick up my mare."

Audra had guessed that Bess might be reluctant to help her with her plan, so she had acquired, by herself, the male attire she had worn to meet Ned.

While the grooms were busy with their morning chores, she had slipped up to their rooms above the stable and had searched through their clothing, helping herself to what she would need. Holding some breeches and a shirt up before her, she had decided they would be a good fit, but the driving coat she tried on was a trifle large and the only boots that were close to her size would still have to be stuffed with paper in the toes. The large hat she had found fitted loosely as well, but she was glad of that as it came down low over her eyes and hid her face well. She had written a note and left some coins in payment for the clothing, coming away well satisfied with herself.

Before going to meet Ned, Audra had stripped off her clothes in her bedchamber, donning the shirt and breeches. It was the first time in her life she had worn breeches and she somehow felt a little naked having her legs thus exposed instead of hidden by long skirts.

She had tried pinning her mass of hair high on top of her head, but she soon decided that would not work and took up the scissors. Bess had discovered her just as she was snipping off the last lock and had cried aloud when she saw the pile of silvery curls on the floor at Audra's feet.

Audra had had to explain everything to her and wasted precious time arguing with the little maid who thought it an impossible scheme and begged her to reconsider.

"You cannot travel alone," Bess had sobbed. "You are quite unused to waiting upon yourself."

But Audra had been adamant and Bess was finally forced to give in. She had helped to finish trimming her mistress's hair, greatly improving the ragged appearance Audra had made, but sniffed all the while at the loss of such beauty.

"My hair will grow again, Bess." Audra had smiled at her.

When the young maid had finished, Audra had glanced into the mirror. Would she pass for a lad? Would she be able to fool Ned? No. The firm points of her breasts were clearly evident through the thin shirt. She would have to bind them flat. Even when this had been accomplished, she felt she looked more convincing wearing the driving coat. In order that her disguise would not be penetrated, she might have to wear the coat even in warm weather.

Before they left for *The Peregrine* that evening, Ned again tried to talk Audra out of her plan, but she would not be budged in her decision. In the end, he reluctantly conceded. He gave her the belt that had come from Castlereagh. It had a compartment on the inside where the captain's new papers were hidden and where Ned now placed some money. Finding it to be too large for Audra's slender waist, Ned cut the belt and adjusted it. He then gave her an old cloak of his to put around her shoulders and hesitantly handed her a muff gun which, he informed her, would fire two shots.

"Its accuracy is only good at close range," he said as she placed it in the top of her boot.

It was not very comfortable, she found, to walk with the little gun there, as it was inclined to rub against her ankle, but she felt safer knowing that she had some protection close at hand in case of trouble.

Audra spent some time striding about her room in a mannish way, trying to get used to taking larger steps than a lady would, trying to make her gestures less feminine. She realized it was going to be more difficult than she had at first imagined.

As soon as it began to grow dark, Audra, anxious to be on her way, joined Ned and the two of them descended to the cellars of Southcliffe and down through the caves and caverns. They came out in the woods and continued along a path to the mouth of the little creek where *The Peregrine* awaited them.

At high tide the sloop had been taken to the

mouth of the narrow channel which had hidden it, and brought about. Now it faced out to sea once more and, as the gentle spring breeze filled its sails, *The Peregrine* headed in a northeasterly direction to France.

Unknown to those aboard, Jean Paul had been transferred to another part of the château dungeon only hours before the attempt was to be made to rescue him. A new plan would therefore have to be decided upon, as this area was not as easily accessible and the compte himself had chosen this particular evening to interrogate his prisoner. The rescue attempt must be aborted.

The fishing boat came out to *The Peregrine* at the arranged time and this information was passed along to Ned. It was decided to make another attempt the next night. Pray God Jean Paul would be able to withstand the compte's attempt to force information from him until that time.

Audra insisted upon returning with the three men who had rowed out to the anchored *Peregrine*. It was explained to them that this was a nephew of the captain who must get an important message through to him on the continent. As Audra spoke excellent French, they were convinced that it would not be difficult to send this lad on his way as soon as proper identity papers could be obtained. In the meantime, he would be hidden in one of their homes.

It was Marie, the comtesse de Lascalles's little maid, who met them on the road as they quietly rode past the château on their way to the village. She explained to them that she had overheard that every house in the village was to be searched that night.

Any sign of anything out of the ordinary might mean more arrests would be made.

Spying Audra riding behind one of the men she asked his identity and was told that this was the captain's nephew who had an urgent message to deliver to him. Marie made a quick decision. She would hide this nephew in *le dit d'amour* until his papers could be obtained and he could be sent on his way.

"It must be done quickly," Audra said, lowering her voice. "I *must* be on my way at dawn tomorrow."

Marie nodded to one of the men. "Do you think you can arrange that, Louis?"

The man nodded. "I will return before daybreak with the papers," he said confidently.

Audra saw little of the room in the flickering light of the candle that was placed on the table by the bed. She was aware she must try and snatch a few hours sleep, for she did not know how long it would be before she would be able to rest again. Her heart was beating rapidly as she removed her coat and hat and lay down on the bed. How could she sleep? She was in the château of a deadly enemy of her country. Jean Paul, the brother of the maid who had brought her to this room, might even now be undergoing torture in the dungeons below.

She lay fully clothed on the cool, satin coverlet and closed her eyes. The faint scent of perfume seemed to cling to the pillow beneath her cheek. Suddenly, she thought she heard a noise outside the door of the room. She shrank back into the shadows of the canopied bed.

The small door was thrown open and one of the most strikingly beautiful women Audra had ever seen entered the room, carrying a long taper. She wore a gown of some sort of diaphanous material that, when she approached the candlelit table, clearly showed that she wore nothing beneath!

"Peregrine, you rogue." She gave a teasing smile. "Where have you been all this time?"

From the dark confines of the bed, Audra stared at this exquisite creature. It was obvious that the lady had mistaken her for someone else. Peregrine! It was the name of Brock's ship! Audra's heart gave a sickening lurch. It was a name Brock might easily have adopted for himself!

"You vanished into thin air, *mon beau capitaine*, so soon after. And our time was so short. . . ." The dark beauty put down her candle. "But tonight, *mon amour*, tonight we will make up for that, *n'est-ce pas*?" She gave a seductive little glance from beneath lowered lids and before Audra's eyes began to slip her gown from her shoulders.

Audra knew she should say something, should stop her, but she was too taken aback to move. This woman and Brock—lovers! It was heartbreakingly clear! Numbed by the thought, Audra lay still, feeling an icy cloak of despair slowly enveloping her. Brock had made love, such tender, beautiful love, to her the night before he had left England and the *next* night he must have come here, here to *this* woman's arms! In that moment any hope that his feelings for her went any deeper than physical desire was swiftly destroyed.

The woman approached the bed, walking as proudly naked as a pagan priestess, her voluptuous body, smooth and white and incredibly beautiful.

"You lazy." She laughed huskily. "Do you expect me to undress you again?"

The "again" echoed in Audra's brain as she sat up, throwing her booted legs over the side of the bed.

"I am *not* your Peregrine, madame!"

At the sound of Audra's voice, Celeste was frozen in her steps, but she made no attempt to cover herself. She appeared quite unconscious of her nakedness.

"Who are you then?" she asked. "I was sure I saw Marie push someone into the cupboard at the bottom of the stairs and I naturally thought—" She peered into the darkness. "But you seem to be a mere boy."

"Looks can be deceiving, madame."

"*Vraiment*?" Celeste smiled and shrugged her lovely shoulders. "Are you implying . . ." Again that throaty laugh. "Perhaps it *would* be amusing to taste a boy's passions. I might be able to turn them into those of a man."

"I am sure you could, madame, but I am afraid what you suggest does not interest me." Audra would not show this woman her true feelings—how completely devastated she felt. She stood up and strode over to the chair beside the table, sitting down straight-backed, her chin set.

"Who are you?" Celeste demanded. A pretty lad, she thought, but so young he might still be a schoolboy.

"I am Peregrine's nephew, madame," she lied. "I have come to France to find the captain. He has been gone for over two weeks. But surely you are aware of that since he apparently paid you a visit." The last words were faintly scathing.

"Only a brief visit. I thought he had returned to England."

"*Non*, madame, there has been no word from him."

Celeste slipped her gown back on and carefully adjusted it. "But why were *you* sent, a mere boy." She frowned.

"I speak better French than the others," Audra replied.

"Patois French," Celeste sniffed.

"True, but a simple farm lad attracts no attention."

Celeste shrugged. She moved closer to the table, carefully appraising the boy who sat so stiff and proper.

"Do you know your uncle well?" she asked.

"*Tres bien.* He has been my guardian since my father died." How easily the lies came to her lips!

"*Vraiment*? Well, I don't think you are very like him. In appearance *or* in actions."

"I should hope not," Audra flared. "I do not condone his dissolute behavior." She was unaware that her voice had risen with her last words or that her contempt was so apparent.

Celeste shrugged. "So the captain has a strong sexual appetite. There is something wrong with that? You are young, *mon petit*. Given a few years, you may yourself—"

"Never!" Audra shook her head vehemently.

Celeste's smile was suddenly enigmatic as she turned away, indicating the room around them. "Do you scorn my love nest then? Surely you did not find the bed uncomfortable? It is large enough for even a man of Peregrine's size. *Mon Dieu*, the passionate times we have shared in it. Such a hot-blooded man! So impatient! He took me there—on that rug before you—and then he carried me to the bed and again we loved." She put a dainty finger to her cheek. "Somehow I think we ended up on the floor again." She laughed her husky laugh. "Never have I known such a stallion!"

Audra jumped to her feet. "Really, madame, I do not wish to hear—"

"Pourquoi?" Celeste's eyes narrowed. "Because it brings back memories?"

"What!"

"I don't know who you are, but you are *not* Peregrine's nephew, mademoiselle." She emphasized the last word.

Audra stared at her. "How—how did you know?"

"Your reactions, *ma chèrie*. The look in your eyes. The jealousy fairly leaped out at me. As I know full well that Peregrine is not one of those men who fancy young boys, you *had* to be female. Furthermore—" she gave a little smirk—"I have never been rejected before."

Silence met this revelation.

"What *are* you to Peregrine?" the comtesse demanded. "That is what *I* would like to know."

"Nothing, madame. I am nothing to him."

Celeste carefully assessed the young woman

before her.

"You are really quite beautiful, I can see that now. Peregrine's enjoyed you, or he's not the man I think he is." She smiled, a rather tight smile. "Did he make you a foolish promise? A promise that made you come to France in search of him? So anxious, in fact, to find him that you cut off your hair and dressed as a boy?" Celeste shook her head. "I am truly sorry for you, *ma pauvre petite.*"

Unwarranted tears had begun to fill Audra's eyes, but now she furiously blinked them back.

"I do not need your sympathy, madame," she said stiffly, anger rapidly screening the hurt.

"Pray call me Celeste. I am la comtesse de Lascalles and this is my château you are presently residing in."

"My name is Audra and I am also a countess. The countess of Latham."

Celeste was a little taken aback. "Have you then left your husband to run off after Peregrine?"

"No. My husband is dead. I am pursuing Peregrine because I have some important information for him."

"How important?"

"It could mean his life."

"Ah, now it is becoming clear. You love Peregrine. So much, I think, you would risk your own life to save him."

"Love does not enter into it at all," Audra snapped.

"I do not believe you, *ma chèrie*, but you are young, you will find other lovers. Peregrine, you see, belongs to me. He is *mine*! Make no mistake about that. He loves *me* and only *me*!"

"Then I am sorry for *you*, madame, if that is what you believe."

"Oh, I have proof of his love for me."

"Really?" Audra raised a skeptical brow. "What proof?"

Celeste placed her hands dramatically on her softly rounded abdomen. "I am carrying his son. Is that not proof enough?"

After Celeste had left her, the engulfing combination of shock and anguish gave vent to scalding tears. Audra collapsed onto the bed, racked by sobs, as uncontrollable waves of pain and sorrow swept over her. She pressed her face into the pillow and again caught the faint trace of perfume. Celeste's perfume! She remembered only too clearly that Brock had made passionate love to the comtesse in this very bed! Audra had to fight an overwhelming urge to scream. No doubt the child Celeste so proudly carried was conceived right here! God in heaven, how could she remain in this room another minute, this room which had served as a love nest for Brock and that woman!

How easily he had deceived her. Kisses, caresses, lovemaking—all had meant nothing to him. Nothing. All the sweet things Brock had said to her, the things she had thought were for her ears alone had probably been said to Celeste as well. He had made a mockery out of love! She felt torn and lacerated by his duplicity.

Thank God she had found out in time. Found out

before she made a complete fool of herself by admitting to him how much she loved him.

Should she return to England? Leave him to his own devices? Clearly he deserved it!

No, she decided. She would continue on her journey, find Brock and give him his new papers. *But*, she vowed, never would she let him near her again! She had weathered Latham's cruelty. She would weather this new torment.

Why then, as she lay there, did she feel so terribly alone and bereft? Celeste was welcome to the deceiving rake! And yet, as Audra thought of them lying together where she now lay, of the voluptuous comtesse writhing beneath Brock's powerful body, a bitter yearning filled her and fresh tears were wet upon her cheeks when she at last fell into a fitful sleep.

Audra awoke to find the dawn had broken and the little room was slowly brightening. Where was the Frenchman with her papers? Surely he must come soon. She lay back and stretched out her arms and it was then that she saw the mirrors that were set into the canopy above her head. How easy it was to imagine them reflecting two naked bodies entwined in frenzied passion! She couldn't bear it! She would go mad if she had to remain in this room much longer!

She sprang from the bed and as she did so she noticed that a stream of light entering through the skylight in the ceiling clearly illuminated a portrait on the opposite wall. It was of a naked man and woman joined in the most intimate of all embraces. The woman was certainly the beautiful comtesse, and the man . . .

Few knew of Celeste's artistic talents. She had painted the original portrait of herself by posing before a mirror and as her model for the man, she had used one of her earlier lovers, who had quite willingly posed with her.

After Peregrine had jokingly complained that the male subject did not resemble him, Celeste had had the portrait taken down and expertly, from memory, changed the man's profile to that of her new lover. It was an astonishing likeness, so real in its crisp, chiseled lines, that upon viewing it Audra gasped aloud.

It was Brock! There could be no question of that! Portrayed locked forever in a lover's embrace with the beautiful comtesse! Had they posed together for the picture? Had he and Celeste blatantly made love before the artist's very eyes? The thought made her feel physically ill. That ultimate moment of ecstasy had been captured so perfectly—so realistically—she could almost see Brock shudder with the intensity of his release.

It was too much! Audra dropped to her knees beside the bed and huddled there as the image she had pictured in her mind while she lay upon the bed now appeared before her in a mockingly lifelike tableau! Hot tears came again and angrily she struck the floor before her with both fists.

"I hate him!" She cried aloud. "I hate him!"

Marie stood in the doorway. Her mistress had told her about the young English lady who had disguised herself as a boy so she could take an important message through to the captain. Celeste had thought it vastly amusing, but Marie had been touched and now as she watched Audra and sensed her despair, tears filled her own eyes. She understood the young woman's feelings so well. Hadn't she felt them herself? Here was another who hopelessly loved the handsome captain.

"*Non, ma petite,*" she said softly, moving over to where Audra knelt, "you do not hate him. You only wish you did."

Chapter Eighteen

Audra had always expected to love France. She had read about the country, and the French servants who had taught her their language had spoken glowingly enough about it to make her eager to travel there. However, the circumstances in which she now found herself were hardly those she had anticipated.

She felt a threatening sense of exposure as she rode over the pleasant countryside, observing the well-cultivated fields. She was always afraid that someone might stop and question her or recognize that she was not French or was not really a young farm lad. When she was asked why she rode at such a fast pace, her excuse was that she was trying to reach her father to inform him that her mother had been taken ill. He was visiting a brother in—and she would fill in the name of a town not too far distant.

Her route, she soon found, was circuitous, and often over rough roads due to stopping at only anti-Bonapartist cottages or inns to change horses, to eat, or to gain a few hours sleep. This route was covered in word-of-mouth stages. Marie had given Audra the name of the first inn and town, having learned it from her brother. The little maid had had to bribe one of Jean Paul's guards, just before dawn, in order to have a few minutes alone with him. Her brother was barely conscious, having been beaten severely during the night, and tearfully she had shaken him awake in order to learn the needed information.

The first day, Audra spent ten hours in the saddle, arriving exhausted at the inn to which she had been directed. She spoke the password, "Peregrine," to the innkeeper and was taken back into the kitchen, fed and allowed to sleep in the stable until dawn. Then, given a fresh horse, she was sent on her way with the name of her next stop in her head. Nothing, it seemed, was ever written down in case it might be found on that person if he were arrested.

The identity papers Marie had given Audra, which had been obtained from Louis, were hidden in the boot opposite to that which held the little pistol. With these papers she also carried a sealed letter written by the comtesse to "her" Peregrine.

How Audra would have liked to break open the seal and read it, or at least destroy it! Every mile she rode that first day made her pent-up emotions turn to burning loathing for the man who had taken so much from her and in return had deceived her. She felt she now hated him as passionately as she had loved him. If it were not that it might hurt so many people, she would gladly have let him be captured.

But as she lay in the soft straw of a stable that night, her mood changed. She remembered how it had felt to lie within Brock's protecting arms, to have him make such perfect love to her, and the tears came again.

"How am I going to live without you?" she cried silently to herself, gripped by an overwhelming loss. Why couldn't she stop loving and yearning for him? From that first night at Southcliffe, when compassion and comfort had turned into desire and he had shown her the sweet joys of lovemaking, she had known she belonged to Brock Deverell. In one glorious night together she had given him not only her body, but her heart and her soul as well. Even as she wept over his deceit with Celeste—and deceit it had been, for hadn't he whispered to her, "You're the best thing that's ever happened to me," and yet the very next night lain in another's arms?—she knew she would still ride as fast as she was able to save him. What a fool love could make of one!

As Audra's arduous journey continued she began to ache all over from the long days spent in the saddle. She felt exhausted from lack of sleep and little food. Never before had she been so completely on her own. Always there had been someone to look after her or to whom she could turn. Now, she had to depend on her own resources, her own strength.

The weather took a turn for the worse and as she drew closer to the German border, a steady rain began to fall. Soon the road became a morass of mud. Audra could not help but think, as she rode through the pouring rain, that if she had been riding for Southcliffe, Bess would be there to greet her with a warm bath and she would have been able to strip off her mud-splattered clothing and sink into hot, soothing water.

Her heavy cloak was sodden by the time she reached the inn that was her stop for the night. Cold and tired and close to tears, she approached the back door and knocked.

A fat, apron-covered woman with a large ladle in one hand answered the door and curtly demanded what she wanted.

Audra asked if she might speak with the landlord and was told that he hadn't the time to speak with the likes of such a filthy urchin. Audra stopped the door being shut in her face by pressing a coin into the woman's hand. The cook looked hard at it, turned it over, shrugged, and allowed her to enter the warm, steaming kitchen that smelled rather sourly of cooked cabbage.

While the woman went off in search of the landlord, Audra removed her wet cloak and placed it over a chair before the fire. She shook the water from the brim of her large hat and set it on the chair's seat. Her driving coat was also damp, but she was afraid to remove it, so she stood before the fire, trying to warm herself as best she could, rubbing her hands together.

The landlord, a flustered little man, bustled into the room and Audra gave him the password.

"You are very young," he said, frowning. Too young for what you are doing, his dark eyes seemed to say.

"I am a fast rider," she said, as if this explained everything.

"The coffee room is warm and comfortable and is empty at this hour," he told her. "I will bring you something to eat there. My wife is away helping her sister with a new baby, so I am short-handed."

He showed Audra down a corridor that ended in the coffee room at the front of the inn.

"Sit by the fire," he instructed. "You look cold as well as hungry."

"I am," Audra murmured. "I have not stopped or eaten since noon."

"You'll be staying the night?" he asked.

"*Oui.* Until dawn."

"Perhaps I can arrange a bed for you," he said kindly. The poor lad looked all in.

Audra smiled her appreciation. "I haven't slept in a bed for nights," she murmured.

As he served her a simple but nourishing supper, the innkeeper and Audra spoke quietly together and she learned her next destination. Afterwards, she curled up on the deep settle by the fire, finishing her steaming mug of hot chocolate. The chill seemed long in disappearing from her bones. Perhaps when she removed all her damp clothing and climbed into a cozy bed . . .

Noisy voices were suddenly heard in the front entranceway to the inn and the door of the coffee room was thrown open.

Four French soldiers laughing boisterously staggered into the room. It was apparent that they had already been celebrating something and were more than a little the worse for drink.

"Where the devil's the landlord?" one of them bellowed, removing his rain-drenched cloak. "Want some food here!"

"Food? Devil with food!" another shouted. "Wine's what we want. More wine!"

Audra tried to quietly rise and slip from the room, but one of them had caught sight of her. He possessed a large, gray moustache and seemed to be the oldest of the foursome, and judging from the insignia on his uniform, the highest in rank.

"You there, *garçon*! Where's the landlord?" he called to Audra.

"In the kitchen, I believe, monsieur," she answered politely. "They are short-handed here tonight."

"Not even a barmaid," another soldier snorted disgustedly, falling into a chair.

"Hey there!" said the youngest of the men, seeing the landlord at last appear in the doorway, "have you no pretty faces about this place?"

The landlord shook his head. "You have the wrong establishment. You will have to go down the road to Le Chat Gris," he said tersely. "I run a respectable inn."

"You would turn us out in all that rain?" the older soldier growled. "I've half a mind to report you to the authorities. Refusing to serve soldiers of the—"

"I have not refused to serve you, monsieur," the landlord broke in, looking a little anxious. "I only mentioned—"

"Then bring us wine and a good, hot supper."

"*Oui*, and be quick about it!" barked another.

During this exchange, the older soldier had come

over to the fire and now laid a hand on Audra's shoulder.

"Sit down, lad. We won't hurt you." He removed his wet, outer clothing and threw himself into a chair across from her. He did not take his eyes from her as he spread his hands out to the fire.

"Where are you from, boy? You seem young to be travelling alone."

Audra did not like the way he looked at her. She could not explain it, because his eyes said nothing, but something about him put her on her guard.

She told him she had come from the coast and gave her story of an ill mother and a father she was riding hard to reach.

He commiserated with her, offering her a drink of wine when it arrived, saying she looked chilled, but she shook her head.

"I have a long ride ahead of me tomorrow and I will be retiring soon," she said, drinking down the last of her hot chocolate. She felt so warm and comfortable by the fire and hated to move away from it. Soon a sense of drowsiness swept over her.

Audra awoke to the raucous laughter of one of the soldiers. She did not know how long she had slept, but the men had obviously eaten and were clearly enjoying more wine.

The gray-moustached soldier was now lolling beside her on the settle. His face was flushed and he was singing a little song as one finger reached out to curl amongst the short locks of her hair.

"*Joli garçon* . . . pretty boy." She caught the words and drew back, feeling a tug as his withdrawing finger became entangled before pulling free.

"I have to go," she said, attempting to rise, but he put a large restraining hand on her thigh.

"Not yet, *mon joli.* I want you to come with me. I promise you, you won't be sorry."

Audra's mouth went dry. Had he discovered her real identity while she slept? She tried to pull away from him, but he grabbed her arm and yanked her to her feet.

There were crude jests and a roar of laughter from the other soldiers as the older one thrust Audra through the door and out into the entranceway.

"Let me go!" she cried, calling for the landlord, but there was no sound from the back of the inn as the soldier pushed her rudely toward the stairs.

Audra fell twice as he forced her to climb and twice her right arm was nearly wrenched from its socket as it was jerked up hard to make her regain her feet.

She thought of the small pistol in her boot, but cast the thought aside. The man would ignore the threat of such a weapon, she felt sure, forcing her to use it. With the other soldiers below, she would not have a chance of escaping.

They reached the landing and Audra was thrust head-first into a dimly lit room and the door slammed shut and bolted behind her.

"We'll have a good time together," the soldier said. "Just so long as you do as I say."

"Let me go!" Audra cried, rising shakily from where she had fallen upon her knees. "I am not what you think. I am not a *jeune fille.* I am a boy!"

"*Vraiment*?" He grinned and the grin was not pleasant. "But you see, boys are my preference."

Horrified, Audra felt her stomach tighten and in that instant he made a grab for her. The soldier was a strong man and although she struggled wildly to escape him, he held her fast and managed to tear off her coat.

Frantically she kicked and twisted and tried to flail out at him as he propelled her backwards across the room. The back of her knees came up against the side of the bed and she knew she could retreat no further. She had one chance. Only one. Her knee jerked upward, jabbing sharply into his groin.

The soldier let out a howl of pain and fell to the floor, groaning and clutching himself, cursing her with an ugly string of profanities.

Whirling away, Audra made a dash around the bed. Quickly realizing he could grab her if she made for the bolted door, she headed instead for the window.

It was not very big, but it opened outward at the push of the latch and Audra was soon up and over the sill. Hearing the angry roar behind her, she did not hesitate, but slid down the wet and slippery drainpipe that descended beside the window.

The moment her feet touched the ground, she started to run around the side of the inn to the back door. The door was unlatched and to the surprise of the cook who was just putting her broom away, Audra flew past her, grabbed up her clothing from the chair by the fire, dropped some coins onto the table, and disappeared again out the door.

When she reached the stable, she hurriedly pulled on the still-damp cloak and hat and, looking about her in the light of a lantern hung from the ceiling, her eyes lit upon the mare she had ridden that day. It had been rubbed down and was quietly eating some oats. The groom was nowhere in sight, so she saddled it quickly herself and led it out into the drizzling rain. Her heart pounded in her ears as she swung herself up onto the mare's back and dug in her heels. She was still trembling from the shock of what had nearly occurred. And she had felt so safe in dressing like a boy!

Once away from the inn, she glanced back and was relieved to see that no one was following her. The rain began to pelt down harder than ever and soon Audra could barely make out the road ahead. She hoped that she was still headed in the right direction.

She rode on for an hour, trying to skirt the deepest puddles in the road. Through the downpour, the shape of a building became visible as she rounded a bend. It looked to be a deserted barn.

Audra urged her horse off the road toward it, cautiously approaching. It was empty, she saw as she entered, and although the roof was open to the sky in places, there was dry straw to lie upon in one corner and, after rubbing the mare down with some of it, Audra made a nest for herself and huddled in her damp clothing. Totally exhausted, she fell into a deeper sleep than she had known in days.

She awoke in the morning to find herself quite thoroughly chilled and with a raw, sore throat. She missed her warm driving coat that the soldier had pulled off her, for the sodden cloak had proved little protection against the driving rain of the previous night.

Wearily, she saddled her horse and set out again.

With no trouble from the authorities, she crossed the border into Germany that day, but the rain that had threatened since the morning started in again about four o'clock and she was soaked clear through when she at last reached her stop for the night, a simple farmer's cottage.

The farmer's wife took pity on the sodden youth and gave Audra more than generous helpings of food at supper, but she found she was not very hungry and after barely touching her tankard of ale, she went straight to bed.

If only the sun would come out and warm her bones, Audra thought the next day. But the bad weather continued and to add to it her horse, a skittish bay, lost his footing in the mire of the road and went down, tossing her from its back.

Deep in mud and water, Audra lay for a moment stunned, her clothes caked and sodden, her teeth chattering from the cold.

She shouldn't have come! This trip was madness! For all she knew Brock might already have started back, been captured and imprisoned. How confident she had been that she could make it in time! How she had laughed at Ned's uncertainties. She had been so sure of herself and her abilities.

Audra let herself cry then, softly and silently. Weeping for the anguish she had suffered at Latham's hands, for the love she had given to Brock that would never be returned. But most of all she wept for the happy little girl she had once been, growing up at Greenleigh, and the bitter, disillusioned young woman she had now become.

She wiped her nose with her sleeve and chided herself for her burst of self-pity. Wearily she rose and tramped back to where her mount waited, her boots sinking deeply in the mire. Rain dripped steadily from the brim of her hat and tears of frustration sprang to her eyes when examining her horse's front legs she found that the left one had a slight swelling. It was what she had feared. He was lame! Her boots were swallowed by mud at each step as she led the limping horse down the road. The relentless wind and rain seemed to assault her from every direction.

It took several hours to reach the next inn, only to find it crowded with soldiers. The innkeeper was afraid to let her enter, so Audra was forced to spend the night in the stable.

An old groom, seeing her shivering with the wet and cold, gave her some dry clothes to wear. A toothless grin spread over his face when she modestly disappeared behind a stall to change.

The next day Audra crossed the Danube into Austria, but due to the severe chill she had suffered, the sore throat had now developed into a dry, rasping cough.

It was late in the evening when Audra arrived at the White Swann Inn in Vienna, and inquired for Monsieur Sabourin.

The landlord, Herr Meister, a stocky, barrel-chested man, eyeing Audra's bedraggled appearance, seemed hesitant until she quietly imparted the password to him and insisted it was a matter of great urgency. Meister, aware that Sabourin was Captain Peregrine, immediately gave her his room number on the second floor where Audra also obtained a room.

She took the key from him and slowly climbed the stairs, stopping once when a fit of coughing overcame her. At the first landing, she passed a plump and pretty maid descending with a tray of dirty dishes in her hands. The girl gave Audra a disdainful glance and swept by her, one hand pulling in her skirt so she would not touch the grubby urchin.

Audra paid her scant attention. All she could think of was that she had arrived in time. Brock had not departed. She had not gone through the hardships and misery of the last few days in vain.

She paused before she knocked at Brock's door. She knew she looked disreputable in her mud-splattered clothing. She had done her best to scrape off her boots before entering the inn, but they were still far from clean, and her big hat was wet and misshapen. Brock was not likely to recognize her and suddenly she knew that she did not want him to.

She would give him his new identity papers and go on her way. He would never know who it was who had delivered them. It was for the best, she told herself. There would be no accusations on her part, no lying denials on his. She could not bear a confrontation now. She felt too weary, too sick.

The door was flung open to her knock and he stood before her, so big he almost filled the whole doorway, so handsome, with his devastating smile, his dark, tousled hair.

Audra felt her breath quicken at the sight of him. How she longed to rush into his arms, to be comforted and protected.

"What is it, lad?" he asked in German.

"I have a message for you, monsieur. May I come in?" she answered him in French. Her voice had deepened due to her cough and was not recognizable to him. Seeing him frown, she whispered the password, "Peregrine."

Brock's smile returned and he held open the door for her. "You look half drowned," he said in French. "Sit down by the fire." He indicated a comfortable chair. "May I take your hat and cloak?"

Audra shook her head. "I cannot stay long."

"Surely long enough for a brandy and a few words."

Sitting down in the deep chair offered her, Audra set about removing the papers from her belt while Brock poured out two goblets of brandy from a bottle on the bed table.

He handed her a glass and lowered his large frame onto the only other chair, a wooden, straight-backed one. He stretched out his long legs before him and when he crossed them at the ankles, she noticed that he was bootless. She also observed that his shirt was only partially fastened, as if it has been hastily donned.

With that thought in mind, her eyes swung to the bed. The covers were rumpled as if he had been lying there. Suddenly she remembered the little maid she had met on the stairs. Had he? Had they? Oh, damn the unquenchable rake! Tears sprang to her eyes and to hide them she took a long drink of the calming brandy. It only seared her throat and made her choke.

"Not too fast, lad." He grinned. "Take your time."

Audra set the goblet down beside her and handed him the papers she had removed from her belt. She told him of the real Jacques Sabourin and what would have happened had he shown the papers with Sabourin's name at the border.

Brock let out a low whistle. "You certainly arrived just in time," he said. "My business is finished here and I was about to depart in the morning."

Audra stared at him. She really *had* saved his life! If Ned had waited for someone else . . . if she had *not* ridden hellbent for leather . . . if there had been even a half day's delay . . .

"What is your name, lad?" Brock was asking as he glanced over the new papers. "It seems I have a great deal to thank you for."

"Leon," she said, and fought to suppress her cough, quickly gulping some more of the brandy.

"Do you work for Jean Paul?"

"*Oui*," she managed.

"Was there, perhaps, another message for me?" he asked casually, swirling the brandy around in his goblet.

Audra's heart fell, but she nodded, and drew the letter from the comtesse from her boot. It was damp and creased, but still quite readable. She handed it to him and Brock's eyes brightened as he saw the handwriting. Perhaps Celeste had discovered the identity of the informer, he thought. But Audra, seeing his eagerness, thought only that he was happy to be hearing from his beautiful mistress.

"I will read this later," he said, rising and setting the letter on the mantel. "Finish your brandy. You still seem to be shivering, lad. You'd best to your room and remove your wet clothing. Could I order something to warm you? More brandy? A hot bath?" He grinned. "Perhaps a willing little wench to share your bed?"

As he spoke, Audra had also risen. "No doubt you have extensive knowledge of the latter," was her quick, unthinking rejoinder, said so scathingly that something sounded in Brock's head.

She had started for the door, but in two long strides he was beside her, snatching the wide-brimmed hat from her head, thrusting her into the lamplight.

"My God!" he cried in English, "it *is* you!"

Chapter Nineteen

Brock gazed into Audra's face in total disbelief.

"How the devil? . . . Where did you? . . ."

"No one else could come," she explained stiffly, angry that she had given herself away.

"You travelled all that way alone?" he said incredulously. "Oh, my love, how—"

"I told you once that I rode well. I used the route you had established. I—" But she didn't finish. Instead she broke into a paroxysm of coughing.

"You've caught a bad chill!" He reached out to draw her tenderly to him, but managed only to tear off the sodden cloak as Audra escaped from his grasp and made a frantic dash across the room to the door.

"What the devil?" Brock growled. He was unable to understand her actions. He had left her in London after a night of love he would always remember, and now she seemed almost repulsed by him. He strode purposefully toward her, while Audra struggled hopelessly with the latch, finally turning at bay, her back against the door.

"Get away from me!" she cried, angry color staining her pale cheeks.

"What's the matter with you?"

"You!" she hissed. "You and your lies and deception."

He was stopped by the look of loathing that darkened her eyes.

She nodded toward the mantel. "I'll leave you," she snapped, "to read the love note from your mistress."

He let out his breath. "So that's it," he said, his face clearing. "I wondered how you had obtained her message. You met Celeste."

"Oh yes, I met your beautiful comtesse." Her words were laced with contempt. "I spent a night hidden in the love nest you shared with her. I saw your charming portrait. A good likeness of you, doing what you do best."

"Portrait?" He looked puzzled. "That was not of me. Audra, listen to me, you do not understand. You've jumped to conclusions."

Don't listen to him! Audra's mind screamed at her as he began to explain. Open that door and run! He has misled and lied to you in a way that will allow no reparation. She struggled again with the door latch, conflicting emotions making tears blur her vision.

"Damn you, Audra, come here!" he bellowed.

An instant later he grabbed her, crushing her

against him, his mouth coming down hard on hers.

"Let me go!" she shrieked. "I hate you, Brock Deverell!"

"I know." He grinned his devastating grin. "I know you do."

She struggled desperately to push him away, managing to jerk one hand free to slap him soundly across the cheek. He barely flinched. His firm, warm lips only pressed harder, willing her to respond.

She must not yield, she told herself! But the emotions she had known before in his arms were resurging through her, his kiss was quickly dissolving her will to resist. She knew he would get his way. Hadn't he always? She felt too weak, too tired to fight him any longer. With a shuddering sigh, she allowed him to draw her body close to his, opened her lips to his demanding kiss. Again she felt the well-remembered feelings slowly encompassing her whole body.

When he lifted his mouth from hers, she gasped for breath, looking up into the glowing hazel eyes that were devouring her.

"Audra," he whispered, and the way he said her name should have told her all she needed to know, but at that moment she began to cough again.

"Soaked to the skin," he growled and reluctantly released her. He rang then for a bath to be brought and made ready for her.

"Sit down!" he commanded, pushing her back into the chair she had vacated and pouring more brandy into her goblet. "Drink it down!" he insisted, and the force of his personality was such that, without even thinking, she obeyed him.

Brock added more wood to the fire and, when it blazed up to his satisfaction, he refilled her glass once more.

The potent liquor was warming her, Audra realized. In fact, she felt warmer than she had in days. She also felt all need for escape slowly draining from her.

Two chambermaids with steaming kettles entered the room, followed by a solidly built young porter carrying a metal tub. This was set up before the fire, and water was poured repeatedly into it as the chambermaids scurried back and forth with more kettles and fetched fresh linens and soap. When the tub was more than half filled, the temperature of the water was tested and approved, and leaving a pail of fresh water behind, the three departed, but not before casting a curious glance in Audra's direction.

"Take off those wet clothes and get in," Brock ordered as the door closed.

"I'll not bathe before you!" Audra declared in a last weak attempt to assert herself. She rose a little shakily to her feet.

"Why not?" He grinned. "I know every inch of that beautiful body of yours." Without more preamble, he began to strip her of her damp clothing with swift, purposeful movements. When she was naked, he scooped her up in his powerful arms and deposited her in the tub.

As the warm liquid enveloped her tired and aching body, a soft, languor spread through her. She leaned back, closing her eyes and uttered a blissful sigh as she luxuriated in the soothing depths. How often in the last few days had she longed for a hot bath to warm and cleanse her?

"You're a pretty grimy little wench." Brock smiled, kneeling down beside the tub, a cake of soap in one of his big hands. Audra reached for it, but he drew back his arm. "My prerogative," he said and proceeded, despite her protestations, to wet her hair and lather the fragrant soap into it, his fingers surprisingly gentle in the tangled locks.

"I'm sorry you had to cut it," he said, his voice very deep. "Sorry for a lot of things."

Carefully he rinsed the soap from her curls with the pail of water and towelled them dry.

"Do you expect your apologies to undo everything?" she asked.

He was lathering her neck now, trailing soapy fingers down over her shoulders. Audra felt her skin warming and glowing beneath his touch, as he massaged the tense muscles in her back. She relaxed beneath the sensitive fingers until they moved gently around to her breasts.

"You shouldn't have bound them," he scolded her. "That may have aided the congestion."

Before he could continue she tore the soap from his grasp. "No! We can never go back to what we had before!"

"Really?" His hazel eyes gleamed as he got to his feet and let her finish soaping and rinsing herself.

When she was ready, he held out a large, soft towel he had warmed by the fire. She reached for it as she stepped from the tub, but he did not relinquish it and instead enfolded her in it and began to rub her down quite roughly, until her skin was flushed and tingling.

"Brock, listen to me—"

"In the morning," he said huskily. "It can wait for the morning."

Relaxed by the brandy and the hot bath, her body refreshed and glowing, Audra offered no more resistance as he lifted and carried her to the bed.

He turned back the top quilt and tenderly deposited her beneath it. Impatiently, he removed his own clothing and lay down beside her, pulling the quilt over them both.

He drew her against his warmth. "Not so cold now? Oh, my love, I've missed you so!" he whispered, his fingers moving with gentle stealth over the soft, fragrant skin.

It was Audra's body that betrayed her. In her mind and her heart she only wanted Brock if he truly loved her. But her traitorous body didn't care about love, didn't care that he only wished to use her to satisfy himself. It was thrilling to the sensuality of his caresses.

With a sense of inevitability, Audra closed her eyes. She could not fight him, even if she'd wished. She was tired and at her most vulnerable and she had missed him so. She offered no resistance as his hands continued their exploration. She loved him still. She could not help it. She wanted him no matter how he had hurt her, no matter what he had done. He was the only man who could make her feel this way. How easy it was to forget everything in his arms!

"Brock," she moaned as his mouth followed the feathery caress of his hands. Languor turned to urgent need and she surged against him, arching her body to his, offering herself eagerly, passionately, wholly, holding nothing back, opening to his touch like a beautiful flower.

Tears filled Audra's eyes as he possessed her, as she moved to accept him when she knew in her heart that she should be rejecting this man who had betrayed her.

They moved together and as waves of pleasure swept over her she strained feverishly against him, urging him on, allowing him to plumb her very depths, to fill her so completely she cried aloud with the joy. The frightening intensity rose and swelled and finally burst over them in a giant, engulfing wave. Audra trembled as the wave began to ebb, leaving her totally limp and exhausted in its wake.

Brock held her tightly and mumbled something in her ear.

"What did you say?" she asked drowsily, snuggling closer to his side.

"Nothing," he replied. "Nothing I had any right to say."

He tucked the quilt about her and with his strong arms holding her tight against him she fell asleep.

It was morning. Audra opened her eyes to see Brock gazing down at her with a look of infinite tenderness. He reached out a hand and gently touched her cheek, but she recoiled, cringing away, and saw the answering flinch in his eyes.

What had made her give herself so easily to him the night before? She felt ashamed, enraged at herself and her weakness. She moved to the other side of the bed and attempted to rise.

What was the matter with her? Her head was swimming. She could hardly swallow. It hurt to take more than a shallow breath.

"You had better lie back," Brock said quietly. "I think you have a fever."

Audra noticed that he had dressed her in one of his warm nightshirts and had buttoned it close about her neck. She began to cough, a hacking cough that caused a pain to shoot through the left side of her chest, leaving her gasping.

"I won't stay here! I hate you!" she cried. "You took advantage of me last night! I was cold and exhausted and you poured brandy into me and—"

"You *will* stay here," he commanded, standing over her. "I am going to fetch you a doctor."

"I don't want *you* to do anything for me," she choked, going off into another spasm of coughing.

"Do you hate me so much?" he asked, shoving his shirt into his breeches as he quickly dressed. "I got the impression you rather enjoyed it last night."

"You *would* think that," she spat, "you conceited, arrogant—"

"Did I ever pretend to you that I was a saint?" he said quietly. "I regret what happened with Celeste more bitterly than you will ever know, but you must realize it meant nothing to me."

"Nothing? Celeste did not think so."

"It started long before I met you. I was blindly seeking revenge, wanting to repay the compte in the way that would hurt him the most."

"So you seduced his wife. How very admirable of you," she scoffed. "You tell me it happened long before we met and yet you know full well you were with her the night—" she could not control the tremor in her voice—"after you left *me*."

"Yes," he admitted, "I slept with her that night. I'm not proud of it, Audra. In fact, I would dearly like to forget it. But at the time it was imperative that I continue in my role. As Peregrine I desperately needed her assistance and it seemed the only way."

"Really? And pray tell me who will take the credit for fathering her expected child, Peregrine or Brock Deverell?"

A dead silence followed her words. Brock stood with his cravat dangling from one hand and she knew by the sudden hiss of indrawn breath and the dismay that leapt to his eyes that he had not known.

"Is this true?"

"Quite true. To Celeste it is proof of your love for her."

He winced at the contempt in her voice and watched her turn her head into the pillow and begin to cough again. He had only himself to blame for Audra's disdain, he thought bitterly. Even if he should tell her of his love for her, as he nearly had the night before, she would never believe him now. "I'll get the doctor," he murmured and left the room.

Brock found Herr Meister downstairs and instructed him to send for the best physician he knew of in Vienna. After this had been done, he told the landlord Audra's true sex and how she had disguised herself as a boy and ridden day and night in order to bring him some papers that were so important they had probably saved his life.

"Brave little *fräulein*," Herr Meister said admiringly. "Was she injured during the journey?"

"*Nein*, not injured, but she caught a bad chill. She was soaked to the skin when she arrived and it seems to have developed into a fever."

"Perhaps my wife can help," the landlord suggested. "Anna is always good with the sick."

When Brock again entered his bedchamber and approached the bed, he could hear Audra's shallow breathing. Putting a hand to her forehead he found that she was unnaturally hot. He poured some water into a porcelain washbasin and dipped a cloth into it, wringing it out and placing it over Audra's temples.

"Go away!" she moaned. "Go away and leave me alone!"

He paid no attention to her, drawing the straight-backed chair over beside the bed and sitting down.

The doctor arrived about a half hour later. He was a middle-aged man with a crisp, black moustache and an efficient manner. Frau Meister entered the room with him and smiled at Brock. She had heard Audra's story from her husband and felt sorry for the poor, young *fräulein* who had travelled so far to save this big, handsome Englishman. Frau Meister was plump and motherly, with a round face that was almost always wreathed in smiles. Now, however, she looked worried at Audra's high color and ragged breathing.

The doctor asked her and Brock to move away from the bed so he could examine Audra. He did this very carefully and thoroughly, placing on the tip of his nose the spectacles he wore on a black ribbon around his neck.

"Her fever is high," he said quietly to Brock when he was finished. "The inflammation seems to be worst in her left lung."

"What can I do to help her?"

"Very little. Keep the cool cloths on her forehead to keep the fever down. Place more pillows beneath her head and shoulders. It is better that she be elevated a little to help her breathing. Give her plenty of liquids to drink and keep her warm. That is all I can suggest. I will return this evening."

Frau Meister shook her head as the doctor left the room. "A good *doktor*," she said, "but with him all is business. He does not show feeling." She approached the bed and introduced herself to Audra. "I am going to nurse you," she said, smiling down at her. "We'll have you well in no time."

"I am so thirsty," Audra murmured. "Could I have something to drink?"

"*Ja*," Frau Meister said. "The *doktor* said you should have plenty of liquids. I am also going to make up some of my extract of malt for your cough and get a croup kettle by your bed. The steam will help your breathing."

She hurried from the room, ignoring Brock, and calling to a chambermaid to find a spirit lamp and bring more pillows.

Brock took the cloth from Audra's head and again wet it and replaced it. His eyes were pained as he said to her, "I'm so very sorry."

"For what?" she gasped. "That I am ill? That you deceived me or that you cannot control your sexual appetites?" She could not go on. She felt so short of breath and the pain in her chest felt like a knife now when she coughed.

"I'm sorry for everything," he answered, his voice rough. "If you hadn't made this trip—hell, why didn't Jean Paul come?"

"Because he was taken prisoner," she said wearily. "Word was sent to Ned to help in his escape. That is why there was no one to come with the papers. No one but me." Audra stopped to cough and this time Brock saw a little, blood-flecked sputum on the handkerchief she used. It sent a chill of fear through him. His mother had died from consumption. As a boy he had watched her wasting away, had seen the blood-spotted handkerchiefs she had clutched so desperately.

True to his word, the little doctor returned that evening.

Audra appeared to be burning up with fever now, her skin unnaturally flushed and hot.

"That kettle is only making the room hotter," the doctor growled at Frau Meister, who stood on the other side of the bed.

"But she said earlier that it helped her breathing," the woman insisted.

"Humph!" the doctor snorted, but he allowed it to remain. "Let me know if there is any change." He placed a little medicine bottle in Frau Meister's hands. "Laudanum," he murmured. "It will help the pain in her chest."

After the doctor had departed, Brock again wrung out the cloth from Audra's head in cool water and pressed it over her burning forehead. Misted by fever, she was completely submissive to his ministrations. It was evident that her coughing was painful and she thrashed about on the bed as a new paroxysm overcame her. When she fell back against the pillows, she was panting from the exertion.

Frau Meister poured a little water into a glass and added a few drops of laudanum to it for Audra to swallow.

"Can we do nothing more, Frau Meister?" Brock's voice was anxious. It tore at his heart to see Audra suffering.

The woman shook her head sadly. "I am just glad that this doctor is not in favor of bloodletting. Some think it helps when the breathing is difficult. Utter nonsense!"

"I would not have allowed it," Brock said emphatically.

"We must keep her forehead cool," Frau Meister said, "and not let the cloth get warm. I have heard that sponging a person down with vinegar sometimes helps. I will get one of the maids to bring some from the kitchen." She went toward the door. "You have not left this room all day, Captain. Why don't you go down and have some supper when I come back? I will stay with her."

"*Nein*, I don't—"

"You will be no good to her if you don't keep up your strength," she admonished him. "I think we should take turns with her. You can stay with her at night and sleep during the day in her little room down the hall. I will look after her in the daytime."

"That is very kind of you, Frau Meister, but I don't wish to impose—"

"Ach, it is no imposition. I feel sorry for the poor, little thing. She could be the daughter I never had."

It was later that night when Audra opened her

eyes and looked at Brock slumped in the straight-backed chair beside her. There was a strange expression on her face.

"Paul . . ." she mumbled. "You want my money, too, don't you? You are all after my money. Brock warned me. Only he . . ." She closed her eyes.

"My love," Brock whispered, but she had drifted back into her shrouded world.

Her fever was still raging the next day and the doctor came and went with a worried frown on his face, shaking his head.

Audra's color remained high and now it almost seemed tinged with blue. There were dark circles beneath her lovely eyes and her breathing had become raspy and noisy. The coughing was always followed by a small cry of pain and the expulsion of more bloody sputum.

Frau Meister stayed with Audra all day, sponging her and making sure she took the broth she fed her, the cool sips of water. The extract of malt seemed to help the spasms of coughing a little, and so that she would no longer cry out in pain, the doctor increased the laudanum she was given.

Brock appeared at noon after only a few hours of exhausted sleep. He looked terrible, Frau Meister thought. Unshaven stubble shadowed his face and his eyes bore a haunted expression.

"How is she?" he asked, and Audra opened her eyes at the sound of his voice.

"Brock? Why won't you leave me? Why won't you go away?"

He looked at her bleakly. "I can't leave you, Audra," he said, and his deep voice broke a little as he said it.

"Pay her no mind, Captain," Frau Meister murmured kindly. "The poor child is burning with the fever. Hand me that cloth in the basin, will you? You can take this one and soak it in the cool water."

That evening when Brock had finished a barely touched supper downstairs and returned to the room, it was to find Audra again ranting deliriously.

"You are like all the others," she cried out, snatching her hand away when he tried to grasp it, "only using women for your own ends."

"She does not know what she is saying, Captain," Frau Meister said sadly. "Poor child." Brock could see the tears in her eyes as she rose from her chair. "Don't leave her side for a moment," she cautioned him. "She has tried to get up twice. She is amazingly strong."

"I will not leave her side again," he replied.

Brock was glad Frau Meister did not hear all that Audra muttered aloud that night. He held her hand and tried to soothe her, but she was restless in her delirium, flailing out at imaginary people and objects. She lived again through her agony with Latham, her confrontation with Celeste, her shuddering encounter with a lecherous soldier, of whom Brock had no knowledge. But most of all it seemed she was disturbed by visions of Brock himself. She cried out to him so plaintively it broke his heart. "Oh, Brock . . . I need you so . . . love you so." Yet the next moment she was chastising herself. "Fool! Such a fool! Doesn't love me. Never has. Only uses women . . ."

Brock tried his best to reassure her, but it was

useless. She could not seem to hear him. He felt so helpless, so frustrated, and cursed himself again and again throughout the long night for what he had done to her.

The fever still continued the next day and to Brock, who kept a constant vigil by her bed, she looked as if she were slowly wasting away. Her large eyes seemed enormous, sunk in her pinched little face.

When the doctor had finished examining her in the late afternoon, Brock called him aside. There was fear now in his voice.

"Will she recover?"

"I can't answer that," the doctor said truthfully. "If she is strong enough. If she has the will. I have done all I can. I think this night will decide. I would advise you to pray, sir. Faith is a powerful healer."

Chapter Twenty

As the hours of the night passed, Brock sat by the bed, his large form hunched over in the chair, his big hands holding one of Audra's small ones, as he prayed to God for the first time in many years.

Suddenly, he realized that the slim body in the bed was beginning to thrash about in terrible, writhing convulsions! As Audra tossed wildly from side to side, her dry skin soon becoming wet with perspiration, Brock jumped to his feet and bolted across the room to the door, calling frantically for Frau Meister.

The woman came on the run, attired in nightcap and dressing gown. "I told Franz to send for the *doktor*," she said breathlessly as she entered the room. "What is the matter?"

"I don't know," Brock exclaimed helplessly.

"Look at her!"

Audra was gasping for breath as the spasms seized her wasted body.

"I think this is what the *doktor* called the 'crisis,' the turning point of her illness," Frau Meister said. "If all goes well her fever will break and she will recover."

"But how can she survive this?" Brock cried. "She has so little strength left!"

Head bent, Brock sat beside the bed, silently willing his strength into Audra, praying as he had never prayed before. He was unaware that the doctor had arrived. The three watched, unspeaking, as the young woman before them fought for her life.

After the fearful pain in her head and chest, Audra felt a wonderful peace slowly coming over her. She seemed in a different realm of consciousness, yet she was aware of what was going on around her bed.

Frau Meister was wringing her hands and the doctor was frantically working over her. There was a glaring light in the distance and she felt it coming closer and closer.

"I'm afraid we're losing her," the doctor said quietly. "I can barely feel her pulse."

"No!" she heard Brock give a roar of consternation. "No! She can't die!" He leaned over her. "Audra, if you can hear me you've got to hold on. Fight, Audra! Fight! It's so easy to let go and drift away. But that's cowardly, Audra. Oh God, don't. . . ."

She wished she could comfort him. Tell him she was all right.

"You love her very much, don't you?" she heard

Frau Meister say.

"Yes, I love her," Brock's voice was hoarse. "But until this happened I never realized how much." He pressed Audra's fingers. "Hold on, my love. I'm here. I won't leave you."

He loved her! Audra let out a long, shuddering sigh.

All at once the room seemed frighteningly quiet.

"I'm sorry," the doctor said, turning from the bed. He put a hand on Brock's shoulder.

No! Audra wanted to cry out. No! I'm not dead!

Brock was loosening his strong fingers from her hand. His face was a mask of grief.

Please don't let my hand go, she pleaded. But he couldn't hear her. She strained and strained but she could not move her fingers to hold onto him.

Gently he placed her hand down by her side. His wide shoulders shook as he leaned over to kiss her one last time.

The doctor pulled the coverlet up to cover her face.

"Wait!" Brock made a grab for it.

"What is it?"

"When I kissed her forehead, I felt—I swear I felt something damp against my chin. Look, *doktor*! Look! She's crying! *Doktor*, she's alive! God in heaven, she's alive!"

The doctor made the announcement a few minutes later, "The fever has broken. Her breathing is normal." He felt Audra's forehead with the palm of his hand. "She is now quite cool."

"*Gott in himmel*! It's a miracle!" Frau Meister declared. "I could have sworn she was gone."

The doctor looked a little shaken himself, but Brock said nothing. He continued to stare down at the little form in the big bed. He was almost afraid to take his eyes from her.

"I'll sit with her for a while," the doctor said to Frau Meister. He nodded in Brock's direction. "Why don't you take him downstairs. I think he could use a good, strong drink of something."

Brock drained the first glass Frau Meister poured for him in the deserted tap room. She quickly refilled it.

"When I thought I had lost her, I wanted to die, too," he told her. "Would you believe I used to scoff at love?" He snorted. "I love that little one up there so much the last few days have nearly torn me apart." He raised the glass again to his lips.

Frau Meister nodded, watching him closely. "Did you ever tell her?" she asked.

"No," he admitted. "No, I never did. I told her I wanted her. Told her I missed her."

"But never the words she wanted to hear," Frau Meister said perceptively.

"The word 'love' has been mouthed too often—been made cheap and meaningless."

"To you perhaps, but not to her."

"I wouldn't know. I've never loved a woman before," he admitted.

"Though I expect you've known many." She gave him a wary glance as she again filled his glass.

"I don't deny it. I've lived my life for the moment. Never planned for the future. Then Audra came along and I . . ." His voice drifted off.

"It will all work out now, Captain."

"No." He shook his head. "She'll never have me after what happened."

"I can't believe—"

"Believe it, Frau Meister," he said harshly. "I am being truly punished or everything I ever did."

For the next twenty-four hours Audra was so weak she did little more than drift in and out of sleep. She seemed content to see the figure of Frau Meister by her bed when she awakened, but if she caught sight of Brock, she became agitated. Brock, therefore, although he still stayed in the room with her at night, was careful to keep to the shadows.

It was a sunny spring morning when Audra finally awoke to total awareness and smiled at Frau Meister.

"*Guten morgen*," that woman said to her. "How are you feeling?"

"Much better, thank you. I have been ill, haven't I?"

"Very ill, *fräulein*. You nearly died."

"I remember bits and pieces . . . faces around me . . . the coughing . . ."

"Does it still hurt you to breathe?"

"No. The pain is gone." She looked up at the woman. "In fact, I feel hungry, Frau Meister. Might I have some breakfast?"

"*Ja*. I will fetch it right away." Frau Meister was all smiles as she hurried from the room.

That afternoon when Brock had risen from his

sleep, she told him that she was sure Audra would see him now.

"No. I only upset her. It is better I stay away."

In the end, it was Audra, herself, who asked for him. "Frau Meister, is the captain still at the inn?"

"*Ja.* Are you not aware that he stays with you in this room every night?"

"What!" Audra struggled to sit up in bed.

"Now, now, do not upset yourself. Ever since you became ill he has not left your side except to eat and sleep."

"He only feels guilty," Audra murmured.

"Is that what you think?" the older woman asked.

"He knows that I caught the chill riding through inclement weather to bring him a message. I suppose he feels responsible."

"He loves you, my child."

"Nonsense. He loves no woman."

"You are wrong, *fräulein.* Very wrong. If you had but seen him when he thought you were dying, you would know."

Brock stood looking down at her, his hazel eyes soft and warm. "How are you feeling, Audra?" he asked.

"Much better, thank you."

She was still white and drawn looking, but her eyes were not so lifeless, her cheeks not so pinched.

Audra, however, was startled by Brock's appearance. Lines seemed to have deepened in his face and he looked drained and tired. Where was the boyish grin? The laughing eyes?

"At the end of the week, if you are feeling strong enough, I would like to take you to the home of a friend of mine in the country," he said. "I think the fresh air and sunshine will do much to speed your recovery."

"That would be nice." She smiled. Her manner was as polite and reserved as his own.

Audra was not aware of what was going on outside the room in which she lay. Brock was anxious to get her away, for all the city was buzzing with the news that Archduke Karl Ludwig had retreated before Napoleon's sweeping attack and the French emperor was marching on Vienna.

On the tenth of May, only two days before Napoleon's arrival, Brock persuaded Audra to leave the White Swann Inn.

With Frau Meister's help, Brock had purchased some clothing for Audra. Not having much money at his disposal, he could not buy all he would have liked, but it was enough to comfortably, if not fashionably, clothe her for the time being.

Brock was profuse in his thanks to the landlord and his wife as they came to the door to bid them goodbye. There were tears from Audra at having to leave Frau Meister's kind and loving care. That woman, herself, offered a prayer that the two young people would forget their pride in the days that followed and admit their love for one another.

One seat of the coach was made into a bed for Audra with pillows piled high at one end. She was carried from the inn by Brock and laid gently upon it. He seated himself across from her for the four-hour journey, hoping it would not prove too much for her. Audra still looked so frail and wan.

The coach moved slowly out of the crowded city,

but soon they were in the open countryside. It was a lovely spring day and Audra exclaimed over the green meadows and wild flowers she glimpsed from the window.

They reached the schloss belonging to Brock's friend, the elderly Baron Von Stead, who was his government contact in Austria, in the late afternoon. The schloss was perched on a small green hill, terracing down to a sparkling blue lake. Mountains rose majestically in the background. The castle looked to Audra, as they approached, like a picture from a fairy tale book, with its many turrets and gables. "How beautiful!" she breathed.

The baron was tall and straight with thick, white hair covering a leonine head and bright blue eyes. He welcomed them graciously to his home.

Brock insisted upon personally carrying Audra to her room and she was delighted by its airiness and bright and attractive floral-patterned carpet and curtains. As if to welcome her, there was a huge bouquet of multicolored flowers on a table, which gave a springlike scent to the room.

"A supper will be brought up to you shortly," Brock said, depositing Audra upon the wide, four-poster bed. He nodded to the little maid who had quietly appeared in the doorway.

"I will dine with the baron, but will look in on you later," he promised her.

"Please don't trouble yourself," she said. "I am a little tired after the journey and will probably go to sleep early."

"Of course," he said tightly, the brightness leaving his eyes.

The following days soon began to run into one another. Audra recovered enough to be moved from the bed to a chair before the window of her room. Still her world was confined to the four walls of her bedchamber. She read the books the kind baron sent up to her and enjoyed his occasional visits when he accompanied Brock to her room.

Every morning she watched from her window as the two men rode out after breakfast and remained in her chair until they returned several hours later. Her window overlooked a pretty hedge-enclosed garden with a marble table and bench in the center. Beyond this was a sweeping gravel driveway that led from the stables.

As the days passed, Audra had a great deal of time to think. Almost too much time. Brock came to see her twice a day, yet there was always that polite but distant manner between them. Neither said what he would like to have said, or made any sign that would indicate what they once had shared.

One warm, sunny afternoon, Brock came to Audra's room and suggested that he take her outside to sit in the shade of a tree overlooking the lake.

He carried her downstairs and out of doors, walking easily with her in his arms. Before, when he had carried her from the inn to the coach, and from the coach to her bedchamber in the schloss, Audra had been too weak to be aware of his closeness. Now, she was disturbingly aware of his strong arms, the warm, clean scent of his skin. She felt a longing to nuzzle her face against his neck. She looked up at him, but he was gazing straight ahead, an unreadable look in his eyes. She thought he appeared much better for his stay in the country. The sun had bronzed his skin and the weariness seemed to have left him, but the lightheartedness had still not returned.

Brock set her down on a carved wooden bench and placed an afghan over her knees.

"You are still treating me like an invalid," she said as he sat down beside her. "I've been walking around my room for a little while each day. I can feel my strength returning."

"I'm glad to hear it. We will have to start back to England in a week or two." How remote we are, he thought. Like two people who are barely acquainted. He looked at her, rejoicing to see that there was now faint color in the pale cheeks. The soft, blond curls had lost their dullness, but the blue eyes still dropped before his gaze. They never quite met his own.

They both sat quietly, viewing the peaceful scene before them, wishing the other would speak out and yet almost afraid that he would. It was the first time they had been completely alone since Audra's illness. Brock finally broke the silence.

"When you left London, was my grandmother well?"

"Yes. Jason had come to visit her."

"Jason? That's not a good sign." He frowned. "He usually wants her to extricate him from some predicament."

Audra smiled. "You're right. He was in debt again, but fortunately a friend came to his aid."

"Really? I'm surprised he has any friends left."

Audra shook her head. "I don't understand your brother, nor why your grandmother puts up with his behavior."

"I gather you did not like him."

She told him then of Jason's proposal of marriage. "You warned me of fortune hunters, Brock," she said. "Would you believe that I had two proposals following one upon the other?" He stared at her as she went on. "Paul arrived in London and asked me to marry him the first time he came to call."

"Did that upset you? I thought you cared for Paul."

"That was a very long time ago. I don't think I really knew him."

"So you refused both proposals," he said, letting out his breath.

"Yes, and wanting to get away from London in a hurry, I headed for Southcliffe. I decided to wait there for your return."

At that time she must have cared for him, Brock thought. He had only himself to blame for the change in her feelings.

"And while you were there you heard of Jean Paul's imprisonment?" he asked.

"That's right, and the very same day a man came from Castlereagh to see Ned about getting the new identity papers to you. Ned was frantic! With Jean Paul imprisoned, who would he get to help you? I had quite a time convincing him that *I* should be the one for the mission. Ned can be quite stubborn."

Audra was happy to see the old grin return to Brock's face at her words. "He can, as I well know."

"I went with Ned aboard *The Peregrine* when he left to assist in Jean Paul's escape," Audra went on, "but the attempt had to be postponed. The compte had decided to interrogate him that night."

Brock's lips tightened. "To torture him, you mean."

"I'm afraid so. Marie was in tears when she came to me. He was barely conscious, she said, when she bribed the guard to see him. She had to find out from him the route I should take—or at least the first stopping place. That was all I was told."

"And Ned, I presume, went back to England?"

"Yes. He planned to return the next night. An escape was being set up by Louis and the other men. Jean Paul is probably safe and sound in England now."

"If the informer didn't intercede."

"What informer?"

"Jean Paul and I were aware that an informer had infiltrated his group of men. You see, someone had got word to the compte that I was moving human cargo as well as smuggling goods. That is why I was shot."

Audra looked at him anxiously. "Could that have been why Jean Paul was arrested? The informer told the compte of his activities?"

Brock thought that might be true. "Do you remember the letter you brought me from the countess?" he asked.

At his words, he felt her body tense beside him.

"I made Celeste promise that she would try and find out the name of the informer for me." He rose to his feet. "I didn't go about it very honorably, I'm afraid." He stood with his broad back to her, looking out over the peaceful lake, shimmering in the afternoon sunshine. "When you were delirious," he continued, "you accused me of using women for my own ends. You were right. I used Celeste. Learning the name of the informer seemed so damned imperative."

He turned to face Audra. "She wrote to me in the letter you brought that someone from the château was definitely suspected, and so Jean Paul had decided to take no chances and use only the village men in his plans. Apparently, the informer must have thought Jean Paul was onto him and consequently had him arrested."

"That sounds logical." A brief pause. "I'm surprised Celeste did not mention the child in her letter."

"She was wise not to. The letter might have fallen into the wrong hands." He looked at her. "I don't suppose I'll ever be able to convince you that there was nothing between Celeste and me? It was her husband who had tortured and caused my brother David's death. I wanted revenge so badly I could taste it. I learned his wife was his dearest possession, that he was obsessed with her. So, hoping to wound him deeply, I . . ."

"Used her as a pawn," Audra said contemptuously. "Even now you don't seem to realize that she loves you."

"No." Brock shook his head. "Celeste loves no one

but herself. What she loves is making others do as she wishes." His lip curled. "As far as she was concerned I was nothing but a stud!" He watched as two bright spots of color appeared in Audra's cheeks. "Now I've shocked you," he said.

"No. What shocks me is that you consented to pose for that portrait in the love nest."

"Audra, I swear to you. That was *not* me."

"How can you continue to lie about that?" Her voice rose. "I saw the portrait myself. The artist had captured your features perfectly."

"You are mistaken."

"There is no use arguing about it," she sighed. "It makes no difference to me. We shared a romantic little interlude, that was all. No commitments were ever made. So you made love to Celeste and the little maid at the White Swann Inn and a dozen other—"

"What little maid at the White Swann?" he bellowed. "Damnit, woman, do you think of me as such a rakehell I must seduce every female I meet? I had an affair with Celeste. I admitted that. But I also told you why and that it meant nothing to me." He gave a snort. "I may have used Celeste, but damn it all, she got what she wanted."

Audra's blue eyes flared. "You were *that* good were you?" she almost burst out. Instead she asked sardonically, "Do you think she wanted your child?"

"That was her risk."

"It was also *my* risk. I only thank God I am not in the same condition!"

He stood looking down at her, his eyes very dark. "Would bearing my child be so distasteful to you?"

"Yes!" she cried, lashing out at him. "I'd rather

bear the devil's!" She jumped up, throwing down the afghan and fled back in the direction of the castle as fast as she could run on her still-shaky legs.

Brock caught up to her before she had covered much ground and scooped her easily up into his arms.

"Put me down!" she demanded, kicking her legs and pummelling his chest with her fists. "Put me down or I'll scream!"

"The baron has gone off to Vienna for a few days. There are only the servants to hear you and I doubt—"

"You are odious and detestable!" She glared at him.

"I know," he said. "You have made it extremely clear how you feel about me. We won't discuss this again."

"Good. I would also appreciate it if you would keep your hands from me!" She gave a shudder. "Your very touch repels me!"

He did not set her down and his expression only became more rigid as he carried her silently back up to her room.

During the remaining week they spent at the schloss, their attitude toward one another returned to polite civility.

Chapter Twenty-One

The baron had returned from Vienna with the glad news that Archduke Karl Ludwig had reorganized his forces and brought them back to the left bank of the Danube at Essling. Napoleon had tried to recross it, hoping to defeat the archduke in a decisive battle, but the Danube was in a rising spring flood which had swept away the principal bridges. Part of the French army and much of the ammunition had had to be left behind and on May 22, Napoleon's 60 thousand men were forced to fight 115 thousand Austrian troops and suffered a disastrous defeat.

"I think it is a good time for us to leave Austria," Brock told the baron. "Before Napoleon has the time to reorganize his men and rebuild the bridges."

"How do you plan to travel?" the older man

questioned him.

"I haven't thought too much about it. It will depend on which roads are open and—"

"Might I make a suggestion?" the baron asked. "The young *fräulein* not being well, the less she has to travel by coach the better. It will take longer, but if I were you I would consider taking a boat down the Danube until it branches southward into Switzerland. Then you can go overland to France."

"That sounds like an excellent idea," Brock considered, settling back in his chair. It was evening and they had just finished dining and had adjourned to the salon for a brandy.

The baron now regarded his guest over his goblet. "May I ask you a personal question? You can tell me to go to the devil if you like, but I've been curious about this since your arrival." He cleared his throat. "You told me, Brock, that Audra had come all the way from England with a message for you, but had caught a chill along the way which had developed into a fever."

Brock nodded, his face expressionless.

"When the young *fräulein* had recovered sufficiently, you accepted my invitation and brought her here, but you have told me nothing about her except her Christian name. Up until now, I have not questioned you, but now it seems she is well on her way to regaining her health. I understand, in fact, that she would like to dine with us tomorrow evening."

"That is correct."

"Then is it too much for me to ask what your relationship is with her? You are too damn polite to be lovers. I simply can't fathom it at all. Why should Audra risk her life to come all this way if she cared nothing for you?"

"We were *once* lovers, *mein herr*," Brock said, his jaw tightening. "Does that answer your question?"

The baron knew by Brock's face that he should drop the subject, yet he intuitively felt that his young friend's changed manner since his arrival at the schloss, his many silences, might be due to this very matter preying on his mind.

"Do you want to tell me about it?" he asked quietly.

"There's little use," Brock declared, jumping to his feet and beginning to pace agitatedly up and down.

The baron watched him for several minutes before he spoke again. "May I offer you some advice, *mein jung freund.* I have been widowed twice and although I would never be so presumptuous as to consider myself an authority on women, I have learned a few things over the years." He took a sip of his brandy. "Tell her, Brock."

Brock stopped pacing and frowned down at him. "Tell her what?" he demanded.

"That you love her, you young fool!" The baron smiled in amusement.

Brock's reaction to his words was to turn on his heel and stalk from the room.

Looking after him, the baron murmured, "Bull-headed *Englisch*!" and shook his head.

Audra lay awake thinking of Brock. How many times in every day did he enter her thoughts? How many times did she yearn to be held again in those strong arms?

She began to feel drowsy. It had been a tiring day, for in an effort to build up her strength, she had taken several strolls up and down the winding upper corridors of the schloss. She planned to join the gentlemen the next evening and she wanted to be able to walk straight and tall without her knees shaking and betraying the weakness that still had not completely left her.

Audra did not fight sleep when it came. She welcomed it for it had become an escape from the turmoil of her emotions. But she dreamed.

She dreamed that she saw Brock running for his life down a narrow road. There were men on horseback pursuing him and she waited beside the road on a chestnut mare, holding the reins of a saddled black stallion. She urged the mare forward to meet Brock, but he paid no attention to her and raced by her. It was then that she saw the lovely comtesse standing beside a carriage drawn by four horses. She had a little boy beside her and was beckoning to Brock. Eagerly he ran toward her open arms.

Audra awoke filled with the same desolation she had felt in the dream. Damn him! It was enough that he was constantly present in her waking thoughts. Did he have to invade her dreams as well?

She had twisted and turned in her sleep; the sheets and blankets were now pulled out from the bottom of her bed and had fallen to the floor. Audra arose and moved to tuck back the covers. Upset by the memory of the dream, she was now wide awake.

The castle was in silence. It must be the middle of the night. Only the wind could be heard blowing gently against her windows, softly rattling the panes.

She climbed back into bed, knowing she would not easily fall asleep again. If only she had something to read. She had given the books the baron had lent her to her maid to return to him only that morning. Audra lay there, tossing from one side of the bed to the other for what seemed to be hours. It was ridiculous. Sleep was never going to claim her this way. She got up and put on her dressing gown and slippers.

Quietly, she took one of the half-burned candles from the branch by her bed and crossing the room, opened the door. She slipped out into the corridor and started down it in the direction of the wide center staircase. Surely it wouldn't be too difficult to find the library below and choose a book that would take away the tension, make her relax and forget her dream.

She stopped. There was a door ajar ahead of her and a light was shining out into the corridor from the room beyond. She didn't stop to think. She walked softly toward the opening and peeped in.

It was Brock's room! He sat alone, sprawled in a large wing-backed chair, a glass in his hand. A near-empty decanter stood on a table at his elbow, its stopper lying beside it. He drained his glass as she watched, then leaned his head back against the chair. A lock of his hair lay over his forehead, his eyes were fixed and brooding.

A dreadful longing rose in her. She wanted to go to him, fling herself on her knees beside him, put her arms around him. How weak she could become at the sight of this man! Why could she not harden her heart against him? He had tormented her for so long, caused her so much pain. She must never forget how easily he had gone from her arms to those of the comtesse. He was a womanizer, a passionate, practiced lover who would never belong to any woman.

Audra stood there in the darkness of the corridor and for a few minutes watched his lonely, quiet drinking. Then she turned to go back to her bed, all thoughts of finding a book completely forgotten. Her candle hit the doorjamb as she turned about and dropped from her fingers onto the parquet floor. Its flame went out.

"Is that you, Schultz? I told you to go to bed, old man."

Brock got to his feet. There was a slight sway in his walk as he started for the door.

Gathering her wits, Audra began to run back down the corridor in the direction of her room.

"Come back here!" he called after her.

She sped by closed doors, not knowing where she was going in the darkness. Then she remembered that she had left candles burning by her bed and looked for a light showing from beneath a door. The room was just ahead of her and she dashed in, closing the door tightly behind her.

Audra was breathing hard as she made her way over to the bed. She doubted that Brock had recognized her in the dark. It was obvious he had been drinking heavily. Nevertheless, she should, perhaps, blow out the candles. But before this could be done, the door was thrown open with a bang. She gave a gasp and whirled about.

Brock stood in the doorway regarding her, his eyes dark and frightening. His cravat hung from about the neck of his shirt, which was unbuttoned, partly revealing the broad, muscular chest with its crisp mat of hair. He strode purposefully into the room and kicked the door shut.

"What the hell are you doing?" he growled.

She didn't move. She stood staring at him, her knees threatening to give way.

"Get back into that bed right now," he ordered, coming toward her.

"I—I couldn't sleep," she stammered.

"So you decided to explore the castle at two o'clock in the morning?"

"I thought if I could find a book in the library . . . You see, I have not slept well since my illness."

"We have that in common," he grunted. He stopped, only a few feet away from her, swaying slightly.

"I think you had better leave." Audra had herself under control now. "You're drunk," she accused.

"Half drunk, perhaps, but not wholly—though the good Lord knows it's not from want of trying. Damn you, Audra," he said thickly. "Do you know how many nights you have tormented me? Tell me how I can stop loving you."

"Loving *me*?" She gave a strained little laugh. "You don't even know the meaning of the word! Did you think of me once when you made love to your eager little Celeste?"

"No! That travesty could never compare—"

"Yet during that travesty, as you call it, a child was conceived."

"Don't remind me! Do you think I don't curse myself for that!" He ran a hand through his already tousled hair. "Damnit, Audra, how can I make you believe that I love you? That I nearly went out of my mind when I thought I was losing you, when I thought you were dying because of me."

"Guilt. That was guilt, Brock. You don't love any woman."

He stood over her now, her words causing a rage to well up inside him. He wanted to take her by the shoulders and shake her until he convinced her. Instead he laughed, a laugh so bitter it made a shiver go down her spine.

"You're right. What would *I* know about love? I only use women."

He reached for her then, pulling her roughly against him. His hands dug into the soft flesh of her arms and as he lowered his mouth to hers she smelled the liquor on his breath. His kiss was long and ardent, drawing from her soft lips as if he were dying of thirst and she was the cool water he craved. Too long he had ached for her, too long. . . . He forced her backward toward the bed and she began to struggle. He felt the sudden fury of her resistance, but he did not loosen his hold. Instead he pressed her twisting body urgently, demandingly against his, desiring an answering hunger to match the passion that already filled him.

"Would you rape me, Brock?" she cried.

"No. I flatter myself that that won't be necessary." Desire, naked and compelling blazed in the hazel eyes as he snatched off her dressing gown. "Will you remove your nightdress or shall I?"

"Don't do this to me, Brock," she entreated. "Everything is over between us."

"Is it?" he said, his voice deep and husky. "You told me you loved me when you were delirious with fever."

She shook her head lamely in denial, straining to break free from the forceful vise of his arms, tears of rage and frustration filling her eyes when she realized there was no escaping.

In one swift movement he had pushed her back on the bed and was pinning her down with his big body, making it impossible for her to lift her knees in defense. She felt the thin gown being ripped from her shoulders, felt his hands find the sensitive flesh of her breasts and begin to move in gentle circles over them. Despite her wish to resist him, the peaks rose, firm and aching and his mouth closed over one, the tingling sensation of his tongue arousing her, though she fought it with all of her being.

She must not respond to his lovemaking! She must not! But his hungry mouth was following his hands as they travelled delicately over her soft skin, caressing, teasing, tormenting her until she wanted to scream aloud.

If only her body could remain passive to him! It remembered too well the sweet passion this man could arouse. It responded to him as it always had, straining against him, yearning to be one with him again, to feel the jolting plunge, the growing surge of ecstasy, the glorious release.

"You lied to me," Brock murmured thickly.

"Nothing is over between us, nor can it ever be."

He took his time now, arousing her inch by inch, his burning mouth trailing soft, little kisses from her tingling breasts down over her navel, moving lower still, finding the secret place of her passion.

"No!" she cried, trying to push him away, as his tongue awoke new sensations, but his hands held her tightly to him. Nerves taut, nearly mad with desire, she reached blindly for him, pulling him up to her, raining kisses on his face, arching her body to his.

"You know full well what you do to me, don't you?" she sobbed. "You know I can't resist you."

"Nor I you, my love," he whispered hoarsely.

Impatiently he claimed her, filling her with his throbbing heat, his movements extracting every ounce of pleasure for them both as the tension rose. Engulfed in passion, she became like a wild creature, revelling in her impalement, twisting deliriously on him, driving him deeper, her nails digging into the flesh of his back.

She clung to him then as the surging, onrushing tide overcame them both. Totally drained, they lay entwined, trying to catch their breath. Audra made a movement beneath him and Brock misinterpreted it.

"No!" His voice was muffled by her hair. "Don't leave me!" He raised his head and looked down at her with such an expression of contrition that she hardly recognized the arrogant Brock Deverell. "Will you forgive me?" he asked.

"I will always forgive you." She smiled, brushing back the lock of hair that had fallen over his temple. "Because I love you."

He gave a groan and sought her lips again. "Don't

stop loving me," he implored. "I'm a brute who has forced himself upon you more than once, but it's only because I love you so."

Her eyes filled. "I don't believe I've stopped loving you since the first time you kissed me in your cabin aboard *The Peregrine*."

A slow smile crossed his face. "I'm afraid it took me longer," he admitted. "I had never known love before and at first I didn't recognize it. I simply desired you. But things changed. I changed. It was in London that I realized you had become an obsession to me, that what I felt for you was more than mere physical desire. But it took your illness, the thought that I might lose you forever, to make me realize how very much I loved you, that I wanted you with me always."

Her eyes were deep pools of loveliness. "Brock . . ." she began.

"Have I exhausted you?" he broke in. "You're still recovering and I should not have—"

"I'm tired, but it doesn't matter. I'm so very very happy."

He kissed her tenderly. "I think we should both sleep well tonight," he said, turning on his back and pulling her against him so that her face rested against his chest. He would have liked to make love to her again, but there was no hurry now. There was always tomorrow, he thought contentedly, closing his eyes.

Chapter Twenty-Two

Audra and Brock bid goodbye to the baron at the end of the week. That man had been delighted to see that the two lovers had again become united. He was quite sure it was all his doing, and Brock did nothing to spoil his belief in his matchmaking ability.

The journey down the river was memorable. The scenery, particularly in the valley of the Danube, was wild and beautiful, with castles crowning every possible summit on the neighboring hills. Still, Audra laughingly told Brock, she had probably seen more of their cabin during the trip than the breathtaking scenery they passed.

It was true that they had spent a great deal of time in the ample-sized bunk, sleeping, talking and making love. Audra soon began to wonder how she had ever lived without this precious intimacy.

Whether by sweet tenderness or fierce passion, they affirmed their love for one another over and over again.

When they took to the road, it was as a farmer and his nephew, travelling in a cart, pulled by a strong but ungainly horse. It felt strange to Audra to be attired again as a boy, but her papers declared her to be a lad and so she travelled in her old disguise.

The weather had taken a change for the better and was warm and pleasant when they approached the French border. They had a few anxious moments as the road was heavily guarded and each person who wished to enter the country was being carefully examined. But, fortunately, both sets of papers appeared to be in order and, with only a cursory glance in their direction, they were able to safely cross the border into France.

The slow trip, though not the most comfortable in the jolting cart, was enjoyable to both of them because they were together. Audra was almost looking like her old self again and her strength appeared to be gaining daily.

Brock teased her, telling her his frequent stimulation of her body was all the restorative she needed. He was simply inbuing her with his strength. She shook her head at his arrogance, but secretly believed what he said might be true. Her body had never felt so blissfully alive and her whole being radiated happiness.

From the start of their journey across France, Audra had noticed how well received they were at each stop they made. It was obvious "Peregrine" was well liked. He took a genuine interest in the innkeepers and people who housed them, in their welfare, their families and their smallest problems.

For appearance's sake, Brock always requested a pallet made up in his room for his young nephew, but Audra never occupied it. She slept each night enfolded in Brock's strong arms. Despite the perilousness of their journey through an enemy country, Audra had never felt so safe and secure.

They did not always wait for the privacy of an inn bedchamber to fall into each other's arms. They made love in the tall grass of a meadow they passed or on a bed of green moss in a wood. Their need for one another was so great it took very little to make it burst into flame.

"I've never been so happy," Audra said one afternoon as they lay in the sunshine beside a little brook, satiated and drowsy from their lovemaking.

Brock nodded. "Or had so little," he said with a grin. "Hardly more than the clothes on our backs and an ancient horse and cart."

"We have each other," she sighed. "That's all that counts to me."

"I wonder . . ." he pondered, thinking of England, only a few days away now—if all went well.

"I know what you're thinking," she whispered, "and you're wrong. Nothing is going to change how I feel, Brock."

"But what can I offer you, Audra? I have no money. No title."

"I already have both and I'd give them away in a moment if you asked me to."

"And live like this?"

"Just like this."

He kissed her and again he drew her to him. It seemed impossible for him to get enough of her, impossible to touch her enough, to taste her enough, to love her enough.

It was when they returned hand in hand to the horse and cart that they saw the ominous-looking man on horseback waiting beside it. His sharp eyes swept over Brock.

"Monsieur Sabourin, is it not?" he asked. "I thought I recognized you this morning at the inn."

Audra stiffened at his words, but Brock, seemingly unconcerned, met the dark gaze. "I'm afraid you are mistaken, monsieur," he said calmly.

"I never forget a face, nor a name," the man said. "Surely you remember me? Several weeks ago we shared a table at the same inn. It was only later at the border that I overheard some officials talking and learned that there was a price on your head."

A pistol suddenly appeared in the man's hand, pointed straight at Brock!

"You will get aboard the cart with the lad and head back in the direction from which you came," he ordered.

The man dismounted and secured the reins of his horse to the rear of the cart. Then he climbed into it and, with pistol cocked and ready, stationed himself behind the box where Audra and Brock had seated themselves.

"Get moving!" he said.

They travelled in silence for a while until Brock spoke, saying over his shoulder to the man, "What is it worth to you to forget you have ever seen me?"

"Don't try to bribe me!" the man growled. "I am a

loyal Frenchman and you, from all accounts, are a murderer and a thief. I also have my own suspicions of what you were doing with that lad down by the brook." He spat in disgust, and poked the pistol into Audra's shoulder. "You are free to go, boy, when we reach the next village. Let it be a lesson to you not to take up with strangers. The only way to earn an honest living is with honest work."

Audra had a terrible desire to giggle at the assumption he had made, but instead she decided to play along with it and sullenly answered, "He hasn't even paid me."

Brock's mouth twitched slightly, but for the man's benefit he glared at Audra. "I fed you, didn't I? Gave you a bed to sleep in and clothes on your back. A lot more than a lad like you has ever had before."

"But you forced me to do things—"

"When did I force you? You told me only an hour ago that you were happy with me."

They couldn't look at one another or they both would have laughed aloud.

"Disgusting!" the man spat again. "Vile!"

Audra turned a little to her right to regard him. "Do you think so, monsieur? If your preference is for the *jeune filles*, I have a sister—"

"Enough! I am a married man and not interested in such depravities."

"Where does your interest lie, monsieur?"

Brock was observing Audra from the corner of his eye. Her right hand seemed to be moving slowly down the outside of her thigh. What was she doing?

"My interest is my work. It is a good and honorable profession," the man said proudly. "I am a gunsmith."

"Really, monsieur? How thrilling! That is a truly fine pistol you hold." Audra admired the weapon as eagerly as a young lad would.

"I designed it myself," the man answered, squaring his shoulders.

Brock was thinking that there was very little time before the road on which they travelled joined the main road. The added traffic might prevent any move on his part to disarm this man without calling attention to themselves. Something must be done and very soon! Only the thought that Audra might be injured by a stray bullet had thus far prevented him from making a sudden lunge at the man to catch him off guard.

"I can see that your pistol is very fine," Audra was saying. "What is engraved on the barrel?"

Without thinking, the man turned the weapon he held slightly toward him to observe the design. In that second, Audra withdrew her own small muff gun from her boot and fired it at the man's pistol. The force of the bullet hitting the barrel sent it flying from his hand and out over the side of the moving cart.

"Now!" Audra cried, grabbing for the reins and Brock responded by throwing himself back at the surprised man.

They grappled for several seconds on the floor of the cart, but Brock was by far the stronger and the gunsmith was soon overpowered.

Brock stuffed a handkerchief from his pocket into the man's mouth and with the man's own cravat tied his hands behind his back. The gunsmith's ankles were soon imprisoned with his own belt.

"Draw over to the side of the road," Brock instructed Audra, and when this was done and the horse brought to a halt, he jumped down and released the man's horse from the rear of the vehicle. With Audra's help, Brock removed their belongings from the cart and secured them to the horse's saddle before helping her to mount the big sorrel. With a wink at her, he said, for the benefit of the gunsmith's ears, "We'll have to change our plans now and head straight for Paris."

He grasped the old nag's bridle and turned it and the cart about on the road. Giving the horse a smart slap on its flank, Brock watched as it started off in the direction from which they had come, the trussed-up gunsmith rolling uncomfortably about in the back of the cart.

Brock's deep laugh followed him. "That old nag won't stop until sunset or until he gets hungry—whichever comes first." He swung himself up behind Audra and pointed the big horse in the direction of the main road.

"Mentioning Paris was good thinking," she said to him as they started off.

"Not nearly as good as your shooting." He leaned over to kiss the nape of her neck.

"I told you I could shoot well," she said proudly. "Ned gave me that little gun for protection."

"I'm glad of that, but I'm also glad you were not forced to use it on that Frenchie."

"So am I, but never fear. I would not have hesitated if it had been a case of your life or his."

"Bloodthirsty woman!"

"You should carry a weapon yourself," she chided him.

"I usually do, but I hid my pistol with my clothing when we crossed the border."

"You must be more alert in future."

"Why? I have *you* to protect me," he teased.

"It's no joke, Brock. If one man recognized you, there may be others."

"Don't worry, my sweet. I won't show my face from now on," he assured her. "I will let *you* do all the negotiating."

"I believe I should have been doing it all along. Were you aware, my love, that your French is pure Parisian? It passed when you posed as a wine merchant, but now that you are a poor farmer . . ."

"That completely slipped my mind," he said, angry at his own carelessness.

"Do I distract you so?" She smiled tantalizingly at him over her shoulder.

"You know you do, you brat!" One arm tightened about her and his voice lowered. "What do you say to . . ."

"No! Keep your mind on business. Right now we have need of another horse. Can we afford one?" Audra had given the small amount of money she carried over to Brock upon leaving the schloss.

"We have enough," he said, "as long as you feel well enough to ride the rest of the way."

"You have helped build up my stamina, monsieur. I don't tire half so easily now."

The incident with the gunsmith had made Brock realize, not for the first time, Audra's remarkable qualities. Again she had revealed her strength in the face of adversity and danger. He marvelled at the calm way she had sized up the situation and planned her move against the gunsmith. In the same position, another female might have broken into tears or confessed everything to the pistol-waving man. Audra, so sweet and yielding in his arms, was made of sterner stuff. Her intrepid behavior only endeared her all the more to him.

As they drew near to the end of their journey, Audra began to wonder about Brock and their future. He loved her, of this she was sure, but he had never mentioned marriage. Would he still be too stiff-necked to share the fortune Latham had left her? That, she felt, was what held him back. It did not matter to her. If he wanted her to live off what he made at smuggling, she would do it and gladly. All that mattered was that they be together.

They reached Lille just after lunch the next day. The innkeeper welcomed Brock with a wide smile and a nod of recognition to Audra. He ushered them into a private parlor and spent an hour exchanging pleasantries with Brock over several glasses of wine. Audra said little, content to sit and listen and sip her own wine. It was when the conversation took a serious turn that the innkeeper informed Brock that word had been sent from the coast that he and the lad should remain in Lille until they were contacted.

"But how will it be known we have arrived?" Brock asked.

"I have already sent word," the innkeeper said.

"To Jean Paul?"

"*Non.* He is in London. He was rescued several weeks ago from imprisonment in the château and taken there."

"I'm glad to hear that. Is Louis running the operation now?"

"*Oui*, with Marie Beaudette's help. That one is clever. Who would suspect the comtesse's own maid?"

It was after Brock and Audra had dined that night and had retired to their bedchamber that there was a knock at the door, and a message given to Brock.

"There is someone to see me downstairs," he told Audra. "It is probably Louis. I won't be long. Get into bed." He gave her his insolent grin. "And keep it warm for me."

Audra tried to stay awake, but an hour passed and then another and still Brock did not return. She wondered what was keeping him and yawned wearily. No doubt much had occurred at the château in their absence. Jean Paul's escape would be discussed in detail and the plans for their return on *The Peregrine*. Audra's eyes felt leaden. She drifted off to sleep.

She awoke to feel Brock's big body sliding in beside her. She turned toward him. "You're late," she murmured sleepily. "I should feel hurt that you preferred Louis's company to mine." She reached out a hand and began to stroke his chest.

He removed it. "Go back to sleep," he said and turned over on his side with his back to her.

Brock had never rebuffed her before. Audra was sure something had happened! She sat up in bed. "What is the matter?" she asked.

There was no answer.

"What is it, Brock?"

Still no answer.

"Don't shut me out!" she said desperately. "We've been through too much together!"

"Will you go to sleep, Audra! This is solely my concern."

"Have I no part in things that concern you?"

"Not in this."

"Yet it has upset you greatly." The feeling was intuitive. The words almost caught in her throat as she asked, "It's Celeste, isn't it?"

He raised himself. "Yes, damnit!" he growled. "Someone told the compte about Celeste and me and he took his rage out on her. Beat her savagely!"

"Oh, Brock . . ." She reached out for him, but he had pulled himself to the edge of the bed and sat there, berating himself.

"I am to blame for his, Audra. Celeste appealed to me the last time I saw her. She was afraid of him, afraid of what would happen if he found out. I told her not to worry." He gave a snort. "Told her that it was me on whom he would want to vent his anger."

"But who would have told the compte?" Audra asked, then answered her own question. "The informer."

"Probably. What matters is that Celeste has been forced to pay for something that was totally *my* fault. I was so intent on wanting my revenge, so—"

"Brock! Celeste is no innocent. Your affair with her was as much *her* desire as yours. From what *I* saw of her—"

"No!" he growled, angrily rising to his feet. "You don't understand. Celeste had no knowledge that I was using her to get at her husband. She has suffered cruelly at his hands and all because of me. All because . . ." He was drawing on his clothes. "Poor little Celeste."

Audra's heart sank. "Where are you going?"

"I can't sleep. Have to take a walk. Think things out."

He was gone and Audra lay alone filled with fear of what Brock might decide to do. She remembered how understanding and compassionate he had been when he had learned how Latham had mistreated her. She had sensed that he would have gladly killed him if the earl had not already been dead. God in heaven! Brock now had more than one reason for seeking revenge on the compte! Would he be foolish enough to storm off to the château tonight?

Audra lay awake sick with worry for him. Remembering too well the softness in his voice when he had said, "Poor little Celeste." It was plain the comtesse had never completely disappeared from his thoughts. And why would she? She was carrying his child. Dear God, had the child been injured in the beating?

It was still dark when Brock returned. He entered the room quietly and lay down on the bed fully clothed, leaving a distance between them. She heard him sigh deeply and in a few minutes his deep, regular breathing told her that he slept.

Brock had made up his mind to do something and having made his decision his mind could rest. Audra only wished she could drift off as easily. It was nearly dawn before sleep finally came.

They left in the morning for the coast. Brock seemed preoccupied, hardly speaking except to answer Audra's questions with a brusque yes or no.

The sky which had been blue and cloudless throughout most of their journey was now gray and threatening. The weather, it seemed to Audra, paralleled Brock's feelings. She cried inwardly for the loss of the sun and the loving closeness they had shared.

They arrived at the outskirts of the village near the château in the afternoon. Louis met them and directed them to the curé's house, where, he told them, they were to wait until he felt it safe to fetch them.

Word had been sent to Ned the past night that he was to anchor *The Peregrine* offshore and await the boat which would carry Audra and Brock out to the sloop. Brock spoke to Louis for a few minutes alone, and then Louis, with a nod of his head, went on his way.

The curé, a white-haired little man, welcomed Brock delightedly, apparently having had dealings with him in the past. As usual, Audra was introduced as Brock's nephew. They were given a hot, nourishing meal by the curé's plump housekeeper and afterwards were ushered into the priest's little study where they sat down to begin their wait.

The curé chatted with Brock until it was time for evening mass. After he had departed, the room became strangely quiet as Brock sat silently gazing into the flickering flames of the fire.

Audra rose and crossed the room to him. They had been so close that it hurt her to be so completely excluded from his thoughts.

"Did Louis tell you anything more today?" she asked, sitting down on the arm of his chair.

He frowned. "About what?"

"The comtesse. Is she all right?"

A hesitancy. "The compte has apparently shown some remorse."

Audra sighed. "I'm glad to hear that. You can return to England now without worrying."

His eyes met hers with a look she found hard to read, but he said nothing.

All went according to plan. A little after midnight they were ferried out from a hidden beach south of the village to where *The Peregrine* lay at anchor. The clouds had drifted off after a light rain leaving a clear, moonlit sky, so the sloop had not come in as close as previously, fearing to be seen from the shore.

Ned and the crew gave them a warm welcome as Brock helped Audra to climb aboard. After the happy exclamations and handshaking were over, Brock motioned to Ned.

"I will take Her Ladyship down below and then I want a word with you."

He led Audra down to his cabin and opened the door. "Will you take a glass of wine?" he asked as they entered.

"No. I just want you to hold me and kiss me. I'm

so happy to be going home."

He took her in his arms and kissed her, quite gently at first, and then more fiercely.

"I must go and speak with Ned," he said, reluctantly disengaging himself.

"Hurry back," she whispered.

He stopped a moment at the door and smiled, his eyes drinking in the slim figure in the ill-fitting boy's clothing.

"I will try not to be long," he promised.

A few minutes later Audra heard the muffled noises from above that told her that *The Peregrine* was preparing for departure. She sighed as she felt the sloop begin to move and looked about her. She did not want Brock to return to the cabin and find the young boy he had left. She wanted him to find a woman.

Entering his sleeping quarters, Audra opened a small footlocker and discovered among some items of clothing one of Brock's frilled shirts. She knew it would hang down about her knees, but it was the best she could do. She stripped off her clothing and drew the shirt over her head, leaving it partly open at the neck to reveal the deep cleft between her swelling breasts. Turning up the long sleeves, she used a silk scarf she had found to cinch in her waist. As she observed herself in the little mirror on the wall, Audra decided she would not now be mistaken for a boy.

Back in the main cabin, she poured herself a glass of wine and sat down to await Brock's return. There was a knock at the door and after adopting a purposely seductive pose, Audra called out:

"Come in!"

The door opened, but it was Ned who entered the cabin!

Blushing furiously, Audra bolted upright, pulling the neck of her shirt together. "Is the captain taking the wheel for a while?" she gulped, trying to hide her embarrassment.

"No, Your Ladyship." Ned hardly seemed aware of her appearance. He was clearly upset about something. "I don't know how to tell you this," he said, "but the captain didn't want you to know until we were underway."

"What are you trying to say, Ned?"

"The captain has gone back, milady. Back to the château. I told him it was madness, but he said he had something he had to settle."

"Oh God, no!" Audra paled at his words.

"He has always hated the compte for what he did to his brother," Ned went on.

"Surely he didn't go alone?" she whispered.

"The captain said it would be easier. He said he had friends. . . ."

"Oh, Ned, he is going to his death! There is an informer in the château! It was because of him the captain was shot the first time! You must turn *The Peregrine* around and head back!"

"No, Your Ladyship. That I will not do. I promised him I would not return until he sent me word."

"Ned, I beg you. . . ."

"No! I take my orders from the captain, and the captain's instructions were to see you safely home."

Chapter Twenty-Three

After Ned had left, Audra remained alone in the cabin while a maelstrom of anguished thoughts spun around in her head. She imagined the compte shooting Brock on sight, standing over him with a smoking pistol, a look of triumph on his dark, evil face. (Having never met the compte she pictured him as a monster.) But the image that appeared most vividly to her was that of Brock comforting the beautiful comtesse. He would tell her how sorry he was she had gone through so much because of him. Audra remembered how he had murmured so solicitously, "Poor little Celeste."

She could almost hear Celeste's husky voice in answer. "It's all right, *mon amour*. For you I would brave my husband's wrath a hundred times . . . a thousand."

Tears filled Audra's eyes as she rose and began to pace the length of the cabin. She did not doubt Brock's love for her now, yet he was still bound to Celeste by a chain he might never be able to sever. Celeste carried his unborn child. Even if Brock were to kill the compte and return to England, would he not want to see his child? Audra knew he would always feel an obligation to it and to Celeste. Duty and responsibility were part of his nature. Because of them he had left the navy and returned to help his grandmother and the tenants and villagers of Southcliffe.

The thought was an agonizing one. Would Celeste always be there? Would she always stand between them?

It was nearly dawn when Audra, again dressed in boy's clothing, reached Southcliffe.

Bess had stayed up to welcome her and the tears ran down her cheeks when Audra appeared. "Thank God you have returned safe and sound," she cried. "We've been so worried, milady."

"We?" Audra asked, giving the little maid a hug.

"Ned and me." Bess's cheeks flushed becomingly. "And Her Ladyship too when she arrived and found you gone."

"Her Ladyship? Do you mean Lady Deverell is here?"

"Yes, she arrived at Southcliffe a week ago."

Louis rode with Brock to a point near the gates of the château.

"We'll leave the horses here." He motioned to a

little grove of trees beside the road where they could tether and conceal their mounts. "I will go ahead and contact Marie," he told Brock. "Wait a few minutes and then follow me around to the east side of the château by the stables. Keep to the shadows and pray no one sees you."

Brock did as Louis suggested, skirting the front gates where he knew the gatekeeper kept a close watch. He made his way silently along the edge of the wooded area that bordered the château, keeping in the shade of the tall, Lombardy poplars.

The bright, moonlit night was making it more difficult for him to remain unobserved. There was a drive up ahead leading from the stables into the woods. When he reached it, he stopped.

He must now move along the driveway, completely out in the open until he reached the shelter of the stable. From here he could see there was a dim light burning from the direction of the kitchens and sculleries. A lamp also burned in the servants' quarters, but the rest of the château was in darkness.

When the moon slipped behind a cloud, Brock made his dash along the driveway. It seemed to take forever before he reached the shelter of the stable. He paused in the shadows, catching his breath, and was startled by a low voice behind him.

"Who goes there?"

Brock spun around, drawing his pistol as he did so. "Don't move or call out," he hissed.

"Is that *you*, Captain?" asked the voice. Its owner stepped away from the building so that the moonlight illuminated his face. "I recognized you by your size," he whispered. "Don't you know me?

Gaston Dubois, the stable master?"

Where had he seen that face before? Brock pondered. Then he remembered. "You're one of Jean Paul's men, aren't you?" He was certain he had seen Gaston in the smuggling cave. He remembered the dark, tanned face, the wide, white grin. Brock lowered his pistol.

The other nodded. "I caught sight of Louis entering the château a few minutes ago. Have you something planned, Captain? May I be of help?"

"I've come to see the comtesse, Gaston. I heard she had been badly beaten by the compte. She was kind enough to hide me once and save my life, now I wish to see if I may be of service to her."

"Isn't it risky, Captain? The compte is still in residence."

"I think, perhaps, it is time I confronted him, Gaston. We have a score of long-standing to settle."

"But the servants fear and obey him without question. If he should summon them . . ."

"Louis is going to take care of the compte's manservant and stand guard outside the bedchamber door while I pay my respects to your master." He considered a moment. "I can also use you, my friend, if you wish to help."

"Of course, Captain. I would be honored to be of assistance."

"Then station yourself outside the servant's quarters and inform Louis if anyone should stir."

"I will do that with pleasure, Captain, but I must warn you. It is said there is an informer in the château. What if he—"

"I will try not to wake him." Brock grinned.

"Don't look so worried, Gaston, remember I have the element of surprise on my side."

A light signalled from the château. Gaston wished Brock well and watched him swiftly cross the open courtyard to the shelter of the doorway, where he quickly slipped into the kitchen.

"*Bon soir*, Captain," Marie whispered as he entered. She gave him a worried little smile. "Do you think this is wise? I had hoped you would return to England." And yet she was so glad to see this tall, compelling man again, to have him standing so close to her. Could he hear how fast her heart was beating?

"I *was* on my way back home when Louis told me about your mistress."

Inwardly Marie called Louis several unmentionable names.

"How is the comtesse now?" Brock asked.

"Her bruises are healing. A rib was possibly cracked, the doctor said, but—"

"The compte allowed you to call a doctor?" Brock was surprised.

"It was necessary, Captain, or she would have died. She hemorrhaged greatly when she lost the babe."

For a moment Brock stared at her wordlessly. Celeste had lost the babe she carried. His babe. Despite his dismay over the conception of this child, he now felt intense anger at the man who had caused its death.

"Was the compte aware of the comtesse's condition before he lifted his hand to her?"

"*Non.* He did not know until later. The comtesse told him then that it was *his* child she had lost. *His* heir. She wanted to punish him, you see. I think she has succeeded. He has not come out of his apartments since it happened."

"You mean he believes he was the father?" Brock was frankly surprised that learning his wife had been unfaithful to him, the compte would still accept the child as his own.

"Well, you see, the comtesse said—" Marie dropped her eyes, a blush staining her cheeks—"she said you always withdrew before . . ."

Brock was incredulous. "And he accepted that?"

"It is practiced, Madame told me, by those of the nobility who fear being impregnated by their common-born lovers."

Brock felt his ire rising. Common-born am I? Then he almost laughed aloud. What was he thinking if? To all of them, even Celeste, he was only Peregrine, a common English smuggler.

"Will you take me to your mistress now, Marie?"

"*Oui.* Please follow me."

They left the kitchen and went through the scullery and down a dark side corridor. Marie carried a single candle to light their way, but as they progressed from the servants' area to the main corridors of the château and out across the immense hall, the moonlight shining through the multipaned windows helped illuminate the graceful, curving staircase they sought.

Both of them knew the way up the marble stairs and across the wide gallery. They paused outside the comtesse's bedchamber and Marie motioned to Brock to let her enter first and awake her mistress. She opened the latch and stepped into the room and

Brock followed her, closing the heavy door behind him and waiting as Marie crossed the room to the large, gilt bed. She lit the branch of candles on the night table and then approached the sleeping form. Gently, she shook the comtesse's shoulder.

"Wake up, madame."

"Wha-what is it?" Celeste mumbled.

"The captain is here to see you."

"Peregrine? Here?" The comtesse pushed herself up on her elbows, brushing a lock of silky hair from her eyes. "Oh, Marie, I look a fright."

"You look beautiful, Celeste," Brock answered, moving closer to the bed. Although the bruises on her face had faded, they were still evident, especially a dark, almost yellowish disfigurement around one eye.

"Peregrine!" Her face lit up at the sight of him, but then her gaze swept over him. "Why are you wearing those dreadful clothes?"

Brock laughed. "I have crossed France posing as a farmer."

Marie moved deferentially away as they began to talk.

"Did your little English countess find you?"

"Yes. She travelled with me."

"Is she here?"

"No. I sent her back to England, but I could not leave when I learned what Philippe had done to you. I had to come and tell you how sorry I am. I feel totally to blame."

"Did you hear that I lost the child I was carrying?"

"Marie just told me."

"It was yours, Peregrine. Did you know that? And

because you had sired it, I wanted it. I truly did. But now I feel I am well rid of it. What would I have done with a child? Even now the thought of being burdened with the bearing and raising of it . . ." She shuddered. "Besides, it would probably have ruined my figure."

Brock had never suffered from any illusions about Celeste. It had always been clearly apparent to him that she thought of no one but herself and her own pleasures; still he had never realized before this moment how completely spoiled and selfish she was. What a poor mother she would have made! He could imagine she would have ignored the child unless it pleased her to see him and as he grew older, he would, in all probability, been only a hated reminder of the passing years.

"You have been through a great deal," Brock found himself saying. "I am sorry for the pain I caused you. If there is anything I can do to make amends . . ."

"There is!" Celeste cried, her dark eyes flashing. "You can kill Philippe for me!"

"Celeste—"

"He made me lose your son, didn't he? I hate him! I hate him! If I could leave this room, myself, I would kill him in his bed!" At her last words she brought her little fist down again and again on the coverlet before her. Her eyes were wild with hate as she remembered what Philippe had done to her, remembered the scene in his study and how it had all started. She recounted it now to Brock:

"You wanted to see me, Philippe?" she had asked him. She had been getting ready for bed when she had been summoned and now stood before him in sheer nightdress and peignoir, her lustrous blue-black hair falling in a cloud over her shoulders.

"*Oui, ma chèrie.*"

The open lust she had at first glimpsed in his eyes when she had drifted toward him now had been carefully masked. He slowly rose from his chair and approached her. Celeste had felt a little stab of fear. There was a dark, purposefulness in his eyes that she had never seen before. He took hold of her wrist and propelled her toward the door. "Come with me," he had said.

They had stood together in the love nest. Celeste's heart had begun to beat wildly once she had realized where they were headed. How had he found out about the room? Who had shown him where to find it? Philippe had pulled her through the château, down corridors and around corners until they had reached the cupboard. He had shoved her into it, had slid open the door and pushed her up the stairs.

"Most delightful, don't you think, *ma chèrie*? Notice the oversized bed, the mirrors placed so strategically in the canopy."

"Philippe, please."

"There is something in particular I want you to see. A portrait."

He had grasped her shoulder and shoved her across the room to stand before it.

"It's an excellent likeness of you, *ma chèrie*. Also, I understand, of your English smuggler. Notice how well he is enjoying you. Was he such a good lover, Celeste?"

She had known it was useless to deny anything.

Suddenly, she had become angry with him. "*Oui*," she had cried. "The very best! There is no comparison between you!"

He had slapped her across the face, so unexpectedly, so savagely, that she had fallen back against the heavy footboard of the bed. She had looked up at him, her eyes wide with surprise. He had never laid a hand on her before.

"Damned little whore!" he had choked.

He had continued raining blows to her face and the side of her head, until reeling, crying out from the pain, her legs had collapsed and she had slid to her knees on the floor before him.

He had stood over her, his hands in menacing fists, his chest heaving from the exertion.

Celeste had lowered the arms that she had brought up to shield her head. Already a deep bruise was appearing under one of her eyes and her nose had started to bleed.

"*Nom de Dieu*, Philippe!" she had moaned. "Would you kill me?"

"You deserve it!" he had spat. "Furnishing a room for your sin and depravities! Hiring an artist to paint your lustful copulation!" Philippe's face had been black with rage as he started for her again, hauling her to her feet and pummelling her with a flurry of blows to the body that made her scream out in agonizing pain.

"Humiliate me, will you?" he had grunted, each time a blow connected. "Cuckold me with that English bastard!"

Celeste had looked up at him through a whirling haze of pain. "Please stop, Philippe," she had sobbed. "I thought you loved me."

"I *did* love you. You were the most precious of my possessions. Now I wish I'd never laid eyes on you! Was the Englishman the first, Celeste, or had there been others?"

Dizzy and confused, she had not immediately answered and he had taken her silence for assent. He had let out a hoarse, crazed roar and come at her again. Feebly she had tried to escape from him, but a kick caught her in the ribs and she had gone down hard on the floor. The second kick had caught her in the abdomen and merciful oblivion had descended.

As Celeste described to Brock all the fear and degradation and pain she had felt, her voice rose, becoming higher and shriller. Although angry and disgusted by what Philippe had done, Brock was alarmed that Celeste might wake the château and began at once to calm her.

"I will do all I can," he said softly, motioning to Marie to come to her mistress's side. "Believe me, the swine will pay for his cruelties." He took Celeste gently by the shoulders, pushing her back against the pillows. "Now you must rest." He nodded to Marie who was now beside him, but as he tried to draw back, Celeste caught at his hand.

"It was the informer who told Philippe," she said. "You must find him for me too, Peregrine!"

"You still do not know his identity?"

"*Non.*" She brought Brock's hand to her lips. "My letter did reach you?"

"Oui."

"Oh, Peregrine, did you think of me at all during those weeks we were apart?"

"You know I did," he said, trying to placate her. "I wouldn't be here—"

"Even when you made love to your little English countess?"

That remark, he thought, did not warrant an answer.

"I didn't expect you to be faithful, Peregrine. It was too long a time and I know your needs." She gave a husky, little laugh. "I should know them, shouldn't I? Ah, *mon amour*, just looking at you makes me . . . But the doctor says I should not." She pouted. "Not for weeks!"

"How hard that will be for you, *ma chèrie*," a scathing voice broke in. "When you are so used to spreading your legs for anything in breeches!"

"Philippe!" Celeste let out a gasp, her eyes wide with horror and Brock whirled about to face le compte de Lascalles at last.

There was a mirthless smile on Philippe's thin lips as his cold, dark eyes looked up into Brock's. He was not as tall a man, but well-proportioned and clearly in control of the situation as he pointed a slim rapier at Brock's chest.

"And you, of course, are the elusive Captain Peregrine, smuggler and lover extraordinaire! I have waited a long time to meet you."

"And I you, monsieur." Brock's hazel eyes had hardened as his right hand went instinctively to the pocket that held his pistol.

"I wouldn't make the attempt, Captain," de Lascalles said, moving menacingly a step closer so that the sharp tip of his sword pierced Brock's coat. "Please remove and drop your weapon on the floor."

Brock did as he was told and then slowly raised his arms, a slow grin touching the corners of his lips. "Do you intend to kill me right here, or are you gentleman enough to offer me a challenge?"

"A challenge, *certainment*, but on *my* terms. *I* choose the weapon." His sly smiled broadened. "Rapiers it will be. It should not take me long."

"*Non*, Peregrine! Don't fight him!" Celeste cried out. "He is an expert with the sword!"

But Brock ignored her, doffing his coat and beginning to remove his boots.

The compte turned to Marie and nodded in the direction of the open door through which he had come. It led to a sitting room and beyond it to his own bedchamber.

"Fetch me the mate to this rapier from the wall in my room," he ordered the maid. He stepped back in his stockinged feet, testing the flexibility of his blade. The lace ruffles of his shirt fell over his hands, but he did not roll up his sleeves as Brock had done.

Brock stood before the elegant compte, looking like a poor peasant in his homespun shirt and heavy, coarse breeches. Yet, the set of his broad shoulders, the strong line of his jaw, showed nothing of the subservient as he faced his opponent. His expression had lightened. It was as if he had been living in expectation of this moment for a long time and was relieved that it had finally arrived.

Celeste on the other hand was still crying out from her bed, "You'll kill him, Philippe! I know you will!"

Her husband turned to her. "Thank you for your confidence in me, *ma chèrie*. If it were not for your wailings, I might not have wakened." He smiled at her. "Inadvertently, you have helped me dispose of him."

Celeste fell back on her pillows, her hands to her mouth, her eyes wide and frightened. As Marie crossed before the bed to hand the rapier to Brock, she gave her mistress a disdainful glance.

"*Bonne chance*!" she murmured under her breath as Brock clasped the weapon. He had no time to test the slim blade.

"*En garde*!" de Lascalles cried immediately.

"At your service," Brock answered, turning to face the Frenchman.

There was the customary brief salute and then the swords rang together.

"So that you will know, monsieur," Brock announced to his opponent, "I fight not only to avenge your foul treatment of your wife and my friend, Jean Paul Beaudette, but also for more personal reasons."

"And what are those reasons?" Only Philippe's mouth smiled as he expertly parried Brock's flashing blade. His eyes were like two hard, black agates.

"I seek revenge for my brother's brutal death at your hands."

"Your brother?"

"Lord Deverell. Surely you remember the man you tortured so slowly and agonizingly in your dungeons?" He gave a fierce thrust toward de Lascalles's chest, but it was deftly blocked.

"So you are not a common smuggler after all, but an aristocrat." Philippe clicked his tongue. At the moment, his head was cooler than Brock's and he was carefully gauging the other's ability. The rapier, he saw, was not his antagonist's weapon. Although Brock's swordplay was strong and dangerous, de Lascalles surmised that he was inclined to take risks. All he had to do, therefore, was to remain patient and calm and watch for his advantage.

Brock could see that Philippe was an experienced and skillful swordsman. He was cunning and careful and it was near impossible to break through his guard. But he knew that on his side he had more strength and at least ten years. If he kept up a murderous pace and drove him hard, perhaps de Lascalles would weary. In the meantime, he decided, it wouldn't hurt to make him lose his temper. The man was too damn cool and composed.

"I'm surprised you even fight me," Brock taunted Philippe. "I thought you only picked on defenseless women and shackled prisoners."

"You English scum! You dare condemn *me*! You, who stole my wife!"

"It wasn't hard." Brock countered a savage thrust. "How did you, a weak, impotent milksop ever expect to please a passionate, hot-blooded woman like Celeste?"

"You filthy, rutting bastard!" Philippe choked, now completely enraged by Brock's baiting. He lunged at him wildly, his cool plan of action forgotten. "Your kind is easy to deal with," he spat. "You should have seen your cowardly brother begging for his life!"

"Liar! By God, I'll kill you for that!"

Each man now fought in a fury of hate. The tempo of the duel increased, becoming more frenzied, more desperate!

Celeste sat erect in her bed, her darting eyes following the swift thrust and parry of the rapiers.

Philippe suddenly grasped the initiative and began to drive Brock backward toward the opposite wall of the room with the flashing brilliance of his wrist. Yet Brock continued to counter well, turning de Lascalles's sword aside again and again.

For a moment, with a swift riposte, Brock seemed to gain the advantage and Marie, watching in the shadows, gave a sigh of relief. Then Philippe's cunning came to the fore. He was wearying in the attack and he knew it. His only hope was to drive Brock into a corner and make a quick end of it. Again he pressed the attack. Steel rang against steel, together with the sounds of the men's labored breathing.

Ruthlessly de Lascalles's dazzling blade thrust at his opponent's broad expanse of chest. Brock was not used to being on the defensive for so long and yet he could not seem to manage to turn the play around. Philippe was coming at him like a madman, lunging and thrusting so swiftly that only by strong, dexterous parrying was Brock able to escape imminent death.

As they approached the corner of the room close to where Marie stood, the maid suddenly saw Brock's guard waver and, thinking he was certain to be run through, gave a despairing cry.

It broke de Lascalles's concentration and Brock was able to sidestep and change the direction of the attack. Wielding his blade with lightning speed he advanced, his strong thrusts causing the tiring Philippe to concentrate his energies solely on avoiding a fatal thrust.

"Had enough, de Lascalles?"

"Go to hell!"

"Perhaps." Brock was panting now. "But I intend to take you with me!"

He lunged violently forward on his right foot, aiming for Philippe's heart. De Lascalles's now-aching arm was just a trifle too slow in parrying Brock's deadly blade. Finding its mark unguarded, it thrust deep and true. Philippe's sword clattered to the floor as he fell.

The room was deathly still. Brock stood gazing down at the body of his enemy, the bloody rapier still held in his hand. At last he had had his revenge on the man he had hated above all others. The man who had robbed his family of its rightful heir, through the cruelest and most dastardly of methods—slow torture! The man who had inflicted similar pain on his friend, Jean Paul, and even on the wife he had professed to love to obsession.

Why then, Brock thought, did he not feel triumphant? Instead, he felt nothing. Absolutely nothing! Only a deep weariness. He sighed and turned away.

"Oh, *mon amour*, you did it!" Celeste let out a cry from the bed. "You killed him for me. Now I am free!" She clapped her hands together.

Brock did not even look at her. Quickly he handed the rapier to Marie, who was holding out his coat and boots to him.

"You must go now. Quickly!" she said.

He nodded and thanked her.

Puzzled a little by his seeming lack of emotion, she

watched him dress. When he was ready, Brock strode to the door, completely ignoring Celeste and her entreaties to come to her. Cautiously, he lifted the latch and slipped out into the dimly lit corridor.

He got no further.

Two men stood before him, pistols pointed in his direction. From their appearance he recognized them as the same men he had looked down upon from the cavity in the love nest.

"I am afraid you are well covered, Captain," another voice said, and a smiling Gaston Dubois stepped out of the shadows.

Chapter Twenty-Four

Audra slowly awoke, blinking her eyes from the brilliant sun which was streaming in through her bedchamber windows. Shading them, she saw Bess, standing at the end of her bed with a tray in her hands.

"Is it very late?" Audra asked, sitting up.

"Past noon, milady, but it was nearly dawn when you found your bed."

Audra looked around the familiar room. How good it felt to be back at Southcliffe! It seemed almost as if she had come home. If only Brock were with her, she thought, feeling again that stab of fear to her heart. Was he all right? Was he still alive? She must not think of that!

Bess set the breakfast tray across Audra's lap. "I only brought you a currant bun and some hot chocolate," she said. "If you would like more . . ."

"This will be fine." Audra smiled at her. "No, don't leave, Bess. I want you to tell me what has gone on here at Southcliffe since I've been gone. How is Ned?"

While Audra sipped at her hot chocolate, Bess admitted to her mistress that she had been seeing quite a lot of Ned. She blushed as she said it, making Audra ask, "You care for him, don't you, Bess?"

"Yes," the girl replied, nodding, a smile of happiness lighting her face. "And he for me. He has asked me to marry him, milady. Can you imagine that? Even after I told him about the earl and all."

"I said it would make no difference if someone really loved you, Bess."

"I know you did, milady," Bess acknowledged, "and you were right. We plan to be married in September. That is, of course, if it should suit you and the captain."

"I see no reason why it shouldn't."

But Bess had not missed the look that had come to Audra's eyes at the mention of the captain's name. Hastily she added, "He'll come back, milady. Ned says he will and Ned is always right."

Audra could not help a little smile at Bess's blind belief in Ned's wisdom, but her eyes still remained uncertain. "I pray he will, Bess. I pray it with all my heart."

Lady Deverell always took a nap after luncheon and so Audra did not see her until later in the afternoon when she joined the dowager in the drawing room. She was surprised when Her Ladyship rushed to meet her, and with tears in her eyes embraced her.

"I have been so worried about you, Audra," she exclaimed. "When you didn't answer the letters I addressed to Southcliffe, I came down here myself to see what had happened to you."

"I'm sorry, Your Ladyship. It was all so rushed. I hadn't time to think or to let anyone know."

"I realize that now," Lady Deverell said. "Ned told me all about it after I had pestered the life out of him."

They sat down opposite one another and the dowager quietly asked, "How is Brock?"

"He—he was fine last night."

"Have you decided anything between you?"

"No. Nothing definite."

"Stubborn dolt!"

Audra looked so uncomfortable that Lady Deverell quickly changed the subject. "I heard about you cutting your hair. I must say it looks very pretty."

"It has grown over the weeks. Bess was able to pin up the back a little."

"It still amazes me to think that you successfully posed as a boy and travelled right across France alone."

"It wasn't quite as easy as it sounds."

"I'm sure it wasn't, and yet you managed to get the message through to Brock. I'm proud of you, Audra. I knew you had grit, but you've shown your mettle admirably."

At Lady Deverell's insistence, Audra told her

about her journey and how, because of the constant rain, she had contracted a fever.

"It is no wonder you look a little thinner, my dear. Are you feeling quite well now?"

Audra assured her that she had regained most of her strength and mentioned the kind Frau Meister and her husband and her recovery at the baron's estate. Lady Deverell asked many questions, so that it wasn't until some time later when the two of them were dining together that Audra finally concluded her story with her return on *The Peregrine.*

"You thought right up until the moment you sailed that Brock was coming with you?" Lady Deverell asked, looking surprised.

"Yes. He didn't tell me he was staying behind."

"Would you have objected?"

"Of course!" Audra cried. "If he should run into the compte, that man would kill him instantly, or at the very least imprison him!"

"But I don't understand." Lady Deverell frowned. "Ned only said that Brock had a mission to complete at the château."

"There is more to it than Ned knows. You see, Your Ladyship—" Audra strove to control her voice—"Brock and the comtesse de Lascalles were lovers."

"Lovers!"

"The affair was something he had instigated long before he met me. Brock wanted to get even with the compte for the torture he had inflicted upon David and a swift death would not satisfy him. He wanted the compte to suffer and suffer greatly for what he had done. Celeste, the compte's wife, is very beautiful and when Brock discovered how much her husband loved her, he—"

"Don't tell me he took the comtesse by force!"

"Surely you know your grandson better than that! He didn't need to seduce her, either, for Celeste fell rather willingly into his arms." Audra swallowed hard. "She was promiscuous, you see, even before she met Brock. But, unfortunately, it was her affair with him that the compte learned of. He savagely took his wrath out on Celeste. That is why Brock went back to the château. He felt responsible for the beating she received at her husband's hands."

"And rightly so." The dowager's face had grown quite pale.

"But he *could* be walking right into a trap!"

"More likely back into milady's arms," drawled a voice from the doorway.

"Jason!" Lady Deverell exclaimed. "What on earth are you doing here at Southcliffe?"

Jason Deverell in puce satin and ivory lace strolled unhurriedly into the room, kissed his grandmother on the cheek, smiled at Audra and sat down at the head of the table.

"You suggested often enough, Grandmama," he answered her, "that the fresh air at Southcliffe was extremely beneficial. So, considering London's present heat, I decided to come down."

Barrow quickly set a place before him and poured out a glass of wine. Jason immediately picked up the glass and took a long sip.

"Now then," he said, his eyes swinging to Audra, "what's this about Brock and a promiscuous comtesse?"

"So you eavesdropped." Audra's voice was

disdainful. "Were you listening long?"

"Not long, but my ears pricked up at *that.*" He smiled. "Who is the lady?"

"La Comtesse de Lascalles."

"Good lord! The wife of David's murderer!"

"Exactly."

Jason chuckled. "Well, that is most interesting. Quite clever of Brock, in fact, to undermine his enemy before he strikes." He glanced again at Audra. "Though I doubt it would appeal to *you.*" His mouth twitched. "My word, what *did* you do with your hair?"

"I cut it."

"Why? Some new style?" He considered her a moment. "I do believe it suits you."

"Thank you," Audra said stiffly.

Lady Deverell was looking at Jason, but there was a blankness in her eyes as if she were miles away.

"Whatever is the matter, Grandmama? Worried about Brock? If anyone can take care of himself, he can."

"How could he have been so foolish?" she murmured.

"Doubtless because the comtesse is very beautiful." Jason laughed, his eyes again on Audra, as if hoping for a reaction. "And probably lusting hotly for him. Our Brock simply couldn't keep away from her. Had to rush right back between her thighs."

"That's enough, Jason!" his grandmother angrily admonished him.

"Dear me, it appears I have been indelicate." Jason gave a little bow of his head in apology but the smile never left his lips.

"Unfortunately your indelicacy appears to increase with the amount of spirits you consume," Lady Deverell snapped.

"Why, Grandmama, I am only on my second glass of wine."

"Humph! And just how many flasks of brandy did you drain on your way down from London?"

"Forgive me, madam, I did not know you were taking a count."

Angrily, Lady Deverell rose to her feet. "Audra and I will leave you to your dinner and take our tea in the drawing room."

Jason merely shrugged. "As you will."

"I hope Jason did not upset you," the dowager said later when she and Audra were settled.

"I am quite used to him now."

"He appears to be aware of your affection for Brock." She put a hand over Audra's. "I think, under the circumstances, your understanding of this unwise affair of Brock's most admirable. Don't pay any mind to Jason's taunts."

"Jason seems to obtain pleasure in hurting people."

"It is because he is unhappy and bitter."

"Both conditions brought on by himself."

"Not altogether."

"What do you mean?"

The dowager shook her head. "Nothing, my dear. What I want to know now is when Ned is to meet Brock off the French coast?"

"All Ned told me was that Brock said he would

send word. Oh, Your Ladyship, it's been nearly twenty-four hours! What can have happened?"

They discussed the many practical reasons why Brock could have been delayed, but they did not mention what was really in the back of their minds. Finally, Lady Deverell rose.

"I am going to have a few words with Jason and retire," she said wearily.

"I think I will remain here for a little while. I doubt I could sleep."

"Audra, my dear . . ." the dowager began, then with a little sigh she shook her head and moved to the door.

It was close to an hour later when Audra left the drawing room and headed for the stairway. She had almost reached it when her eye caught sight of the open door of the library. Eager to put off the moment she had to go upstairs to her lonely room, she approached it.

A fire was still burning brightly in the fireplace and candles were ablaze on the mantel. Audra remembered so well seeing Brock's tall figure standing there. He had been attired in evening wear, a dark green velvet coat, and at her appearance he had raised his glass in a silent tribute to her. She could still hear that deep, resonant voice saying, "What a lovely vision you make, Audra. Do come in."

Audra entered the library as she had done then and moved to the couch beside the hearth. The very couch where she and Brock had first made love! She ached, remembering it all so clearly. She must push away the tormenting thoughts!

On the table before the couch she saw a cut glass decanter of brandy and a half-empty goblet. Her mind came back to the present. "Jason," she said aloud. He had probably been in here after dinner. She thought it rather surprising that he hadn't finished his drink. It was not like him to waste good brandy.

She moved across the room to the window overlooking the garden. This end of the room was in shadow and in the starlit night she could clearly make out the outlines of shrubs and bushes outside. How much better they looked now that they had been pruned and shaped.

Hearing footsteps, Audra turned her head toward the library door in time to see Jason enter the room. She stepped back. She could not bear another confrontation with him, more supercilious looks and taunting remarks. Quietly, she slipped behind the long, velvet curtains beside the window. Through a crack in the edge, she watched Jason head straight across the room, not looking to his left or right in his haste to reach the table where the brandy decanter and goblet sat.

Audra saw him withdraw what appeared to be a vial from the pocket of his coat and add some of its contents to the half-filled goblet on the table. Even from across the room, Audra could see that his hands shook as he lifted the goblet in both of them and downed the whole in one long swallow. He replaced the glass on the table and stood for a few moments regarding his hands, as if watching them steady themselves. Letting out a deep sigh, he seated himself at the end of the sofa.

Audra continued to watch as he poured himself another brandy and this time he sipped at the liquor, leaning his head against the back of the sofa. She wondered what had been in the vial he had added to the brandy. Was he taking some form of drug? As she continued to stare at him, she saw his head sink in the folds of his cravat and a moment later the left hand which held the brandy goblet relaxed, spilling the last of the liquid onto the rug beside the sofa as it tipped from his fingers. Jason slept.

Audra was relieved. She could now slip from the room without being observed. She quietly emerged from her hiding place, her eyes not moving from Jason's slack form. He slept on.

She had just tiptoed past him and was starting toward the door when a dry voice remarked from behind her:

"Looking for a drink?"

Startled, Audra spun around. Jason had raised his head and was regarding her with his usual mocking smile.

"No. I—I just wandered in here," she stammered.

"Don't leave on my account."

"I don't wish to disturb you."

"You won't. I don't sleep for long periods anymore. Even with the brandy."

"Why?" She couldn't help but gibe. "Does your conscience bother you?"

He regarded her. How lovely she looked in the candlelight. The short curls seemed to form a little halo about her head. Yet, he was sure, beneath that angellike exterior lurked a most passionate nature. He realized now that he had desired her from their first meeting. An idea entered his head, an idea that so greatly appealed to him that he immediately put it to work.

"I'm afraid I offended you tonight," he said, his eyes asking for her forgiveness. "I'm very sorry."

Puzzled and a little suspicious of his apology, Audra remained where she was, gazing straight at him.

"Will you sit down and have a brandy with me?" Jason asked quietly. "I think I'm going to have a long night of it." He winced and ran a finger along the inside of his high collar.

"You drink too much," she said. "That is your trouble."

"I only wish it were." He gave a little snort. "At least *that* could be cured."

"What do you mean?" Audra frowned, coming a little closer to him.

"Nothing." He shook his head. "I shouldn't even have mentioned . . ."

"What is it?" she insisted. "I saw you pour something into your brandy earlier."

"Only laudanum," he told her.

"But why? To help you sleep?" She stood directly before him now.

"No. I take it for a little problem I have. You see, it helps the pain."

"The pain! I did not know you suffered from pain. Have you seen a doctor?"

He laughed. "Many, many good physicians, I'm afraid. They all gave me a similiar diagnosis." He paused significantly. "I suffer from a type of malignancy. It is only a matter of time."

"What!" she cried, in surprise and disbelief.

He lowered his voice. "No one knows about this but Grandmama. And now you. It all started when the glands in my neck began to swell. It was not painful at first, just uncomfortable, but lately I've felt this pain in my chest. That is one of the reasons I came down here. I thought, perhaps, the clean, fresh air . . ."

"Can't something be done for you?"

"No. I am told other glands are enlarging in my body and pressing in on the neighboring organs. That is what causes my shortness of breath. My breathing and swallowing will slowly become more difficult and painful. When the process reaches the spine, I will be paralyzed."

The blue eyes were wide now with horror.

"I'm sorry," Jason again apologized. "I shouldn't have blurted all this out to you. The brandy has loosened my tongue. This disease is supposed to affect the liver and the doctors have forbidden me to drink. Stupid fools! I'd rather drink myself into my grave than go through all that hell. . . ." His voice drifted off.

"Oh, Jason," Audra said sympathetically, "I'm so sorry." She was kneeling by the sofa now, picking up the goblet that had dropped from his hand.

"Pour me another?" He smiled down at her. When he smiled in that way he reminded her so of Brock it tore at her heart.

She obeyed him and handed the goblet to him.

"You won't join me?" he asked.

She shook her head. "Jason, I think I have probably misjudged you." She sat down on the sofa beside him.

"No, you haven't misjudged me. I'm still a bastard. Anyone else if he discovered he hadn't long to live would be trying to redeem his life, trying to help people and leave behind a good mark beside his name. I don't feel that way." His voice rose. "I feel cheated and bitter. I don't give a damn for anything or anyone."

"How long has your grandmother known about this?" she questioned him. It explained Lady Deverell's actions to her grandson, why she had done so much for him and been so lenient with him.

"From the start," Jason said. "It was she who made me seek medical advice, although a fat lot of good it did me."

"Tonight she almost said . . . It explains a lot of things," Audra murmured.

"Does it? I hope you will keep this to yourself. Brock does not know and I would prefer he didn't."

Audra nodded. "If he comes back," she said under her breath.

But he had heard her. "He's *got* to come back!" he almost shouted. "Someone has to carry on the Deverell name! Damn the fool for going back to that château! Always had to play the bloody hero! Always had to defend—"

"I cannot blame him for returning. It was the honorable thing to do."

"Why? The beating is a matter between the comtesse and her husband. Why should Brock become involved?"

"Because she is carrying his child," Audra said quietly.

"Good lord!" Jason exploded. Then, after a moment, "Does Grandmama know?"

"No, and I'm sure he would rather she didn't."

"Brock has craved revenge for our brother for a long time," Jason pondered. "Now, with *this* added to it, it would be just like him to challenge the compte."

"Surely not! Not when he is completely surrounded by enemies! It would be suicide!"

Jason's arm went about her shoulders, but she was hardly aware of it. "I think I have alarmed you unnecessarily. It is more likely that Brock has only gone to see for himself the condition of the comtesse. That is all." He paused. "He may even be with her at this moment."

Oh, why had he said that? Audra wailed inwardly. She immediately pictured the little love nest in the château across the channel. She could see the portrait so clearly in her mind—Brock's strong profile, the intimate embrace. She felt a heavy feeling in the pit of her stomach as she imagined Brock consoling Celeste for the hurt her husband had inflicted upon her, taking her in his arms . . .

Jason's own arm tightened about Audra's shoulders, pulling her closer to him. She felt his warm breath against her cheek and yet she did not push him away. Poor man, he needed consoling even more than Celeste. Why, he was dying! Dying a slow and painful death!

"He may even now be holding her like this," Jason whispered to Audra. "Kissing her, caressing her.

Can't you imagine them together?" He lowered his head and found her lips and she let him kiss her lightly, tentatively.

"I've wanted you since the day I met you," he muttered hoarsely. "Come with me to my room, Audra. I need you so. We need each other."

"Jason . . ."

"A little happiness. It may be my last chance."

"Jason, I . . ." Oh, how had she got herself into this position? Audra thought, suddenly aware of the warm closeness of his body. She didn't want to hurt him. Gently, she pressed his hand and raised sympathetic eyes to his. In that instant, as their eyes met, she caught something before it was quickly masked. It was a look of triumph!

Damn him! He had been purposely working on her emotions! On her pity! Now he was sure he had succeeded. The conceit of the man! Angrily she pushed herself away from him and jumped to her feet.

"You are vile!" Sparks of indignation leapt in her eyes. "I doubt that you are ill at all! You've only been playing on my sympathy! Taking advantage of me when I'm worried half to death! You know I love Brock. You know and yet you tried . . ." She stumbled across the room to the door.

Jason Deverell frowned after Audra's departing figure. For the first time in his life he felt a twinge of conscience. It amazed him to realize that he actually cared what that chit of a female thought of him.

A little too late for that! He loosened his cravat, poured himself another brandy and settled down for a long, sleepless night.

Chapter Twenty-Five

While Brock had been escorted down to the dungeons below the château, Gaston had remained behind to issue instructions for the removal of the compte's body. With this accomplished, he entered Celeste's bedchamber. Calmed by Marie after an hysterical outburst, she now sat sobbing quietly in her bed.

"I'm sorry you were a witness to all this," Gaston said, swaggering a little as he approached her and giving an impatient gesture of dismissal to Marie.

"What are you going to do with him?" Celeste managed, watching Marie's tightly compressed lips as she turned and left the room.

"Your husband will be laid out in his study. The priest has already been summoned."

"I don't mean Philippe!" she cried. "The captain!

What do you intend to do with *him*?"

"He will be punished, madame. He is a seducer of women and a murderer."

"*Non*! That is a lie!"

Gaston ignored her exclamation. "He not only dishonored Monsieur la Compte, he stole what belonged to *me*."

Celeste's eyes widened. "You don't mean . . . You actually thought . . . I *never* belonged to *you*!"

"Oh, *oui*, you *were* mine!" he insisted. "You even painted us together—joined as one. We shared that love nest. Just the two of us. Until *he* came!" Cold fury showed in his dark eyes. "Now he will pay! Oh, *oui*, he will pay dearly!"

"You would not have him killed?" she asked fearfully.

"Eventually, perhaps. But first I want to repay him a little. Punish him until he begs for mercy!" His laugh made Celeste shiver.

"You would torture him just because he hurt your pride? Why, that's inhuman! You must be mad!"

"Am I? I cared very much for you, madame, and you rejected me for him. An Englishman! An enemy of our country!" He barked the words at her.

She knew then, if she had not sensed it earlier. "*You* were the informer, weren't you? It was *you* who told Philippe about the captain's movements!"

He nodded. "It was so easy to gain Jean Paul's confidence and become one of his men. I worked hard to try and convince him of my sincerity to his cause. He was so sure I was a valued anti-Bonapartist. The fool!" He laughed again.

"And you reported everything to Philippe. You

even had Jean Paul arrested and tortured!" Celeste's eyes narrowed. "*You* were responsible for telling my husband about the captain and me! It was *you*! He abused me because of *you*!"

Celeste flew at him then, using her nails to claw at his face. He gave her a rough shove back that made her fall sideways from the bed and crash onto the floor.

"Filthy pig! Judas!" She screamed at him.

He wiped the blood from his cheek and glared down at her. "Just remember, madame, that I am now in complete charge of this château. You will do as I say. I will be rewarded well for capturing such a valuable prisoner for France and stopping an enemy escape route." He smiled his wide, white grin that she had once found so appealing. "In a way I should be grateful to your captain for disposing of the compte for me. I was very tempted to do so myself. Bonaparte, in his gratitude for all I have done, may see fit to bestow the compte's title upon *me* now, since there are no heirs. In any case, I intend to make you my wife."

"Wife! You are suffering from delusions of grandeur, Gaston. You are only a servant! A common stable hand!"

His jaw tightened. "You took pleasure in me once."

"Ha!" she taunted him. "You were a fumbling clod compared to the captain. You—"

"Is that the reason you changed my face in the portrait?" he asked, his voice deadly calm. "Why you painted his face over mine?"

"How did you discover that?"

"It was after the captain was shot. *I* was behind that," he boasted. "I had learned you two had become lovers." He lent her no assistance as she crawled back into bed. "No trace could be found of the captain after the shooting. Some said he must have been picked up by his ship that same night, but I was sure he had been hidden somewhere. I searched the caves myself and the woods around the château. It was then that the compte decided to go back to Paris and asked me to accompany him and bring back some horses he had bought. I was away a week and in that time I got to thinking of where the captain could have been hidden and not discovered. I didn't like to believe you had taken him to *our* love nest. But I went there after I returned to the château and when I saw how you had changed the portrait, I knew."

"Gaston."

"It is too bad you are still too weak to accompany me down to the dungeons. I would like you to see your lover grovelling at my feet."

"Peregrine would *never* grovel!"

"You could, of course, prevent him from being tortured."

"How?" she asked suspiciously. "What would you have me do?"

"Why, marry me, of course. As soon as the compte has been buried."

"Never!"

"Then, I'm afraid your poor Captain Peregrine must take his full punishment."

* * *

The damp, stone cell in which he had been thrown had only a high, barred window. Through it, as the dawn approached, came a faint and indistinct light.

Slowly raising his head, Brock's first sight was of a large rat running by his outstretched hand as he lay on the dirty, straw-strewn floor.

The men who had dragged him down to the dungeon the night before had all taken a turn at him. While the two largest, despite his struggles, held him fast, the others went at him with their fists and pistol butts—first at his ribs and stomach, then at his head.

Blood had clouded his vision after a while and now his whole head throbbed in agony from the punishment it had taken. Every inch of his body seemed to be racked with pain.

He had been writhing on the floor after the beating, when Gaston had arrived and prodded him impatiently with the toe of his boot.

"Get up, Captain! Stand at attention before me!"

Brock had staggered to his feet, reeling before the grinning Dubois, who had nodded to the men to hold him upright.

"You don't look quite as handsome as you once did." Gaston laughed. "I doubt the comtesse would find you so attractive now."

"Traitorous bastard!" Brock spat, and a small mass of bloody spittle landed on Dubois's coat.

Gaston lifted a fist and drove it straight into Brock's face. Blood spurted out from his split nose and streamed down his chin.

"I would advise you to keep your mouth shut, Captain," he said, angrily brushing at his coat. "When we're through with you, you are going to be so ugly no female will ever look at you again!" He again punched the helpless man.

"That is for dishonoring the comtesse de Lascalles and murdering her husband!"

Brock glared back at him through eyes swollen almost shut and in the wavering lantern light he suddenly realized just where he had seen Dubois's face before. It was *he* making love to Celeste in the portrait in the love nest! Gaston Dubois must have been Celeste's lover before him! Jealousy was behind all this! Not devotion to the compte or loyalty to Bonaparte!

Now, several hours later, Brock tried to raise himself from the cell floor. The room swam before him. He did not remember when he had finally blacked out from Dubois's brutal beating, but unconsciousness had been a blessing.

And this is only the beginning, Brock thought to himself. It had taken his brother David days of torture before *he* had died.

He tried again and this time he pulled himself up and staggered forward, holding his side, past the slop bucket and over to where a pile of straw served as a bed. Falling back onto it, he lay there, gasping. He could hardly breathe through his nose and his mouth was dry and tasted of blood. God, but he had never been so thirsty!

The comtesse had demanded that Marie stay with her for the rest of the night. She was almost irrational, alternating between tears and rage, at the position in which she now found herself. Never once did she mention the captain or her recently deceased husband. Her thoughts were centered totally on herself.

It was nearly dawn when she finally closed her eyes, and Marie was able to slip from her side. She found that Brock was being heavily guarded in the dungeon and there was no possible way she could see him. Weary and disconsolate, Marie slowly made her way back to her mistress's bedchamber and fell asleep curled up in an armchair beside the comtesse's bed.

"Wake up, Marie!"

It was morning. The little maid raised her head and rubbed at her eyes.

"I've made a decision," the comtesse said. She was sitting up in bed with her hands clasped around her knees. "With Gaston threatening me, the sooner I leave the château the better."

"Leave, madame?"

"Don't look so stupid. It is quite intolerable for me here now. I will insist the funeral for the compte be held tomorrow in the chapel. Everyone will understand why I am not present, but the servants must *all* attend. All, that is, except you, Marie."

Marie was now sitting bolt upright, staring at her mistress. "But why—" she began.

"Sometime today you will arrange for a carriage to wait just outside the side gates at the time of the funeral service. Then, while everyone is there, you and I will make our escape." Celeste smiled at her maid. "Now, isn't that simple?"

Marie looked clearly distressed. "But where will we go?"

"Why, to Paris, of course. I have influential friends there. They will see to Gaston Dubois, never fear."

"But, madame, you are not well enough to travel," Marie declared.

"It has been a week and my strength is returning." Celeste's eyes shone. "Oh, Marie, I have not been to Paris since before I was married. I'm so looking forward to it!"

"Madame, have you forgotten the captain? We cannot just leave him."

"Word can be sent to his smuggling friends so that they may rescue him."

"At least Louis managed to escape last night before he was captured," Marie murmured.

"There. You see. Your Louis will send word," Celeste said, brushing the matter aside. "The captain is no longer our concern, Marie. What is most important is that we arrange for *our* departure without Gaston having the slightest suspicion. Now then, I wonder what gowns I should take with me?"

Although she moved almost in a daze, Marie was able to make the arrangements for the funeral as the comtesse had requested. Gaston turned out to be in full agreement with the small, quiet service. Yet, as she went about doing the tasks required of her, Marie's mind screamed at her: "You cannot leave the captain! His friends may be too late to save him! You must stay and help him escape!"

It was during the afternoon that she realized that her mistress was weaker than she thought. After being out of bed an hour trying to decide how much could be fitted into the small portmanteau, which was all they could carry with them, Celeste had fainted. Marie knew then that she would have to be there to assist the comtesse in her escape from the château. Her first duty lay with her mistress, no matter what her feelings were. Someone else would have to see to Captain Peregrine.

Marie waited for dark to escape from the château and arrange for the carriage's arrival the following morning before noon. She would seek out some friends who lived close to the château and where Louis, himself, might actually have taken refuge.

Louis. He had proved such a good friend. If it hadn't been for him Jean Paul's escape might never have been accomplished. Had Louis been able to send word to England of the captain's imprisonment?

She knew he would have done this if it had been at all possible. Louis would remember the cruel torture Jean Paul had been subjected to—how he had been beaten almost senseless. Louis was a kind and sensitive man and very courageous. Jean Paul had pointed this out to Marie many times. She knew her brother hoped she would be attracted to the big, shy man who clearly worshipped her. She must accept the fact that the captain was beyond her reach. Perhaps it was just as well she was leaving the château for a time. She would have time to think things out.

* * *

"Good evening, Captain. You *are* Captain Peregrine, are you not? One would hardly recognize you," Gaston Dubois sneered as the two burly guards dragged Brock to his feet.

"Water . . ."

"Of course. I imagine it is quite difficult to talk through those swollen lips. Give the captain some water, Emile."

Brock did not mask the eagerness with which he swallowed the cool liquid that was held to his mouth.

"Better? It's too bad you would not eat what was offered to you today. You must keep up your strength, Captain." He nodded to the two men. "All right, you may begin," he said, moving back as the two guards shoved Brock to the opposite end of the narrow cell.

There were chains embedded high in the wall and these were fastened to Brock's wrists, so that he would have hung from the wall by his arms if he had been a shorter man. As it was, his arms were almost yanked from their sockets.

"Strip off his shirt!" Dubois commanded, clearly enjoying his new authority. The men obeyed, standing back after this was completed and Brock faced the wall, his bronzed back bared to the waist.

"You have a fine body, Captain. Very strong. I was going to begin with ten stripes this first time, but I think you will be able to stand at least twenty."

Brock said nothing.

Dubois only shrugged, but as the largest of the two guards uncoiled a wicked-looking cat-o'-nine-tails from his belt, he licked his thin lips in anticipation.

And so it began. The first man administered ten murderous lashings of the whip before handing the bloodstained instrument over to the other who added ten more.

Brock's back was crisscrossed with deep, bleeding welts, but he had not uttered a cry of pain. He would not give Dubois that satisfaction.

"Leave him there!" Dubois ordered the men as they moved over to release Brock. There was a pleased smile on his face as he swaggered over to the heavy door. "You'll be begging for mercy by morning, Captain."

Brock knew that he must have lost consciousness, for the night was becoming a lighter gray when he again became aware of his surroundings.

The pain was excruciating! He felt it right through his torn flesh to his bones. As he tried to straighten his sagging body, perspiration ran down his forehead and into his eyes. He blinked to clear them. He had no feeling at all in his arms, and with the broken ribs pressing so hard into his left lung, his breathing had become a rasp.

This was a hell of a way to die! he thought. And die he would, he was sure now, for who was there to rescue him?

Louis had no doubt been captured with him, which left only Marie. She could never manage it alone. How could anyone escape from this place, deep in the bowels of the château? It was only because Jean Paul had been taken from here to supposedly show the compte where he had stored his English gold that an ambush was accomplished and he was freed and spirited away to England on

The Peregrine.

The Peregrine—he could almost feel the sea spray on his face, see Ned standing at the wheel. How his thoughts had begun to ramble! Ned. Ned knew he was here at the château, but Ned was waiting for a message from him. By the time he realized no message was coming, it would be too late.

Had it been worth this anguish, Brock wondered, to kill de Lascalles? To avenge David's death? Yes. He could not regret it. It had been something he had had to do.

But what if he had stayed on *The Peregrine* that night and returned to England with Audra? She might even now be lying in his arms. No! He must not think of Audra. He would go out of his head if he thought of her and what he had given up!

But she would not leave his mind. What must she have thought when she learned he had gone back to the château? He had felt responsible for Celeste's beating and yet she hadn't cared a whit about the child she had lost. His child. Perhaps now, he would never sire a son or daughter of his own. It was doubtful Jason would marry, so the Deverell bloodline would end. Unless . . . Could he have planted his seed in Audra on the trip back from Austria? Oh God, if he were to die, he hoped he had! He sighed deeply and his head fell again to his chest.

It was daylight. Bright daylight. There was a noise at the door of the cell. With an effort, Brock lifted his head on his aching neck. Dear God, was it Dubois again?

"*Mon Dieu*!" said a familiar voice. "They've left him hanging! Can you get him down?"

Someone started working on the manacles on his wrists.

"Can you hear me, Captain? It's Louis." A flask of water was held to his lips and he managed to drink a little, but most of it ran down his chin.

"Louis . . ." The word was said hoarsely, through lips barely able to move.

"I've come to rescue you. Henri and I have taken care of the guards. The other occupants of the château are all in the chapel attending a funeral service for the compte."

"How did you . . ." Brock muttered, but Louis shushed him.

"We'll talk later. We haven't much time. We have to get you out of here."

As Henri unclasped the iron manacles around Brock's wrists, he collapsed into Louis's arms.

"Captain," Louis said, staggering a little, "we are going to help you." He switched his support to one side of Brock's heavy body and Henri quickly took the other. "But you are going to have to walk. Do you think you can?"

Brock nodded and took a step forward. A tearing pain shot through his side and made him groan aloud in agony.

Henri looked hopelessly across at Louis.

"Gag me!" Brock demanded, "so I won't cry out."

With his free hand, Louis unclasped the neckerchief he wore, rolled it into a ball and stuffed it into Brock's mouth. They then began their slow, halting walk toward the open cell door. Perspiration stood out on Brock's forehead and his teeth bit down hard into the cloth jammed in his mouth.

Fortunately, it was not far from the cell to the stone steps that led up from the dungeon to the cellars of the château. The steps, however, were difficult for Brock to manage and he fell twice, taking the two men down with his heavy frame. Each time they fell, they were sure someone would hear them, but after waiting a moment, they continued on their way.

From the cellars, they were forced to traverse a long corridor and up another stairway to the pantry above. Brock almost blacked out once, and they had to wait agonizing minutes before he could continue. As they went on, Brock's weight grew heavier and heavier on the two men, although he was doing his best to keep himself upright.

"We'll never get him outside to the woods," Louis gasped. "We'll have to hide him in the château."

"But where?"

"The love nest. It's the closest place and no one but us and the comtesse and Marie know of it."

The two men practically had to drag Brock up the steep stairs to the hidden room. They paused just outside the door to regain their breath and then struggled forward again, entering the room and depositing Brock on his stomach on the big canopy bed.

Louis pulled the gag from his mouth and he and Henri sat down on the edge of the bed themselves for a minute, breathing deeply and rubbing their sore shoulders. Louis removed the top from the flask of water he carried in his coat pocket and held it to

Brock's lips. "Are you all right, Captain?" he asked after Brock had greedily drained the flask.

"Feeling's coming back in my arms," Brock gasped.

"Hurts like the very devil, I'll wager," Louis said. "Wish we had thought to bring something stronger to give you."

He pushed Henri aside and began to strip back the bedclothes from under the big man until Brock lay only on a sheet. From the washstand, he brought back a basin of water and a cloth and did his best to bathe the torn flesh of Brock's back. The wounded man flinched as the dried blood was washed away and clamped his teeth together hard.

"We've got to leave," Henri urged his friend.

"You just sleep, Captain, and get your strength back," Louis said, placing a pistol on the bed by Brock's right hand and pulling the second sheet over him.

The last thing Brock remembered was hearing a key turn in the lock.

Chapter Twenty-Six

It was very early that morning when Ned got the message brought across the channel by the same French smuggler who had delivered the previous ones.

Captain killed compte in duel. Imprisoned in château dungeon. Imperative be rescued as soon as possible.

—Louis

Ned looked at the words a long time and then decided, although it went against his better judgment, that he must share this information with the young countess as soon as she awakened. She was the only one who knew the château. Perhaps she would be able to offer some suggestions as to how they should proceed. The captain would not be as easy to rescue as Jean Paul.

After arriving in England, Jean Paul had been taken to London to see Viscount Castlereagh. He had remained there, his injuries being treated by the viscount's own physician. If only he could have been part of the rescue party, Ned thought. If only Jean Paul could lead them.

At Ned's summons, Audra went to the library to see him as soon as she was dressed. "You've heard from the captain, haven't you?" she asked as she entered the room.

"Not from him personally, milady. I had a message from Louis this morning that the captain has been imprisoned in the château dungeon." He handed her the note to read and Audra read it aloud, the color draining from her cheeks at its contents.

"It must be tonight, Ned," she whispered, not daring to think of what torture Brock might have already suffered.

He nodded. "I know that. You have been to the château. Have you any suggestions as to the best way to attempt this rescue?"

Audra shook her head. "I was taken in at night through a back way and up to a secret room," she explained. "I was hidden there until dawn and then taken out the same way. I know little about the château or where the dungeons are located, but would not Louis or Marie have already devised a plan?"

"Perhaps, but they will no doubt need our help. The château will be well-guarded."

"Who can be in command now that the compte is

dead?" Audra frowned. "Certainly the comtesse would never imprison Brock."

"The compte must have had loyal men who—"

"The informer!" Audra broke in. "He seems the most likely leader and the compte's men could be working with him. Ned, I don't think this is going to be easy."

"I have always enjoyed a challenge," drawled a voice and Jason Deverell rose from the sofa before the fire where he had been lying unnoticed since the night before. He yawned, delicately covering his mouth with a lace-trimmed handkerchief. "When do we start?"

"How much have you overheard?" Audra demanded.

"Enough to know that Brock has managed to kill the murderer of our brother and has been imprisoned as a result."

"Jason, please don't speak of this to anyone," Audra begged him. "Especially to your grandmother. Ned and I will cross the channel tonight on *The Peregrine* and enlist the aid of Louis and his friends—"

"And I fully intend to accompany you. Brock's life is in danger and he is Grandmama's only hope. I think you know what I mean, Audra." He looked steadily at her. "You will not find me an encumbrance. I am quite deadly with a pistol."

"Jason, I don't—"

"I think we should accept his help, milady," Ned said quietly. "We can use every man we can get."

And so it was decided. Audra did not like the thought of Jason coming with them. It was not like him to think of anyone but himself and she did not wholly trust him, wondering if there was something behind his decision.

She found it hard to hide her anxiety from Lady Deverell when she was with her that day. Her mind would not concentrate on anything for long and twice the dowager asked her if she were well.

Ned met them in the downstairs hall as they were about to go in to dinner that evening. There was a smile on his face and a look of relief in his eyes.

"May I speak with you a moment, milady?" he asked Audra.

She stepped aside to confer with him, urging Lady Deverell and Jason to go ahead.

A miracle had occurred, Ned explained to her. Jean Paul had arrived from London late in the afternoon and was anxious to return to France. When he heard that they were already planning to leave that night, and why, he was even more eager to make the trip.

"But is he well enough?" Audra questioned Ned.

"He appears to be. Now you will not have to go with us, milady. Jean Paul has knowledge of every aspect of the château."

"I am still going, Ned," Audra declared. "There is no way you can stop me!"

"I was afraid you would say that," Ned sighed.

"I will dress as a youth again, but you will have to find me a better pistol than that stupid little muff gun!"

Ned smiled and told her to meet him at the entrance to the cellar as soon as it began to grow dark.

During dinner that night, Lady Deverell kept glancing at Audra, as she toyed with her food, but Jason, surprisingly sober for once, managed to keep the conversation flowing smoothly.

Ned and Audra had been impatiently waiting by the cellar door for half an hour when they heard footsteps approaching and an anxious feminine voice.

A clearly upset Lady Deverell appeared from around a corner, followed by a rather shamefaced Jason. "I'm afraid she caught me slipping down here," he explained.

"Jason wouldn't tell me where he was going," the dowager declared. "Now, I see all of you are . . ." She looked at Audra dressed as a boy and put a hand to her heart. "It's France, isn't it? You're all going after Brock."

Audra nodded, but before she could say anything, Lady Deverell began directing her appeal to her.

"Surely you don't need Jason. I doubt he has spoken French for years and he is not too well. You heard him say he had come to Southcliffe for his health."

"They didn't ask me to go, Grandmama. I insisted," Jason said tightly.

Audra noticed, for the first time, that he was dressed not in his usual dandified clothing, but in a plain, dark coat and breeches.

"Jason, I forbid you to go!" Lady Deverell cried, clinging to his arm.

Firmly he removed her hand from his sleeve and then, with a smile, raised it to his lips.

"I must, Grandmama," he said quietly. "You see

that, don't you?" He smiled down at her a little sadly and tears sprang to her eyes.

"Then God go with you," she whispered. "God go with you all."

The moon was high and bright and shone down through the skylight into the little room. Brock groaned, rousing slowly as the light penetrated a corner of the big bed and made something glimmer above him. His eyes lifted and he surveyed the mirrored canopy.

Devil take it! He was lying in the love nest!

He tried to move and felt the searing pain of his striated back, the breathless agony of his broken ribs. Louis and a friend had rescued him from his dungeon prison and brought him here, he recalled. It had been daylight then and now it was night. Were they coming back for him?

He couldn't stay here! Just why, he wasn't able at first to remember. Then it came to him. Gaston Dubois knew about the love nest! It had been *his* face in the portrait! He had also made love to Celeste in this little room!

Louis and several other men were on shore to greet the boat returning from *The Peregrine*. Jean Paul was eagerly welcomed by his men and they would have conversed longer except for a nervous Louis, who hurriedly directed them off the beach and into the woods. Horses had been tethered for them there as they were several miles south of their destination. Before they mounted, Louis told them as quickly as he could all that had occurred since the captain's arrival two nights before.

He told them how he had gone to the compte's bedchamber in the château as the captain had instructed him, and had come upon the compte alone, sleeping in a chair by the fire. Louis had hidden himself, he said, in the shadows, witnessing de Lascalles's awakening at the sound of his wife's hysterical voice and the subsequent duel between the compte and the captain.

Afterwards, he had been about to join the captain, when he had seen Gaston Dubois and the compte's men take him prisoner. It had been pure luck that he had managed to escape unseen a little later.

"So it was Dubois who was the informer." Jean Paul's eyes narrowed. "I can hardly wait to get my hands on him!"

"Has the captain been in the dungeon since his capture?" Audra asked.

"*Oui*, until this morning," Louis continued. "While the compte's funeral service was being held in the chapel, Henri and I were able to take the guards by surprise and rescue him. We hid him in the love nest."

"He is all right then?" Audra's voice was anxious.

"We rescued him in time."

"Then he *was* tortured?" she cried in dismay.

"He requires medical attention. I have obtained some medicinal salves and linen bandages from the doctor in the village."

Audra closed her eyes. Oh God, she thought, what had they done to him? She had visions of Brock maimed or crippled.

"Where is my sister?" Jean Paul was asking.

"She helped the comtesse escape by carriage at the same time as we were rescuing the captain."

"But why would—"

"On the death of the compte, Dubois and the others took over the château. It appears Dubois wanted the comtesse to become his wife and she would have none of it. She planned her escape to coincide with the compte's funeral. Dubois believes the two women took the captain with them. He's livid with rage and called in a local army detachment to go after them. I believe they got away, for no one has yet returned, but the château is still alive with soldiers. I don't see how we can get the captain out tonight."

"But we can't delay!" Audra pleaded, looking first at Jean Paul and then at Louis. "Isn't there some way?"

"Not without an open confrontation." Jean Paul shook his head. "Unfortunately, we really do not know their full strength," he added.

Audra turned to him. "Would it be possible to get me clothing so I might pose as a maid of the château?"

"Of course, but—"

"I know the way to the love nest. I'm sure I could slip into the château without much difficulty at this time of night. At the very least, I could attend to the captain's wounds."

"It would be very dangerous." Jean Paul frowned. "If Dubois should see you, you will be stopped. He knows all the servants on sight."

"Can you describe this Dubois to me?" Audra asked quietly. She was resolute now in her decision.

It was nearly two in the morning by the time Audra, suitably garbed, crept with Louis, Jean Paul and Jason close to the rear of the château. Ned had been anxious to join them, but had been dissuaded due to his lack of the French language. He and the others were instructed to remain in the woods with the extra horses until they were signalled.

As the four reached the shadow of the stables, they saw to their consternation that a soldier was stationed by the door that led to the kitchens of the château. Louis shook his head. "There is no way any of us can get by him without being seen."

"I will get by him," Audra declared.

"But you can't—" Louis began.

Audra paid him no mind but moved out into the moonlight of the courtyard before she could be stopped.

A moment later the soldier's gaze was attracted to an approaching female form.

"*Bon soir*," Audra said huskily, swaying her hips as she came abreast of him.

The soldier was a good-looking young man with a rakish grin. "Where did *you* come from?" he demanded, his eyes brightening as he viewed the bold beauty before him.

"I was visiting my sister," she gave him a saucy smile as she stopped before him, one hand on her hip.

"I'll just bet you were." His grin now resembled a leer. "Came from the stables, if I don't miss my guess. Some stableboy take your fancy tonight?"

"I don't see that that's any of *your* business." Audra attempted to flounce by him.

"I'd like to make it my business." He put a hand out to stop her. "Where's your room, *ma petite*, so I can find it when I go off duty at dawn?"

"And what have you got to make it worth my while?" Although her heart hammered within her, Audra managed a seductive little smile.

"I've coins to please you and something in my breeches that that stableboy wishes he had," he said proudly.

Her eyes were full of promise as they swept boldly over him. "The corridor off the pantry," she agreed after a moment. "Second door on the left."

Audra outmaneuvered the arms that reached out for a sample squeeze and fled through the door of the château.

It was dark in the kitchen, the only light coming from the embers that still glowed on the hearth. Audra crossed to the fireplace, discovered a stump of candle on the mantel, and lighting it from the fire, hurried from the room.

She was surprised to find that she had no difficulty remembering her way and had soon reached the cupboard and was ascending the steep stairway to the hidden room. She took out the key Louis had given her from the deep pocket of her apron and opened the door to the love nest, slipping in and locking the door behind her. Even in the dim light of her candle, the sight of the room brought back a wave of unwelcome memories and she bit her lip as she crossed the floor to the bed.

After his first awakening, Brock had again fallen

asleep, only to be tormented by dreams of Audra lying warm and soft and responsive in his arms. Fiery heat flooded his loins as he drew her closer to him and abruptly he awoke, immediately aware of a dark shape beside his bed.

His right hand stole toward the pistol Louis had placed beside him as he eyed the shadowy form. In the soft candlelight, he recognized the figure of a woman and he relaxed.

"Marie? I didn't hear you come in," he said and to his own ears his voice sounded oddly hoarse and thick.

She said nothing as she lit the branched candelabrum beside his bed. It was when she turned back to him that they both gasped in unison. Brock, at the sight of the woman of his dreams suddenly materializing before him, and Audra, at the battered vision of the man she loved, his face bruised and swollen almost beyond recognition.

"Oh, my love!" she murmured, tears filling her eyes. "What have they done to you?"

She did not wish to hurt him, but she wanted so desperately to touch him, to kiss him. She did so as tenderly as she could, running gentle fingers through his tousled hair as her lips brushed his cheek.

One big hand came up, grasping her chin and bringing her lips down to his, drinking in the warm softness as if he had never expected to do so again. "That's better," he breathed. "Now I know it's really you."

She smiled at him as she straightened. "I'm going to do my best to fix you up so I can get you out of here," she said, reaching in the deep pockets of her apron and bringing out the medicinal salves and bandages Louis had given her. She had to get busy. It nearly broke her heart to look at him.

"I thought at first you were Marie," he rasped.

"No. Marie and Celeste should be far away from here by now. They escaped from the château at the same time as Louis and Henri released you and brought you here."

"Escaped?"

"Apparently Dubois was eager to marry the comtesse and claim the lands and château as his own."

"Dubois! Good lord, I've just remembered!" Brock attempted to push himself up, but Audra cried out, seeing the sheet that covered his back was adhered to his skin by congealed blood.

"Lie down!" she ordered and ran around the bed to the washstand. The cloth and basin of water Louis had used were still there, but she ignored them, taking up the half-full pitcher and coming back to the bed.

"I'm going to dampen the sheet that is covering you so I can pull it off more easily. Grit your teeth, because it will probably hurt."

"I have endured more than that." He grinned, but he winced as the covering was gently tugged from his back.

"Oh, God!" Audra moaned, fighting down the nausea when she saw the raw strips of flesh. "They whipped you like a dog!"

Tears rolled unchecked down her cheeks as she set to work cleaning the gore away, dressing his wounds as gently as she could and binding the cracked ribs.

She covered his torso in linen bandages, even covering his face where his nose had been split and broken. It would likely not heal in the same straight lines as before, but what did it matter? All that mattered to her was that he was alive! Oh, how much she loved him! Even more, it seemed, now that he lay there so helpless and in need of her. He had always seemed so big and strong before, so sure of himself. He had taken care of her when she had thought she had murdered Latham, when she had nearly died from the lung inflammation. Now it was her turn to care for him.

Brock was urging her to hurry. "We must leave here," he insisted. "Dubois knows of this room. He was one of Celeste's lovers. It is him in the portrait with her."

"You need not worry," Audra soothed him. "Dubois thinks you escaped with Celeste and Marie. He will not be searching for you." She looked over to where the portrait still hung on the wall. "I'm going to help you sit up for a moment," she told him.

When this was accomplished, she braced the soft pillows at his back and picked up the branch of candles from the table beside the bed. Walking to the wall before him, she held up the candelabrum and let the light from it shine on the portrait.

"Now, is that Dubois?" she asked Brock.

In shocked amazement he stared at it. "But—but the face has been changed!" he exclaimed. "That's *my* face!"

"I told you."

"But it was Dubois's face I saw before in that portrait. I swear it!"

"Surely it isn't possible that Celeste has the portrait changed whenever she changes lovers?"

He gazed at it and then he gave a crooked smile. "Not the portrait. Just the face. That's not my body."

Audra moved closer to observe it. "You're right! His shoulders are not as broad as yours or his body as muscular." She turned back to him, lowering the branch of candles. "All the time I thought you were lying to me."

"I've never lied to you, Audra. I love you." He held out his arms to her. "Come here," he said softly. "I want to hold you. I never thought I'd see you again."

She went to him, sighing as she felt his arms enclose her, kissing the swollen lips.

"I love you so," she whispered. "You had no right going off and leaving me that way."

"The trouble is that I know you too well, my love. You would have insisted upon coming with me."

"You're right, but you put me through a thousand deaths wondering what had become of you."

"I finally met the compte face to face. Killed him in a duel."

"I'm glad I didn't witness that." She shuddered. "But what of Celeste. Was she badly beaten?"

"Enough to have lost the babe."

"Oh, Brock, she seemed so proud to be carrying your child."

"Really?" His voice was sardonic. "She told me she felt well rid of it, that it would probably have ruined her figure."

Audra looked surprised. "Perhaps she was just

trying to compensate for its loss," she said. "I can't believe—"

"Can't you? You told me once you'd rather bear the devil's child than mine."

Her hasty words had obviously hurt him deeply. "You should have known I didn't mean that."

"Then you would like to bear my children?"

"With all my heart."

He tried a smile. "It might be more conventional if we were to marry first."

Two luminous blue eyes looked deep into two hazel ones. "Then you no longer . . . You don't care anymore about my money, or—"

"It doesn't seem to matter now. Not after all that has happened. When I was lying in that dungeon, I thought if ever I were allowed to see you again, I would never let my stupid pride stand in the way of our happiness. I love you, my darling, and I want you to be my wife. That's all that matters."

"I love you, too, and I'll marry you any time . . . any where."

Again they kissed and so lost were they in each other that they did not hear the footsteps ascending the stairs outside the room and only started apart when there was a loud knock at the door.

Gaston Dubois had been playing cards with the compte's two men and an army officer who was housed overnight in the château. He had lost money, but he did not care. Wasn't this *his* château now? Celeste, too, would belong to him again when she was brought back. And the soldiers *would* bring her back, he had no doubt of that.

By the time the men went their separate ways, Gaston realized it was after two in the morning. He had imbibed more than usual, but the claret had been of the finest quality and had passed smoothly down his thirsty throat. He made his way from the study to the bottom of the curving, marble stairs. He was about to ascend them when he thought how much nicer it would be to have an eager little wench sharing the compte's huge bed with him. He changed his direction and made his way toward the back of the château and the servants' quarters.

As he left the main area of the house and entered a long, narrow corridor, he took down a lantern that had been hanging by the entrance and shone it ahead of him to light the way. It was in its light, a few minutes later, that he saw something that made him come to an abrupt halt.

On the plain wall beside a door at the end of the corridor was a dark blotch. He lifted the lantern so that he could see it better. He had been right! It *was* a smear of blood! Someone had brushed up against the wall, someone who had been bleeding!

He looked again at the door. Wasn't it the very one that led to the love nest? He entered the empty cupboard and with his right hand felt along the back panel for the hidden spring. It swung back to his touch and he saw another smear of blood as he went through the opening. He smiled to himself. It looked very much as if the English smuggling captain had not left the château at all!

Chapter Twenty-Seven

"Open this door!" a deep, angry voice demanded.

"Who is it?" Audra whispered to Brock.

"Dubois!" he hissed, fumbling beside him on the bed for the pistol.

There was silence for a moment and then the sound of heavy footsteps descending the stairway.

"He's gone." Audra let out her breath. "Thank God I locked the door after me."

"He's only gone for help," Brock warned her. "Get out of here, Audra! Now! I'll be too slow, but you can escape before anyone returns."

"No! I won't go without you!" She looked frantically around the little room. "If only there was someplace you could hide!"

"There is," he said, grimacing a little as he pushed himself off the bed. "And it's probably a better idea than trying to stand up to them alone." Shoving the pistol in his belt, he moved to the end of the bed and gingerly knelt down to pull back the rug. Audra was instantly at his side, helping him lift the trap door and climb into the open cavity. Brock could not help emitting a groan as he painfully fitted himself into the narrow space, lying on his best side and drawing up his knees.

"Hurry!" he said as Audra lowered the section of flooring over him. Carefully she pulled back and adjusted the rug.

She started then for the door, remembered the branch of candles by the bed and raced back to them, grabbing one taper and blowing out the rest. Once out on the landing, she locked the door behind her and pocketed the key. With skirts raised in one hand, she descended the stairs as quickly as she could and was just stepping out of the door to the cupboard when she was brought up short by someone shining a lantern in her face!

Gaston Dubois, for it had to be he from the description she had been given, stepped forward into the light. His puzzled gaze swept her up and down.

"Who are you?" he demanded.

"I'm Thérèse, monsieur," she said, bobbing a curtsy. Louis had told her what to say if she were caught. "I'm Sofie's sister."

"But what are you doing here?"

Audra could see now that there were three soldiers with him in the narrow corridor. One of them, she recognized as the soldier she had encountered on the way into the château. He winked at her.

"I was on my way to bed when I saw that this door

was open," Audra said to Dubois. "I—I was curious when I looked in the cupboard and saw an opening at the back. I shouldn't have, I suppose, but I went through it and when I saw the steps I wondered where they led. Would you believe there is a room up there? A hidden room! I was just looking around it when I heard someone coming and being afraid, I locked the door. There was a knock at it, but I was too frightened to answer. Then I heard him go away and I rushed down the stairs."

"Likely story!" Dubois growled. "You're coming with us!" He pushed her back into the cupboard, through the opening and up the stairs. As she climbed ahead of the others, Audra managed to extract the key from her pocket and when she arrived before the door to the love nest, she slipped it into the lock, as if she had left it there.

"Shall I open the door?" she asked, her hand on the key.

"Of course, *imbécile*!" Dubois snarled impatiently. He pushed Audra aside in order to enter the room first.

"It's empty," she said, following him, "but you can see that someone has been here. Look at the bed, monsieur, and the basin on the washstand."

"Quiet!" Dubois snapped at her angrily, although he carefully eyed everything she had mentioned as he strode around the small room.

"How do I know you didn't help him escape?" he asked, coming to stop before Audra and looking down at her in the light from the lantern he carried. For the first time he noticed that the maid before him was a beauty.

"Help who escape, monsieur?"

"The prisoner. The man who has hidden in this room."

"But I only . . ." she began. Then she pointed at the soldier with the rakish grin. "He was stationed at the kitchen door. He will tell you I only entered the château a short while ago."

"That is correct, monsieur," the soldier agreed.

"I was on my way to bed when I saw the open door," Audra repeated.

"*Oui, oui*, I know all that. What I want you to tell me is why you were returning to the château at such a late hour?"

Audra looked up at him and then let her eyes drop coyly. "Surely, monsieur, one as handsome as you is not a stranger to *l'amour*."

His dark eyes brushed over her and he smiled. "Why haven't I seen you before, *ma chèrie*? Sofie's sister, you say. Was it not she who had an accident in the kitchen this week?"

"*Oui*, monsieur. That is why I am here to help in her place. Poor Sofie, she was badly burned about her arms and hands by grease from the fire. It may be weeks before her bandages can come off and then she may not be able to use her hands for some time. The doctor says—"

"Never mind what he says." Dubois waved his hand impatiently. "All right. All right. Be gone with you and see that in the future your curiosity doesn't take you where you don't belong."

"*Merci*, monsieur." Audra bobbed another curtsy, which, this time, unfortunately gave Dubois a delightful glance down her blouse as it gaped forward.

He grasped her arm as Audra was about to start past him. "Not so fast, *ma petite*." His strong white teeth showed in a sudden grin. "Who's the lucky man you bestowed your favors upon tonight?"

She gave him a teasing little smile from below lowered lids. "I would rather not say, monsieur."

He laughed. "So you can hold your tongue about some things." He released her and lowered his voice. "Do you know where the master bedchamber is located in the château?"

"*Oui*, monsieur."

"I will expect you there in fifteen minutes," he said with a bold gleam in his dark eyes.

Audra glanced at the soldier standing beside Dubois, knowing he had surely overheard this exchange. She gave him a significant shrug of her shoulders before running from the room.

Dubois was silent as Audra could be heard descending the stairs. It wasn't until a door banged shut below that he turned to the soldiers.

"She is a liar!" he said tightly. "There was blood on the sleeve of her blouse!"

Beside him, the soldier's eyes widened in disbelief. "But, monsieur—"

"I believe that *jeune fille* took the prisoner from this room and hid him somewhere else in the château. Possibly in her own room. She returned for something that he had left behind and we caught her going back to him."

The three soldiers looked uncertain.

"What would you have us do?" one of them asked.

"I doubt she will be long. She will want to get him out of the château as quickly as possible. I believe we should station ourselves outside the rear door and when she leads him out that way, it will be an easy task to capture them both!" With a last look around the room, Dubois motioned for the uniformed men to follow him.

Audra almost ran into Jason and the two Frenchmen in the dark kitchen.

"We came in when the soldier left his post," Jason explained, smothering her gasp with his hand. "Where is Brock?"

"I hid him," Audra explained when Jason removed his palm. "We must hurry! I promised to meet Dubois in fifteen minutes."

"You ran into Dubois?" Jean Paul exclaimed.

"*Oui.* I haven't time to explain now. Just come!"

Dubois and the soldiers, turning a corner, heard the voices up ahead and ducked into the corridor leading to the main part of the château, quickly extinguishing their lantern. They stood in silence as Audra and the three men hurried by them without even a glance in their direction.

"She's not leading those men to her room," the soldier with the rakish grin hissed.

"So you know where it's located," another laughed, but was quickly shushed.

"The rear door!" Dubois scowled at them and set off, letting the others fall in behind him.

* * *

Audra opened the door of the hidden room.

"Where the devil did you hide him?" Jason looked about in the dim light from Audra's candle.

"Over here!"

The small rug at the end of the bed was quickly thrown back and Audra searched for the finger slot to lift the door. Seconds later the men had drawn Brock from the cavity in which he had been wedged. They sat him up at the end of the bed and he began flexing his cramped arms and legs, new pain added to that which already throbbed unceasingly through his battered body.

"You've wrapped him up like an Egyptian mummy!" Jason snorted to Audra.

At the sound of his voice, Brock's head shot up. "Jason! What the devil are *you* doing here?"

"Come to rescue you, old fellow. Couldn't let little Audra here do it all by herself."

"I'll be damned!"

"We have to hurry, Brock." Audra's voice was agitated. "Dubois expects me—"

"Like hell he does!" Brock growled. "I heard their whole conversation. He's on to you, Audra. After you left he told them he had seen some blood on your sleeve. He and those soldiers are just waiting to pounce on us when we leave by the rear door."

Jean Paul looked at him. "Then we must go another way," he said quietly. "I know. It will take longer, but we'll help support you, Captain." He nodded to Louis.

"*You*? Support *me*!" Brock exclaimed. "Why, you've only just recovered yourself from—"

"I'm fine, Captain," Jean Paul assured him, "and so will you be once we get you out of here."

Jason had withdrawn a flask from his pocket and now he held it out to his brother.

"Take a long swig of this, Brock. It's brandy, laced with laudanum. Will help your pain."

Brock surveyed him a moment and then he did as Jason suggested. When he was through, he wiped his mouth with the back of his hand and made a motion to give the flask back to his brother, but Jason waved it away.

"Keep it. You may need more before we get you safely home."

Jean Paul looked around him. "Has everyone his pistol ready?" he asked, patting the weapon at his belt.

Audra withdrew her own pistol from the pocket of her apron and with the candle held in her other hand said to Jean Paul, "I'll go ahead, if you will tell me the direction I should take."

He did this as quickly as possible and, after assisting Brock to his feet, the two Frenchmen helped him toward the door, followed closely behind by Jason Deverell.

"They should be here by now," Gaston Dubois said to no one in particular. "Even if they had to carry that damned smuggler."

"Could they have gone another way?"

"Not by the front door, it's too well-guarded, and I left a soldier at the side." Dubois suddenly straightened. "The double glass doors leading from the salon to the garden!" he cried. "Come with me!" He nodded to one of the men. "You others stay here!"

Audra and the four men had emerged from behind a tall hedge bordering the garden, and were just starting out across the wide lawn in the direction of a stand of trees beyond, when Dubois and the soldier came around the side of the château.

"There they go!" Dubois shouted, firing a shot at them without so much as aiming his pistol. He hoped it would attract the two soldiers he had left behind. The bullet whipped over the heads of the fleeing group.

"Save yourselves!" Brock pushed Jean Paul and Louis away from him. "I can make it on my own." He pulled the pistol from his belt and turned to fire in the direction of their pursuers.

The soldier with Dubois jerked back, clasping his shoulder, but he still managed to let off a shot. It sailed uncomfortably close to the two Frenchmen who had paused to look back at Brock.

"Go on, damn you!" he yelled at them as he started into a loping run.

Audra had gone on a little way and now turned to come back to Brock.

"Take her with you!" he commanded the men.

But Audra had seen a window light up above in the château. A figure was silhouetted in it. She caught the glint of a musket barrel as it was raised and fired her pistol directly at it. She just had time to see the man fall back into the room when Louis grasped her hand, pulling her along with him as he dashed for safety.

Jason had come up beside Brock and now fired at the two soldiers who had suddenly appeared on the run from around the side of the château. One of them let out a cry and fell forward in his tracks.

"Come on!" Brock dragged at Jason's arm.

"Right behind you!" His brother grinned, removing the second pistol from his belt.

"My thanks, Jason," Brock gasped and, holding his side, sprinted for the trees.

Dubois had stopped long enough to take careful aim at the man he had grown to hate more than any other. It was not hard to recognize him in the moonlight with those white bandages swathing the top of his body. His pistol roared and the bullet would have entered Brock's back and pierced his heart, if at that moment he had not stumbled and fallen to his knees. It therefore shot over his head and smashed into a tree a dozen yards in front of him. Shaken from the jolt of his fall, Brock staggered to his feet and was again running before he realized that Jason was not behind him.

He turned in time to see Dubois clutch his chest and fall from a shot Jason had fired.

"Jason, for God's sake!" he roared, but his brother only waved him on, crouching to reload his pistols. A bullet whizzed by Brock's ear and this time he did not delay, but made straight for the woods. There was no point in remaining a target. He had no more ammunition with which to return the fire.

Audra had watched the two brothers from the woods and didn't realize she had been holding her breath until Brock had gained the tree line.

With Ned in the lead, the horses now came charging into view. More shots were fired in the direction of the château and the horses started out across the lawn.

Brock had reached Audra's side when they both saw Jason hit. He fell sideways onto the grass, but almost immediately was seen struggling to sit up again. Louis's hard hand reached out and gripped Brock's shoulder.

"Ned will reach him," he said, stopping the big man from returning to assist his brother.

They watched as Jason rose to his knees, steadied his pistol with both hands and took aim at a soldier who appeared to have a perfect bead on Ned. Jason's shot was true, but in that same instant, another bullet found its mark and Jason dropped like a stone to the grass, a round hole in his temple.

Ned was beside him immediately, scooping him up in his strong arms and laying him across his saddle as he raced back in the direction of the woods.

The men with him let off a volley of shots in the direction of the château before turning to follow him. By the time they reached the line of trees, the others were mounted and ready to ride.

Soon, all that remained of the rescue party was the distant thundering of hoofs as they headed southward, leaving the château far behind them.

Chapter Twenty-Eight

Like his brother, David, before him, Jason Deverell was returned to England and laid to rest in the small family cemetery behind Southcliffe.

The weeks passed and Brock mended quickly, due to his excellent physical condition and the constant and loving ministrations of Audra and his grandmother. When he began to feel more like his old self, he insisted that Audra set a wedding date, refusing to bow to convention and wait until the mourning period was over. As it turned out, the thought of a wedding proved to be just what Lady Deverell needed to take her mind off her loss of a second grandson.

Unknown to Audra, Brock sent word to her father and Sir George arrived by himself the day before the ceremony. When she caught sight of him standing in the lower hall, Audra burst into tears and ran straight into his arms.

Sir George was looking much better than Audra remembered him. In restoring Greenleigh to its old splendor, he seemed to have gained back the self-assurance he had lost. Audra was so happy to see him that she never thought of the price she had been forced to pay to bring about that transition.

"Where is Emily?" she asked him. "Did she not come with you?"

"No. I thought it better I come alone." He looked down at her and Audra caught a glimpse of the old twinkle in his eye. "Fancy an old hand like your father allowing a filly to run completely free! Needed to feel the reins a bit." He smiled. "Even have her on an allowance now."

The simple ceremony took place outdoors, at Audra's request, before the recently restored gardens of Southcliffe. It was a beautifully clear summer day and the only witnesses to the event were Lady Deverell and Sir George, the members of the household and some of *The Peregrine*'s crew.

Audra wore a softly flowing gown of blue silk that made her porcelain skin glow and emphasized the amethyst shade of her eyes. Adorning her silvery blond hair was a coronet of flowers.

Despite the abrasions which were still apparent on his face, the new Lord Deverell was an arresting-looking man. Broad shoulders strained at the immaculately tailored dove-gray coat as he stood so tall and commanding beside his bride, seeming to be aware of no one else as his eyes consumed her.

Audra looked up with love into Brock's face as she

repeated her vows: "In sickness, and in health, to love, and to cherish . . ." This time, she was not hoping for a knight on a white charger to sweep in and rescue her. This time, he was already at her side.

Through the whole ceremony, Sir George gazed intently at his daughter's choice. He had made inquiries about this new Lord Deverell. There were rumors that he might be involved in the smuggling trade and despite being told a tale of him being involved in an accident, he wondered about those injuries. Still, it was obvious that this rugged-looking man loved his daughter dearly and after talking with Audra, there had been no doubt in Sir George's mind that she shared the same feelings. He thought now that she had never looked that adoringly at Latham. In fact, observing the profound look of love that passed between the two of them, he was deeply moved.

It was evening and Audra and Brock had finally escaped from their guests and were standing before the wide-open windows of their bedchamber, watching the sunset. The sweet perfume of the rose garden below drifted in on the cool evening air.

Brock's hands were gentle as they closed over Audra's shoulders, caressing them as he pulled her back against him. His lips found the sensitive spot at the nape of her neck.

Audra's eyes gazed out over the wide, green lawn to the line of trees beyond. "How beautiful Southcliffe looked today," she murmured.

"Southcliffe is a home again, thanks to you."

"*Our* home," she corrected, turning in his arms. The love in her eyes was almost tangible. "And you, my dashing smuggler, the lord of the manor."

"Lord of the manor," he repeated. "But at what a price!" His voice had a ragged edge.

"Dear heart, you grieved and avenged David's death," Audra said gently, "and Jason would not have wanted you to grieve for him. It was the way he wished to die. He could not bear to contemplate a slow and painful death."

"Yet I still wish I had understood what was tormenting him, known the cause behind his self-destructiveness. I always thought Grandmother so weak with him. If I'd only known then—"

"No!" Audra put a finger to his lips. "He would have hated your pity. It was better this way."

Brock reached out to smooth back a curl from her cheek. "Did I tell you that Jean Paul sent his blessings?"

She nodded.

"He also said the smuggling and escape route is open again, now that Dubois and the others are dead."

Audra felt a cold shiver of fear. "Does that mean you will return as Peregrine?"

"I will continue to manage the smuggling operation, but I doubt that I will be making many runs. I have too much to occupy me here."

"I'm glad." Love shone from Audra's eyes as she reached up to lightly touch his nose. "It's healing well. I think there'll be only a slight bump. No doubt it will make you look even more arrogant."

"And odious." He laughed, remembering her favorite word for him.

"How hard I tried not to love you." She shook her

head. "What a fool I was!"

"We were both fools." Gently he cupped her chin, making her eyes lock with his. Her heart caught in her throat at the tenderness in his gaze. "I will never stop loving you, Audra. Remember that. You are my very life, my darling."

Audra felt suddenly that she could see far beyond this moment and what she saw made her smile with happiness. "We'll be together always," she whispered.

He echoed her last word as his arms tightened around her and pulled her even closer.